Magick in the Desert Night

Pamela.

It was Rosa's voice—  calling to her.

I hear you, Rosa, she

Come to me.

What? Where are you? Pam asked.

In the night. Come to me in the night.

The next thing she knew, she was standing on the desert plain beside Scorpio Rose. Twenty feet away, Max and Diana were lying beside a huge boulder. The two women were in shadow, but Pam stepped back instinctively.

"They cannot see us," said Scorpio Rose.

In truth, Pam could hardly see herself. She seemed to be, if not a ghost, then something made of fluid light, now visible, now not visible.

"Where's my body?" Pam asked, surprisingly calmly.

"See for yourself," Rosa said. And Pam did. Without even turning her head, she looked back at the campsite, at least a mile away. She saw her unmoving body sprawled in the dust.

"In the future, you will want to lie down before flying," the witch said.

· · · · · · · ·

"With a well-developed magickal system and a cast of intriguing (and sometimes bizarre) characters, Englehart provides the perfect vehicle for a rambunctious and enjoyable joyride." —*San Francisco Book Review*

Turn the page for more raves for* The Plain Man *and Max August

Knight, and he created the comic book character Nightman. I highly recommend that you check out *The Plain Man* and the entire Max August series of books, and I can hardly wait for the fourth book in the series to come out: *The Arena Man.*   —*BookSpotCentral*

"Who is Max August? Think a supernatural, twenty-first-century version of James Bond. Or maybe, better yet, Harry Potter for grown-ups."   —Richard A. Lupoff,
author of *The Comic Book Killer*

"For an almost superhuman span of time, with care, skill, intelligence, and brio, Steve Englehart has been blowing the minds of readers around the world—including, blessedly and irrevocably, my own. *The Long Man* adds another dazzling burst of storytelling power to the ongoing display of his brilliance."   —Michael Chabon,
New York Times #1 bestselling author of
The Adventures of Kavalier and Clay
and *The Yiddish Policemen's Union*

BOOKS BY STEVE ENGLEHART

ABOUT MAX AUGUST
*The Point Man**
*The Long Man**
*The Plain Man**
The Arena Man (forthcoming)*

CHILDREN'S BOOKS
Rustle's Christmas Adventure
Christmas Countdown
Easter Parade
Countdown to the Moon
Countdown to Flight

DNAGERS SERIES
DNAgers 1: *Legend of the Crimson Gargoyle*
DNAgers 2: *Legend of the Crossbones Key*

*A Tor Book

The Plain Man

· ·

Steve Englehart

A TOM DOHERTY ASSOCIATES BOOK / NEW YORK

This is a work of fiction. All of the characters, organizations, and events portrayed in this novel are either products of the author's imagination or are used fictitiously.

THE PLAIN MAN

Copyright © 2011 by Steve Englehart

All rights reserved.

Edited by James Frenkel

A Tor Book
Published by Tom Doherty Associates, LLC
175 Fifth Avenue
New York, NY 10010

www.tor-forge.com

Tor® is a registered trademark of Tom Doherty Associates, LLC.

ISBN 978-0-7653-6427-2

First Edition: June 2011
First Mass Market Edition: February 2012

Printed in the United States of America

0 9 8 7 6 5 4 3 2 1

This One's For
My Sister
Anne Englehart Carpenter

He was not "a thinking machine"; for that is a brainless phrase of modern fatalism and materialism. A machine only *is* a machine because it cannot think. But he was a thinking man, and a plain man at the same time.

—G. K. CHESTERTON,
The Innocence of Father Brown, 1910

The reason why *time* plays a great part in so many of my tales is that this element looms up in my mind as the most profoundly dramatic and grimly terrible thing in the universe.

—H. P. LOVECRAFT, 1937

Pope Gregory commissioned a calendar based on rigorous science, to accurately reflect the turning of the Earth. The result is now the international civil standard.

The Plain Man covers the lives of Max August and Pam Blackwell from
Monday, June 15, 2009
through
Sunday, June 21, 2009.

The Mayans, who worshipped Time itself, devised a calendar made of two interlocking cycles. The first, consisting of numbers, goes around every 13 days, while the other, consisting of images, goes around every 20. So each day's name consists of a number and an image. Altogether, there are 13 × 20, or 260, distinct day names, and each has a meaning.

The Plain Man covers the lives of Max August and Pam Blackwell during

5 Jaguar	Empowering Clarity
6 Eagle	Responding to the Storyline
7 Candle	Engaging with the Matrix
8 Earth	Connecting with Humanness
9 Flint Knife	Being Magick
10 Milky Way	Personifying Alchemy
11 Sun	Owning All
12 Nipple	Fulfilling Reality

The Plain Man

. . . .

5 Jaguar (Empowering Clarity)

"A sex caper?" Pam Blackwell said skeptically. "My name isn't Mata Hari."

"And I'm not Heidi Fleiss," Max August answered. "But honey traps have existed as long as spies have, because they work."

"I suppose so, but still . . . kind of *ballsy,* no?"

Both of them chuckled in the sweltering night.

They were lying on a blanket spread over the sand, on a hill in the ass-end of Arizona, watching the sky above. An hour after midnight, it was still eighty-seven degrees with no breeze at all. But this far from pollution and city lights, the sky was brilliant, blazing with stars, planets, and the satellites that swept across the expanse like clockwork. Pam was twenty-nine years old. Max was thirty-five even though he'd been born in 1950, and he'd be thirty-five until somebody killed him, because he was Timeless. Both were blond, he with hazel eyes and her with blue. They could have been two lovers on a picnic—which, in fact, they were—but they were also two alchemists, and they were going to war.

Max said, "Everybody thinks with their body sometimes, lady." His features were striking, dominated by the full mouth of the deejay he'd once been. That mouth produced a voice just as striking, deep and rich and round.

Pam studied his silhouette against the night, and said,

"Everybody wants a relationship. Every*thing* wants a relationship, because everything is related—the first magickal secret you ever told me."

"Mike and Di are no different. They want each other and they're coming together like crashing meteors." He gestured toward the sky, which was devoid of meteors. "See if you can shoot this down. We've got time."

"Okay." She put her hands behind her head and stretched.

"Well," he said, "Dave does data mining for me. It's small-scale, but he's only looking for a few things. One is intelligence concerning Michael Salinan and Diana Herring."

Pam's eyes narrowed as she ran the information she'd gathered over the year and a half she and Max had been together. Dave was his computer jedi. Michael Salinan was a well-known political guru, usually but not always right-wing, and Diana Herring ran Full Resource Channel, which owned radio and television stations of all networks all across America. Several years before, Dave had uncovered a relationship between Michael and Diana that suggested a love affair, though they'd tried hard to hide it—just as they'd tried to hide their membership in a cabal known only by the initials "FRC," or three words beginning with those initials. The FRC had run the American government during the Bush/Cheney years, embedding its people throughout the bureaucracy to maintain as much control as possible after Obama took over, and judging from the results, they'd succeeded. Rather than end the wars as promised, the government had recently announced its intent to assassinate American citizens if it wanted. This was duly reported to the citizens months afterward at the bottom of page A-12 and most people missed it. But for Max and Pam, "of, by, and for the People" was not just a slogan, the way it was to the FRC.

"Dave discovered a run of credit card numbers that seemed to have been dropped down a black hole," Max went on. "Everything before that run was issued, and everything after, but those cards were just gone. So he kept an eye out. One of them was used last month to buy tickets for Wickr under an assumed name, and Dave applied his standard cross-checks. He traced the transaction as far as KSN-TV in Wichita and then hit a brick wall, at first, but he checked the station's FedEx shipments and found one to a hotel on the south side of Chicago. There was no record of what happened there, but Diana operates her FRC out of Chicago, so he kept going and found airline tickets on the same card, from O'Hare and Dulles, both to Las Vegas, arriving later today. And Wickr starts today, three hours north of Vegas."

"Nice work on Dave's part," Pam said. "I couldn't even master Windows. But what's the deal with Wickr? You've been before, right?"

"I went in ninety-eight. It was a whole lot smaller and more intimate than it is now, but I doubt if the vibe has changed. It's a festival in the high desert during the week leading up to the Midsummer solstice. Upwards of fifty thousand people, all ages and persuasions, come together to live in an instant city far from view; there is a lot of energy. It's held at the base of the Silver Peak Mountains, at a point where the hills sweep into the distance like stone wings. On either side of that point, Wickr plants two two-hundred-and-twenty-foot towers. A fifty-foot sphere made of curved wooden slats, like massive rattan, simple and primitive, hangs one hundred feet in the air, suspended from a cable on an arc between the towers. That's the Sun; it hangs above the landscape, swaying in the breeze, all week. Then, at the Midsummer solstice, it's raised all the way up to two hundred feet and set ablaze against the sky. The solstice moves forward a quarter of a day every year, so the Burn takes place whenever Midsummer comes—morning, afternoon, evening, middle of the night. You get a different gathering every year, depending on who's awake. This year's the evening year; the best blaze, biggest crowd, biggest party."

"Is it a straight takeoff on the old Wicker Man festival?" Pam asked, interested. *When we started,* Pam thought, *there was so much to take in. But you get inside it and it's simple.* "Eight festivals mark out the year, at each of the four seasons and the four points halfway between. We met on one— Hallowe'en. Wicker Man's for Midsummer, the longest day of the year, when the Sun reaches its highest point in the sky and the Earth is in the fullest of bloom below. Both sides at their most radiant—because after Midsummer, the Sun will grow lower in the sky and the Earth's vegetation will fade, and we puny humans certainly have *no control* over whether they'll do it again next year. So everywhere in the world, humans came together and showed off their own considerable life-force with sex and sacrifice—usually an animal but sometimes a man if they were really worried about how things were going."

Max's hand found hers on the blanket, and he chuckled. "As far as I know, the *Wickr* festival's just a festival. Nobody's into human sacrifice, but there's almost any other thing you want if it doesn't hurt somebody else. There's dancing and drugs and conversations and costumes and art and wacky cars and vision-quests and girls on stilts, with a permanent techno soundtrack from dance floors in all directions. Wickr is essentially an alternate reality you live in for a week; it's a very cleansing experience. There just happens to be plenty of sex if you want it, and Mike and Di want it."

"Are you and I having plenty of sex?" Pam wanted to know.

"With each other. If we want it."

She jabbed him with her elbow. "Not other people?"

"Up to you, my love, but I'm not."

"No, I'm good." She pulled her hand from beneath his and placed it on top. "We'll keep our magick to ourselves."

There was silence for a while.

"Anyway," Max said finally, "Wickr's like a free-thinker's Renaissance Faire that you get to live in."

"So that brings up the question," Pam said, "of why two members of the FRC would choose it."

"Two members having an affair," Max reminded her. "They've kept it quiet because they don't want their bosses to find out about it. Now comes a chance for a week of heavy petting, in a place their bosses would never go. As Di would be the first to say, 'Win-win!'"

"Still, there will be fifty thousand people there, and both Mike and Di have been on TV a lot."

"But how many of those fifty thousand, who like a little alternate reality in the desert, watched *Meet the Press* clips like us? Probably not too many. Plus, Mike and Di *can* disguise themselves."

"With wigs and makeup, maybe," Pam responded with ironic dismissal. "*We* can bend light to actually change what people see."

"True, but *we* won't actually be dealing with them."

"Right. Because then we'd have to sleep with them."

"Yes, but also because the more I reveal of myself to the FRC, the more openings I give them to come after me. I prefer to remain invisible as long as I can, because soon enough I'll be right up in their face and I want every advantage I can get."

"*We* can get." Pam rolled over in place onto her side, supporting her head with her hand. "So this is where Sly and Rosa come in."

"Right."

"Why them, particularly?"

"They're both creatures of illusion."

"And *they're* good with the sex?"

"Sly is ecstatic."

"What about Rosa?"

"If she didn't want to do it, believe me, she wouldn't."

"That's hardly a ringing endorsement."

"With her, it is," Max said. "She's not what you'd call demonstrative."

"So that's another question," she said. "Are you sure they can pull it off?"

"Pull what off?"

"Seducing Michael and Diana."

"Sly and Rosa can seduce anybody," he said with confidence.

"And why is that?" Pam pursued. "I have no way of evaluating them because I don't know them and you can't tell me much about them, thanks to the frikkin' code of the magi. But what else *can* you tell me, Max?"

He hesitated, then said, "Nothin'."

"You know," Pam said darkly, "you're adorable when you do that deejay folksy thing, but I still heard 'nothing.'"

"Their secrets are their secrets, Pam. That *is* indeed the code. Nobody wants his secrets spread around—we wouldn't want them spilling ours."

"But you can't trust me to *keep* their secrets."

"That's exactly right. *I can't* trust you," Max said. "It's not up to *me*. Only *they* can trust you, which they will, once they get to know you."

Pam thought about her one meeting with the pair. They had been strangers in the night—jostling through the crowd of a Mixed Martial Arts match in Barbados. Sly and Rosa both looked to be teenagers, almost like kids playing dress-up in that crowd, but even then Pam felt that they were far older than Max was. Creatures of illusion, indeed.

"So how are they going to work it?" was all Pam said out loud.

"That's up to them. We'll brief 'em and then turn 'em loose," he responded. "But we might get a few ideas. What's today going to be?"

"Ah," she said, and looked down across her hip at a thick manuscript lying beside her, gray in the night. It was her well-thumbed copy of the latest version of Max's *Codex,* which he kept current with everything he knew about the occult systems he'd mastered. The Mayan calendar was a basic one, and he put her through her paces every day.

"In the Mayan system," she said, "days have names, created from a simple shorthand: a verb plus a noun. In the calendar that counts the days for average people, there are thirteen numbers corresponding to verbs, times twenty names corresponding to nouns—for a total of two hundred and sixty days per calendar cycle. Every day begins at dawn; until then, it's still the old day. So right now, at . . . one thirty-four in the morning, we're still in Five Jaguar. 'Five' is 'Empowering' and 'Jaguar' is 'Clarity,' so the energy around us now is *Empowering Clarity.* Which is probably why I'm trying to get everything clear before we begin."

"Probably," Max agreed.

Pam said, "Yeah, so you've done this longer. It's still hard to grasp that we're living in the midst of all this energy." She tapped his chest. "The energy flows forward forever, we call it time, and alchemists make use of it. By the time we get to Wickr, it'll be after dawn, so the day will be Six Eagle, which means *Responding to the Storyline.* We'll be surrounded by other people, all of whom have their own agendas, and the energy will be there for improv. Which, I remind you, we would be doing on *any* day that Wickr got under way."

"Sure, but on Six Eagle it'll be the dominant concept. On other days, other things would be more important—bad weather, cranky vehicles, the things we brought, the things we forgot to bring. This day, the flavor of the flow is

Responding to the Storyline, so you and I are going to scope out Mike and Di and have everything nailed down before Sly and Rosa get here tonight. We'll get them ammunition they can use tomorrow—then we'll kick back till their part is done."

"Yeah, that's the part I still have trouble with," Pam said off-handedly. "Mike's hot."

"If you think a bald-headed guy with big ears is hot—"

"It explains why you made the cut, too; is that what you were going to say?"

"No."

"It *would* explain a lot. . . . But it doesn't explain why I haven't left you for some slightly less hideous guy. Maybe there *is* no one less hideous. . . ." She touched his face. "Ah, well," she said, smiling, "I like hideous."

"Me, too."

They nuzzled in the sweltering night.

MONDAY, JUNE 15, 2009 • 1:49 A.M.
MOUNTAIN STANDARD TIME

5 Jaguar (Empowering Clarity)

After a while, they packed up their deli wrappings, shook and folded their blanket, then half slid down the sandy slope to their rented Volkswagen camping van, parked in a turnoff by U.S. 95. They could have chosen something roomier or newer for their ground transportation, but both of them had fond memories of trips in VWs—Max in one of the original puke greens. So they'd flown into Tucson from Acapulco yesterday afternoon and picked up the rental. They had used assumed names they'd never before assumed, and paid cash (a suspicious circumstance with airplane tickets but not camping vans, at least if you were obviously white Americans). They checked the van thoroughly for bugs both physical and metaphysical, just to be sure, then drove to a Big 5, a Costco, and a Walmart, where they outfitted themselves for a week of camping—and finally, found the Goodwill for a week of costumes. As the sun was lowering, they left Tucson and traveled over 250 miles, taking a nonobvious route around Phoenix toward Blythe on 10, then up 95 toward Lake Havasu, staying out of California to avoid the agricultural inspection stations at the border. And nowhere along that journey had Max sensed anyone or anything paying the slightest bit of attention to them, though he never for a moment stopped checking.

Now, as they pulled back onto the two-lane blacktop, heading north, he savored the hot desert breeze. It might well have been cooler with the windows up, let alone with air-conditioning, but he liked nature as it was. He glanced at his watch with its luminous dial and calculated the distance. "We've got to get to four-tenths of a mile past milepost 378 by two forty-five. Should be a piece of cake."

Pam, uplit by the dashboard greens and ambers, still thinking over what they'd discussed, said, "Okay, we're sure the FRC isn't tracking us, but we're on our way to meet someone they could have tracked. What's up with that?"

"They can't track Dave."

"Why not? He's a computer genius, but he's not an alchemist or a mysterious pair of whatever Sly and Rosa are."

"No, but I got him a power *stone* years ago, and they don't know he knows me."

"He does more than know you. He's your right-hand man in the straight world. He contacts you and you contact him. He may have a magick talisman, but all it takes is one slip—and everyone makes one, sometime. Isn't that what both you and the FRC count on?"

But Max just laughed. "With Dave, it's mostly a matter of timing. Computers got going while I was learning alchemy from Agrippa in the early eighties, and Agrippa wanted to learn them, even though he knew he only had four years to live. So I asked around on the down-low and people said Dave was the best guy in Marin—a geek out in Forest Knolls. If we'd lived in the South Bay, I'd probably have contacted Steve Jobs or Steve Wozniak and the whole world would have changed, but I got in touch with Dave, talked with him until I figured I could trust him, and told him he could build his dream system if he kept it absolutely quiet. He agreed, and I introduced him to Agrippa, who agreed with my assessment. So Dave outfitted us with *the* cutting edge computers, *Osborne I*'s."

"Never heard of 'em."

"They were a portable computer—only weighed twenty-five pounds. And they were very cool for the time, by the way. Anyway, he kept us on the edge till Agrippa died. By then we had the very first Mac Plusses, and he and I were good friends. When I had to disappear, no one knew of our connection. He's stayed out on the edge through all the technology changes since; he uses a proprietary 1024-bit symmetric encryption scheme now, four times the government's Top Secret standard, and twice the FRC's. When we communicate, there's really no way for anyone else to track us. My skills are alchemy and combat; his is artificial intelligence. I've taken him places he can't go on his own, and he's taken me, many times. I trust him."

"You've said that twice," she said. "I rarely hear you say it once."

"Dave has never let me down, in over twenty-five years."

She snorted. "I forget how old you are sometimes."

"I'm thirty-five," Max answered equably. "It's my *history* that's old."

5 Jaguar (Empowering Clarity)

An hour later, Max's eyes flicked to the rearview mirror, and saw nothing but the low Pisces moon behind them, its half-lit face a pale gray-green. Ahead was darkness, split by his headlights along the asphalt road. They were south of Vegas, in the dead zone between Sunday night and Monday morning, between no radio worth listening to and no radio at all. He was running his iPhone through the van's sound system, playing Neko Case, "Prison Girls."

Two-tenths of a mile to go.

He checked his rearview again, then looked back at the highway. There was no sign of life. Coming up on his right was a ranch road. With no hesitation, he turned into it, slowing as he trundled over the cattle guard. The gate was open, the road a pale ribbon running toward distant mountains which blacked out the desert stars. Max flicked off the lights and drove with practiced ease over the rutted dirt, keeping it slow to mitigate the plume of dust rising gray in the night at their passage.

"One thousand one, one thousand two . . ." he began. Pam counted along with him, in her head, and when they reached one thousand twenty-six, they came to a turnaround, a wide spot in the road. A dark Tacoma was parked to the left. Max pulled to the right and braked.

Pam's eyes were adjusting to the dark. She saw a man climb out of the truck and step into the road. Max opened his door and got out. They were surrounded by great silence and the scent of sage.

"Wilhelm," Max said, just barely loud enough for the other to hear.

"Scream," he replied just as quietly.

It was evidently the right answer, something just between the two of them. Max went quickly forward and hugged the other man. Pam saw the other's teeth, grinning widely over Max's left shoulder.

Max saw the past.

APRIL 24, 1982 • 3:18 P.M.
PACIFIC DAYLIGHT TIME

11 Nipple (Owning Reality)

He was standing by Dave's record player, spinning the disks from Dave's incredible 45 collection, inside Dave's bungalow in Forest Knolls. He was bullshitting like the best deejay in town, the legendary Barnaby Wilde, though he'd retired a year before to work with Agrippa. Agrippa, wearing his usual impeccable black suit, was dancing barefoot on the hardwood floor with Val. She and Max had been married one whole month now and their love was growing like the spring orchard outside the house. Marriage to the legendary Barnaby Wilde had only pushed her farther up the pop-goddess ladder, and if she wasn't at the top she was damn close. She had big wild hair, dark-mascara'd eyes, a figure the whole world was in love with, and an enormous lust for life. But Agrippa, nearly five centuries older, was enjoying himself as much as anyone in the room, even with a death sentence over his head; all those years as a wizard had taught him to live for the day, and his years as Val's manager had taught him to breakdance. He gave Max an insouciant wave as he did the splits. All the while, Dave was waving his own loose hand, lounging long-limbed on his couch. They were riding the waves of the day.

Sharp knuckles sounded on the front door.

Max let "I Can't Go For That" spin on as all concerned looked quickly around for any telltale evidence, and all concerned realized that the room was completely filled with smoke.

The knuckles rapped again.

Dave got up. Agrippa motioned him back, preparing to defend them. But then the door opened, and two cops from the Fairfax Police, under whose jurisdiction Forest Knolls fell, stood there. The smoke wafted through the open door into their faces and curled around their caps.

Dave said, "Jesus, Bernie, you scared the hell out of us!"

The cop said, "Gonna need you to turn it down a little, Dave."

"Sure. No problem."

The cop saluted the room. The others in the room saluted back, with Agrippa clicking his heels. Dave closed the door and they fell about laughing.

MONDAY, JUNE 15, 2009 • 3:05 A.M.
MOUNTAIN STANDARD TIME

5 Jaguar (Empowering Clarity)

Max had Dave in a bear hug. "How're ya doin', man?"

"Pretty good *now*," Dave said. They stepped apart, and Dave's grin was unmistakable in the gloom. "It's always a good day when I see you, bud. If you can call this 'seeing.'"

Max waved his hand in a precise, wiping motion. An

outside observer would have seen no change in the desert's darkness, but both men became visible to each other's eyes, and to Pam's. "I can see fine. You've lost weight."

"I was turning into a caricature of a geek," Dave said, sticking his stomach out, rubbing it. "Junk food and no exercise. I decided, if you can do what you do, I can get off my ass. I've lost thirty-three pounds."

"You look good, man."

Pam opened her door, slid out, and walked around to the driver's side. Dave caught her shape in the night. "Is this Pam?" he asked.

Pam reached up and put her palm against his forehead. She became as visible as the men. "Yep, it's me," she said, as she and Dave looked each other over frankly.

Dave wasn't exactly thin even now, but his clothes were loose. He had thin brown hair and looked to be a well-worn midfifties, pale from lack of sun.

"Damn," he said.

"Hi, Dave," Pam said. "I've heard a lot about you. It's a pleasure."

"I've only heard a little about you," Dave replied. "Our friend here keeps our conversations short. But he really undersold it."

"I did not," Max said.

"You said she was smart and pretty. That's *way* underselling it."

Pam dropped her hand, returning herself to a mere shape in Dave's view. She didn't want him to see her blushing; she *had* to learn to control that. But Dave was the first person in over a year who knew her for who she was. She'd gotten compliments and innuendos often enough in that time, but always for the woman she was pretending to be. This was directed at *her,* and that was unusual. A break in the routine.

"Pam's learned a lot in the past year," Max said, casually

drawing attention from her, knowing her embarrassment. "She can protect herself, which is key, and it turns out she's got a natural flair for mental projection. She had telepathy from the jump."

"I never could get the hang of any of that," Dave sighed. "Alchemy. Even astrology. I tried for a long time, but I guess some brains are just wired differently."

"I certainly could never do what you do," she told him sincerely. "I can use computers, but their innards are a complete mystery."

"I'll record some stuff and give you a DVD next time we meet up."

"Thanks. That'd be cool."

But his words had evidently reminded Dave of why he was there, and that reminded him of who they were up against. He abruptly pulled a manila envelope from inside his shirt and thrust it on Max. "Here, bud," he said. "Two tickets to Wickr, as requested, and a little something extra from your Uncle Dave."

"What's that?" Max's voice betrayed his quick interest. Dave smiled with satisfaction; he liked holding up his end of the deal with the master alchemist.

"Well, I've got a pretty good idea how the FRC encrypts their stuff now. I made the assumption that these guys would use three-word combinations beginning with F, R, and C, because we've seen that's how they like to roll. So I had a place to start off. Their encryption is awesome after that, so I'm only partway through uncovering it, but I'm makin' progress. Well, it occurred to me that Michael and Diana would certainly bring their laptops, even if they're flying under the radar. If you get the chance, stick this thing in a USB port and it'll transmit the hard disk data, securely. I should be able to read at least some of what we come up with."

Pam had rarely seen Max surprised, but he was now. "You're not serious."

"It's what I do," Dave said.

Max took the device from the envelope and turned it back and forth in the ghost light, studying it. It looked something like a flash drive, but maybe 50 percent longer, widening out at the end. Probably the transmitter.

"You're saying you can *decrypt* FRC files," he said.

"I hope so. I think so. But I didn't test it. That could leave a trace, and you don't want me to do that."

"No."

"It was fun, though," Dave smiled, "reverse-engineering what I got." He looked at Pam and added with a shrug, "I have a funny idea of fun. And not enough real challenges anymore."

Max looked at Pam. "They don't know! Jesus! That changes everything!"

"Empowering Clarity," she said.

"In spades!" He turned back to Dave. "Thank you, man! Even if it doesn't work, that's above and beyond."

"No way, bro. I'm behind you all the way, and all the way behind you. No, I'm serious. You're doin' good work here. Old man Agrippa'd be proud. I'm happy to be in on it." His eyes flicked to Pam again. "So, there's just that one last thing . . ." he said.

Max understood. He said, "It's okay. You can talk in front of her."

"Well, it's about Val."

"I know."

Valerie Drake August had died in 1985, three years after that day at Dave's, but had kept her spirit alive after death—until she vanished on Hallowe'en, 1991. Now it appeared that she had been reincarnated, somewhere on Earth, as a seventeen-year-old girl. Dave gave it one more beat to be sure Max was cool, then went ahead. "I've got a pretty complete list of girls born that Hallowe'en night, worldwide, with complete records for Europe and America—partial everywhere else. I'm crunching their lives looking for any connection to you that I can find. So far there's nothing, but I've got a long way to go."

"There'll be a connection," Max said. "It probably won't look all that significant, but I am certain there'll be one."

"Why?"

"Because Aleksandra likes to fuck with me." Aleksandra was the other-worldly diabola who'd killed both Val and Agrippa.

"Well," Dave said, "as you can imagine, getting info on all those kids, even knowing their names, is a long process. They're not old enough, most of them, to be in the system. But anything I come up with, I'll let you know ASAP. Meanwhile, check the list to see if anything jumps out at you."

"As soon as I can," Max said. "I'm a little busy right now."

"Understood." Dave pulled out a second package. "But once you get some real free time, I burned the latest seasons of *Dexter, Burn Notice, Mad Men,* and *Hustle,* in case you haven't seen 'em. And season one of *Party Down,* highly recommended. For your voluminous free time."

"Thank you, Dave. And for you," he said, handing over his own package, "here's music from Barbados and Mumbai." The mention of *Mad Men* sparked a memory. "Hey, you hear anything from Heather and Bill?"

"They're still livin' in Ashland, still doin' advertising. Their oldest just got out of med school. And McGrady's salesman of the year for the third time. Tangier's got an estate with a gate and a private sound studio, but nothing much comes out of there; he talks about submitting a movie to Cannes but never does. Jan said some nice shit about you a couple of months ago, wondered where you were. They all think you're livin' back East, you know. And, what else? . . . KQBU switched formats again."

"Unbelievable," Max said.

"Which is why I've got six terabytes of the music *I* want on a portable hard drive. But none of it is from Barbados."

"You'll like it."

"I know I will. Nobody knows music like you do. Back in the day . . ." Dave paused, clearly remembering where they were right now, and why. Max understood.

"No one knows we're here," he said. "And you've got your *stone,* right?"

"Right," Dave said.

"We're cool. Trust me."

"Okay. Sure."

"So what about *you,* man?" Max asked.

"Me? Oh, you mean Kate?" Dave said.

"Mmmm."

"We broke up. No big deal."

"I thought you guys were doin' good."

"We were, for a while, but she wanted to live in the city. That's not me."

"You could give it a try."

"Nah, I know who I am. I like my little bungalow. It wouldn'a worked."

"Well. Too bad," Max said. "I liked her."

"Yeah, well," Dave said. "Life happens. I'm better off. Listen, I think I'll get rollin'. It's a long way back."

"I hear you," Max said. "We've got to go, too."

"There's a Grand Slam breakfast with my name on it in Bakersfield. Good seein' you, buddy. Really good meetin' you, Pam. Sorry about the Val thing. . . ."

"Not a problem," Pam said.

"Stay careful, man," Max said.

"You, too, guys."

The two men hugged again, then Dave hugged Pam, and she hugged back, fully aware that he could use a hug from a woman just then.

Dave went back to his truck and Max and Pam got back into their van. Dave started his truck and drove away along the dirt road, lights out. Max, also without lights, turned the van around and watched Dave drive halfway back toward the highway. Watched the highway. Watched for anything that bothered him, on the ground or in the sky. Still a point man.

When he was satisfied they were still in the clear, he followed his friend out to 95. At the junction, Dave turned south and Max turned north.

Pam, in the passenger seat, waved a hand at the world ahead of them. "All this," she said. "Wickr, the FRC—so many things on your plate." And, after a barely perceptible beat, "And no time to read the list of possible Vals?"

"I'll read it. But I can't give it my full attention while we're trapping Mike and Di, and I know any clue will be subtle so I need my full attention."

"Shouldn't you," Pam asked, "make looking for Val a priority?"

"Looking for her has always been a back burner thing," Max said seriously, his gaze far down the road. "When she was still a spirit, I only reached her on All Hallows' Eve—the rest of the year involved some preparation for the next one, but mostly, other stuff altogether. Now I have no way to reach her, so progress will have to come to me. All I can do is stay open to the signs."

"She could have been reborn anywhere."

"It doesn't matter. All the magick involved will have set up waves in the Flow. I wouldn't be much of an alchemist if I didn't believe those waves will have effects. And if I'm enough of an alchemist, I'll feel them wherever I am."

"Good," Pam said. "I want you to find her, Max."

"I know you do."

"You told me, you won't know how you'll feel—about her, about me—until you do. So the sooner you find out, the better."

Max abruptly pulled the van off the road, onto the dirt shoulder. He put it in park and put his hand on Pam's shoulder . . . then drew it sensuously down along her arm, down to her fingertips. . . .

"Well," Pam said, several moments later, "I think that empowers all the clarity I could ask for."

6 Eagle (Responding to the Storyline)

Eva Delia Kerr meandered along Oxford Street, enjoying the sound of "Mama Do" bouncing out of Whittard's tea shop on a summer's day. The bright morning was comfortable, not too hot and not too cold, with sun peeking through billowing clouds. Those clouds were building; it would rain later. But all that meant was, she was outside, in the open air, and not in some home somewhere. She was surrounded by other kids in their late teens, just like her. And her meds were working. She felt quite at home in Soho.

It seemed so long ago that she'd been in a home in Cambridge, labeled a schizophrenic. They had kept her so sedated that it was like a dream, anyway. Like another life. The voices in her head had always been at cross-purposes— they were *bad* then, yes they were. But the meds she got kept her from listening too hard, and that was a good thing for a while. Only, when the drugs were dialed back and she started listening better, she heard things she needed to hear.

One voice was Eva Delia, and that was the one they said was her. The other she just called the Voice. It was a woman's voice with a foreign accent, American maybe, and she didn't so much *talk* as *sing,* which just made it weirder and harder to shut out when Eva Delia wanted to believe she was Eva Delia. The Voice was like the earworm to end all earworms. And if she listened to its song long enough, she couldn't believe she was Eva Delia, no matter what the nurses told her.

Eva Delia *knew* she wasn't Eva Delia. But that didn't mean she was the Voice. Far from it. The Voice was beautiful. Eva Delia knew she wasn't beautiful, and although she tried, she couldn't sing at all. She dreamt about singing almost every night, but in the real world she could hardly even whistle.

"Little black butterflies deep inside me," Pixie sang.

So she was nobody, and she had two voices competing for her head, and everyone agreed that that made her mental. But with the meds dialed down, she had finally heard a third voice. That one reminded her of a drunken clown she'd seen on an outing, staggering along a Cambridge mews, holding on to the buildings for dear life, puking on his shoes. But that drunken clown had come from somewhere, and was going somewhere, and with the staggering and puking, it seemed like *her,* the girl with the voices. Her life had been so strange and erratic, but it was her life.

So the Clown-Girl listened to Eva Delia but didn't believe her. She listened to the Voice and didn't believe her, either. And by listening to both of them, bouncing off their walls, she was able over time to be the Girl. Just the Girl, but at least she wasn't nobody, she was somebody, even if she really had no name whatsoever. She was glad to know that. *Finally.*

And with her new meds, she could stagger a great deal less.

"Uh-oh, uh-oh," Pixie sang.

The first step in survival, the Girl had realized as realization became possible, was getting free of Cambridge. She knew they couldn't hold her once she turned sixteen, but they'd be *there,* watching her. Talking to her: more voices. So she had to go, and she forced herself to walk all the way to the M11 to see if someone would take her away. She had staggered a little, but she didn't throw up, and she didn't give up, and she got there. She knew men could be bad so she said no to the men who asked her to ride with them, and when Carla Lambert said she'd give her a ride to Liverpool, she'd said no, too, because it just didn't feel right in her addled state. But soon enough Betty Gerard had spoken to her, and Betty had said she was driving down to London, and Eva Delia said her father lived there, and it was done. That was more than a year ago, now.

The Girl dodged the cars to cross the wide street and duck into Rathbone Place, then continued into Soho Square. Here, suddenly, it grew darker as the ancient trees shaded the sun, and she began walking unconsciously to the beat of the Voice. But that didn't worry her the way it would have in Cambridge. She passed the melting statue of the old king or whoever, and the homeless kids sitting endlessly on the worn grass behind the benches, and the boy in the wool cap playing the public piano. There was some sort of festival setting up—there was always some sort of festival, it seemed—but she exited into Frith Street, and the light from the sky came back.

Just down the block was the National Health clinic ("Soho Centre for Health & Care"). She went up the ramp and crossed the waiting room filled with people with hurt bodies, to take the lift to the third floor. The waiting room there was nearly empty; not so many people with hurt minds. There was only Fred, the rasta. As usual, he stared at her but said nothing. It had bothered her the first few times he'd done it, but now it was familiar, comforting, like the clinic. The pretty nurse behind the counter was expecting her, and passed her through to her psych nurse, a nice woman with pretty skin and lots of it. Her name was Sunita

Koomari, which was *so* pleasant; it always made the Girl smile, even on the bad days.

"Hello, Eva Delia," said Nurse Koomari. "How nice to see you again."

The Girl knew not to say she was not Eva Delia. "I never forget to come, Nurse Koomari," she said carefully. "I want to get better as soon as I can."

It seemed as if Nurse Koomari's face grew a little sad then, just a little, and the Voice sang, "You'll never get better," but Eva Delia said, *"Yes I will! Shut Up! Shut Up!",* and the Girl with no name closed them both out firmly. They weren't welcome here in the clinic, or anywhere else when they argued.

Nurse Koomari asked her the usual questions, making sure she was all right, making sure the hostel they'd found for her in Greek Street was treating her correctly. To prolong the conversation, the Girl told the truth but elaborated on her answers until she felt perhaps she'd started rambling. She enjoyed talking to Nurse Koomari, and she thought Nurse Koomari enjoyed talking to her, so long as she didn't ramble. That was the same as staggering, and that made Nurse Koomari unhappy. But evidently, the Girl had pulled back in time because Nurse Koomari gave her the same prescription, 10 mg of olanzapine, and said she was doing very nicely, indeed.

It was such a good session that the Girl kissed Nurse Koomari's cheek, and let the Voice sing without interruption as she made her way back to the lift. She wanted to go down, but the sign there said, as always, "Press Up button for lift." Nurse Koomari had told her the Down button was broken, and the lift would come anyway, which it did.

But that kind of thing, the Girl thought, could make you mental.

6 Eagle (Responding to the Storyline)

The sun had been up for forty-five minutes in Manhattan, but the temperature wasn't all that bad for mid-June. Early-morning dog-walkers, even runners, were hardly breaking a sweat. Inside his brownstone on East Thirty-fifth Street, Lawrence Breckenridge was sweating, but he was communing with the only power in the universe that he submitted to, the diabola known as Aleksandra. She had been human once but existed on a different plane now, and though she could appear in something very like flesh if necessary, she preferred to have the sixty-eight-year-old Breckenridge lead her FRC. He was, as both friend and foe often noted, "remarkably well-preserved"—thanks to her.

Coraxo cahisa coremo, od belanu azodiazodore . . .
Das Daox cocasu ol Eanio vohima . . .
Ohyo! ohyo! noibu Ohyo! casaganu!
NIISO! carupe up nidali! NIISO I A I D A!

Suddenly she appeared before him, burning with a red fire that highlighted her perfect, naked form. It was a false form of high, perky breasts sweeping into smooth curves of hip and leg, and Breckenridge, like any man, had no trouble lusting after fantasy. He felt her hand wrap around his heart, like the world's most skilled courtesan caressing his balls. That pleasure, he knew, could so easily turn to pain, and she'd given him one heart attack already. But still, he was confident.

Aleksandra! he cried out. *Diabola!*

She looked back at him impassively. He ruled everyone below him, and she ruled him, which put her at the pinnacle of the world—but she took that for granted and found no special pleasure in it.

What's the news on Max August? she asked, her communication a form of *call,* direct from mind to mind.

"The three teams sent to destroy him and his woman remain close," Breckenridge answered, orally. He could approximate a *call* to her, if he had to, but why? Speaking was easier. "Each of them has a different skill set, so each seeks him on a different level."

"Close" is not what I expect from you, Lawrence.

"We're on track, diabola," Breckenridge responded crisply, still on his knees but straightening his thighs and rising as high as he could, to look right into her crimson eyes. He had failed to kill August the first time the cabal had targeted him, and Aleksandra had threatened to replace him, but she had not done so. It told him that there was no one better suited to act for her on this level, and the terror he had felt when he'd failed her had rebounded to become a sort of surety. He knelt because she was worthy of awe and respect, and even love—not because he feared her. She could destroy him but she needed him, so they were collaborators. "You know better than I how hard it is to track someone with powers like his. He's damn good at using all of them, but we have mercs, ninjas, and demons. One of them will find a weakness and move in for the kill, because he's only human, in the end. We're closing in. It's just a matter of time."

Isn't everything? But the last time anyone found him was two months ago, in Mumbai.

Breckenridge said nothing. It was true but ultimately irrelevant in his view, so he waited for her to continue.

What about your new wizard, Quince?

"I'm seeing him tonight. I gave him three weeks to study

Jackson Tower's records, and he'll give me his conclusions at sundown, in Duluth. If I'm impressed, he'll have passed the first hurdle in taking his place in the Necklace. If I'm not impressed, Dick Hanrahan will terminate him on the spot. But I expect to be impressed."

The FRC was the outer order; the inner order was the Necklace, a chain of nine men and women. Each of the Nine was responsible for one sector of power in society, like media, politics, finance . . . and wizardry. The Necklace had existed long before Aleksandra took it over, and had prospered over the years by using every form of power available. Wizardry gave them an edge; only the Nazis had ever staked out the same ground, and they had been undone by their direct assault on their enemies. Magick was powerful but so were enemy armies; therefore, the Necklace had *almost* always chosen to operate in the shadows, through pawns and fronts. They'd been operating without a wizard since August killed Tower and stole his power, a year and a half before, but Breckenridge had searched long and hard before settling on Peter Quince, an associate professor of philosophy at the University of Wyoming in Laramie, as Tower's replacement. On the one hand, Breckenridge's association with Aleksandra made him uniquely qualified to judge magickal skill, and he had sought the best candidate out there. On the other hand, his association with Aleksandra was a secret that could never be revealed, so he had to feel certain that he could maintain the secret. Quince had struck him as a man with such a high opinion of his magickal power—a perfectly valid opinion—that it would never occur to him to wonder if anyone else in the Necklace had more than he did.

What do you expect him to offer you?

"No idea. The real point is for him to demonstrate his thought process."

If he doesn't offer something substantive, that means another delay.

"I don't expect that to happen. But if it does, it does. We need to make sure our own house is in order. August, after all, is a temporary problem, but we are here for the long term."

Unless Max August destroys you in the interim.

"I don't expect that to happen," he said again.

But if it does, it does. She was mocking him. Again, he showed no response. This, too, was true.

In any event, you'll be without my aid for the next several days.

Finally, he was caught off guard; this had never happened before, not in all the years they'd been linked. "What are you saying, diabola?"

I have a quest. I won't be available if you CALL, so don't CALL.

"But—why?" Now it was she who did not respond, except for a mocking smile that played over her face. It was not his place to question her; he couldn't push it. So he simply said, as if it didn't matter, "Good luck, then. You can rely on me." Still, he did love her—how could he not, with her overwhelming beauty and power?—and he hated the idea of losing her for any length of time. "Can I be of any help—?" he began.

But she had vanished.

The man who ran the world was well and truly alone, for the first time in years.

5 Jaguar (Empowering Clarity)

Peter Quince stood spread-legged on a flat, metallic plane that stretched away forever everywhere. High above him, two lights, a sort of sun and sort of moon, threw twin shadows down over him and the center of the plane. He knew it was the center, at least for him, because four lines led from it, at right angles to each other, in four different colors. The red line led straight out ahead, as far as the eye could see.

It was another world, and he was alone in it.

Peter Quince was a stocky man. His face was stocky as well, with all the features compressed into the middle of it. But some people, given a second look, saw the reverse: the vast brow and the tough chin. The brow was further expanded by his receding hairline, though he was not yet forty; the remaining hair was combed backward in smooth waves. His shoulders were wide, his arms heavy; he looked far more like a linebacker than a wizard.

Quince gazed above the red line, through crystalline air, at the images hovering before him. Centered among them was the horoscope of Max August, born July 31, 1950, 11:56 A.M. Miami. He had studied it for hours today, and hours on several days before this one. He saw the planets and their intricate, ancient patterns.

He was certain that Jackson Tower had taken notes on Max August, but he was just as certain that they'd gone up in flames along with the old wizard. So he'd begun from scratch. He saw things, and the next night he saw more things, more complex patterns. It was always that way with a chart. You had to live with it for a while, get to know it, just as you would get to know a person. And in this case, he had to know it, because Tower, who was reputed to be a sharp old sonofabitch, who'd survived a long time for a wizard to the all-powerful Necklace—had lost to August. There was something in the Code Red that Tower had not seen.

Or perhaps something Tower had *seen,* but not fully *understood . . . !*

Quince swiped his hand, four o'clock to the center of the air. The horoscope moved up to the left, retreating, shrinking, while the National Security Agency dossier on August moved into its place, expanding. Quince flipped seventy-three pages with a mind-thrust, read:

In Vietnam, August was his unit's point man. The other men would move through the jungle as a group with August on his own somewhere ahead. His job was to hunt for the Viet Cong or their booby traps, to protect his men. He was said to be very good at it.

Staff Sergeant Oliver Mendelsohn, interviewed 27 Feb 81: "The guy had a real knack. You can either go out there and sweat bullets, or go out there and make a game of it. He made it a game, though he knew the stakes as well as any of us. He was never reckless that I know of, but he liked it out on the edge."

Lieutenant Gene Polansky, interviewed 24 Feb 81: "There was something seductive about the war. Danger—weird danger—in the jungle, and hookers and dope in Saigon. You could hit a nice rhythm between the two, rocking back and forth, in and out of the darkness. But August played it straight in town, which made him a real motherfucker in the field."

Spec4 Dantron Weeks, interviewed 2 Mar 81: "He thought the war was a huge mistake, but if it had to be, and he had to be in the damn middle of it, he was going to do what he had to do. He was going to do his job, to the best of his ability. And I think he found out that he did love the job."

The images in the air faded, as Quince's concentration on them faded. He was inside his head, reading signs in those words, savoring them. *That* was what Tower had missed. Because Tower practiced the old ways of abstinence, so Tower did not love.

But August did.

Quince waved the book aside and called up Pamela Blackwell's chart, July 9, 1979, 1:24 P.M. Alamogordo, New Mexico. Seven, nine, seventy-nine. He appreciated the cleanliness of it.

She was a strong other half for him, with a real connection. Tower must have seen it, but it didn't mean enough to him. Max and Pam, as Quince thought of them now, would reinforce each other. The way a *stone* augments a wizard, the two together were more than the sum of their parts. To attack one, you had to attack both, and the bond between.

He let the plane boil and bubble away beneath his feet, dissipating like fog in the mountains. He felt himself falling, though it seemed as if he stood quite still, and when the final tendrils vanished, he was standing in a large, private room in Duluth, Minnesota. Despite its specialized design, it wasn't a room he'd ever have chosen, but he didn't have to stay there. He could rise to the plane whenever he wanted. Or he could walk out the room's door, down the narrow wooden hall, down the narrow wooden stairs, and open another door.

Peter Quince was a lover, too, and Rita Diamante was waiting for him downstairs, naked.

Day One

·······························

6 Eagle (Responding to the Storyline)

When Max and Pam crossed into Nevada, the change from Mountain Standard Time to Pacific Daylight Time was mere semantics, so when Pam took over the wheel, she drove through Vegas with the night shift going home, the day shift reporting for work, and, for the first time, other vehicles clearly on their way north to Wickr. These last ones were packed with supplies, whether or not they flew flags with the Wickr sphere on them, or plastered that design on their windows. Most of them had old bicycles attached to their trunks. She had no trouble spotting them, and no trouble spotting the traffic cams along the freeway, which she could have avoided by taking the long way around through Pahrump. But now that the energy was Responding to the Storyline, she made the decision that they'd be less conspicuous in the crowd. She drove with the traffic, while Max dozed.

KLUC was offering Ne-Yo's "Mad" and "Closer" back to back as she made her way along 95, dancing in place to the snap of the beat. She passed miles of subdivisions behind sound abatement walls, until coming to the ring road finally let her see the vast sweep of the land she was in by daylight. Born in New Mexico, it had been a while since she'd seen a Southwestern desert, and it made her realize she missed it. It surprised her. She didn't like what the FRC had done to

America but she liked America just fine. All she and Max had to do was get it back.

Tearing her eyes from the vista, Pam looked over at Max. *We've been together twenty months now,* she thought. *I was twenty-eight when I met him; in three weeks I'll be thirty. And Val or no Val, we've become a couple, just the two of us.* She remembered his earliest attempts to explain magick to her, and her first attempts to keep up. He'd tried to use words because he was a deejay and she was a doctor, but they'd soon figured out that she was really someone who learned by doing. So they developed her natural abilities, like the *call,* and built on that—letting things like the Mayan calendar and festivals of the year come when they came. Through it all, they became a team. *Now we're going to have two more in the mix,* she thought. *It's going to be a change.*

She drove north along 95, past Lathrop Wells and Beatty to the junction with 266, where she took a left past the Cottontail Ranch, following and followed by the other Wickns. Pink sang "Please Don't Leave Me" and Jeremih sang "Birthday Sex." Ten miles later, 774 cut off south toward Gold Point. The Black Eyed Peas sang "Boom Boom Pow." Ten more miles into increasingly empty vistas got them to the few scattered houses of the old mining town, where the Vegas deejay talked about Michael Jackson's upcoming tour, and then a reddish-brown dirt road marked with the bright golden circle of the Sun to put them on the last five miles of their journey. Lady Gaga broke up in the midst of "Poker Face," and that was it for the outside world.

Max sat up, stretching. He could see dust rising in the air from far across the subtly rising plain, churned by dozens of other vehicles ahead of them. They drove along a low ridge overlooking the plain until they caught up with the cars, then settled in for a good ninety-minute crawl to the entrance kiosks.

"I've got nothing to do until we hit the ground, so I'm going back to sleep," he said, and sat back, pulling his cap low over his eyes. "Home, James." Pam gave him an indulgent look and soldiered on.

At the end of the crawl, a ticket-taker took their tickets and passed them forward to the greeters. These were people dressed in costumes of one sort or another, from elaborate to all-but-nonexistent, who asked each arrival to step out of his or her vehicle and chat a little, one on one, making the first of the human connections that really defined the festival. Those who said they'd been to Wickr before, like Max, were welcomed back with enthusiastic hugs, but those who were new had to grab a handful of dust and throw it up into the air. Pam threw, and her little white dust cloud was one of dozens down the kiosk line, a continuing fireworks show to celebrate discoverers. Pam's greeter gave her an enthusiastic hug then, dipping her, and she joined the energy of Wickr: when they stood up, she dipped him. The car behind them emitted applause.

They were in a large, relatively flat area at the base of the chocolate brown mountains. Even in mid-June there was snow on the mountain peaks, thousands of feet above, but down in the desert it was already better than ninety degrees. Max and Pam got back in their van and drove into the charmed circle of the new city, like Dorothy beginning to follow the yellow brick road.

They trundled at five miles per hour around what was actually the dusty circumference road until they found a view of the mountains they both liked, then worked their way inward on the spoke road. When they came to Venus Street, Pam pointed out a likely looking camping spot with some crazy-looking vehicles around it; Max agreed, and she pulled to a halt so Max could lean out his window and ask one of the campers already in place if they and some friends could join them. With the guy's ready affirmative, Pam pulled into a large empty spot, stopped the van, and got out again, stretching hard in the heat of the sun.

Max got out, looked around, and casually made a wiping motion with his left hand, as if cleaning a windshield. In fact, he was cleaning the world he saw, looking through that world into another world for anything that might be a danger to them in either world. When he was satisfied that there was nothing, that they were still safe, he gave Pam the slightest of nods.

The other campers here had come in vehicles ranging from cars to trucks; Max and Pam had the only van in sight. Some of the others had tents or other shelters erected, others were in the process. The tents ranged from low Army pup-tents to vast domelike creations, some limned with lights. There was also an even larger structure built to resemble the curl on the top of a soft-serve ice cream cone, with a window cut into the side and the twelve-foot cone lying nearby; someone was planning an attraction.

Max and Pam walked back to where their new friend was lounging in a low fold-out chair alongside a woman his age, under a canopy made of three layers of mosquito netting stretched from their car's roof to corner poles. The guy was wearing knee-length shorts and nothing else; the girl had on a see-through muslin top over a pale green skirt. Glasses and a pale green pitcher were arrayed on a small wooden table between them.

"Mojito?" the guy asked.

"We would love two," Max said. "Hi. I'm Paul and this is Olivia." Pam noted the names; it was one of Max's jokes, or maybe tests, to spring new names on her when needed. Paul and Olivia.

"Randy and Sara," said their new friend, and his girl raised a hand. Randy scrunched himself forward in the sunken seat of his chair to reach the fixings, and poured out two drinks that he handed around.

Pam, taking a sip, felt the kick and said, "Damn! That goes down good."

"It's our official Wickr whiskey," said Sara. "Starts the day off right."

"Where are you guys from?" Randy asked.

"Chillicothe, Ohio," Max said.

"How long a drive?"

"Six days," Max said. "We came out Route 66." Pam knew that he'd actually motored west on 66 at some time and would be able to talk about it accurately. She wondered, not for the first time in these situations, *when* he had done it. "How about you guys?" Max continued.

"Salem, Oregon," Randy said. "One long day."

"One very long day," Sara echoed. "But there are springs just before we get to Nevada, so we broke it up."

"How many times have you been here?" Max asked.

"Three," said Randy.

"This is the second for me and first for Olivia."

"How do you like it?" Sara asked Pam.

"So far so good," she grinned. Sara grinned back.

Max said, "We've got some friends coming in tonight, so I'm gonna set up two tents in my space if that's okay."

"Knock yourself out," Randy said. "You need any help?"

"I don't think so, thanks. We'll stop back after we get squared away."

"Putting up tents is thirsty work," Sara said. "That's why we don't. So stop on back for refills whenever you need them. We'll probably head out after a while but we'll leave the pitcher full."

Max and Pam went back to the VW and slid open the side door. All of the equipment they'd picked up in Tucson was packed expertly, and still filled the interior almost to the roof; it took a fair amount of stuff to spend a week self-contained. But right on top, ready to be pulled out, was a Volkswagen tent designed to attach to the side of the van, wrapped in a carrying bag. A standalone tent lay in another bag. They got them both out onto the ground, then climbed inside to get the rest of what they'd need to erect them. Pam touched Max's leg with her hand, a small signal, and pulled the sliding door closed. It immediately became an oven inside.

"Max," she said.

"Yeah?"

"That test back there."

"You did fine, as always."

"That would be my point," she said, looking meaningfully into his face. "I'm both your girlfriend and your disciple. I like both parts, but being at Wickr makes me think that maybe we've gotten 'em out of balance. How about if we let the girlfriend part predominate this week—when we're not planning doom for the FRC? After all," she added, warming to her brief, "Sly and Rosa are doing all the heavy lifting—so to speak. Most of the time, we won't be involved."

"We're always involved," he said, but he was nodding. "Your point's well taken, Pam. Whenever we can, we will party—" his voice became the resonant one he used on-air in his radio days "—LIKE IT'S TWO-THOUSAND-AND-NINE!"

She laughed, and softly paraphrased Fergie. "I'm so two-thousand-and-nine / you're so far out of your time. . . ." She smiled her crooked smile. "Thanks, sweetie."

"Believe me," he said, opening the door again, "it is *not* a problem." He stepped outside and gazed around at the burgeoning city. "I like Wickr, too."

6 Eagle (Responding to the Storyline)

"Back . . . back . . . hold it, that's good."

Michael Salinan brought Diana Herring's American Heritage luxury coach to a halt, directly across from his own, facing the other direction, at a distance of twenty feet—far enough apart to allow them some semblance of separation, near enough to discourage anyone from trying to park between them. They'd chosen a spot far out on Saturn Street where there were few other vehicles as yet, and none even approaching the size of theirs. Soon enough they'd set out travel chairs and tables to further mark their territory, and the thirteen-foot heights on either side would go far to shield their world from view. All in all, it seemed to be about as much privacy as one could have at Wickr.

Diana slid down from her seat and exited down the passenger-side steps. It had not been a long drive from Vegas, but she wasn't used to driving anything as big as this behemoth, and the five miles of dirt road had been a real pain. Literally: her shoulders ached. A luxury coach was indistinguishable from a tour bus in shape: forty-five feet from squared-off front to squared-off back. She would not have minded at all having someone else drive it, but no one else was allowed to know she was here. She would not have minded coming with Mike on one bus, but that left no plausible deniability if one or the other was found out. So she drove "hers" and he drove "his."

His was identical to hers except for color; hers was Sandrift, all beiges and tans, while his was Cashmere Blaze, aswirl with whites and maroons. She approached her behemoth as he opened the door with a hydraulic whoosh and stepped out. Then he walked behind her up her steps. Then he took her in his arms.

Michael Salinan, the political guru of the Necklace, was forty-two. His head had been shaved bald since the Clinton administration, highlighting his wide, pointed ears to make him easier to caricature, since he appeared in political cartoons and on the Sunday news shows from time to time. But at the moment, he was wearing a curly brown wig beneath a wide-brimmed straw hat, and aviator sunglasses. The wig was exquisitely made and looked completely natural. It had been attached to his head with an adhesive guaranteed not to loosen with sweat. It made him look both normal and nonthreatening.

Diana Herring was thirty-eight. She had the strong willowy body of a news anchor, and curly black hair, naturally, but *now* her hair was straight and blonde. Her face was normally slightly asymmetrical, which didn't mar her striking beauty but gave her greater gravitas. *Now* it was carefully balanced, with extra shadow under the cheekbones. Her best friend would have had a hard time recognizing her. She had worked local news, followed by a brief stint with NBC, before moving into management at the age of twenty-nine. Six years later, she was tapped to head the Media link in the Necklace. Her secret to success was her ability to always appear completely sincere; right now she *was* sincere as she pulled Michael into the interior of her coach and led him toward the queen-sized bed with the beige satin coverlet.

"Hang on," Michael said. "What about security?"

"This thing's got an alarm system," Diana said, and let him go long enough to reach out and press a wall switch. The door to the van hissed shut and a red light came on beside it.

"That's fine," Michael said, "but *my* coach isn't set. Anyone could get in." He broke the clinch altogether and turned back. "Open up," he said.

Diana made a disparaging sound but pushed the switch again and let him out; then watched through the side windows, beneath the shades and past the flowerpots with real flowers, as he walked back over to his coach. He looked around, then checked inside, before coming back out and thumbing a button on his keys. His door slid closed.

Michael was a hale fellow well met, but he was a chess player at heart. He loved the game, and he loved the win, and Diana loved that about him. She herself was all about the big picture, and her love was an air war for men's minds.

When he came back up her steps and into the coach, he said, "Okay, babe, here are the rules. Anything goes at Wickr. It's all about being exactly who you want to be, and the worst thing we could do is hold each other back. I want to be here with you, big time, but I also want to enjoy the time and place."

"And I'm good with that, Mikey. Though I, personally, have more than sex on my mind."

"So do I, babe. Part of what I need to know here is the mind-set. We've got to turn the tide on the youth vote, so I'm going to be studying these kids."

"And I've got to stay up with the demographic, so I'll be doing a lot of empathizing. Win-win." She smiled, and spread her arms. "All right?"

"All right," he said, and had the decency to smile.

As they fell backward onto the bed, Michael's hands undid her silk blouse and slid inside. He ran his hand along her rib cage with a delicacy no one would have suspected in him; it made her moan and twist to offer her breasts. He took what was offered, deftly snapping open the clasp on her bra. It parted to reveal her breasts, flushed and hard-nippled.

"Hi there," Michael said brightly, "I'm Ron."

"Stacy," snickered Diana. "Pleased ta meetcha!"

They were going to enjoy this week big-time.

MONDAY, JUNE 15, 2009 • 2:00 P.M.
CENTRAL DAYLIGHT TIME

6 Eagle (Responding to the Storyline)

Kevin Stallworth paced the basement of his parents' down-sized house in Fort Worth. It was hot outside, cool in here; he wanted to be out there, wearing a heavy wool suit, with a tie. Instead he was here in his skivvies. He put three Hot Pocket Sideshots in the microwave, went into the bathroom and peed. He flushed, washed his hands, went back to his room to get dressed. The NASCAR calendar above where he'd dropped his jeans read JUNE 2009.

For the one millionth time, Kevin asked himself why he'd had to graduate when there were no jobs.

Monday was the beginning of another week, and the early bird had the best chance of catching the worm. But he'd been trolling the net since 8 A.M. and there was no more there than there ever was. He pulled on a DaVinci tee shirt and slid his mini-burgers onto a plate and checked his e-mail for any responses to his morning's work. There were several, ranging from turndowns to not hirings at this time. So then he worked his way through the Web sites again, applying for anything that sounded even remotely plausible.

Finally, out of all other options, he called his uncle.

"Uncle Craig?"

"Who's this?"

"Kevin. Your nephew."

"Oh, hi, Kevin. If you're still looking for work—"

"I am, I guess, Uncle Craig."

"Well, I'm sorry, buddy. I asked, but they're not hiring."

"Oh. Well . . ."

"Sorry," Craig said. "They may even be downsizing, tell you the truth. And sales work—I don't think that's for you anyway. You've got a degree."

"*Anything* would be for me right now. Even door to door." Kevin got himself under control. *Remember that it's not his problem, that he's not the enemy.* "That's cool, Uncle Craig. I'll find something."

"Sure you will. You're a smart kid. Someday we'll all look back on this and laugh." A voice in the background said, "Time, Craig."

"Gotta go," Craig said. "Good luck, Kevin. It'll work out."

Kevin punched END and checked his e-mail again. It went quick; there was nothing for him there.

MONDAY, JUNE 15, 2009 • 12:35 P.M.
MOUNTAIN STANDARD TIME

6 Eagle (Responding to the Storyline)

Craig and Aaron walked into Sanders' Rental Cars on South Tucson Boulevard. There were no other customers at the time, because the two men had waited until that was the case.

"Hi there," Jeff Grundy greeted them cheerfully. "What can I do you for, guys?"

Aaron said, "We're looking for some friends of ours, who may have rented from you yesterday."

"Sure," said Jeff. "What are their names?"

"That's what we want you to tell us," said Aaron, slowly lifting a Keltec .380 pistol from his pants pocket. Jeff's eyes grew huge. His hands went up, palms out.

"Whatever you want," he said, trying to stay calm. "I can show you my receipts. Whatever you want."

"Put your hands down," said Craig, who now had a Colt .45 automatic in his hand. It looked huge. He went to the Open sign on the front door and turned it around. Then he pulled the yellow plastic shades that kept the sun out in the late afternoon. Satisfied that no one could easily see inside, he returned and leaned his back against the counter, keeping watch on the front door.

Jeff's hands fumbled a bit as he opened his receipt drawer, but once he'd done so he stood aside with his hands in plain sight. He was clearly no threat at all.

"Put your forearms on the counter, palms up," Aaron said. Jeff did as he was told. It caused him to stand awkwardly, bent over slightly. His back began to pain him almost at once.

Craig started working his way through the papers. As he turned each one up, he typed the name, address, and credit card information into his BlackBerry Storm. Then—

"Here's a couple that paid cash for a Volkswagen Vanagon."

Jeff said, "The man had dark hair—"

"Shut the fuck up," Craig said. "It doesn't matter what they looked like." He talked to his partner. "They took it for two weeks, to be returned here."

"Did they say anything about where they were going?" Aaron asked Jeff.

"California," Jeff replied.

"Okay," Aaron said, talking to himself. "They'll be out *less* than two weeks, and *not* to California." He looked at his partner. "Let's check the camping stores."

"Where are the best ones?" Craig asked Jeff.

Jeff told him about the malls down the road.

"Anything you can add to that?" Aaron asked.

"No . . ." Jeff faltered.

"Let's go in the back," Craig said.

6 Eagle (Responding to the Storyline)

Living without Aleksandra was a strange thing for Lawrence Breckenridge. He'd been in thrall to her for seventeen and a half years, since January 20, 1992. He was returning from a Necklace conclave in Wheeling, West Virginia, that night. The Nine had been strategizing for the coming transition to a Democratic president, as it was clear that Bill Clinton would defeat George Bush Senior. Breckenridge was just drifting off to sleep in his private jet when his blood pressure tripled. His fingers stiffened; his eyes bugged from his head and the veins above them burst. He thought they'd been struck by lightning; he thought it was a heart attack. And then he was overcome by the most erotic rush he had ever known. He came in his pants and the pressure inside him lessened; he slumped in his leather chair as if dead. But he was unbelievably alive.

A scarlet mist flowed into his vision from the blood above; the world turned red. The mist flowed *from his eyes.* He could see the ripples in its fog, radiating from him into the cabin, until they swirled into a perfect oval, a scarlet egg, floating directly in front of him. Then slowly, but with thrilling purpose, the egg began to grow thicker in rhythmic parts, like blood coagulating . . .

. . . forming curves, in-out-in-out . . .

. . . the shape elongating, top and bottom . . .

. . . the whole thing solidifying, starting with slim white perfect hands raised like a dancing girl's . . .

. . . ending with the most beautiful woman he had ever

seen, standing in his cabin. She was dressed like the goddess of all dancing girls, in low-slung skirt and veils.

But Breckenridge had never expected goddesses when he died. "Who the hell are you?" he demanded, his hand moving toward the Glock Model 21 beneath his suit jacket.

She smiled a dazzling smile. *If you shoot at me, Lawrence, you'll blow a hole in the aircraft and depressurize it. You don't want to do that.* Her English had a faint New York accent, but it seemed to issue not from her mouth, but from . . . her, in general. Whatever; he knew she was right. He lowered his hand, meeting her halfway, and stood up.

My name is Aleksandra, she said. *Or it was. I've transcended my incarnation, but I remain INTERESTED in this world, the same way you are, Lawrence. I lived here long enough with the same dreams. Your Necklace is the leading force for world domination today, and I have had an arrangement with Tom Jeckyl since 1988.*

Tom Jeckyl had led the cabal since the '50s. He had personally recruited Breckenridge as their political link in 1976, and they'd worked on many projects over the past sixteen years. Breckenridge was astounded: Tom, with *this?* And no one *knew?*

Tom and I have worked together in complete secrecy for four years, but as of tonight, we are one year away from a change in American government, Aleksandra said.

"We have allegations of an affair, a woman named Gennifer Flowers. Tom wants me to put the word out tomorrow. But you would know that, wouldn't you?"

Will it work?

Breckenridge hesitated. "It's all court of public opinion stuff, and Clinton's damn smart."

Will it work, Lawrence?

". . . I don't think so."

I don't, either. But Tom thinks it will.

"Tom's been at this longer than I have."

Will Tom take you where you want to go, do you think? Or has Tom run out of gas?

Breckenridge took a step forward. She might be real and she might be unreal, but he wasn't afraid of her. No, fear wasn't what he felt at all. "What is it that you want, Aleksandra?"

I want a man tough enough to ask me that question, she said, looking him straight in the eye. *I want YOU to be the Gemstone of the Necklace.*

Breckenridge reached out and took her arm. She felt solid, but she was scarlet, in the mist, waiting on him. "What are you? A demon?" he demanded.

A diabola. The difference is subtle but important.

"Like what?"

She smiled. *I don't want your soul. I want OUR success.*

"And how much power do you bring to the table, miss 'diabola'?"

Power beyond anything you can imagine, Lawrence. I'm in a realm twice the size of this one now. It takes work for me to put on flesh like this, so I need a human agent on the scene. I've taken my time and studied all the members of the Necklace, and I want you to be that agent.

Breckenridge shook his head. "I'm not 'agent' material," he said flatly.

Ah, but MY agent is the most powerful man on Earth. He'll RULE the Earth in time. She spread her hands. *Your cabal has chased that dream since Frederick the Great, but you and I together will finally achieve it.*

Breckenridge thought furiously, weighing all the factors. "It's tempting—but you say we *will* rule. When?"

That mostly depends on you.

"Give me a ballpark."

Twenty years.

"2012." He imagined it. "I'll be an old man then."

I'll give you vitality. You'll be one of those old men who never gets old, and you'll live as long as you want to.

"Hunh." He perched his butt on the arm of his chair. "Tom's not likely to step down. He enjoys being the Gemstone. And he probably enjoys the same deal on life-extension with you." He looked at her. "He'll have to be killed."

You'll have to kill him, she agreed.

"I can do that," he said, and the deal was done.

She flowed toward him, around him; he experienced ecstacy such as he had never known or even dreamed.

In the seventeen years since, he had experienced *power* such as he had never known, and she had always been available when he needed her input. Their plan for domination had proceeded almost flawlessly, just as she'd predicted. But now, for the first time ever, and so close to the end, she had left him . . . for something even more important?

And yet . . .

He had to admit there was something refreshing in the change. One thing he talked about a lot was "freedom," which he let others believe meant freedom for them. He was the Gemstone of the Necklace—but Aleksandra *was* always above him. They worked together, each had unique strengths—but Aleksandra was always above him. Now she wasn't. It happened to feel good. Not good the way her touch felt, but good the way life had felt when life was simple.

Breckenridge looked out the window of his brownstone. It was *quiet* now, lacking the buzz of her presence. He walked to the bar, poured himself a healthy slug of the absinthe he was savoring that year—Vieux Pontarlier—and added crushed ice from the refrigerator. He took the drink to his wide desk, sat back in his great leather chair, and propped his feet up. He studied his glass as the green liquid grew cloudy and white from the chill. He took a sip and savored it, along with his options.

He'd been fighting a dozen brush fires from this room for most of a year. He'd had to make sure no one from the Bush administration was investigated, let alone tried, for their war crimes. He'd had to make certain the Obama people would continue their security state and their wars. He'd had to make certain no banker lost anything for ruining the economy. He'd had to make certain the oil giants didn't lose, and the health care giants. None of that had been easy, with so many little people, and even some big ones who should have known better, thinking their vote would lead the other way. But he'd managed it so far, and he would continue to do so.

Now, though, he was on his own—and goddammit! for the first time in a long time, he was going to have some *fun*, the way he used to. Enough with the weight of the world!

He put his feet down and picked up his telephone. He punched one speed-dial button, waited only briefly for an answer, and then spoke just three words.

"Hit Senator Ensign."

–o–

Aleksandra hovered, floating, in the Abyss. She had been like this since leaving Lawrence Breckenridge—it was impossible to say how much time that had been because she was no longer in SpaceTime. This was just Space, where Time meant nothing. The hovering woman-form glowed with an angry red light, which dissipated into the unlimited darkness like foam on a breaking wave and faded to deepest black. But the red light was beginning to curdle, to form tendrils of darker shadow at the edges, like clotting blood. The tendrils were twisting around themselves, like serpents, creating larger shapes, larger shadows, like film being developed.

She was a diabola, and this was hard for her now. Squeezing herself into SpaceTime always required real intent. But she had the intent, so she searched through her memories, seeking a hook, a grain of sand which she could build a pearl around. If she could isolate one human emotion, she could impose it on human reality, and create a human self.

The self she once had been.

I was barely six years old when the two women drove their small black automobile to our farm in the Samarkand. It was classic theater: the lone black car, the long, trailing dust plume, the high lonely clouds. 1955, it was.

They got out like city people, stiff from the journey. They were wearing black as well, though each had a bright-colored scarf. One was yellow and the other green. I felt excitement rise inside me. All of us children had taken a test several months before, but I knew these women had come to see me. I knew it to a certainty. And I was barely six years old.

They talked to my mother, and strangely, I thought, ignored the baby. Women never ignored a baby. But maybe Dmitri was ugly or squally; I can't recall. It's beyond the human wall. Looking back on it now is like looking through glass from a broken Coca-Cola. Thick, green, distorting . . .

My mother agreed with the women, and the three of them escorted me into the next room. It was smaller than the parlor, but that seemed to please my visitors.

"Now then, Aleksandra," the woman in the green scarf said, "I'm Drysi—"

"What does that mean?"

She smiled, kind. "It means 'one who comes from Demeter.' Demeter was a Greek goddess. But I am not a goddess and I don't come from Demeter. I come from the School Board."

The one with the yellow scarf spoke. "I'm Svetlana. I'd like you to hold my scarf for a minute." She leaned toward me and I grasped the cloth. It felt yellow; I don't think there was anything more than that.

"Now I'm going to go outside," Svetlana said, and she left the room. Drysi didn't say anything for a while, watching to see what I would do. I sat quietly, waiting for them.

She said finally, "Now, I would like you to tell me where Svetlana is standing."

I remember staring at her. No one ever ignored a baby, and no one ever asked me to Witness. But I sat up in my chair, back straight, head poised atop my spine, and closed my eyes.

I saw the yellow, trailing like a fern in a brook. I FLEW to it, caught hold of it mentally, then pulled myself along it to Svetlana's neck. I turned and looked and saw the barn, the mule. "She's in the barn," I told Drysi. "Beside the mule. It's the southwest corner."

Drysi blinked. Stood up. Said, "Please wait here," and left.

After maybe four minutes, Svetlana came in and sat down across from me.

"How did I do?" I asked, but I knew the answer. I wanted to Witness her saying it. But instead, she said, "Aleksandra, please tell me where Drysi is standing."

Well, right away I knew she wouldn't be standing. She'd be sitting or lying down. But I still needed the "where," so I took up the posture again.

I hadn't touched the green but I'd had it in front of me the whole time. It was a little harder to make out, especially as it blended with the grass and some trees, but there was a limited area to search. I found the scarf whipping back and forth—and since I hadn't touched it, I didn't have to touch it to know it. It was whipping back and forth because Drysi was swinging on our old tire.

I told Svetlana, and asked again how I had done. She smiled, and said I had done well, and they would be in touch with my mother.

Then five months went by. Soviet bureaucracy.

It wasn't until February that we heard from the ministry (not the School Board, no). And of course, then I was given just one day to prepare, and be prepared by my mother. Like all parents, she was upset at losing her daughter but proud to have contributed to the state. It sent her up and down emotionally throughout that twenty-two hours, and Dmitri caught her mood and squalled for certain.

But I was tremendously excited. I kissed my mother and brother good-bye and took the four-hour bus trip to Tashkent, where I boarded the Trans-Aral Railroad for Arys. There I transferred to the Turkestan-Siberia rail line running north. The birch and aspen outside the grubby windows grew increasingly barren, leaving the landscape to the old, green pines. I saw reindeer and elk among the trees, and a single fleeting fox. But I could hardly sit still, for I was going to Novosibirsk.

Novosibirsk—"New Siberian City"—was the largest city in Siberia, and the third largest in the Soviet Union. A tattered flag fluttered on the fender of the thick black car that met me and drove me through the city and then over a bridge above the river Ob. I didn't know anything about cars at the time, but if I had, I'd have registered that this car was a Chaika and known Chaikas were the next step below Zil limousines, available only to government officials. Nikita Khrushchev was entitled to a Zil but he preferred his Chaika.

But I didn't know cars, and my driver answered questions as briefly as possible, so I soon stopped asking any.

Eventually we came to a curious compound. It consisted of four cinderblock buildings forming a rigid square. The layout spoke of a purpose, but the buildings themselves were shabby, stained, cracked. Then Drysi came out of the nearest one, now wearing a red scarf, otherwise still in black. She was smiling. "Come with me, Aleksandra," she said, and offered me her hand.

She led me across the wintry courtyard between the buildings to the one at the opposite corner.

"You mustn't mind this place," she said, and I wondered if she could read my mind. "The ministry is building Science City just thirty kilometers south of here, right beside the Ob. It was supposed to have been finished by now, but isn't. That's all right. You'll like the people here. Especially our Comrade Director."

We went through the door, out of the cold, and into a dark hall. There were lights but they were dim. Drysi took me to the end of the hall, and knocked on a metal door.

"Enter!" called a thin voice.

Drysi opened the door and motioned me inside. "Comrade Director, Aleksandra Korelatovna is here," she said as I walked forward.

The man behind the desk was small, and looked to me to be a hundred years old. He was dried up, fragile, and his face had a cowlike stolidity. . . . I instantly knew he was not like me, not even like Drysi and Svetlana. If I had thought that was all the school was ever going to be, I think I'd have turned around and gone home, no matter what they did to me; I could already sense the scope of my life and this little man could only thwart it.

But when I looked at him, I Witnessed another man, a man who was coming. In my vision, he wore a white suit, with a rose in his lapel. I had no idea who he might be, but I knew to a certainty that he would not thwart me.

"Hello, Aleksandra," said the current Comrade Director. "My name is Colonel Bek. Welcome to your new home."

"Yes," I said, my face breaking into an almost painful grin. "Yes! I am HOME!"

• • •

Aleksandra had found her human emotion, to build a human form.

6 Eagle (Responding to the Storyline)

The rain had been falling in London for several hours when a large cumulonimbus suddenly blew up, bringing thunder, lightning, and a torrential downpour. For some twenty minutes water fell like a monsoon, overwhelming the storm drains and leading to sudden flooding in some parts of the city, especially near the Thames. People everywhere ran for shelter under canopies and bridges. People remember that night to this day.

But a seventeen-year-old girl named Lexi strode purposefully through the pouring rain, across the open expanse of Leicester Square, dressed in a LIFE ON MARS tee shirt and well-washed jeans, as well as high heels, which were an anomaly in this city. What did she care? They pleased her. The tee shirt was plastered across her perky breasts so the boys who spotted her were instantly smitten, and she wanted to take them, one after another, right here in the rain—but that was not what she was here for. Sex, she knew, was one of the great benefits of flesh, but there were others. When she came to a market on Charing Cross Road, she popped inside and bought a ninety-nine-gram Cadbury Fruit & Nut bar. She paid for it, having a little trouble finding the correct change, then went back into the street. The clerk stared after her, focusing on her butt in those tight, tight jeans. Lexi unwrapped the Cadbury and bit off one end . . . and staggered for a step, gobsmacked by how good it tasted after all this time.

Ahead, on her left, was Rusterman's bookstore, which had stood in this location since 1853. Lexi went inside, very properly dropping her candy wrapper into the rubbish bin beside the streetlight.

The shop was a labyrinth of bookshelves, perhaps too much aware that the original owner had never even thought of standardization. The shelves were as long as they'd once needed to be, and no more; placed where they'd needed to be, and nowhere else. Now there was no thought of changing any of it. It was London, the city, and it was "London," the tourist attraction. As prosperity had come to the generations of owners, neighboring buildings had been bought, low doorways had been knocked through walls, so that now, Rusterman's lurched along for quite some distance, with an upstairs and a downstairs as well. But Lexi strode the aisles with confidence.

• • •

Seven rooms away, the Girl people called Eva Delia was fingering a leather-bound volume of ancient writing. The book meant nothing to her, but the store was a haven from the street. The absence of meds had allowed her scrambled mind to form some pathways it hadn't had before. She would be the first to admit that it still resembled Rusterman's labyrinth, jumbled and narrowing, but as with Rusterman's, she had learned her way around. It might be jumbled but it was solid and real.

She had learned most of London by now. She knew where free food could be had, and where good food could be stolen. She knew where she could sit for a while, where she could linger, seven rooms away from the entrance, and force herself to think. This was her favorite spot for thinking, because they kept the oldest books here. The many volumes, orderly on their shelves, with their orderly pages and orderly lines of type, seemed to help. She couldn't read them because they were in some foreign language, but it wasn't the words that mattered. She opened the books one after another, letting her eyes run along the lines. She particularly liked the really old books because the lines were uneven, like her mind, but they were still lines, like she wanted her mind to be. She especially liked this leather-bound one; it might be the oldest one of all. She carried a worn bag, never knowing when she'd find something she needed, and she could have slipped the book into the bag. But she was not a thief if she didn't need to be.

"Penny for your thoughts, luv."

The Girl looked up, startled. Boys talked to her sometimes, but rarely girls. This girl was about her age, seventeen, and her hair was a striking shade of scarlet. She was dressed in well-washed jeans and a LIFE ON MARS tee shirt that ended at the navel. There was a ring in her navel above jeans that rode low across perfectly proportioned hips to reveal half a tattoo—possibly an eagle. Did the girl think she was going to steal the book? The Girl felt dowdy and abashed, and turned to go.

"My name's Lexi," the newcomer said, her voice warm and friendly. "What's yours?"

"I don't do that," the Girl said doubtfully.

Lexi laughed, sparkling. "I'm not looking to snog you," she giggled. "I just—well, my birthday's coming up this Sunday, and I just got a check from my auntie, and I wanted to do something nice with it. If I had to guess, I'd say you could use a nice meal, and I don't know a soul in London, so I'd be as pleased to have you as anyone come join me. I was thinking of steak."

"Steak?" That couldn't be right. "Steak?"

"Steak. With wine, because I'm turning eighteen. And perhaps a nice pie for dessert."

"You mean cake," the Girl said.

"No, I like pie. But you can have cake."

"I don't think so."

"We can go to Covent Garden if you like."

The Girl had seen the restaurants there, near the Opera,

but had never been inside one. They were filled with prosperous people, dressed in gowns and suits and even tuxedos. (People *sang* there.) Go there? How would that even work?

Lexi suddenly became solicitous. "Say, you've had rather a worse time of it than I thought, haven't you? Won't you please come with me? When the night is over, you can go where you like. I won't try to stop you. But it would make my auntie so happy, and me."

The Girl thought the poor girl really needed company, and realized that for once *she* could help another soul. That was something new. The Voice and Eva Delia began jabbering, but the Girl shut them away. "Okay," she told Lexi. "I guess we could do that."

"Super!" said Lexi, taking her hand. "We're going to be *such* great friends. What's your name, luv?"

The Girl hesitated. But she was committed. "My name is Eva Delia," she said.

MONDAY, JUNE 15, 2009 • 2:30 P.M.
PACIFIC DAYLIGHT TIME

6 Eagle (Responding to the Storyline)

Max and Pam surveyed their work, and found it good. The freestanding tent reminded Pam of some Bedouin chieftain's abode in *Lawrence of Arabia,* since it was easily big enough to contain a four-man conference. By contrast, the VW tent attached to the van was comfortable for two people and that was about it. Since she liked being a twosome with Max, that was not a problem. Neither was the space between the two tents, since there was plenty of desert to go around, and the stabilizing ropes from the corners of the tents set up obstacles that discouraged other people from using the space as a walkway.

Everything was out of the van and into one tent or the other, so Max and Pam were sitting on the floor of the van, their legs stretched into the attached tent, eating peanut butter and jelly sandwiches. All food had to be considered against a week with no refrigeration. They'd bought block ice in Tucson and kept it in a cooler buried under the supplies; it had held up surprisingly well. When it was gone, they'd buy more; the only two things you *could* buy at Wickr were ice and coffee. So the two of them had given some thought to food that wouldn't last, to be eaten early on, and food that could; Pam had even snagged some Chinese chicken salad that could stay frozen till Thursday. PB&J could certainly last, but acclimating to the desert heat, now somewhere north of one hundred, would take at least a day and simple comfort food was all they wanted after tent-raising. That and lots of orange Gatorade.

But finally Max asked, "You ready to find Mike and Lady Di?"

"I was born ready," she replied. "But how will we do that? There's got to be twenty thousand people here already."

"At least," he agreed cheerfully. "But we've got an edge."

"We know the energy of the day."

"Yep. Responding to the Storyline." He took a long slug of Gatorade. "The Storyline is made up of the bright, shiny things that attract our attention. There's nothing wrong with bright, shiny things *per se*—we all like 'em to one extent or another, and I once played pop records for a living— but they distract you from what else is out there. Your *response* to the Storyline is what matters, because as anyone who's watched cable news knows, Storylines can easily be manufactured.

"For example, I've seen a lot of comedies and commercials in the past ten years that present men as slackers, so their level-headed and much better-looking wives have to hold them together."

"What's your point?" Pam asked sweetly.

"Level-headed wives I don't have trouble with. Clueless slackers who can't handle life sounds too much like crowd control. Watch old commercials. The men in those Storylines had a lot more balls, and men in real life were active."

"You're one of those guys."

"Those guys exist at any time. They're just not part of the Storyline now."

"But is that a plot, Max, or is it just change?"

"Couldn't tell you yet," Max said. "I only know it's happening, and television is paid for—and if it *is* FRC mind-control, Di's involved, so that's one of the things we're going to find out."

He gestured toward the surrounding city. "Mike and Di are running an *extensive* Storyline for Wickr. That they're not here, that they're somebody else. Everything they do is designed to make us pay attention to some things and not pay attention to others. A lot of people at Wickr like to play at being somebody else for the week, but they're not over-stressing it. If somebody recognizes them from their life back home, so be it. But Mike and Di are stressing all the time, to hold their Storyline together, so their energy is distinctive."

"Well," said Pam, "if you and I can do anything, it's recognize energy. If we get out there on the dark wave, the odds are excellent that we'll feel them."

"That's how we roll," Max said, grinning. "Unless my much better-looking *girlfriend* doesn't want to do alchemy."

She inclined her head derisively. "Alchemy is your *girlfriend's specialty,* pal."

So they moved out of the van and into the tent, tied the flap behind them, and sat cross-legged on the canvas floor, invisible to the outside. Though it was hot inside the canvas structure, it was cooler sitting low. Without making a big deal out of it, Max had consulted a compass while setting things up, so the tent was aligned with the four directions. He sat in the north and Pam sat in the south.

She remembered her hours in Jackson Tower's slave room, twenty months before, trying to send her thoughts to Max along the dark wave. She hadn't known how to do it, but, with the help of a sorcerer's *stone,* she'd kept trying until she'd found out. That was her particular strength.

She extended her hands. Her right one closed around Max's left; his right closed around her left. Their knees touched. Their alchemical energy began to circulate around and around, first inside each of them, then inside their duality. Like a dust storm in the desert, it grew and began to rise. It became a towering thing, invisible—then it widened out, its circular sweep spreading from a spot on Venus Street, inward to the Sun and outward to Earth Street, Mars, Jupiter, Saturn. . . .

On Saturn, Max found the twin coaches with no trouble at all. But Mike and Di weren't in them now. He "leaned" inward and surfed what he called a "psyclone" back toward the Sun at the center. Soon enough he found two discords at Mars and Noon.

He rode down and in, until he could see his quarry—not the way he would see them with his real eyes; he had never been really good at that—but he could see their auras. The reds and oranges clearly signaled their stress and excitement. His mind reached out to Pam's, to tell her it was time to move on, only to find her excited in her own way. He decided to let her have her head, and waited quietly for almost a minute before she acknowledged his presence. Then the two of them spun the psyclone back to its towering shape, back to its circular shape. . . .

They opened their eyes, and unclasped their hands.

"Mars and Noon," Max said.

"Brown wig and blonde wig," Pam answered.

"You saw that?"

"Sure. You didn't?"

"No. Congratulations."

"Thanks. It's just my thing." Her tone was casual, the same as his when he brushed off his accomplishments, but she was proud nonetheless. Here was something she did better than he did; she was making progress. She almost leapt to her feet as she added, "Let's go check 'em with our eyeballs!"

6 Eagle (Responding to the Storyline)

Michael and Diana were walking the dusty streets on Wickr in their disguises and a state of intense excitement. Part of it was their own horniness, only intensified by their mid-morning delight, but most of it was the festival itself. Now that thousands of people had pitched their tents, hundreds of people were taking in the sights the way they were. Those people came in all sizes and colors, all genders and costumes; this was not a place to hide one's light. And even if many of them were just playing, they were playing for keeps. The costumes ran from elaborate, closely worked gaud to simple but offbeat mélanges, and dozens of people wore nothing at all. These were primarily but not exclusively men, while an equal number of women, not quite willing to go all the way, wore only thongs and pasties. No one was going to be offended, and no one was going to attack anyone; the energy was all the more positive because of that. Plus, on all sides, little theme parks were arising—open-air lounges for dancing, clusters of wire sculptures, tubes that spit fire in time to the techno-beat that suffused the desert air. Strangely redesigned vehicles drove slowly past, showing off. It was like living in a circus. Michael and Diana had never seen anything like it.

"This is unbelievable," Michael kept saying. "I've seen far more flesh at some political dinners—and Bohemian Grove? forget about it—but that's all, you know, bought and paid for. This is spontaneous."

"It's freedom," Diana agreed. "It's what these people want to do. That's terrible for you; you need people who want protection. But it's heaven on earth to me; I have to keep their attention, and every new idea is a new way to do that."

"I am loving it," he replied. "Loving it!"

She took his hand. "I wish we didn't have to keep it hidden all the time, Mike."

A shadow fell across his face. "Don't go there, babe."

"I'm just saying—"

"Breckenridge and Hanrahan would cut our throats without a moment's hesitation if they didn't approve. I'm not chancing it."

"You're overdramatizing," she said.

"Am I? They don't do political compromise. Like you, they renew or they cancel."

"But why would they cancel *us*? We've done everything we were supposed to, and we've done it well. Why should you and me together be a problem?"

"The Neck—" he said, but then reconsidered; they could be overheard. "Our group has nine people. Each has his or her own specialty, based on principles that have worked for generations—a lot more generations than Breckenridge admits to, I think. But we're supposed to be nine separate entities. It's the Gemstone who puts it all together."

"We work together. We *have* to be together."

"Work, not sleep."

She shook her head irritably. "All right. We agreed, and I won't force it on you. But I think you're wrong. It's the work that counts, and not the sleep."

Michael smiled. "It's the sleep that counts for *me,* babe."

She kissed his neck.

Ahead, on their left, a guy wearing a purple wife-beater and camouflage pants was standing in front of a large open tent filled with loungers, holding out a tray. "Chocolate?" he asked the world at large. His tray was covered with broken-up chunks of Heath Bars; the chocolate was melted, exposing the toffee, but chocolate always looks great. Diana reached for a piece but another hand got there first, dipping in and out quick so as not to forestall her. It was attached to a good-looking guy with red hair and beard. By his side was a girl who might have been his sister, they looked so much alike. He handed her half of his booty; she had to detach it from his hand.

"Don't mind me," the guy said to Diana, sticking his chunk in his mouth and crunching it. "You looked like you were thinkin' about it and I'd already made up my mind."

"I was just deciding on which piece," she said.

"Did I take yours?"

"Not at all."

"Then it's all good," he drawled. "Have you guys been out to the Caterpillar yet?"

"No," Michael said. "What's that?"

"Giant caterpillar," replied the redheaded girl. "Out on the plain. It's huge, and you can climb through it, or just admire it. At night I think it shoots flames. Where are you guys from?"

They went through the introductions—Ron and Stacy started out, then the redheaded girl jumped in to say "Julie and Elmer."

Elmer grinned easily. "I go by 'Flash.' So, you all want to take a run out there after dark?"

Stacy said, "I'm up for a little adventure," but Ron stepped in. "We're still scoping the place out. Where are you located?"

"Sunup and Mercury," Flash said—an intersection of the east side of the city.

"Well," Ron said, his eyes on redheaded Julie, "we'll try to catch up with you tomorrow maybe."

A little more talk and they were all on their way, blending back into the masses.

Pam made a grimace of distaste. "Both of them had a faintly superior vibe, like they were slumming."

"You think it was faint?" Max asked. "But I've got a pretty good idea what she likes. To her it's all a sort of reality show, and everything's on camera without a second thought. We're only her extras, but she was ready to roll."

"He was, too," answered Pam. "But he's a back-room guy. He doesn't want anyone watching him, especially Diana. If half the stories out of Washington are true, he'll do a little acting out if given the chance. Are you *sure* Rosa should get into this?"

"I'm telling you, don't worry about Rosa."

"Okay, Flash. And by the way, you passed your test."

"Oh, good."

"So then, I guess I can escort you to this caterpillar— unless you made him up."

"I'm afraid I did. But I'm sure there'll be three things even better." He pointed down the length of Mars Street. "What the hell is *that?*"

6 Eagle (Responding to the Storyline)

Eva Delia and Lexi were having a wonderful time. The food had been unbelievable, the wine even better, and then they'd switched to champagne. Eva Delia was feeling completely satisfied for the first time, maybe in her life. She knew she was drunk because she'd seen people drunk, and she remembered what Nurse Koomari sometimes said about mixing wine with meds, but there was nothing wrong with this. It felt so good. Was it a bad thing to thank God for Lexi's arrival?

"Here," her friend said, tipping the thick bottle to pour the last sparkling drops into Eva Delia's glass. "Finish it off."

Daringly, Eva Delia did, tossing it down with a flair, almost toppling backward from her chair. She had been this spacy many times in her life, but always on downers, not sparkles. The room around them was slewing up and down. Staggering like a clown. She burst out laughing.

"I've got to go," she managed to say, and looked obliquely, suddenly, at Lexi. "That's okay, right?"

"I told you, E.D., I don't want your lily-white body. Hey, can I call you 'Eddy'?"

"My name is not Eddy. I don't even think it's Eva Delia."

"What do you mean?"

"I don't know what I mean. Never mind."

"No, really. What's up?"

"I don't know," the Girl said. "I've never known. I just feel it, inside."

"We all feel stuff inside," Lexi said. "That doesn't make it real."

"I know. That's what everybody says. I know all sorts of things. That's the trouble. I know more things than I can fit together. I hear a Voice . . ." But she let that go with a guilty look. Other people didn't like that.

"Well," said Lexi, "*I* will think of you as Eva Delia. You look like an Eva Delia to me." Eva Delia wondered how spacy the other girl was. She didn't seem spacy. More like watchful. But smiling as she went on. "This was a wonderful evening. You certainly saved my birthday party."

"Your birthday's not till Sunday."

"But the party started today. I plan to devote the week to it."

"You're nice, Lexi."

"I'm just looking for a friend," Lexi said. "Just one special friend."

"I haven't had many friends," Eva Delia said. "In the hospitals and houses, kids come and go. But you remind me of my first friend. She was my best friend. Her name was Sandy."

"Really?" said Lexi, cocking her head. "How do I remind you?"

"She had the same dark blue eyes."

"Really. And what happened to Sandy?"

"I don't know." All at once, Eva Delia felt great sorrow, as the past washed over her. "They used to give me drugs, so I missed things, and one day when they let me alone so I was me, she was just gone."

"She probably saw that they were keeping you under control."

"What? No. That doesn't make any sense. They just transferred her."

"Ah. I'm sure that's it. It's not my area, after all." Lexi waved her hand without looking around, calling for the check as if she'd eaten in fancy restaurants a hundred times before. But she kept her eyes on Eva Delia. "Like I said, this was a wonderful evening. Shall we do it again tomorrow?"

"Oh, I'd love to, but I can't—"

"Take advantage of me? You're not, really. But we won't eat in a fancy restaurant. I told you my brother paid for this treat, so we'll do something different."

"I thought you said your aunt—"

"No, my brother. But tomorrow we'll be on our own, and we'll find our own fun."

"Well, okay." This girl still liked her! "Where do you live?"

"Why don't we meet where we met tonight? In the bookstore. That's simplest."

The waiter arrived with the bill. Lexi said, "You go on now, Eva Delia. I don't want you seeing how much this cost. I'll meet you tomorrow at nine again."

Eva Delia got to her feet. The room was really swinging now, but the prospect of tomorrow, with a new best friend, was more than enough to counteract the sorrow of the past. On impulse, she bent down and gave Lexi a hug, but not a kiss. Any time she'd ever kissed anyone, she'd been spacy, drunk; kissing reminded her of the bad times. She hugged Lexi, then whirled gayly and made her way more or less toward the door. She was staggering again. . . .

But she couldn't remember a happier time in her whole entire life.

6 Eagle (Responding to the Storyline)

Breckenridge had worked for nine months on his plan to eliminate Tom Jeckyl. Often he'd thought that having a baby would be easier. But finally, on October 8, 1992, Jeckyl died of what the most determined autopsy by Necklace doctors later called a pure heart attack. That night, in Wheeling, the other links in the Necklace voted him the new Gemstone—and then Aleksandra gave him a talisman for his victory.

In a few moments, a meteorite will fall across the eastern half of America. It'll break up over Kentucky, and the largest fragment will pass within a quarter mile of this aircraft before destroying a Chevy Malibu in Peekskill, New York. That fragment will weigh twenty-nine pounds. Send men to retrieve it and I'll fill it with power the next time I come to you, to make a weapon for you alone.

He had men sent. He also had men analyze the trajectory of the meteor, the dynamics and the makeup. Everyone agreed that it was a real meteor, which Aleksandra knew about before it happened. So he presented his trophy to her, and she turned it into a magickal *stone*—the largest *stone* on earth. No man on Earth had had more power than Lawrence Breckenridge for the past seventeen years. . . .

• • •

"We're here, Renzo."

Breckenridge came back from his private thoughts and looked out at the house of their wizard. It was still several hours to dark this far north, but the sky was heavy with rolling black clouds. Lightning flickered far out over Lake

Superior, followed just three seconds later by the crack! and the boom. On the horizon, a gray curtain descended and began to march across the waters toward them.

Dick Hanrahan studied his old friend covertly. It was absolutely clear to the Necklace's chief of espionage that something was going on with him—something secret and new—and Hanrahan disapproved of secrets in others.

He'd had bugs on his old friend for the past ten years. He already knew that Renzo had one big secret. It had to do with an unidentifiable static that blotted out all else on his digital recorder at random intervals, but since the static was unidentifiable, Hanrahan couldn't put the picture together. At first, naturally, he suspected drugs or women, but his own personal surveillance—none of his many operatives could be involved in this—proved beyond a doubt that that was not the case. So he'd added Renzo's rooms and jet to the list of his many private taps.

On the night Jackson Tower died, a continent away from Renzo, Hanrahan heard that unique static from Tower's death site. Renzo could not have been there, so it was something else—but what? It had been eating at Hanrahan for a long while.

And now there was something new.

"Would you like me to see if they're ready?" Breckenridge's driver asked.

"No, Roger," Breckenridge said. "We're ready." Then, to Hanrahan: "Right?"

"Sure, Renzo. Let's open things up."

6 Eagle (Responding to the Storyline)

The house was a large Renaissance Revival, with a half tower on the front wall, designed by famed architect Issac Vernon Hill in 1898. Like most of Hill's houses, this one boasted a carved wooden head that gazed from under the corner eaves of the front porch. In this case, it was an eagle, gazing not at the great lake before it, but the dark forest around it.

The two highest-ranking and longest-serving members of the Necklace exited their Range Rover limo and hurried to the front porch, as the sound of the rain on the lake grew loud behind them. Beneath the eaves, Breckenridge rang the old, familiar doorbell just as the storm swept over them and began to pelt the roof.

The door was opened by Rita Diamante, dressed in her usual sprayed-on jeans and stylish top, now accessorized by a light, clinging sweater in honor of the distance north from her native Miami. Both men enjoyed the view, and she knew it. "Welcome, Mr. Breckenridge, Mr. Hanrahan," she said, smiling brightly.

"Is he ready?" Breckenridge asked her in low tones as the two men came inside.

"Yes, sir," she answered. "He's been working deep into every night. Whatever he does, he does it balls-out." Her accent was Miami-Cuban, tightened by years of harsh, uncompromising command. She was beautiful and she was charming when she wanted to be, but she was always tough. Acting as the majordomo for their new wizard was a test for her, set by the two old men before her. She knew it, and they knew she knew it. "Follow me, please," she said cheerfully, and led them into a high hall, whose well-trodden hardwood floors sent their footfalls echoing around them.

Rita knew that lesser men might not have understood why she'd been forced to flee Suriname. The fact that they did understand, that they saw how she'd played a losing hand as well as anyone could, had only strengthened her desire to join their organization. When they'd told her to run their potential wizard's household while he communed with the cosmos, she traded Miami for Duluth without a second's hesitation. It might not seem like a promotion, but it was. In the FRC, the alternative to promotion was termination. Everyone kept moving forward, like sharks.

They entered the old house's solarium, kept warm and humid by dozens of plants and small trees beautifully arranged around the circumference. The windows were intricately made, with the slight wave of hand-crafted glass, and now awash with the rain. More lightning blasted the sky above, and the resulting thunder rattled the glass almost instantaneously. But a single tranquil butterfly wove its way among the leaves inside the solarium. There was no other animate creature. Rita looked around with sudden impatience and said shortly, "I'll go see." —but at that moment, Peter Quince strode into the room.

His dark hair and dark eyes seemed to absorb the light around him. He was wearing a black robe, but it was the man himself who was dark—a strange mix of common clay and something ethereal.

"Sit, please, gentlemen," Quince said, his voice a soothing baritone. "I apologize for keeping you waiting." His years as a professor had given him command of a room. But he was the one facing an exam as Breckenridge and Hanrahan sat on the padded lawn chairs of the solarium, causing the butterfly to move on.

"This is the time and place agreed upon for your recommendations," said Breckenridge succinctly.

Quince nodded. "I'm more than happy to perform like a seal, Mr. Breckenridge," he said, "but afterward, we need to discuss this place."

Breckenridge snapped, "What about this place?" and there was no mistaking the warning in his voice. But Quince, while acknowledging it with a slight bow, was not to be deterred.

"I'm happy to begin there," he said. "Happy to work with you gentlemen. But wizardry is first and foremost a matter of the mind, and my mind is more at home in the wide open spaces of the West. If you approve my performance, I would like to return to Wyoming to continue my work. I know a spot far from real civilization, but not unconscionably far from an airport—"

"No," Breckenridge said definitively. "Our wizard always lives in this house. Get on with your recommendations."

Quince took a step forward, quick to anger. "That's ridiculous," he grated. "A wizard must have total peace of mind—"

"Fuck," said Breckenridge, "you." He started to get up from his chair. "The wizard lives here, for reasons you're not yet able to know, so move on!" He stood and awaited the response.

Quince took a step back. This was not what he had expected, not what he'd counted on. A simple request . . . "I have to believe you," he said slowly, "if you say it's necessary, but *you* have to admit, I was speaking as a professional—"

"Shit!" said Rita, from the shadows of the ferns. No one had paid the slightest attention to her since Quince had entered the room, but now she stepped into the gray light, her attention focused on the wizard. "You spend a lot of time outside the reality the rest of us are in, Professor Quince," she said, "but you still work for these gentlemen and they have their own reality outside yours. Deal with it."

Quince glared at her. She glared back, unmoved.

He snorted, but he backed down. He smoothed his robe. "All right," he said, as if he'd made the decision. "To business then." He turned again to the old men, relegating Rita to the background even as she stepped back into the shadowy vegetation.

"I say again, I am unaware of the larger scope of your activities. You've been careful to keep it that way. I apologize if I've overstepped my boundaries. Now, I have reviewed Jackson Tower's logs, and Señorita Diamante has been useful in telling me of his last days. I have spent long nights seeking his spirit—since, as you may not know, a man at the moment of his death can sometimes hold his spirit together." He looked from Breckenridge to Hanrahan, but they were waiting for him. "I'm sorry to say that I've been unsuccessful. If we assume that Tower died in combat with Max August, and I don't think there's much doubt on that score, August inherited all his power, as is the way when wizards die. Tower had no magick left to maintain himself in the great beyond. But I have had more success with his logs, and the logs of his predecessors, concerning his knowledge of August. Roland Stavros, in particular, had a stream-of-consciousness approach to his wizard's life that is intensely appealing. And Tower had good first impressions—wizardly impressions—of Pamela Blackwell. So I am fully prepared to make five recommendations concerning August's destruction."

He looked behind him, as if forgetting for a moment that he had no classroom blackboard to hand. "First—August gets his power from sex magick. In point of fact, all magick is closely related to the sexual power, but it was his specific starting point in magick, back in 1980. Beyond that, he is traveling with a woman who is his lover. So I recommend making all those who pursue him on your—our—behalf, groups consisting of one man and one woman. The two sensibilities will catch more clues along his trail than either sex alone."

The two old men showed absolutely no reaction, and Quince took that as a signal to continue.

"Second," he said, "these teams should concentrate on areas of what I would call sensual pleasure. This does not mean they will never visit the South Pole if required, but given multiple options, they as a couple will tend toward locations which heighten their senses. This is not simply because they *are* a couple now, though that's a factor; more important is the fact that Blackwell likes pleasure. August likes it but he's compartmentalized, able to live on his own as needed. Blackwell, on the other hand, is a sensualist at heart. She will influence his thinking in that direction. So what I am saying is, seek them anywhere your intelligence takes you, but once close, keep a special eye on the more stimulating options. And should you lay a trap for them, go heavy on the honey.

"Third, August did receive magick from Tower when Tower died. Such magick does not contain specifics—that's not the nature of magick—but there could well have been bits of data, impressions, things that could give him a direction of inquiry. And because of August's orientation toward sex magick, such impressions would most likely be of people, and their relationships. It's clear from his logs that Tower did not believe in squandering his energy in sex, which is fortunate for us; had Tower had a lover, August might have been led directly to her, or him. But Tower had acquaintances—you and the other members of the FRC. So I recommend keeping a close eye on those members. I'm sure you keep tabs on us all," he added easily, speaking to Hanrahan, "but keep a *close* eye." This time, Hanrahan nodded curtly. Quince took it as a good sign.

"Fourth, elementals."

"What are they?" Breckenridge sat forward in his chair, appearing quite interested, and Quince smiled inwardly. At last he was certain that he offered something they did not have. Breckenridge was continuing. "I don't know much about your business, but I've worked with a number of wizards over the years. Explain it to me, and let's see if I get it."

Now Quince's voice took on an unconscious lecturing quality, being as clear as he could. "Elementals are the forces of nature, personified, or at least solidified. They exist everywhere in the world, on land and sea, in the air and in fire. People sometimes see them from the corners of their eyes, but they dismiss that. A wizard, however, can communicate with them, to learn—well, 'the lay of the land' is very accurate. So I will contact the beings here—though I don't know them as well as the ones in Wyoming—and make my interest in August known. It's a long shot, since the farther from here he is, the less likely that these simple creatures will be able to convey my interest outward, or convey any answer back to me, but I've seen some surprising results. In my opinion, it's worth a try."

Breckenridge's earlier interest seemed to have evaporated. Quince hurried on to his big finale.

"Fifth and finally," he said, "I will devote myself to carrying the battle to our enemy. There are no definitive answers in magick, so I cannot guarantee success. Nevertheless, I have a plan, and I will pursue it if you agree."

"What is it?" Breckenridge asked. Interested? Not interested? Quince smiled craftily.

"You know about *stones*, right?"

"I think so," Breckenridge answered, slowly. "Meteorites that you people charge with magick, to be used as weapons."

"That's exactly right. Well, most *stones* are old; the majority were first used in the Middle Ages. It's very rare to encounter a fresh one, just fallen from the heavens. But eight months ago, on October 5, 2008, the Catalina Sky Survey at the University of Arizona spotted an asteroid on a collision course with Earth. They were quickly able to determine that it was tiny—just a few meters across—so *it* would bear the brunt of its collision with our planet, rather than the other way around. Just twenty hours and three minutes later, the asteroid, now called 2008 TC$_3$, broke up twenty-three miles above the Sudan and showered the Nubian desert with fragments.

"On December 6, Dr. Mauwia Shaddad of the University of Khartoum, aided by Dr. Peter Jenniskens of the SETI Institute in California, led a line of students and faculty on a search for the fragments. Their sweep began at station six on a lonely desert train line and moved out across the plain, with each member of the search team ten meters from the next. Because the asteroid had exploded at such a great height, they expected that any remaining meteorites would be scattered over a large area, making them particularly difficult to locate. But only two hours into the search, one of the students, Mohammed Alameen, found the first chunk.

"The team ultimately collected some 280 small meteorites, with a total mass of about five kilos. Doctors Shaddad and Jenniskens gave 2008 TC$_3$ the permanent name of 'Almahata Sitta,' Arabic for 'Station Six,' and set about studying their treasure, every piece of which was guarded in the scientific community as if it were gold.

"But there have been whispers in occult circles that one of the students kept one chunk for himself, slipping it under his jacket while his fellow searchers had their eyes locked on the ground. I have now proven that the whispers are true, and identified the student, so I intend to obtain that *stone* for us. The magick that goes into it will be all ours, unadulterated by anyone else. Long term, it will be a very valuable addition to the Necklace's arsenal—and short term, it will give us a weapon against Max August that he cannot possibly be prepared for."

Hanrahan spoke sharply. "Won't that divert you from searching for August?"

Quince was measured but firm in his response. "If I am to be your wizard, you will have to trust me until I prove untrustworthy. Of course, if you don't trust me, that means I will not be your wizard. It's your call." He knew full well that he was taking a big chance. That was the thing of it, though; a wizard by his very nature *has* to take chances— and *likes* to take chances. His world is made up of leaps in the dark. He has to believe that he will land safely.

The room grew silent. But at last, Breckenridge nodded. "I'm prepared to back you on this, Quince," he said, "so long as you remember that you *are* still being judged on your results."

"That's fair enough."

Breckenridge and Hanrahan looked at each other, conveying something Quince could not read. After a beat, Breckenridge cocked his head back at Quince and continued, "Now, what about *you* as a lover?"

"Excuse me?"

"Do you put *your* sex energy to use?"

Quince said nothing.

"Does he, Rita?"

Quince looked at her. She shrugged, acquiescing. He said, "Rita and I have an arrangement. Do with that what you will."

"Oh, we approve wholeheartedly," Breckenridge responded, as Hanrahan nodded beside him. "As it happens, after years of working with wizards, I have formed the same opinion as yourself. Fuck her silly if that will charge you up." Breckenridge turned again toward Rita. "Fuck *him* silly if that will charge *him* up." She laughed.

Breckenridge stood up, and Hanrahan followed. "You've made a few promises here tonight," the Gemstone said. "Now deliver. We'll show ourselves out."

MONDAY, JUNE 15, 2009 • 7:00 P.M.
CENTRAL DAYLIGHT TIME

6 Eagle (Responding to the Storyline)

Peter Quince walked slowly to the door at the end of his upstairs hallway, carrying a steaming mocha in his left hand. When he arrived, he found Rita waiting for him. Their eyes locked but they kept their mouths shut. Quince unlocked the room with a large nineteenth-century key and made a series of mystical passes over the door. His right hand did not glow, but it left a glowing trail of almost ultraviolet, like the afterimage on the retinas when a sparkler cuts the night. The door suddenly *felt* different to Quince, and even to Rita—somehow *relaxed*. He reached out, pushed it with his forefinger and little finger; the door swung wide, silently, upon its nineteenth-century hinges. The wizard bowed Rita in first.

She entered a large Midwestern room with no windows, no openings of any kind save the door, and no furniture. It was painted exquisitely, with trompe l'oeil landscapes of the four directions on the four walls. To the east was the bright blue of Lake Superior, looking out along the finger over a stand of pines. To the south the entryway cut its rectangle in a field of golden wheat, ringed by sycamores. To the west was the flat plain of North Dakota, almost devoid of trees. And to the north was the majesty of the Great

North Woods surrounding dark Lac Seul. The floor contained an exquisitely detailed circle, with strange markings at the four corners and the center. Rita immediately thought of Santería, and felt a cold hand clutch her soul. A year and a half in and she still couldn't control her atavistic response— but she could control her response to that response. The FRC used magick, and if she was going to make her way in this world, she was going to accept it as casually as she had the drug wars' bloodbaths that had brought her to her first platform of power. Besides, if she knew anything here, it was that Peter Quince meant her no harm. Just the opposite, in fact. And anyway, this wasn't Miami; this was cool, blue Duluth. No Santería here.

Quince closed the door behind them, locked it, and made passes that were the mirror image of those he made before. "Jackson Tower kept this cupola as his sanctum sanctorum, completely insulated from electronic *and* from magickal surveillance. I've renewed and reinforced his spells because, despite my formal recommendation, chica, I don't plan to be monitored myself. And neither should you be, so I've made certain we won't be." He turned and grinned at her, his features compacting even more. Rita found his face not really handsome, but it was interesting, and his position on the council of the FRC made him handsome enough, for now. "Moreover," he said, setting his mocha on a low shelf tucked in the southeast corner, the only addition to the plain room, "Breckenridge and Hanrahan know far more than they were telling."

"How could we have faith in them if that weren't true?" she asked sensibly.

"Exactly. They're our masters." He snorted. "So we have to learn their secrets in order to become masters ourselves."

Rita, never shy, tapped him on his chest. "I was right about telling them *our* secret, Pete. It made us look open and honest."

"And normal, with the two of us spending so much time together, and you so blazingly hot."

She laid her cheek against his chest, began massaging his bicep. He stroked her smooth black hair, down over her shoulders. "In any event, it worked," he murmured to her. "You and I both passed their little test. And now we won't stop till we're at the top of this heap."

"Thanks for including me, Pete," she said. "It'd be a long time before I made it to your level, let alone higher, under other circumstances. I needed a mentor."

"I prefer the term 'faculty advisor,'" Quince said with broad irony.

"I'll bet you do," Rita responded. "Well, I knew your predecessor personally, and though I didn't like him very much, he dropped a few hints about his life that I can check into while we're stuck up here in Duluth. That's *my* best shot at learning what they don't want us to know."

"See if you can find out *why* we're stuck here."

"Sure. Of course."

"With all deliberate speed, my love."

"I know."

"Hell, you may find August before I do," Quince said. "For all his magick, he likes his humanity, and humanity leaves its own traces."

"I don't see *you* giving up on *your* humanity, Pete," Rita said, running her hand down his flank.

"No," he said. "I'm a good ol' country boy. But I learned to use my power to rise above the Earth, for power over the Earth. August stays in the dirt."

"So you can beat him?"

"I wouldn't be here, either in *my* estimation or those two old men's, if we all didn't think so. But magick—"

"I know. Tower told me, too. There's nothing cut and dried. That's why I prefer working in the dirt myself. You want somebody dead, you kill him. But I want August dead any way possible, the way he left me hanging out to dry in Suriname, so I'm with you all the way to the end."

"I know you are," Quince said, his hand rising to her breast. Rita began writhing against him.

"I *do* love sex magick, Pete. I had no idea what I was missing."

"You and most of the world, chica," said Quince, starting to remove his clothes. "That's a wizard's ultimate edge over men like Breckenridge and Hanrahan. They don't understand what people like me and August are really capable of."

MONDAY, JUNE 15, 2009 • 7:15 P.M.
CENTRAL DAYLIGHT TIME

6 Eagle (Responding to the Storyline)

Breckenridge and Hanrahan sat back in their limousine as it made its return trip to the airport, slowed by the heavy rain and an accident on East Central Entrance. The rain beat on the roof of their solid and roomy compartment, and the windows were dissolving kaleidoscopes.

Breckenridge said, "I'm prepared to accept Quince so far. He's arrogant, but I don't believe we've ever considered anyone who wasn't. The male/female idea is a good one, so make that happen. And I'm excited by this idea of a new *stone,* if he can pull it off. I've never heard of anything like that before." He smiled, eyes half-lidded. "But how could he imagine that we don't keep the *closest* of eyes on everyone already?"

"He's just new, Renzo," said Hanrahan.

Breckenridge snorted. "There are too many new members just now. Diana and Michael have been with us for some time, but they're still not completely assimilated. Now Quince.

And not for any slot, but the Wizard. It took a long time to pick him; I don't want to have to go through it again. But none of them thinks big enough for the Necklace yet."

Hanrahan grinned, unconcerned. "That's why we're here. Crafty veterans, to teach them."

Breckenridge shook his head. "That's fine as far as it goes, but I don't like having that much uncertainty in my equations. We need to *force* them into their rôles."

"And what rôle do you envision for Señorita Diamante? We have no slot for her among the Nine."

"I like her spirit. I'd like to see what she can do in the FRC. I don't like uncertainty but it always comes calling."

"We've never had anyone who uses sex like a weapon, the way she does."

"*As* a weapon, I'd say." Breckenridge laughed. "Our kind of woman."

"Maybe that's worth a tenth center. A sex center, up past Boston, in Spruce Head?" Hanrahan joined him in jocularity. "No, it's not about her head."

Breckenridge's wristwatch emitted a low beep. "I've got to make a call," he said, and picked up his secure phone. Hanrahan sat back, as he so often did. In a moment, Breckenridge told the phone, "Gordon Brown is going ahead with a British inquiry into the war. Tony Blair will have to testify in public. These fucking guys have more cameras than we do, and then they hold an open inquiry. So I want Yevkurov dead within a week. No, that's more than enough time."

Hanrahan sat back and watched him without ever seeming to.

6 Eagle (Responding to the Storyline)

Craig and Aaron were parked in the lot across from the Public Works Building at 201 North Stone in Tucson. They were watching for anyone who might notice them, but not really worried; local government had no money to hire parking lot guards. The building they were looking at was grimly functional, with four rows of square windows marking four floors of civic officialdom overlooking a no-frills beige brick façade around the ground floor. Government chic.

Craig, in the passenger's seat, had a picnic basket in his lap, but the contents of the basket had nothing to do with picnics. Instead, the basket was neatly outfitted with a heavy piece of electronic equipment that could not be bought at Best Buy. From their car, Aaron and Craig could reach invisibly into the PWB and tap the computers that stored the feeds from the twelve traffic cameras the city had set up along I-10. One by one, those feeds were being studied, looking for a beige VW van, license plate ZAR9197, leaving town yesterday afternoon.

"Not going to California, but outfitted with camping gear," said Craig.

"If the clerk at Big 5 was right about who we're after," answered Aaron.

"I would have taken him outside—"

"I know you would, Craig, God love you. It was a fucking superstore in a mall—a little different from an isolated car rental office. We had to take what we could get."

"There are plenty of places in a mall. Service tunnels, untenanted stores—"

"You just like to kill," said Aaron.

"You killed the car rental guy," said Craig.

"I don't mind killing when it simplifies things. I do when it doesn't."

"Working with you is a pain in the ass."

"And working with *you*— Wait a minute." Aaron leaned over Craig's computer screen. "There they go," he said. "Right onto the Ten-North, at seven twenty-seven P.M.."

Aaron turned the car's ignition key. "Twenty-two hours. That's the closest we've been in four months!" He laid rubber onto Stone.

MONDAY, JUNE 15, 2009 • 8:11 P.M.
CENTRAL DAYLIGHT TIME

6 Eagle (Responding to the Storyline)

In the cupola of the old Hill house, Peter Quince was now alone. He and Rita had performed their sex magick with abandon, and when they'd finally finished she'd left him to his own devices, as was their arrangement. Still buzzing with that energy, he popped two Provigils and washed them down with his mocha. These tablets, a perfectly legal stimulant for the treatment of narcolepsy, had crossed into the gray market of self-medication as cognition enhancers. They were very popular with his students and everyone else's; Rita had told him it was the fastest-growing segment of her market. Small wonder. When Quince took two one-gram hits, his consciousness soon grew in a focused, driven manner that psychedelics never produced. His mind became almost painful in its clarity, sharp enough to slice worlds.

He walked into his circle, calm and jittery at the same time—walked to its center and stood silent, letting the jitters fade. Then he began to chant, slowly at first, building on the rhythms of words used by wizards for over a thousand years, riding on the rhythms. Minute after minute, he went on. Slowly, his naked body began to pulse with his rhythms . . .

dissipating in waves . . .

becoming a mist . . .

• • •

Quince was a mist above a plane, the highest realm he could imagine. The two lights shone high above him, throwing vague shadows through himself onto the center of the plane. Four lines led from that center, stretching away forever everywhere at right angles to each other, in four different colors. The red line led straight out ahead. The black line led to the left, into a rolling fog.

It was another world, and he was alone in it as he turned, no more than a cloud, and moved along the black line toward infinity. But as he moved, the fog began to thicken around his mist, forming translucent shapes, shadowing the light. Like blood coagulating. The world around him began to throw shadows, which grew clearer to his eyes. He was walking now in a shadowed passageway, with stone pillars to his left. He saw a series of beige arches over his head, running into the dark distance. Pale light spilled onto the tiled floor, split by the pillars' ebony shadows. Traditional Egyptian music came softly from a distance, as well as Lady Gaga's "Poker Face." This was the University of Khartoum in the Sudan.

Quince was physically a mist in his cupola room, but he was also physically a mist in Khartoum. Neither mist required all of him, so he could be both. Only his eyes, glowing dark blue, seemed solid, floating in both of the clouds he'd become.

6 Eagle (Responding to the Storyline)

Eugène Tenebre strolled the night streets of Khartoum. For several years now, he had enjoyed traveling, just taking off on the spur of the moment to visit any place that took his fancy. He knew he deserved such a lifestyle; three years before he had had the wit to cash out of adjustable-rate mortgages while they were still going up, and now money was of no consequence to him. He spent his days working out, eating healthy but well, and pleasing himself as much as possible.

Yesterday, he'd had a hankering to visit Khartoum. He didn't know much about it, except that its name had a ring to it, and that was sort of the point. He'd just go and have a look. Since his arrival this morning—yesterday morning, actually—he had visited the vast open market of Souq Arabi, working his way through its many sections, and lingering in the one focused entirely on gold. Afterward, it was but a short stroll to the Great Mosque, Mesjid al-Kabir. He worried that a Westerner might have some difficulties there, but nothing had happened to him. Then he'd taken a tram to the botanical garden, where he'd admired the sausage trees. By rights, he should have been dead tired, but sleep did not come, and now it was nearly dawn as he approached the clock tower at the University of Khartoum.

From out of the sky above him, a gray cloud fell like a stone, just missing his head and striking the back of his neck with the impact of a cloud. His body never wavered as the mist penetrated the base of his brain.

Peter Quince looked out through Eugène Tenebre's eyes for the eighth time.

Quince had the range of skills one would expect from a wizard, but his starting point, his special power, was as a Passenger, able to project his essence inside that of certain other people—a very few other people, relatively speaking. It required these people to have thirty-seven aspects of their psyche in synch with his, and he had once calculated that of the nearly seven billion people on Earth, no more than four hundred filled the bill. That was why, once he had found Eugène Tenebre, he had made him rich so that he could be "on call." He had found seven other such Hosts in the past five years, and he guarded their existence tenaciously, but Tenebre was his favorite because he was a man in his prime and in Europe, which made him useful for many jobs. Like this one. When Quince decided he needed a man on the ground, he only had to instill in Tenebre a desire to see Khartoum, which the man would take as a whim of his own.

Now Quince/Tenebre made his way surreptitiously across the campus. It would not do to be too memorable, since Tenebre would be no good if he were arrested for this night's work. Fortunately, in the predawn hours of a Tuesday morning, there was almost no one else around. Two male students, chattering high on coffee, engrossed in their discussion, came toward him. He melted into the shadows. They did not make him out, and he encountered no one else.

When he came to the room of Ja'afar al-Burabi, he tried the knob and found it locked, as he'd expected. It was not a problem. He placed his palms on either side of the knob, his forefingers and little fingers extended, touching the door. Dark indigo energy flowed between Tenebre's hands, forming a box around the knob. Slowly, Quince rotated his hands, keeping the relationship between them constant, and the knob turned with them. He pushed with his fingers and the door clicked softly wide.

He stepped inside, a mere silhouette. Light through the door fell dimly on a sleeping student. The wizard closed the door and drifted to the bed, darkness in darkness.

Suddenly al-Burabi opened his eyes. He was in that dead-of-night state where he couldn't tell dream from reality, or consciously move his body. He wanted to sit up but found he couldn't move; his pounding heart counted off long moments in his chest as he lay paralyzed. At last he forced one arm off the blanket—and then the spell was broken. He made to sit up—and two fingers jammed into his throat. He gagged, fell back coughing. A great weight fell upon his chest.

His eyes were becoming accustomed to the dark, enough to make out a man kneeling on him, arms pressing down on his shoulders, squeezing his breath. The man—it was only a man-shape—spoke English with a French accent.

"Where is Almahata Sitta?"

Al-Burabi's eyes all but popped from his head.

"Speak or you'll regret it!"

But al-Burabi had dreamed too long of the riches he could make from the stone when the time was right. He was going to wait until all the known fragments had been studied and catalogued. A new piece then—

He roared with pain, as the man-shape leaned down and bit his nose. He felt cartilage breaking, blood spurting, and he bucked with all his power, but he couldn't dislodge his attacker. And he couldn't hear his roar. The sound had been in his throat but it never reached his ears.

The man bit the tip of his nose right off.

Al-Burabi jabbered, "Behind the lower drawer!" He couldn't hear himself, but the man, evidently, did. He sat up above al-Burabi and pulled his right arm back, then drove his fist onto the boy's jaw. The jaw broke and the boy passed out.

Quince moved to the room's desk. The lower drawer was

larger than the others, to hold A1 papers. He pulled it out and saw that it was artificially shallow, front to back. He pulled it all the way out to reveal the space behind it. The *stone* was indeed there, shiny even in the gloom, and bigger than he'd dared hope. It was the size of a softball, roughly spherical, with one flat side where it had broken free of its parent body and edges smoothed by final heat. Quince picked it up and savored the heft of it.

Behind him, the door clicked open again.

He turned to witness Daniel Cheever in the doorway. Cheever was from Alabama or someplace, a wannabe magician who had e-mailed Quince several times based on Quince's published work, thinking he'd found a kindred spirit. But Cheever was a dilettante, full of theories but without the drive for concerted effort. Quince had stopped answering the e-mails, only to find Cheever on the doorstep of his condo a month later. Quince had told him quite clearly to quit screwing around, but evidently, Cheever hadn't listened.

The man crept almost silently into the room, cupping his penlight with his hands. He probably thought al-Burabi was still asleep, and he never noticed the other man in the room.

Quince reached out from behind the redneck punk. This was going to be a pleasure. . . .

MONDAY, JUNE 15, 2009 • 7:45 P.M.
MOUNTAIN STANDARD TIME

6 Eagle (Responding to the Storyline)

Aaron and Craig pulled into the Petro Shopping Center south of Phoenix, and parked by the air pump. Craig looked sourly around. "I hate this fucking town," he said. "There are four different ways out of here!"

Aaron said, "We'll just have to do some old-fashioned legwork—talk to the people at the gas stations and restaurants and see if anybody saw them go one way or the other."

"You sound like you don't mind it."

"Sure, I mind it, but we were never gonna find this guy without some hard work—work that those other teams are too pussy to do. It's a marathon, not a sprint."

"That's what I like about you, Aaron," Craig said. "You get a pile of shit, you think it means there's a pony around."

"And you get a pony and think it's going to shit on you."

"Working with *you* is enough of a pain in the ass."

"Oh, but working with *you* is just a walk in the park," Aaron said. Just then his secure phone vibrated. He held up his hand for an end to the discussion and answered.

"Hello, sir," he said. Then he listened for a while. His face grew tight.

"Yes, sir," he said finally. "But we're running down a hot trail right now. Less than a day behind. Phoenix, Arizona." He listened some more, then said, "Absolutely. As soon as we run down this lead." Finally, "Thank you, sir. We won't let you down."

He clicked off the phone and said precisely, "Mother-*fuck*!"

"What?" Craig demanded from the passenger seat.

"Hanrahan wants to reconfigure the teams—male and female."

"He wants to split us up? That's ridiculous! We've got a track record."

"Don't tell me. And you *know* you don't tell *him*. I told him that we'd comply—just as soon as we run this lead to ground. He's letting us go ahead for now."

"What the fuck? I don't want to break in a new partner."

"Me either, man. Which is why you and I have to bring this Code Red down by ourselves, this week."

Craig swung his door open and got out. "I'm on it," he said, and started long-legging it toward the office.

6 Eagle (Responding to the Storyline)

Night had fallen over the Nevada desert, and Wickr had taken on an entirely new reality. The structures, the art pieces, and the strange vehicles stopped being structures, pieces, and vehicles, and became lines of light in the dark. On the vast open plain, it was like being in Luke Skywalker's space colony on Tatooine, light-years from everyone else; red and green and blue and yellow lines of light formed nonstandard shapes against the black, flowing and pulsing. It was now a comfortable seventy-six degrees, and the festival of Wickr was finally fully alive.

Max donned a haori and sandals, leaving his chest bare; Pam wore a bikini with fake feathers on the top, a stylish fedora, and calf-high boots with platform soles. They had had a good time at the Goodwill, stocking up on all their coming needs; Pam was glad Max knew what to prepare for. They broke open a box of light-sticks and created some intriguing accents for their necks and arms. Then they grabbed a couple of plastic glasses and swung by Randy and Sara's shelter. The couple was gone again, but a fresh pitcher of iced mojitos was set out for anyone passing by. Max and Pam filled their glasses and launched themselves into the streets.

Night was when the fire projects really got going. A whale made of connected cars snaked through the throng, blowing flame from a hole on the top of its head, five feet above even the tallest celebrant. Fire-cannons on one side of the Sun-circle fired their flames into the air, and were answered by other cannons on the far other side, half a mile away. It was almost too much to grasp, even for a woman who had stood (or felt she'd stood) in the middle of interstellar space. She took Max's arm.

"Do you ever get bored?" Pam asked. "Like Dave? No new challenges."

"There are always new challenges," Max answered. "Do *you* get bored?"

"Not so far," she responded. "Not by a long shot. But I'm seeing it for the first time, and you've seen it before, the same way he has. By now, you've seen lots of things before."

"Yeah, but hell, Pam, even chronologically I haven't been around *that* long. Agrippa was here five hundred years, and he never got bored, for the same reason: no matter how many times people repeat history, there are always the odd-balls and the breakouts, and that's what I appreciate. Every time I'm tempted to think, 'Jeez, another inspiring movie about the outcast team that won the championship,' or 'teens trapped with a maniac,' I see things like this. And if I came here often enough for this to get familiar, I'd end up discovering Ragga Soca or the Morning Banana Diet somewhere else. There's always somethin'. So unless I decide to just close my eyes, how can I ever get bored?"

"How can Dave?"

"Listen, I love Dave, but he's not an alchemist. He doesn't get the *size* of life."

People who'd outlined their forms with cool neon wire were sauntering past them like two-dimensional cartoons. A giant pirate ship rolled across the plain, followed by a gleaming silver rocket shooting bright light from its tail. Techno was beating from all the dance floors that had been assembled during the day; the nearest one proclaimed itself in scarlet neon, DOME O'AREGATO. When they'd met, Pam had told Max that she loved to dance, and she'd gotten him, who hadn't danced in a while, back into it. There was none of her beloved salsa here, but anything was fine with both of them. Max enjoyed all music, and since techno was just a fragment of what he listened to most of the year, the immersion in it here was, indeed, something different.

So they danced at the Dome, and then made their way along the edge of the circle 'round the Sun, moving from club to club, stopping to gawk, or participating in street theater. They ran into Randy and Sara at a venue limned with trailing red and white streamers of light; they all filled their glasses at the free bar and danced together for a while. Then Paul and Olivia moved on. The hours rolled by and the crowd only grew; partying all night was the norm.

As Nevada moved toward midnight, in a club called the Pang-Toon where an anime rabbit ran endlessly overhead, they saw Michael and Diana across the floor, and as one pivoted toward the exit, as if it were a dance move. Max was certain the duo hadn't spotted them, and there was no sense registering on their consciousness twice if that could be avoided. It wasn't as if there weren't still more places to dance.

They were getting down and funky in an open-air arcade filled with carved totem poles when Pam became aware of two people dancing the exact same moves right next to them, like mirrors. She looked and saw two strangers looking back; the guy was smirking. Then she saw Sly and Rosa, just for one coordinated flash. Pam was in the moment, so she stuck her finger in her nose, and watched as the girl over there did exactly the same.

Then the four of them left the dance floor for the dark of the desert night.

6 Eagle (Responding to the Storyline)

The lights on the horizon of Wickr formed a long flat arc, like a multicolored Milky Way, or an organic Vegas. They were far away from the lights, on the dark and empty plain. By common consent, Max made the choice of the spot he judged the most secure.

Then they stood and listened to the night. It was something Max and the newcomers were accustomed to, evidently. Pam at least understood it, and went with it. They all four let the night sounds soak in. . . .

Across from Max and Pam two people appeared, mentally lit as Dave had been lit. Automatically, Pam lit herself just as Max lit himself, but she was all too aware that she'd have to touch the newcomers if she were lighting them on her own. All at once, she was the new girl. Sly was looking at her and probably caught the emotion, because he held out his arms and gave her a hug, then a kiss on the neck, quick and playful, almost a nip. He was wearing faded jeans and nothing else—his chest, with its thick pelt of hair, was warm against her own chest. Max meanwhile hugged Rosa, who accepted his embrace with the smallest of meaningless smiles.

"She's not what you'd call demonstrative," Pam thought.

Rosa's face was Slavic, with cheekbones and eyes both a trifle slanted, and a strong, straight nose. She wore a deep purple gypsy skirt and vest combination over an indigo leotard; her crimson hair was in short braids below a wrap-around gray scarf. There was no jewelry or bangles, but a packet made of old and well-rubbed leather, very dark, hung from her belt along her slim left hip. She stepped back deliberately from Max. She said to Pam, "No, I am not."

Pam started.

Rosa's small, polite smile didn't change. "May I call you 'Pamela'?"

"Sure," said Pam, nettled. "That's my name."

"Yes it is. Now Pamela, I read people's fortunes, in their cards, their atmosphere, their body. I read you." She took Pam's hand, her long, slender fingers touching Pam's palm, her wrist. "But Pamela, you are what we who travel our road call a *friend*—of Max's, and thus of ours. That means something, so I will leave you your privacy, as I leave Max his."

"Don't let her throw you, Pammy," Sly said, drawing Pam's attention with a touch of her other arm. "She's always this serious, but the good thing is, she means what she says. I live with her, and if I can stand it full time, you can put up with it for a few days."

"No, I'm not—I just—" Pam said, feeling called upon to explain, feeling like an idiot for explaining. "I've only really known Max, what he can do. I just met you guys for five minutes, if that. And he won't tell me anything about you."

"'Course not," said Sly sagely. "Good for him. Only we can tell." He squeezed her arm in a convivial fashion.

"So tell," Pam responded, surprising even herself.

"In time," Sly said, his grin growing mischievous. "We need the right time and right place. Atmosphere!"

"Okay, here we go," said Max. "Watch out for this guy, Pam."

"Yeah. Watch closely, Pammy," Sly said. "Here's a taste of my tale. I'm a shapeshifter." In the shared alchemical light, he suddenly became once more the dancer on the dance floor, spinning in a sharply executed move, then just as suddenly returned to his normal self. There was only a slight ripple of energy along his frame as the changes overtook him. "We're not talkin' Max's little tricks with gravity and light, to make people *think* I look different. *I* really *do* change—" He stopped in mid-sentence, raised a hand. "Hang on."

Pam became aware of several people riding bikes making their way across the plain, more or less in their direction. They were still more than two hundred feet away, their headlights spraying through the night as their tires jostled over the dirt. Those lights came nowhere near reaching the foursome in the dark; Pam would not have noticed the approach, let alone marked it as a problem, for some time to come. But Sly had. Max set his neck, held his hands with the first two fingers out, like pistols—swept those hands across a slice of the night. The bikers came upon ruts in the land that took their bikes in an oblique direction, so that they went past the foursome, twenty feet on the right.

"So I shift shapes," Sly went on easily, evidently not worried that they'd overhear him. "Who would you like me to be, Pam?"

"*You*," Pam said at once. "I want to know who *you* are."

"Can any of us ever really be certain?" he asked, dropping a faint hand to his forehead like the oldest of old-time thespians.

"Oh yeah," Max responded. "You're *real* complicated, Sly."

Rosa spoke, and it almost came as a surprise to Pam. "If I can live with him full time, you can put up with it for a few days." It could almost have been irony, if her words had had more vivacity. She seemed preternaturally calm.

In the few minutes since she'd been let into their world, Pam's ideas about these newcomers had changed dramatically. Because they both looked to be the same young age, because they both had far older eyes, because they traveled together, she had thought of them as a couple. But whatever bound them together was obviously a lot more complex than that. She was excited at the prospect of learning a lot more in the next few days.

Max said, "So let's go over the plan. We've got it pretty well worked out for you, but you're the ones who'll be executing it."

"Aww, c'mon, Plan-Man," Sly protested. "I know how to sleep with chickies." He gave him a heavy-lidded grin, dissolving into a wink, then threw another at Pam. "Sometimes I think he's one of those Puritans, straight from Plymouth Rock. A big square rock. Is he a Puritan, Pam?"

"Not hardly," she laughed.

"I'll take your word for it. But Rosa and I are nothing like Puritans either. I'm looking forward to sleeping with your chicky for the sex, and she's looking forward to sleeping with your charley for the justice."

"Justice?" Pam echoed.

"The things they do to this world must be stopped, Pamela," Rosa said softly. "I have sworn an oath to destroy such darkness." She still seemed calm but now it was the calm before a storm.

Sly nodded. "So who's up for more dancin'?"

"All in good time, brother," Max said. "We know things whether you like it or not, and we're going to be damn sure you're fully prepared before you get your freak on. Sleeping with the enemy is just the entrée for what we want here."

Sly shrugged at Pam, one *friend* to another. "A Puritan for sure."

6 Eagle (Responding to the Storyline)

Michael and Diana were in a bar, up a thirty-foot flight of steps, festooned in tikis and overlooking a fenced-in yard filled with pink plastic flamingos. To be precise, she was on the bar, on her back, and he was drinking shots from her navel. Every time he slurped another down, sending her into fits of laughter, the blonde bartendress poured another.

And this is just the first night! Mike thought.

6 Eagle (Responding to the Storyline)

Dick Hanrahan sat in his bunker, inside his house in Wheeling, West Virginia. It was at the back of the mansion he was obliged to live in (but had no objection to), inside a secure area that was inside a secure area—a large command center with everything a master spy wanted at his fingertips, and nothing that he didn't. He could live in this room for fourteen days if it came to that. He could catalogue the secrets of the world in here. No one else, not even Renzo, ever entered this room without Hanrahan. It was his sanctum sanctorum.

He was listening to his recordings of Renzo and of Jackson Tower, to the breezy whistling noise that neither he nor his computers could identify. He listened to those recordings several nights a week now, looking for the slightest clue that would deliver the key to the mystery. He had solved so many mysteries; the meaning of this sound was his current Holy Grail, or Great White Whale.

What linked Renzo and the wizard? Or was the link between Renzo and the Code Red? It was Hanrahan's job to know secrets.

It was his life to know.

And he needed just one more piece to fall into place so he could move forward. That would happen in less than a week—maybe much less. Get through the Necklace's current plan, see if the trigger existed, and if it did, pull it. Simple.

He didn't mind the indeterminate wait. Intel came when it came. Not a moment sooner, but not a moment later, either—not for the spy chief of the Necklace.

Day Two

7 Candle (Engaging with the Matrix)

When their wristwatch alarms went off, Aaron and Craig rolled out of the twin beds at their motel in Phoenix. They had showered the night before so they could simply slip on their clothes and go. By 6:15 they were having breakfast in the Denny's down the road. The lighting there was bright but their waitress was tired. She was probably working two jobs.

Aaron and Craig were working their one job, and they were damn glad to have it. By 6:45 they were headed up 17. It was going to be another hot one.

7 Candle (Engaging with the Matrix)

LAS VEGAS—Republican Sen. John Ensign of Nevada, a leading conservative mentioned as a potential presidential candidate, admitted Tuesday he had an extramarital affair with a woman who

> was a member of his campaign staff. "Last year I
> had an affair. I violated the vows of my mar-
> riage," Ensign said at a brief news conference. "It
> is the worst thing I have ever done in my life. If
> there was ever anything in my life that I could
> take back, this would be it."

In the midst of a soundproofed steel vault in the exact
center of an unobtrusive building on East Forty-seventh
Street, Lawrence Breckenridge was eating eggs Benedict
with Adrian LoBianco, host of *Newstime,* weeknights at
eight Eastern. There was a faint scent of vanilla in the air.
Surrounding the vault were the outer walls of the building,
reinforced with thick steel beams, and the intervening space
on all sides boasted a fully deployed assassination system
which would kill any intruder as soon as he intruded. The
vault's interior was something out of old New York, an ele-
gant Knickerbocker dining room, with fastidious décor and
soft lighting from what looked like gas lamps. Since this
warm space was surrounded by a kill zone, there were no
windows. The only way into the vault was through two tunnels, both of which began in buildings three blocks away
and ran parallel to the existing subway and utilities tunnels.
When Breckenridge used this meeting place, he entered
on Madison Avenue; his guest entered by the only doorway
guests ever knew about, in suite 107 of a condo on Forty-
fourth.

LoBianco had never been to this room before, and had
never met Breckenridge directly. His contact had always
been Diana Herring. LoBianco knew about Breckenridge,
and felt privileged to do so, but he never expected to meet
the great man in person, let alone share a breakfast with

him. In LoBianco's opinion, this meeting was a definite sign of respect.

"That was delicious," he said as he wiped his lips with his napkin. "Outstanding. It's always a pleasure to be on the team, Mr. Breckenridge."

"Lawrence, please. And we've always appreciated your efforts, Adrian."

"Thank you, Lawrence. Diana and I work well together. Where is she, by the way? I trust she's all right."

"She's fine—just taking a short vacation, I believe. In the meantime, I'm enjoying the opportunity to get back in the field, and connect with people I should have connected with far sooner."

LoBianco nodded. "Am I what you expected?"

"Oh, absolutely. You are what you appear to be on television."

LoBianco laughed a little. "I play a version of myself there."

"We all play a version of ourselves," said Breckenridge. "Your version appears far more straightforward than most."

"I want people to know I believe what I'm saying."

"Even when you don't?"

"Even when I don't, *sometimes*," LoBianco ventured. "I find it easier to believe, if possible. And usually it is."

"You have mastered your medium."

"Thank you." LoBianco knew it was the truth. "Interesting revelations about Ensign, don't you think?"

"No one ever could have predicted," agreed Breckenridge.

"I love the stories behind the stories," LoBianco said. "Though this one's getting a *lit*-tle familiar. Why is it always the guys who lecture others on their sins who turn out to have sins of their own? This guy was a huge critic of Clinton. Wouldn't it be smarter to crusade on sins you don't share?"

"Ah, but if there's one constant in politicians, it's self-delusion. He goes out seeking votes thinking people will love him enough that he'll get them, and if he's right, he soon convinces himself that he can do anything."

"But reality still exists."

"And so does the Village in Washington. I imagine everyone in that town could be brought down for something or other, but in fact it rarely happens. They play by their own rules."

"So why did the system break down here? Do you know?"

"I believe the woman's husband was about to complain."

"But he'd kept silent for months."

"Something pushed him over the edge, I imagine." Breckenridge pushed a button on the edge of their table, summoning the silent valet with the shaved head who served them. "Coffee? Tea?"

"Coffee. Cream."

"Certainly. So what are you working on for tonight, then?"

"After Ensign, we're taking a look at the depression—a thumb-sucker on why we're where we are."

"And why are we? According to your report."

"It's actually pretty simple," LoBianco said. "When the depression hit, companies naturally started laying off people. Getting lean and mean has helped them weather the storm, so even though the stock market is starting to turn around, no company is going to jeopardize its recovery by staffing up again. And the people who still have jobs are in no position to complain if their workload has increased with no increase in pay. So it's going to be several more years before there needs to be any significant hiring."

"But all those people with no jobs aren't buying anything," Breckenridge pointed out.

"It doesn't matter. The stock market provides all the money the companies need right now. At that level, nobody took a hit."

"You might want to go easy on the market, then," Breckenridge said.

"Sure," said LoBianco, very attuned to his master's voice. "Not a problem."

"In fact, I think the main problem is foreigners, taking Americans' jobs."

"I see your point."

"It's all due to the hard left that runs this country."

The coffee arrived, piping hot and delicious. Its aroma filled the small room, mingling with the vanilla.

"I have another story I'd like you to work on," Breckenridge said, after LoBianco had poured his cream.

"Whatever you want."

"I need you, on tonight's show if possible, or tomorrow's if not, to do a hit piece on nuclear power. You know the drill. Nothing major or alarmist, but I want the subject out there, tonight or tomorrow."

LoBianco laughed. "I hate to say it, Lawrence, but you didn't have to go to all this trouble for that. I can roll out that report in my sleep. Nobody likes nuclear power."

"But at the moment, it's an abstract dislike. It hasn't been reinforced lately. And meanwhile, the price of gas has gone up a dollar since the first of the year. If it continues to climb in a vacuum, people might forget that they dislike nuclear, and I don't want that to happen."

"Not a problem," LoBianco answered.

"Good." Breckenridge sat back, satisfied. Step by step, and so easily, everything was falling into place. He really didn't need Aleksandra to run the world.

7 Candle (Engaging with the Matrix)

In Wheeling, Dick Hanrahan sat in the bunker eating a bowl of Post Shredded Wheat—his breakfast of choice for more than fifty years—and made a telephone call. He hadn't slept, because he'd had to wait for his man to get up out west, but he didn't mind; he'd always done his best work at night. He would grab a—what did they call them now? a "power nap"—as soon as he was done here.

The man answered on the first ring, expecting his call.

Hanrahan spoke without identification or preliminary, knowing the transmission was secure. "Everything square?"

"Yes, sir."

"Any second thoughts?"

"God, no! Not on my part . . . if my wife gets the money."

"The payout is tomorrow, as scheduled. It will appear completely random if anyone ever checks, which they won't. But we've got her covered. Check with her after one P.M. your time. There won't be a problem."

"Then I don't have any problems, either. Hell, man, I'm damn glad to have the chance. I feel like I can *do* something."

Hanrahan heard nothing in the man's tone to belie that. "We know that. Good, then. Contact me after you talk with her, and that will be our last scheduled communication, so think of anything you want to ask before then. Contact me after that only if anything comes up on your end."

"Nobody here has the slightest inkling."

"Let's keep it that way." He hung up, the call having lasted just forty-three seconds.

7 Candle (Engaging with the Matrix)

Duluth was overcast, but it looked like the rain would hold off for a while. It was definitely gloomier than Miami, in Rita's opinion, but the cleanliness was amazing. Rain was a common occurrence in the Caribbean, but it was usually followed with sweat.

She had not spent much time with Jackson Tower, but she had been very interested in him because of who he represented, and she'd learned as much as she could in the time she had. One thing she'd learned was, he was familiar with fine whiskey. On their flight to Suriname, she had seen his eyes light up at her offer of a forty-five-year-old Laphroaig in a way that they had not lit up for her. So, bright and early, dressed in a conservative blue suit, she presented herself as a revenue officer at Duluth's top wine merchant. Her credentials were in perfect order, because they had once belonged to a legitimate ATF agent in South Florida. That agent had been pumped full of lead and left halfway to Cuba, the result of an offshore meet between Rita and her suppliers that went wrong, but her ID had gone to Rita's top forger and come back with Rita's picture and particulars. So now, Special Agent Carolina Tiburón sat in the back room at the Lake Aire Bottle Shoppe on London Road and examined Tower's invoices. Agent Tiburón didn't have to explain herself, so she hadn't. She found plenty of invoices, almost all for superlative Scotches, but everything was paid in full, in cash, once a month like clockwork. There was nothing there that gave her any kind of leverage.

It was boring as hell for a woman who'd ruled an empire

in her time, but it was part of her long-term plan. And in the part of her mind that would always think like a gang leader, she had to admire the way the organization she wished to join never left its fingerprints on anything.

TUESDAY, JUNE 16, 2009 • 11:30 A.M.
PACIFIC DAYLIGHT TIME

7 Candle (Engaging with the Matrix)

Max, Pam, Sly, and Rosa were lounging in camp chairs between their two tents, eating blueberry pancakes provided by the campers across Venus Street. That group all wore turquoise tee shirts with an incomprehensible logo that Max gathered had something to do with Chinese blow-up dolls. In any event, Max wore only shorts and Sly wore only jeans and the pancakes hit the spot. Rosa wore her usual costume, which fit right in, and Pam was down to a sports bra, a wrap-around skirt, and a spangled top hat. The four of them had crashed somewhere around five.

Sara came out of her shelter to get a bottle from their car. She was as topless as Max and Sly. Max looked, of course, but this was Wickr; she could do whatever she wanted, and he could do whatever he wanted, so he took the opportunity to appreciate the female form in motion. Sly, on the other hand, sat up and craned his neck for a better view. He started to say something, then thought better of it.

Pam hissed. Rosa said nothing.

Max made a distinctive hand gesture past his right ear, as if smoothing a head of hair three inches thicker than his own. Sara could now look at them on her way back, but all she or anyone would see was four people sleeping quietly in their chairs. Sara did exactly that, smiled at their comfort, and went back under her shelter. Max said, "What's today, Pam?"

"Today," she said promptly, "is Seven Candle, Engaging with the Matrix—the flow behind the Storyline. Today Sly and Rosa not only get laid, they get into the private worlds of Michael and Diana."

"It is also Bloomsday," said Rosa placidly.

"What's that?" Pam asked, thinking of magickal days like Midsummer—though she added, "I think I've heard of it, somewhere. . . ."

"It is the day on which everything took place in James Joyce's *Ulysses*," Rosa answered. "Leopold Bloom took his first walk with his wife-to-be, Nora Barnacle, from Dublin to Ringsend, on June 16, 1904. Now it is an annual day of celebration for Joyce-lovers."

"Which does not include me," Sly said with a derisive smile, looking around with an expectation of general agreement. He got it from Max.

"You like *Ulysses*?" Max asked Rosa, skeptically.

"Yes," she said. "Why not?"

"I know it's supposed to be great, but I've gotta say, it drives me crazy," he said. "I've tried it twice and gotten nowhere."

"Wait," interjected Sly. "There's something you can't do?"

"Yeah," said Pam, jumping in after him. "I thought you had a line into everything, Max."

"Epic fail," Max said. "I have lots of lines into lots of things, but I can't have a line into everything, and *Ulysses* is one of those things where I said my time was better spent elsewhere." His palms went up. "I have a lot of Time so I *really* don't like to be bored."

Rosa said quietly, "The vast complexity of Joyce's thought becomes more manageable when you have seen as much as I have, Max. In fact, it approximates my own worldview, and I believe it will come to approximate yours. But for everyone, Leopold's walk with Nora should be the hero's journey in our time. A template. A matrix, as you say."

"1904 is not our time," Sly said.

"All times are our times," Max told him. "Since I stepped off the people-mover, it's like I stand in one place while Time goes past. I've become aware of Time itself."

"Like I haven't," said Sly.

"Like you haven't," said Max. "You reinvent yourself all the time."

"I'm a shape-shifter!"

"Exactly. You're always someone new. It's the furthest thing from standing still."

"And by nature," said Rosa, "you are also a drifter. You cannot stand still."

"But you *do* live forever, too, don't you?" Pam asked.

The conversation came to a dead halt.

"Sorry!" Pam blurted, growing pink to the roots of her sun-blonde hair.

"Gotta set the stage just right, Pammy," Sly said cheerfully. "*My* story is *really* the hero's journey of our time."

"We do not know you well enough, Pamela," said Rosa, matter-of-fact.

"And it's a really cool story," added Sly. "Can't just toss it off."

Pam felt the heat in her face, but she looked him in the eye and asked, "How will you *get* to know me if you and Rosa are away, doing the actual magickal work?"

Sly laughed as he popped up out of his chair, and let that be his answer.

7 Candle (Engaging with the Matrix)

Diana let herself out of Michael's coach without waking him. They had staggered home at dawn, drunk out of their minds, and loving every hazy moment of it. Michael had announced in the last fading moments after sex that he'd sleep in and orient his time more toward the long dark hours of the night, but Diana came from twenty-four-hour cable news and found energy in all the times of the day.

The heat outside hit her hard, but she was from Chicago; she knew heat. She walked leisurely to her own coach and marveled at the number of tents and vehicles that had sprung up around them in the twenty-four hours since their arrival. There was hardly any open space left, all the way out here on Saturn. But the area between the coaches was still all theirs.

Half an hour later, after a refreshing shower—something not available to those in tents—she put on a tee shirt and wrapped a sarong around her waist. She used the coach's full-length mirror to twist the cloth to reveal the most flattering expanse of leg, then lathered on sunscreen, put a wide straw hat on her false blonde head, and went out into the noonday sun.

Unlocking her bike from the side of her coach, she rode off in the opposite direction from yesterday's explorations. The hard, dry desert plain was pretty good for riding, and it certainly speeded up the covering of long distances, but it was still thirsty work. She found a rough wooden bar where free iced coffee was being dispensed by twin girls, about twenty -one or -two, one wearing just the top of an orange bikini and the other just the bottom. *No wonder 90210 is back again,* she thought. *That kind of life is always ready to be reinvented.* Impulsively, she reached underneath her sarong and removed her own panties, then hung them on a nearby totem pole—before riding quickly away. She wasn't looking to attract a man, she just wanted to show she was undaunted.

Turning onto Four O'clock Road, heading inward toward the Sun, she didn't notice when she passed two young men among many. She didn't notice one of them move his hand in a certain way. What she noticed was her sarong getting tangled in her bike's chain, and the suddenness with which that brought her to a halt.

She got her feet down quickly, awkwardly, standing straddle-legged over the bike. She twisted to survey the situation and did not like what she saw. The sarong was wound tight against the gear wheel. She tried to pull it loose but it wouldn't come. She tried harder and heard it rip, just a little, and she stopped. Now what?

TUESDAY, JUNE 16, 2009 • 12:25 P.M.
PACIFIC DAYLIGHT TIME

7 Candle (Engaging with the Matrix)

Coyote stepped away from Max and sauntered forward. This little chicky was really hot—a little older than he might choose, but a nice little cougar nonetheless, posed with her butt over her bike, which made up for a lot. It was a great trick and he owed Max for bringing him in on it. But he could take it from here. Coyote consciously loosed his pheromones and quickened his step to reach the chickadee before anyone else. "Need any help?"

She lifted her gaze from her sarong and saw a handsome guy with an engaging smile, somewhat younger than she was, but with eyes that had seen a few things. His face and body were tanned and lean; his only clothing was an open short-sleeved bright red shirt, a pair of khaki shorts, and some well-worn sandals. She gave him a nice smile, not overly embarrassed, and answered, "I think I'm stuck."

"So you are." Coyote knelt beside her back wheel and began to tease the cloth free, little by little. His fingers were limber, wiry, and his forearms lean and muscular. He knew what women thought of that. He looked up at her with an impudent grin. "You have really gone and done it this time, cutie. We're gonna have to cut this loose."

"Ooo," Diana grimaced. "It's from Mount Kinabalu." Seeing his blank look, she reacted with her newswoman's experience, adding almost without pause, "Borneo, where sarongs originated. It's an original. I can't cut it up."

"Pretty pricey for Wickr," he said, cocking an eyebrow.

"You may well be right. I didn't think," she said, her eyes on his.

"Virgin?"

"At Wickr, you mean?"

"What else could I mean?" His eyes twinkled.

"Right. So then yes, I'm a virgin."

"You'll get over that. The simpler the better out here. Simple and primal."

"Primal versus virginal."

"That's what makes it simple. A very simple story, and a very old one." The energy between them was hanging heavy. It was up to her as the woman to dial it back.

"You've been here before?" she asked him, bending her knees to allow more slack in the material.

"I stop by pretty much every year."

" 'Stop by'?" she responded tartly. "It's pretty pricey to just 'stop by.' "

"Well, I live in Vegas but I'm out in the desert a lot," he said easily. "I know the folks who put it on, and they cut me some slack."

"You mean you don't pay."

"I don't pay for anything if I can help it," he said, and there was no mistaking his second meaning. He was a little direct for Diana's standards, but her standards were up for grabs at Wickr. This could be an adventure.

"Well, I paid a pretty penny for my sarong, and besides, like I said, it's got some history. We can't cut it."

"Then undo it at your end. I'll carry your bike—"

"Umm, I can't do that, either," Diana said, and was astounded at the strength of the surge of mortification through her. *Jesus! What the hell did I do?* "I—don't have on any underwear."

The guy gave her the goofiest grin. He really was cute for a hunk, saying, "What if you get in an accident? You're not wearing patent leather shoes, either. Or maybe that's what you're supposed to do. I'm not good on Catholic schoolgirls."

"Where is this conversation going?" Diana demanded.

"I dunno. You had me at 'no underwear.' But how about this? You can have the shirt off my back to wrap around you while you drop your high-priced chain rag."

Diana looked around. There were dozens of people on all sides of them. The guy was so lean his shirt wouldn't close completely around her. Someone would see something. But hell, she'd already seen everything the coffee twins had to offer. She'd rolled with that. *I'm not a Catholic schoolgirl.*

"I'll take that shirt," she said with real conviction, her eyes on him. "And maybe I'll raise you one. Later." He looked her right in the eye and nodded, quite self-assured. Well, self-assured was good. She held his gaze and said sincerely, "I'm Stacy, by the way."

"Greg," Coyote answered with unabashed enthusiasm.

Not only was the trick working like clockwork, this chick was gonna be fun to romp with.

He slipped off his shirt and handed it to her. His hand took hers, and she held it for a moment, before slipping free. She began tying the shirt around her waist. Coyote turned his back like a gentleman, and gave his old pal Max a big wink.

TUESDAY, JUNE 16, 2009 • 12:37 P.M.
PACIFIC DAYLIGHT TIME

7 Candle (Engaging with the Matrix)

Scorpio Rose lingered among the patrons at the snow cone shack, courteously conversing with those around her, completely still and quiet within her mind. The shack was just a large tent, naturally well-populated, though snow cones to her taste had always seemed too sweet on the outside, too cold at the core. The two parts were only connected, not joined. And she knew full well it was a metaphor for herself. She had known it the first time she saw a snow cone, at the Texas State Fair in 1919.

Today she played the part of a calm but good-natured eighteen-year-old French girl. She wore a simple blue leotard and a reddish-orange scarf tied around her neck, which was a common costume for her but also fit right in at Wickr. A second scarf encircled her waist; her leather case hung from it. She was chatting with the raw-boned couple leaning against the snow cone bar next to her. They were down from Manitoba, and could not believe the world of Wickr.

"Two days of driving, we took turns, lots of people from Canada actually, we met a guy from the Netherlands, are you from Paris?"

"Yes, I live in Montmartre, of course tourists, a madhouse, like this but different, but still it is wonderful, did you see the sunset last night?"

While her mind sat still and quiet, keeping an eagle eye on the two massive coaches across the street.

TUESDAY, JUNE 16, 2009 • 12:45 p.m.
PACIFIC DAYLIGHT TIME

7 Candle (Engaging with the Matrix)

Michael came down the steps of his coach holding one eye closed against the glare and scowling. He had wanted to sleep till dusk, but his internal clock was still on East Coast time, and the coach's AC, fancy though it was, had the stale stink of the Greyhounds he used to take on campaign tours, back in the day. He hadn't heard the technobeat that hit him now like the heat, but that made it certain: he was up.

With his sun hat shading his face, shorts covering his nakedness, feet encased in sandals, he padded over to check Diana's coach, but she was gone, as she'd said she'd be. Her product went to people directly; she had to be amongst 'em. His product went, you could say, *in*directly, so he went back inside his own vehicle and started frying up some ham. He was not a desert guy but he knew that salty meat was a good thing. And lots of liquid, and sunglasses, and sunscreen. He wore sunscreen on his face, and a hat, all year long. When you shaved your head, a red face and white head did not work, even with blue eyes.

The doorbell on the coach rang.

He went to the front door and found a girl there, no more than eighteen. She was the most striking thing he'd ever seen—breathtakingly beautiful. Striking red hair, curling to the shoulders of a shapely dancer's body, and deep, dark eyes—eyes that looked a lot older than eighteen. *Down, boy,* he thought.

"Yes?" he said, professionally.

"Hello," Scorpio Rose said, with her light French accent and her prettiest smile, a smile that lit up her whole face. "Could I please trouble you for a shower?" She was standing hip-shot, with one hand smoothing her hair back. She knew what others found attractive, and she did it well. Any more and it would become parody, but she knew how to take the edge off, ease it into reality. Michael liked young, unworldly girls; he was easy to read.

Just now he wasn't sure he'd heard right. "Say what then?"

"A shower," Rosa said. "I would love to come clean, and I think you have a shower in your huge autobus. I came to Wickr on my own, you see, not understanding how dirty it can be, and I am hoping you will take pity on me."

Michael was thinking furiously. He could not let an outsider into his coach, but he couldn't let her walk away.

"I'd love to help you out, but if I let one person do it, I'd have to let all your friends do it, and I don't have enough water. Maybe . . ."

"I do not have friends here," the girl said, her eyes widening. "I am camping by myself."

There had to be a way. "I wish I could—Mademoiselle—?"

"Maya."

"Mademoiselle Maya. But the truth of it is, I'm an . . . artist—"(for some reason, she smiled a little at that; an enchanting smile) "—I've got paint and canvas drying all over the place, and I can't disturb it. Dust in the air, you know. But what if I got you a tub outside—strung lines from my coach to that other one, and hung some blankets—give you total privacy—"

"I do not need privacy," said Scorpio Rose. "It is Wickr."

"Well, yes," Michael's hands spread, "but I think *I* do. I've got neighbors."

She smiled impishly. "They will not mind."

"One of them might," said Michael with a grimace and a glance at Diana's coach.

"Then I will certainly accept your blankets with great pleasure, Mister—?"

"Ron."

"Enchantée, Ron." She made a mock curtsy.

French, Michael thought. *She's never seen me on TV.* Michael realized that he had been looking at her for quite some time, so he said, "I'm not a lord," just to be saying something. And really, how much more did he have to say? "I'll get those blankets up right away."

Scorpio Rose moved with a dancer's loose-limbed grace to stand where Michael indicated. He grabbed a handful of bungees from the coach's supplies and connected them in two strands, which he strung across the back of his and Diana's area. He hung the blankets. Only now did he notice that the noonday sun, high in the south, threw her shadow on the northern blanket. She pretended not to notice it herself, let him admire it for almost thirty seconds, then called, "Water?"

"Coming right up," Michael said. He dug out a large red plastic tub, as big as a child's wading pool, and attached the hose to the faucet on the side. The hose had a spray nozzle, so when he turned on the water, the closed nozzle simply fizzed a little. He carried hose and tub between the blankets, set the tub down, and handed Rosa the hose. "You can fill it," he said. She gave him that pretty smile again and began spraying water in the tub. "These coaches are really amazing," he said, leaving her area, "and this from a man who hates buses."

"Really? What do you do, Ron?"

"I'm a political reporter."

"Obama or McClain? Is that right, 'McClain'?"

" 'McCain.' And I was an equal opportunity wretch."

"A . . . 'wretch'?"

" 'Ink-stained wretch.' Time-honored expression for 're-porter.' " He was standing again with a view of her shadow on the cloth. She turned off the water at the nozzle, put the hose down, and began, all unaware, to slip out of her leotard. Not that her silhouette was much different with or without the skin-tight garment, but now he knew she was naked, and that was enough. She turned sideways, displaying the shape of her breasts. She approached the tub and bent from the waist to feel the water. She slid into the water.

"Maybe," said Michael in a slightly husky voice, "we could meet up tonight. Hit some clubs."

"I would like that, Ron," said the seductive snow cone.

TUESDAY, JUNE 16, 2009 • 12:51 P.M.
PACIFIC DAYLIGHT TIME

7 Candle (Engaging with the Matrix)

Max sat in the shade of his tent, a gallon jug of Gatorade at his side, and read through Dave's list of girls born on Hallowe'en, 1991. Names, last and first, father's name (if known), mother's name, addresses lived in, schools attended, clubs joined . . . every scrap of info Dave could dredge up. The guy really was first class.

But within that mass of information, there was no thread that Max could spot on first glance. There were only three Valeries, and nothing about them struck a chord. Nobody named Drake. Nobody born in Louisville or San Francisco. Overall, there seemed to be a lot of Ashleys, Jessicas, and Brittanys, but also Elizabeths and Emilys. A lot of the more traditional names were also the names of asteroids, like Diana and Elsa, Eva and Maria, Julia and Barbara. There was even a Penelope—no, two Penelopes. And three Rosas. But none of those asteroids had anything to do with Val, as far as he knew.

He kept flashing back to the night he first met Val, at KQBU—the day he saw her sunbathing on Agrippa's deck— the night they made love in the Great Pyramid—the night they were married—the night she died, hanging—the night he saw her spirit in the moonlight, and she saw him. . . .

He looked up, to see if Pam was around. But she wasn't.

The heat was causing sweat marks on the pages, so he put them on the ground and laid his running shoes on top of them, to keep them from blowing. The weather was calm now but it could change at any time. He stretched his legs out in front of him and slid down in the camp chair, pulling his hat over his eyes. In a little while he would sleep, but first, he had to work out the means that he and either Mike or Di would use to communicate once they had an arrangement. It had to be simple, so it wouldn't freak them out; it had to be as undetectable as possible. What sort of paperwork would they be accustomed to sending and receiving? Polls for him, of course, and ratings for her, broken out any one of a hundred ways. They could easily generate lists where the code could be hidden, and he had just the code in mind—an inversion of a KGB special, based on the price of oil. All you needed was the ability to read and to count, but the results could not be predicted. The original had served the Russians well, and they'd had no Internet for *minute-by-minute* updates. In his version the code would modify itself sentence by sentence.

He wished Coyote and Rosa extremely well in their labors of love.

He took a long pull of orange G.

. . . and saw Val all but naked on Agrippa's deck . . .

When our school moved to Academgorodok in 1957, it seemed to be a fairy tale, compared to the four-square campus. There were research universities, libraries, apartment buildings, houses, hotels, hospitals, stores, restaurants, cafes, cinemas. There was the Ob Sea, an artificial lake built from the river for a hydroelectric power station. This station, being Soviet, did not supply enough power for the new city, but the fields and forests were flooded, creating open space where the wind speed doubled, causing dust storms as it returned to the land. Still, we were not there to look outside.

Our little school was dedicated to telepathy, telekinesis, teleportation. The purpose was military—Moscow saw great potential in spies able to communicate invisibly and untraceably—so it was run by the military, in the person of Colonel Bek, with all the feel for telepathy that a military machine would be expected to have. My fellow students and I made progress, but slowly, and probably mostly because we were growing older.

But in 1958, a new man took over. A man in a white suit, just as I'd Witnessed. His name was Wolf Messing, and he knew exactly what we were going through, because he'd gone through it himself.

At the start of the Second World War, Messing was performing a stage act as a psychic in Germany. With their emphasis on controlling all magick in the Reich, the Gestapo arrested him. He was taken to headquarters for questioning, but was able to escape by mentally suggesting to the guards that they go into another room and leave him alone. From there he fled to Russia and offered his services to Stalin. To demonstrate his abilities, he underwent two tests. First, he gave a Moscow bank teller an empty briefcase and a blank piece of paper; then he mentally told the teller to hand over

100,000 rubles, which the teller did. Second, he penetrated Stalin's headquarters at Kintsevo, which was heavily guarded by the Secret Police, by walking past them in plain sight, with no attempt to disguise himself in any way. But he mentally suggested to the guards and servants, "I am Beria. I am Beria."—the head of the Secret Police. So Messing became Russia's top psychic agent for the duration of the war. Afterward, he resumed his stage career to increase his income and feed his substantial ego, but he remained a military operative.

After Stalin died in 1953, the same Soviet stolidity that had sent us Colonel Bek disregarded all past evidence and declared Wolf's powers impossible. He was forced to present himself as a "clever trickster," in keeping with the new party line. But in 1957, the Navy's complaints that there was no way to communicate with submarines beneath the surface of the ocean caused one intrepid general to consider the benefits of telepathy, and that led to an official review of Wolf's file, and finally a revised party line. He was rehabilitated and assigned to Academgorodok.

All of these reverses and counter-reverses bred a deep fatalism in him. His favorite expression was "Decay is coming. In the end as in the egg—Naught." But he knew the power of Naught.

All of this he told us over our first months with him. Did I mention his ego? He loved himself and showed it off with all the flamboyance twenty years of vaudeville had instilled in him. But his powers were absolutely genuine. I was constantly examining him just as he was examining me, and I had no doubt. With him as Director, I knew that the path I desired was finally open to me.

Over and over we sent messages, received messages; that was our main concern. But those of us with different abilities worked them as well, to see what use they might be. I found my ability to Witness growing steadily, so that by the time I *was twelve, I could tour Novosibirsk from one end to the other without leaving Academgorodok. And I was learning Moscow—specifically the Kremlin. That was my little secret. Or one of them.*

The other was that Wolf became my lover.

It was not much of a secret. I wasn't the only young girl he took to bed, and as Comrade Director, he was not to be censured for it. His wife was no obstacle; she was already far gone in dementia. So he told me the usual lies, that he loved me, that his power would help my own. I didn't believe him because I was too bright, and he knew that, but he tried to use his power to make me believe it. When he saw that I could resist him mentally, but accepted him physically, he was content with the situation. That was his mistake.

Because at Academgorodok, I was learning far more than telepathy; Witnessing him, I was learning the WAYS of POWER.

Once again her emotion took her back down to the world.

TUESDAY, JUNE 16, 2009 • 9:00 P.M.
BRITISH SUMMER TIME

7 Candle (Engaging with the Matrix)

Eva Delia was waiting outside Rusterman's bookstore, looking both ways for Lexi. She looked left, then she looked right, then she looked left, and it began to seem to her like her own brain, with two sides battling for attention. Ping-pong, like they had in her Cambridge home. But she didn't want to miss her new friend.

And there she was! Lexi was striding up the street toward her with great resolve. "Hi, Lexi," Eva Delia said, as the girl reached her.

Lexi swung her fist and hit Eva Delia as hard as she could,

flush on the jaw. The fact that it didn't knock her cold was more happenstance than anything else, or maybe Eva Delia's brain, already scrambled, was able to take a punch better than a normal person's. It still buckled Eva Delia's knees, and she started to fall to the sidewalk. But Lexi grabbed Eva Delia by the blouse, keeping her upright, in order to slam her against Rusterman's front wall. The Voice sang, "No one's watching! No one's doing anything!", and it was true, as if the other people on the sidewalk couldn't even see them.

"Stop!" Eva Delia shouted, but Lexi bore in on her.

"You're a fucking retard, Eddy! A loony!"

"No! No, I'm not!"

"Don't lie to me! You can lie to yourself all you want, but you lie to me again and I'll cut your heart out!"

"I don't understand—"

"No, you don't, because you don't understand anything. This whole world is full of normal people and you don't measure up to a single one of them! Not the lowliest scumbag junkie whore!"

"Why are you doing this, Lexi? I thought you liked me!"

"I'm doing this because you disgust me, and you always have! Don't you get it? Everything we did last night was a big joke, and I was laughing my ass off the whole time. I don't have an aunt or a brother. I picked you out because you were easy prey, and I won't be the last! Everyone knows you're retarded and weak, and they'll come after you, one after another, until one of them drives an ax through your brain! Maybe that'll split the voices up for good, but you'll be dead, bleeding on the pavement—"

"Stop! Stop!" Eva Delia twisted hard, fighting to get free, but Lexi's one hand had her pinned against the wall like a butterfly. Eva Delia lost all control and bit Lexi's arm, trying to make her let go, but Lexi didn't seem to mind at all. Huge tears began pouring from Eva Delia's eyes, coursing down her cheeks. Lexi snorted, a sound of pure disgust, and shoved Eva Delia to her knees—then kicked her in the rear, sending her sprawling on her stomach.

Lexi crouched down beside her and hissed in her ear, "You're crazy, Eddy! Admit it!"

"I'm not crazy. I'm sick—"

"Crazy! Lunatic! Admit it!"

"No!"

Lexi grabbed her hair and yanked it, painfully, then slammed Eva Delia's face into the sidewalk. "Admit it!"

"I'm crazy! I'm crazy!"

"Don't ever let me see you again, or I will kill you, you crazy *cow*!"

Lexi stood up, gave Eva Delia a final kick in the ribs, and then stalked away, leaving her moaning and sobbing. No one came to Eva Delia's aid. They walked past as if she weren't even there. Gasping for breath, she knew why. They all hated her, and thought her insane. She was insane! She would never be normal. She was crazy to think she would be. That was the proof. . . .

After another two minutes, the girl got to her hands and knees, then slowly to her feet. She leaned dazedly against the wall, her mind a maelstrom of conflicting thoughts/ needs/pain, and that was good because she couldn't dwell, and bad because she shouldn't be like that. She fumbled in her purse for her meds.

But they were gone. Lexi had stolen them!

There was to be no relief for Eva Delia Kerr. Not on this night, and maybe forever.

··

7 Candle (Engaging with the Matrix)

When Rosa got back to her camp, she found Max, Pam, and Sly lounging deep in their camp chairs, knuckles dragging in the dust beside their plastic cups. It was hot.

"How'd it go?" Max asked her.

"As one would expect," she replied placidly. "I am seeing him tonight." Looking at Sly, she added, "And you?"

"We're hooking up around ten, beside a rock I know at the base of the mountains to the west."

"I shall make certain that we stay well to the east."

"You're slipping, Red," Sly said. "You didn't get him on the first try."

"Neither did you."

"Girls like courtship. Men, on the other hand . . ."

"It's going fine," Max said.

"Yes, it is," Rosa said, "but the real reason Michael didn't make his move was, he does not want Diana to see him betraying her."

"Diana may have the same problem," said Sly. "But I'd have to say no."

"So the only reason she had to wait was her dissatisfaction with the dog who was after her," responded Rosa. As always, Pam was surprised when the gypsy showed any flash of personality, and she wondered how she could possibly have made a hit with Michael. But of course, Michael was a man; he didn't need much.

Sly was unruffled by Rosa's riposte. "She wants seduction. She likes being the center of attention. She was on TV, you know. I seduced the hell out of her and she ate it up."

"It's going fine," Max said again. He got up and patted the arm of his chair. "C'mon and take my chair, Rosa. Have some Gatorade, or some wine."

"I am fine, Max."

"No, really. I've *been* sitting. Sly, you wanna play some Frisbee?"

"Sure." Sly came up out of his chair in one acrobatic leap, getting his feet down and holding his balance as he came vertical.

Max looked at Pam. "Likes athletics," he said.

"Well, I'm no athletic supporter," she replied. "You two go play. I'm staying right where I am, next to Rosa—especially if you refill my wine before you go."

Max took the glass and ducked into the tent, so Rosa did take his chair. "I'll bring two," he called.

Pam looked up at Sly. "*You're* a confident guy," she said.

"Always," said Sly. "But seduction's not exactly rocket science."

"Sly could charm the birds from the trees," Rosa said. "If there *were* any birds, or trees, on this plain."

"How about buffalo gnomes?"

Sly grinned at her. "He told you about that, huh?"

"He told me how he thought of it. Not what it meant, or any details." She wondered if she'd said too much. But Sly continued to smile at her, so she relaxed . . . except he continued to smile, which made her uncertain. He was not supposed to be charming *her*.

Max came back, glasses in each hand and a Frisbee under his arm. He handed one glass to Rosa and the other to Pam, then he and Sly went out in the dusty street and began to play.

Rosa took a sip of her chilled Chardonnay, then sighed, relaxing into her chair.

"Hard work?" Pam asked her.

"Not especially."

Pam regarded her quizzically, but didn't say anything. Then she remembered it didn't matter.

"You must not hold back," Rosa said, turning to look at Pam directly. "I know that this is new to you."

"I don't want to break the rules," Pam answered her.

"Ask and see."

"Well, then," said Pam, blushing, "how do you do it? Sex without involvement. I can sort of see it, and at the same time . . ." She stopped under Rosa's unwavering gaze, feeling stupid as she'd expected. But Rosa's next words changed all that.

"I am going to tell you my story, Pamela."

That was not what Pam had expected. "I—I'm honored, Rosa—" she began, but the gypsy waved her off.

"There is nothing that special about me, in the grand scheme of things. And I feel that I can trust you."

"You can," Pam said, providing space.

Rosa made a pass with her hand. "I am assessing our common shields," she said. "This is for your ears alone."

Pam nodded. "I understand," she said, sitting even farther forward.

Rosa said, "My birth name is Rosa Kalderaš, and I was born the first of November, 1593, deep in the Carpathian Mountains of what is now Romania. My drabardi name is Scorpio Rose."

Pam. Calculating. *Four hundred and fifteen years.* "Drab-ardi?"

"I am of the people the world calls 'Gypsy.' We call ourselves 'Roma.' We are wanderers, because we refuse to be limited to one land when all the others beckon. Wherever we wander, we blend into the background, because we refuse to be limited. We are not furtive—we simply do not allow others control over our lives. The best of us can become, in time, impossible to see. The best of those become *drabardi*. The world calls drabardi 'fortune tellers,' because drabardi stand outside the world.

"When I was eighteen, I was well on my way to mastery of our craft—much farther than you are now, Pamela. But I was still a maiden in the mysteries, as well as in the flesh.

"One night at sunset, a pilgrim came to our camp in the mountains. He was a large, handsome man, gentle and polite, asking to spend the night with us. I saw a use for him, and so I danced for him, around the flames of our fire. I did everything an eighteen-year-old Scorpio maiden instinctively knows how to do to capture his attention. And I succeeded.

"As the evening died down, I convinced him to walk with me beneath the silver moon. All about us the pines whispered, and the peaks were like the breasts of yearning women. I attempted to convince him to take me with him on his journey, away from the cloistered world I knew.

"In response, his man-shape vanished, and I was standing with a demon, large, powerful, unstoppable. He threw me to the cold ground and raped me."

"Oh my God!" Pam blurted impulsively, reaching out to her. "I'm so sorry!" But Scorpio Rose seemed not to notice.

"There was a horrible stench in the air, burning sulphur. I was drabardi, I had power. I threw it all against him but I could not stop him. He tore into me. It was a crescendo of pain, powerlessness, and grinding horror . . . and then nothing. I was conscious, but I was not in pain, I smelled no sulphur, I was simply there. I was involved, but I could feel nothing. I thought it was a blessing. Perhaps it was in that instant.

"But in the days and weeks and months that followed, I learned that I had been changed. My human soul had been permanently detached; I had become an empty vessel, bereft of everything that makes one human. To me, since that fateful night, all life is a play of the mind. It is simply *there*.

I do not feel anything for it, though I can pretend that I do—quite well, if needs be. I have my likes and dislikes, but I do not care, the way you do. I do not feel sorrow, or joy, or fear, or lust. I am like the silver moon, watching from afar."

"Oh, Rosa. That's horrible!"

"And it has continued for nearly four centuries," Scorpio Rose said matter-of-factly.

"Did you ever catch the demon?" Pam asked, trying to steer them to less sensitive ground.

"Yes. I swore my oath to close the doorways to darkness wherever I could find them so that others might not fall through. It was all I could do. In time I found him, and the gods who drove him to his depravities. They will not harm any other soul. I have closed many, many dark doors in my years."

"And none of that gives you even satisfaction?"

"No," said Scorpio Rose. "And thus it is that sex without involvement means nothing to me."

"Not even, with the . . . rape?"

"None of it affects me now, as anything more than a story—what Max calls the Storyline. To have sex I must counterfeit sex, but I must counterfeit everything. The plan Max offers promises the defeat of darkness. I choose to be involved, and so I involve myself."

Pam looked around. The guys were still tossing their Frisbee, apparently as carefree as birds. She asked, "Why do you stay with Sly, then? If you don't feel love?"

"I have my likes and dislikes," Rosa said. "If I did nothing, I would go mad, and madness was denied me that night and forever. I must interact. No one can exist in human form without interaction."

"Max taught me that."

"Sly accepts me for what I am, and I certainly accept him, for I can do no other. He offers a good Storyline. My existence is better with him."

"But I think all this involvement means you do feel. You just don't know that you do."

Rosa just looked at her.

"No. Of course. Sorry," Pam said. "Who am I—?" She stopped, got ahold of herself, and started over. "You don't feel."

"I do not. But Michael Salinan chose politics because he enjoys intrigue and shadows, and Michael Salinan likes young girls," said the drabardi quietly. "He will have those in spades from Scorpio Rose."

TUESDAY, JUNE 16, 2009 • 1:30 P.M.
PACIFIC DAYLIGHT TIME

7 Candle (Engaging with the Matrix)

Max and Coyote stood forty yards apart, tossing the Frisbee with practiced expertise, and *called* to each other in silent communication. At least, Max called it *"call"* because that was what his teacher, the vodou mambo Mama Locha, had called it. He had no idea what Coyote called it. Probably something to do with "wind." Or maybe he just thought that because the wind around them was picking up—not something you wanted when throwing a Frisbee. There might be a dust storm on the way.

Rosa's telling Pam her story, Max said in the brightness of his mind.

How can you tell? came the response.

Look at Pam's face.

Coyote held the Frisbee, cocked his head, and picked out the twosome between the vans and tents. Others might well have missed it from that distance, but his eyes were sharp. *Her deep concern is wasted,* he said finally.

Pam doesn't know that! Max snapped back.

No, 'course not, Max. Everybody does it; that's the thing. They all reach out with compassion and it drives home to Rosa that she can't. It doesn't hurt her but it's hard for her, letting other people into her life.

And yet, Max said, *she does it anyway.* He plucked the Frisbee from the air. *I'm still working my way through being Timeless, still finding new things about it. I can't imagine doing it without emotional reinforcement.*

She has me, Coyote said.

Max started to say something, then let it alone. Instead, he changed the subject. *Remember, when you and I first met, and you revealed you were a shape-shifter—I asked if you'd ever met a shifter named Aleksandra?*

Sure.

Anything new on that front?

Not a thing, Coyote said. *But I've just been keeping an eye open; I haven't really been looking. Why?*

Not sure. I'm feeling something that's got her name on it, but I don't know what it is. It's not around here. . . . But it's something.

Instinct, said Coyote positively. *I'll keep my ears perked.* He caught Max's throw, then tossed the Frisbee high in the blue desert sky and ran to catch it as it soared back over his head. The wind was picking up. *Maybe I'll go on a hunt for her.*

No, you won't.

So she's a diabola. You should meet the spirits in the Black Rider Mine. Bad things happened down there, believe me.

Believe ME—

A cloud of whitish dust swept over them. The Frisbee, momentarily invisible, sailed off to the left. *Dust storm,* Max *called. Let's get inside the tent.*

You're a prairie dog, Max, Coyote jeered. *Hiding in a hole.*

No, I just have sense enough to come in out of an alkali storm. You can stay and play with yourself if you want.

I'm going for a run.

If it gets bad there'll be a complete whiteout.

More fun runnin' blind, said Coyote.

Okay, you're a Trickster, Max said. *But sometimes you trick yourself, too. C'mon inside, Coyote.*

But when the next cloud cleared, Coyote was gone.

TUESDAY, JUNE 16, 2009 • 2:21 P.M.
MOUNTAIN STANDARD TIME

7 Candle (Engaging with the Matrix)

"That's the last of them," Aaron said grimly. "We've covered every gas station and restaurant on the main routes, and nobody saw them."

"All right, but Vanagons go about two hundred, two twenty miles on a tank of gas," Craig answered. "Phoenix is one twenty, so they were never likely to stop here. If they had, it'd've been great, but now, we just need to drive out another hundred miles in each direction and canvas those areas. We might have to drive a thousand miles covering the whole area, but if that's what it takes, that's what it takes."

"*You* say that?" Aaron asked.

"*I* say that," Craig declared. "I'm not givin' up my partner."

"How long can we stall Hanrahan?"

"As long as *that* takes." The two men exchanged a long look. They had known each other since the first three months of Desert Storm, and their decision to become mercs-for-hire had been based on how well they'd embraced the suck in the Iraqi Sandbox. There was nothing else they needed to say.

So Craig said only, "Which way first?"

"It's a total crapshoot. We don't know why they're here. But I say, they wouldn't have gone straight east; if they were headed over there, they'd have gone direct from Tucson. So let's head north, toward Flagstaff. Then we can work our way west from there if we have to."

Craig nodded.

The two men drove into the American Sandbox.

7 Candle (Engaging with the Matrix)

Eva Delia's physical pain subsided once she made her way home and fell into a deep sleep. But her mental pain only increased as she dreamed a dream that had tormented her for many months. In her dream, she was on stage, and in the audience was a certain blonde girl. Eva Delia could never see the girl's face, only her golden hair, but she could hear the girl laughing at her. Laughing like Lexi, at her. But the girl wasn't Lexi.

Who *was* she, and why did people hate Eva Delia even in her dreams?

What had she done to deserve this?

7 Candle (Engaging with the Matrix)

Michael was lounging on his coach's couch, sipping a Coke Zero, reading Politico on his laptop, and enjoying the air-conditioning. On the one hand, Obama had reneged on the Defense of Marriage Act, and on the other, Senator Ensign, one of the act's prime movers, had been caught cheating on his wife. It miffed Michael just a little; Ensign had been his catch. Why hadn't Breckenridge informed him when he pulled the trigger? Well, maybe because Michael had asked not to be disturbed for anything that wasn't earth-shattering. . . .

People, even Breckenridge, tended to give Michael what he wanted. He'd come up through the old Chicago knee-capping politics, and no matter how smooth he was now, how much of a caricature he presented to the world, he got things done however they needed to get done. Breckenridge gave him what he asked for because when he asked for something, he delivered in return, and never abused the privilege—except when Breckenridge didn't know. That was fair enough; politics was the art of the deal. But if no deal could be made, like Breckenridge's approval of him and Diana, then Chicago politics came back into play: just get it done.

So it was funny that the political link had always been in Columbus, Ohio, while media was in Chicago. But politics was in Ohio because Ohio politics was a model for the nation, while Chicago politics had always been too obvious. You didn't need knee-caps now, you just needed electronic voting machines, and he was proud to say that Ohio had led the way.

But you couldn't get a decent hot dog there, and that was usually the tipping point when it came to whether Diana would come to him or he'd go to her. She was his baby but a Superdawg was a Superdawg.

TUESDAY, JUNE 16, 2009 • 9:00 P.M.
EASTERN DAYLIGHT TIME

7 Candle (Engaging with the Matrix)

"He won't do a damn thing because he's spent his whole life *not* being scary, Gerry. You'll get your bonuses, don't worry." Breckenridge rolled his eyes above his secure phone, miming disgust for Hanrahan's benefit. "Limits? Don't make me laugh. You'll make more this year than last. Yeah, really. Okay. See you Sunday."

Breckenridge put the phone away. "These geniuses are so fucking dumb." Hanrahan nodded with a half-smoked Coyolar Puro between his teeth and pressed the pad on the portal to the secure area inside his Wheeling mansion. The doorway unlocked with the sound of compressed air, then shooshed aside so he and Breckenridge could enter.

They stepped into a T-shaped hall presenting three more doorways. Hanrahan led the way into the middle one, his conference center. It was a much smaller counterpart to the room where the Necklace met, in the outer part of the mansion. Nine people could enter here, maybe, if they all stood and crowded together. It was really built for no more than five.

The old man closed the door behind the two of them. There was not a chance in hell that they could be overheard after that. Silent, invisible fans drew the cigar's smoke smoothly through the ceiling, into a sanitizer that would release unscented fumes into the center of ten acres of restricted forest seven miles to the east.

"This is our last chance to make any substantive changes, Dick," Breckenridge said. "Is there anything I need to know?"

"Nothing, Renzo. Everything is on track and moving smoothly. Our guy is still solid, and once we pay off his wife, everything will be locked down."

"It would only be natural for him to have second thoughts."

"Not him. He's a true believer. He *wants* this."

"And money for his wife."

"We all love our wives, Renzo." It was a joke because neither man was married—and yet, it sparked a quick light in Renzo's eyes which Hanrahan spotted and noted.

"Listen, I want to witness that payoff."

"What? Don't be ridiculous."

"I want to see it. I haven't been close to the action in years."

"Which is a good thing. We don't want to lose you."

"Just witness it. Set me up a spot where I can see through a view-finder."

"A scope, you mean?"

"Whatever you call it, set it up."

"All right, if you say so. But why, Renzo? Is there something you want to tell me?"

"Not at all. I'm just bored with doing everything from rooms like this. I want to get out on the street again, even if I'm two blocks away."

"Yeah? Because you seem different."

"Drop it, Dick."

"Sure. Fine. But let me ask you something else."

A flicker of annoyance crossed Breckenridge's face. His great ability was the ability to lie without conscience, so he never showed even that much of his true feelings except to his oldest friend—his friend who could annoy him. "What is it?"

"Why are we keeping this operation between ourselves, and not sharing it with the group?"

"I have my reasons."

"I'm sure you do. But—"

"Don't hector me, Dick. I don't have to explain myself to you or anyone." It was only in his head that he added, with satisfaction, *Now.*

TUESDAY, JUNE 16, 2009 • 6:00 P.M.
MOUNTAIN STANDARD TIME

7 Candle (Engaging with the Matrix)

By the time Aaron and Craig reached Flagstaff, the sun was a fireball in the west and they were certain the VW had not come up this way. They checked until they were almost in the city, well beyond the VW's range, and found nothing. So they grabbed Frappucinos and muffins at Starbucks and took I-40 west, directly into the fireball, to cover the hundred miles toward U.S. 93.

They were swallowed up quickly by the beautiful solitude of the cool Arizona mountains.

7 Candle (Engaging with the Matrix)

Peter Quince knelt on the floor of his sanctum sanctorum. The circle around him shimmered like heat lightning, and a haze like peat smoke hovered over his head, filling the top half of the room. It was one reason he was on his knees; the continued breathing of it did not feel at all healthy to his lungs. The other reason was, he was draining himself, pouring every bit of magickal energy at his disposal into his invocations.

But he could not charge his *stone*.

The process was almost blindingly simple. These chunks of space rock had functioned as magickal repositories for centuries; anyone who penetrated the mysteries could learn how to perform the ritual; the trick was finding the rock. Quince had done it with older *stones* half a dozen times. But this new *stone* seemed as inert as a block of salt, resisting his every attempt.

He rested, letting the room settle, before mystically attacking the problem one last time. Again, he failed.

Was it the murders that had attended his appropriation of it? No. Murder was no bar.

Was it some counterspell by Daniel Cheever? Please. The man was third rate at best. Anything he could have erected, Quince would have sensed and then shattered. But there was no sign of such a spell.

Had al-Burabi done something while he possessed it? What *could* he do?

Or was this some new kind of *stone?* Possibly, since there were known to be many types of asteroid, but Quince had never heard of anyone before him failing if he performed the rites correctly.

The night was rolling onward, and Quince had no answers.

He gestured and the haze above him swirled up and out the solid ceiling. He stood up, trembling slightly. He had to find the answer, not only for his own sake, but for the sake of the promise he'd made to Lawrence Breckenridge.

TUESDAY, JUNE 16, 2009 • 10:47 P.M.
CENTRAL DAYLIGHT TIME

7 Candle (Engaging with the Matrix)

Half an hour later, an even more frazzled Peter Quince found Rita in her room downstairs, talking on a secure line with her lieutenant in Miami. "Shut it off!" he told her.

Rita looked at him with a hard glare . . . then deliberately modified her gaze and spoke into her phone. *"Te llamaré, Mérides,"* she said shortly, and closed the connection.

"What is it, Pete?" she asked. Her voice was flat. She had to please Quince, but never in her life had she enjoyed being told what to do. "You want more sex?"

"If I thought that would help . . . ," he began, and for the first time, she saw him at a loss.

"What is it, baby?" she asked with quick concern.

"There's something going on here," he said, "something blocking my work. It's got to be this damn house, or this city. At least, it better be."

"I'm still digging into Tower's past," she said. "Maybe that'll tell you."

"Well, dig deeper and faster, first thing in the morning. We've got to get this figured out or we're gonna end up out on our asses!"

"I hear you," she said, and she did. If he went down, she'd never survive a second failure with the FRC. "Have you ever powered a *stone* before?"

"No, but the books are clear and the books *work!*"

"Calm down, Pete. I'm not saying it's your fault."

"But it *is!*" he almost shouted at her. "Because I can't see the answer! If I were the wizard I'd like to be, I would see it! And I'd deal with it because that's what wizards do! But if I can't see it, I'm not enough of a wizard. Not enough for the FRC!"

"Pete," Rita said, taking his hand. "Chill. You're a *hell* of a wizard. Just the parts I've seen have blown my mind. Sit down and we'll talk about something else, take your mind off it. It'll come to you."

It better, she thought.

TUESDAY, JUNE 16, 2009 • 9:35 P.M.
PACIFIC DAYLIGHT TIME

7 Candle (Engaging with the Matrix)

Michael and Diana were in his coach. It was sparkling clean, in contrast to the dust-covered world outside. Michael had prepared a fine meal of roast pork and au gratin potatoes, which they ate with a 2000 Grgich Hills Chardonnay. They were listening to Hank Mobley's *Blue Note Years,* offered by Diana. The air-conditioning hummed just on the edge of Hank's tenor sax.

They drifted into silence, inside the bop. But not a sensual silence. This was mellow, very mellow, but *only* very mellow.

Michael noticed it and thought, *She suspects something.*
Diana noticed it and thought, *He's tired. Good.*

Michael said, "Long day, huh?"

Diana smiled. "You slept longer than *I* did!"

Michael smiled. "*I* know. I also flew from Columbus."

"That's *three hundred miles* more than me. Big whoop."

"Still . . ."

"Still what?"

"I just wanna take a walk, by myself, tonight. Wind down."

"No lovin'?"

"Plenty of lovin', baby." He got up and came around the table. Leaned down, took her face in his hands and kissed her like he meant it. He did mean it.

She felt it. He loved her. Well, she loved him, too, but *This is Wickr, for God's sake! There are no rules, and I'm sure you know it! You'll do it, too, before the week's out.*

"Okay, baby," she said, taking his shoulders. "I'll see you tomorrow. Get a good night's rest."

"Okay," Michael said. "Sweet dreams." He kissed the top of her head.

Natural-born conspirators.

TUESDAY, JUNE 16, 2009 • 9:42 P.M.
PACIFIC DAYLIGHT TIME

7 Candle (Engaging with the Matrix)

Michael stepped out into the warm desert night. Half the stars in the universe blazed overhead; there was no moon to blot them out. Neon blazed in spots in every direction, throughout Wickr City. The air was dry and fresh unlike any Michael Salinan had breathed in the last four years. From the moment Ohio reported Bush winning 2004, Michael had been working Obama versus McCain for the Necklace. It was his job as Political Link to have puppets in both parties, able to push things one way or another as the situation demanded. And so, as two wars and the economy dragged America down around them, Michael had worked the fringes of the battle, trying to turn whatever happened on either side to the Necklace's advantage. And he had delivered. Almost every minute of that long and dangerous campaign had been a pleasure for him. Now, all of a sudden, he was looking around and seeing stars in the sky.

All of a sudden, he was going to meet Mademoiselle Maya.

Apparently, Diana had not suspected, or she wouldn't have let him go that easily. But if she ever found out, she'd have no cause to complain. Politics was the art of the deal, no? Still, he suspected she wouldn't be too thrilled if she knew, so it was better to keep her in the dark if he could. Diana was damn sharp in many ways, but she sometimes saw people as an audience viewing her, and forgot that they all had secrets themselves that they weren't revealing while they were watching.

He walked down Saturn to Four and turned outward, toward the empty desert beyond Neptune. The techno grew softer but never quite vanished. The world grew almost pitch-black in this direction, this far from the center, with only occasional camp lights, light sticks, and random bicyclists' head- and taillights to help mark his way. Also ahead of him, the stars clearly drew out one of the very few things he recognized in the sky: the constellation of the Scorpion, rising in the east. The red star in its head was unmistakable.

He passed beyond Neptune, the city's ring road, and entered open territory. Oddly, his world grew brighter. This was where large art projects were stationed, and each had lights around it. The closest one was still a quarter of a mile away, and the one after that a quarter mile to the side. Out here there were attractions, and sightseers like himself heading between them, but mostly, there was empty desert, under the empty sky.

He set off toward the closest thing, a sculpted set of giant nuns, three or four stories tall, clustered around a leaping fire fed from some gas line. The sculptures blocked much of the light, allowing only shards of it to twist and writhe across the plain.

Michael had gone perhaps a hundred feet when he heard someone coming toward him in the dark. It took a moment before he could make her out. It was, as he had hoped, Maya.

"Hello," he said. "I thought we were meeting at the statues."

"We were," she said with her delightful accent. "But I took the chance to find you sooner, since I knew you would come out Four Street."

"Well, you did it perfectly," he said expansively. All of his earlier caution was gone, now that the chance of his being caught was gone. "Do you want to keep going, or head somewhere else? What would you like?"

"Why do we not just walk on the desert for a while?" she asked.

"Fine with me. Smell the air."

"Yes, it is wonderful."

"Are you feeling clean now?"

"As opposed to 'feeling dirty'?"

"Ha!" Michael said. "That's not what I meant, but it'll do."

"If I were not, I would not have been seeking you like a cat in heat," said Scorpio Rose, coming into his arms. Suddenly, there was no pretense or the need for it. They both felt what they were there for. Michael looked around and saw no one anywhere around. Of course, he hadn't seen Maya either, so you never knew. But that was enough thinking. He crushed his lips against hers, felt her tongue slide into his mouth, and he reached to unsnap her leotard.

7 Candle (Engaging with the Matrix)

Diana looked back at her coach. No lights burned there; clearly, she had gone to bed for the night. Or, she'd gone out. But there was no way to learn the second option without risking the first. Michael wouldn't know, and that was enough.

She walked out the back of their camp onto Uranus and turned toward Five, passing it, passing Six, until she got to Seven. The odds of her running into Michael were pretty much nil as she made her way inward toward the Sun from here. She turned again on Venus, passing Eight and arriving at Nine. Nine ran straight west from the Sun, along the side of the mountain. She turned toward the empty desert, and the stars. The big triangle of Leo the Lion was burning in the black sky, and there was some sort of planet nearby. She could almost believe the stars lit her way.

As one of the main thoroughfares, Nine had attractions lining both sides. She guessed "attraction" was the right word. There were bars, dance floors, a stage show, a roller rink, an outdoor movie, and bowling lanes. There were hundreds of people and a now-familiar electric enjoyment. Everyone there, including her, was happy to be in the magical city tonight.

She remembered, as she always did now, that there was a difference between magic and magick. *Magic* was a night like this. *Magick* was what the Necklace wizard practiced. She hadn't known that magick was real, in a certain few hands, until she'd joined the Necklace. Now that she did, she had to be certain that when she wrote the word, she always spelled it without the K, because other people weren't supposed to know. Since they didn't, the Necklace had a huge advantage in controlling the world.

Controlling the world. It was something everyone had heard about, usually as the ultimate plan of the menace the hero had to take down, every Monday at nine. The "big bad" of paranoid fiction. But the Necklace was no boogeyman to jazz the 18–49 demographic. Everything the Necklace did was pointed in one direction only, and they were always moving.

Diana was completely serious about the Necklace and what she could do in it. She had known she was ruthless long before she'd encountered them. She was climbing, climbing toward control of her personal world. And then Dan Rather had been deposed, and Brokaw retired, and soon thereafter, she'd started noticing odd little things. People who might have been following her. Clothes put away just slightly differently from the way she did it. There was nothing she could report to the police, even if she'd been so inclined, but she paid more attention to her surroundings. As she found out later, this was one of the things that made them pay attention to her. She wasn't dumb and she wasn't asleep.

She found out when Michael took her aside after the third Bush-Kerry debate and had a private word with her. After she'd done a piece on Carole van Dusen her bosses had assigned. After meeting Lawrence Breckenridge at a charity do. After almost literally running into Jackson Tower along the lakefront. After—

"Hey there, cutie."

She looked right and saw Greg leaning up against a huge boulder, one foot on the ground and the other back against the stone. She'd left the city behind several minutes before, continuing into the desert. Greg had told her he'd meet her out there, beyond the city lights, and she'd never doubted he'd show. If she knew anything, she knew he wanted her as much as she wanted him.

"Hey yourself," she responded, turning toward him.

"It's a beautiful night in the desert," he said with such enthusiasm that it made the people she'd passed on the street seem suddenly glum. His gusto was contagious. Where she lived, in Chicago, there was nothing like this—the sweeping darkness, split horizontally, with the bottom half jet-black and the top half spangled with stars. There might have been just the two of them in all the world.

She went and leaned her own back against the stone, still slightly warm from the day. Her shoulder touched his. She could smell him, a warm smell, not off-putting at all despite his lack of bathing. The dry desert air deodorized, and really, Greg was a primal sort of guy. Just the sort of guy you'd like to have all to yourself in the night.

Nevertheless, she touched the gun in her fanny pak. A girl couldn't be too careful, and neither could a link in the Necklace.

"You're lucky," she said. "To get out in places like this so often."

"You're right," he agreed equably. "I've been east to the cities, and it's really amazing what people can build, but I like what's here without people."

"Misanthrope," she teased him.

"I hate people who call me that," he responded, showing a heretofore unexpected intelligence while flexing his shoulder to give her a slight nudge. She responded with a nudge of her own. He nudged her again, she nudged him again. He took her hand, turned her, and took her in his arms. She kissed him fiercely, decided to go with it, and moved her other hand to cradle the back of his neck. He let her hand go so his hands could slide along the small muscles of her back, up and down. At which point he broke their kiss.

"You see how much I hate people," he murmured, his lips in her hair.

"Shut up," she responded, and that was the last coherent word either one of them spoke for the next ten minutes. But there was a lot of growling.

TUESDAY, JUNE 16, 2009 • 10:31 P.M.
PACIFIC DAYLIGHT TIME

7 Candle (Engaging with the Matrix)

Max and Pam were seated on their tent floor, he in the north and she in the south. Small circular lights were also on the floor, before each of the four tent walls, providing soft illumination up the canvas. Max and Pam were drinking Tanqueray and tonics. Techno music pounded from outside.

"You feel it?" Max asked. "The sexual energy?"

She rolled her eyes. "Who could miss it?"

"Non-alchemists."

"There's only alchemists here, sweetie."

Max looked at her, the glow from the southern light behind her haloing her hair. "That's twice you've said something like that," Max said soberly. "But you're not an alchemist yet, Pam."

"Thanks."

"I don't mind your calling yourself an alchemist. That's your path. I just don't want you to forget exactly where you stand on it, Pam. That's dangerous."

"I know where I stand, Max. But I *have* come a long way, you have to admit."

"I do admit. And that's not what this night is about, anyway. With all this energy around us, here in Wickr, it's a good night to take another step along the way."

Pam sat up straighter, feeling the thrill run through her. There had been other nights and days like this, when he opened up other doors. This was the path she'd chosen, and every step forward into an unknown that soon became known had given her that thrill.

Max leaned forward, savoring her blue-eyed face. Pam leaned forward, savoring his green eyes, till they were in a space that held only them. The techno went unheard. When Max spoke, it was for her ears alone—and she knew it.

He said to her, "Everything in the Universe is in a relationship with everything else. Nothing exists completely untouched. And each one of those relationships has a specific energy. How does that sound?"

"So far, it seems to hold true," she agreed forthrightly. "I'm watching, and it's definitely a world of duality. And its primary attribute is Relationship—all the relationships between two things that make up the world."

"So that's a total of three things: the two halves and the energy between them. One-two-three. That's everything in the Universe." Max picked up the pitcher between them and poured himself another drink. He saluted her with the glass. "That's what I told you, and it's true, but there's more. You will never know all of it until you do, or until you die. So you have to learn it before you die."

Pam listened.

"Three things: the two halves and the energy between them. One-two-three. But if that's all there was, we wouldn't know it. It would be a complete, self-contained system and there would be no 'we.'

"But 'we' do exist, so the system is not self-contained. One-two-three is not all there is. There is one more number."

"Four," Pam said.

"Why four?" Max asked.

"What do you mean?"

"Why not pi?" Max said.

"Oh. Well . . . ," Pam said. "If you're asking, because one, two, and three are integers, and so is four. Pi is something else—'irrational,' I think." Her eyes were bright: the research scientist. "And if you're looking for a number larger than three that encompasses the universe, why not 'infinity'?"

"Absolutely," Max said. "Why not infinity? So have you ever heard of 'squaring the circle'?"

"Huh? Where did that come from?"

"Squaring the circle is a problem proposed about 2000 BC: to construct a square—having four sides—with the same area as a given circle, using a compass and straightedge for a finite number of steps. That's called a plane solution. But it turns out there isn't such a solution, because the relationship between the curve of the circle and line of the square can only be determined using the number *pi*. If the side of the square is 1, then the circumference of the circle inside the square is pi. Completely scientific, used every day in the real world, with a key on your calculator and everything. So, what *is* pi?"

"3.1415926," Pam said.

"Keep going."

"That's all I remember. It goes on forever."

"Yes," he said, "it does."

She regarded him closely. "You go on," she said.

"Pi is essential to our reality, because to build things, you need to be able to measure both curved lines and straight lines—but as it turns out, you can't measure pi. It turns out, pi is a *transcendental* number, which means that no sequence of algebraic operations can come out equal to it. That means it is impossible to construct, using physical tools, a square whose area is equal to the area of a given circle. *Impossible*.

"And pi is indeed an *irrational* number, which means that its value can't be expressed exactly as a fraction. The closest is twenty-two over seven, but that's not exact, and even if you put an incredibly large number over another incredibly large number, it's impossible to get the right answer. Our regular numbers just can't encompass it, no matter how we come at it. Pi exists outside our concept of structure, and yet it's essential to our concept of structure. *Pi is impossible but essential.*

"There's an alchemical saying that Agrippa liked, called the Axiom of Maria Prophetissa. It's very old and it goes like this: 'One becomes Two, Two becomes Three, and out of the Third comes the One as the Fourth.' Most people would hear that 'one-two-three-four,' because we never count 'one-two-three-pi.' We can't have pi things in our world of duality, so we count 'one-two-three-four.' Four is a useful substitute in our world, but it's *not even close to an accurate representation of the Universe.*

"An accurate representation of the Universe is a number that never ends. The Universe, in short, is *impossible but essential.* And its symbol is pi."

And all at once, Max's face split in an uncontrollable grin as his deejay brain could not repress his next words. "So while you and I partake of the power tonight . . . ponder pi, Pam."

TUESDAY, JUNE 16, 2009 • 10:46 P.M.
MOUNTAIN STANDARD TIME

7 Candle (Engaging with the Matrix)

Aaron and Craig came to the junction of I-40 and U.S. 93. It was a desolate spot in the middle of nowhere; they took the standard-issue cloverleaf from the sparsely traveled interstate and circled to head south on the U.S. road, which was just a two-lane blacktop, disappearing into the desert night, completely forsaken except for them. The road was flat; the land was flat; the sky was vast. They were hunting wizards but they had no sense of wizardry, so the empty darkness held nothing extra for them. It was just the world.

The Dodgers were still playing the A's on the West Coast and the radio from far Bakersfield came and went with Vin Scully's story of the Bums' thrilling comeback. When it went a Mexican station filled the void for a while. The long day and the urgency of their mission had drained the two men of conversation; they just listened to whatever came their way and drove, mile after mile. They were farther away from Phoenix than a VW could have gone on one tank of gas, but that would give them a margin of certainty as they worked their way back down the highway toward the big town.

They drove as far south as Wikieup before seeing any civilization, and there they checked into the Trading Post Motel.

It was then about midnight.

WEDNESDAY, JUNE 17, 2009 • Midnight
PACIFIC DAYLIGHT TIME

7 Candle (Engaging with the Matrix)

Stacy and Greg lay on the ground beside his rock and looked up at the Universe. There was no moon and no planets up there; just crystalline stars. She recognized the Big Dipper, and followed its edge to the North Star. The desert night was only slightly too cool; draping her blouse across her chest made it perfect. Greg seemed comfortable as he was, which was entirely naked. Diana felt damn good, in every way there was to feel good. Her body was sated and her mind was plotting. Now she really didn't want Michael finding out about this guy. Michael was a good lover, often inspired; there was no problem there. Long term, with their shared and secret associations, he was a perfect match. But Greg was an animal, tireless, energetic, enthusiastic . . . everything a girl could want. The very definition of a fling. And she had found him the first time she went looking.

Finally, her internal interviewer felt the need to ask a question. "Do you know the desert stars, Greg?"

"I know what the local Indians say about them," he drawled. "When the North Star was on the earth, he was known as Na-gah, the mountain sheep, the son of Shinoh. He was daring, sure-footed, courageous—and always climbing. He hunted for the highest mountains.

"One day he found a very high peak. Its sides were steep and smooth, so around and around the mountain he walked, looking for a trail. But he couldn't find any trail. He climbed as far up the rocks as he could, but he always had to turn around. Na-gah had never before seen a mountain he couldn't climb.

"Finally, he found a crack in the mountain that went down, not up. He went into it and soon found a hole that went upward. He began to climb with the greatest of pleasure.

"But soon it got so dark that he couldn't see, and the tunnel was so full of loose rocks that he slipped too often. His courage began to fail him, and he was also getting tired. 'I will go back and find a better place to climb,' he said. But when Na-gah turned to go down, he found that the rolling rocks had closed the cave below him. There was only one thing he could do: keep on climbing until he came out somewhere.

"And after another long climb, he saw a little light above him. When he finally came out of the hole, he found that he was on the top of the highest peak in the world. There was scarcely room for him to turn around, and looking down from this height made him dizzy. Nowhere on the outside could he get down, and the inside was closed. . . .

"Now, about this time, his father was out walking over the sky. He looked everywhere for his son, but could not find him. He called loudly, 'Na-gah! Na-gah!' When his son answered him from the top of the highest cliff, Shinoh felt sorrowful, and said to himself, 'My brave son can never come down, but I will not let him die. I will turn him into a star, and he can stand there and be a guide mark for all the living things on the Earth or in the sky.'

"And so Na-gah does not move around as the other stars do, and the Paiutes call him *Qui-am-i Wintook Poot-see*—North Star. The other mountain sheep wanted to go on up to him, so Shinoh turned them into stars, too. You can see them in the sky at the foot of the big mountain, going around and around."

Diana said, "That would make a wonderful children's special. I wonder if PBS has ever done it."

"Are you in television, Stacy?"

"Me?" She laughed. "God, no. I'm a legal secretary. But it would make a good show, wouldn't it?"

"I dunno. I hate television."

"What?"

"I hate television. I'd rather be outdoors."

"You," Stacy teased, "are some kind of Communist."

"You like TV?" Greg asked innocently.

"I do."

"So," he said slyly, "we're not compatible."

She gave him a gentle elbow in the ribs. Greg chuckled. "What kind of law are you in?" he asked.

"Intellectual property. Unfortunately, I can't tell you anything about it because it's all highly confidential."

"Does it involve TV?"

"I can't tell you. Forget TV. What do you do?" Stacy asked.

"Professional gambler."

"Really?"

"Uh-huh."

"Do you win?"

"More than I lose. I do all right," Greg said.

"Have I seen you on ESPN?"

"You're really into TV, huh?"

"I like to play cards, too," Stacy said.

"Poker?"

"Yes, poker. Other stuff, too. But you and I should play sometime. Strip poker."

"I don't play with friends."

"Why not?"

"They lose. Then they're not friends," Greg said.

"I usually win. I might take that challenge."

"But I won't. I like you too much as a friend."

"With benefits," she bantered, while filing away that *"I like you too much."*

"Definitely benefits." This time he laughed. "And if you can't play my game and I can't play yours, then everything we have is right . . ." his hand strayed over her body, and settled on a landing, ". . . here."

"Works for me," she said urgently, twisting his way.

7 Candle (Engaging with the Matrix)

Ron and Maya were almost run over by a herd of bicyclists, and had to scramble for cover while snatching up their clothes. The bikers laughed but kept on going, not interested in causing any real distress. Ron gaped after them, as he stepped into his briefs.

"This place is crazy," he said.

"Why, Ron?"

"Where I come from, the best we'd get is a horselaugh, and the worst you don't want to know."

"Where is this horrible place?" Maya asked.

"Pretty much anywhere."

"You sound cynical."

"It's a fact of modern life."

"Oh, I imagine the dark ages weren't much different," Maya said.

"Yeah . . . Which makes Wickr that much more amazing. It's not some hippie fest, but people are just nice." He caught himself and laughed. " 'I'm good enough, I'm smart enough, and dog-gone it, people like me.' " He laughed harder, and decided not to put his pants on just yet.

"Why is that funny?"

"It's what the new senator from Minnesota used to say when he was a comedian. And I don't like the new senator from Minnesota. But it's true right here." He took her hand and drew her to him. She came so easily. It was easy to lie to her. "Forget all that. It's not what we came here for." He held her close. "This is the best night of my life, Maya."

"Ummm." She snuggled against him.

"I've never met anybody like you. And I've met a few girls in my travels. But there was never anyone I wanted to be with like I want to be with you."

"You are just saying that."

"No, I mean it. I hope we can see each other this entire week."

"Only if I can shower indoors tomorrow."

"Well, why not? Since I know you're coming, I can clean up."

"Come, go there now. Spend the night on clean sheets—"

He considered it, but then his earlier lie would be exposed when she found no artwork. "I can't, Maya. Things are still too spread out. But I'll put it all away in the morning. You won't see a stitch of art."

"It is as if you are afraid to be seen with me," she pouted.

"Not at all! I have a friend, but she won't mind. Come tomorrow." He began to stroke her. "Tomorrow is a long way off. . . ."

8 Earth (Connecting with Humanness)

In the morning, Eva Delia rose early, still stiff and sore from her beating at the hands of the girl she'd thought was her friend, hurting still more from the betrayal, without her meds. She brushed her teeth carefully, her face red and swollen, and dressed in nonbinding clothing, before hurrying to the National Health. Today she would sit in the downstairs room and have her body fixed. But first, the meds.

As she approached, the air became unpleasant, even nasty. Sometimes people had parties in the park and burned stuff. But, she decided, this was different. Or at least that's how she felt. Feelings were all she had now. She wanted her mind turned off. Cascada was singing from a window overlooking the Square: *"Our souls are divided."*

But she began to meet people walking her way, handkerchiefs to their faces, crying. It frightened her and she felt very deeply that she should turn and walk away. Run away. But the Voice was chanting again, a simple, unaffected beat, the beat of her footsteps on the concrete, and it propelled her forward even as it calmed her down.

Then she saw the police and the tape and the crowd.

She needed her mind off! She shouted, "Where's Nurse Koomari?" Somehow she knew.

The counter nurse bustled to her side and took her hands with hands that trembled themselves. "You have to be calm, Eva Delia," the nurse said.

But Eva Delia shouted again, "Where's Nurse Koomari?"

"Nurse Koomari is dead," the nurse said, and went on from there, but Eva Delia didn't understand her anymore. And she certainly didn't think to ask the nurse for more meds as she broke away and finally ran all the way back to Greek Street, the way she'd wanted to all along. All she knew was, this was Lexi's fault.

WEDNESDAY, JUNE 17, 2009 • 1:15 A.M.
PACIFIC DAYLIGHT TIME

7 Candle (Engaging with the Matrix)

When the moon rose over the eastern mesa, Stacy and Greg decided it was time to call it a night. For Wickr, the night was young, but they'd made love three times and she was ready for sleep. In the bright moonshadows, they said good-bye to each other beside their rock, and they took their time. She didn't want him walking her home, because now she really didn't want Michael to find out about him.

She set off back down Nine, sauntering with a delicious lassitude. When she came to Uranus she turned and took the longer but easier orbit back home. Making her way through the dark streets, passing patches of light and sound, she ran back the tape in her mind of what had transpired—not just the sex, though she lingered on each time, but also on what had been said. She made certain she hadn't given anything away, and she catalogued everything Greg had told her.

When she came to her coach, she looked carefully for any sign of Michael. Finally secure in the idea that he wasn't waiting in the dark, she quickly went inside her coach and locked the door behind her. She went to the nightstand beside her bed and removed what looked like a small pencil flashlight from the drawer. Crossing back to one of the two storage cabinets beside the forty-inch flat-panel, she opened its door and removed the factory-installed false floor, revealing the coach's safe, which she opened with the supplied key. Inside, apparently no longer protected, was her armored laptop, based on a Vaio but almost completely rebuilt by Hanrahan's people. She played the beam of her flashlight across the lower right side of the case. Had she not done that, touching the computer would have shot 900 kilovolts through her body, causing at least unconsciousness and quite probably death. Once that protection was turned off, however, she had only to reverse the "flashlight" and fit its back end into the computer's special lock to open it for use. Her left ring fingertip held against the power button was the final hurdle.

When her desktop came up—an image of herself with ridiculous hair, doing the news in Tulsa, surrounded by an old-style TV screen—she connected to the secure Necklace net and ran an all-out background check on Greg. She assumed Hanrahan was monitoring her usage but she ran background checks all the time; there was no reason to think this one would stand out, and even if it did, she could explain it innocuously. If the results turned up nothing, there was not even a problem, and if they turned up something, she was just doing due diligence on a suspicious acquaintance. If they turned up something, she would like to know it just as much as Hanrahan would.

She went and poured herself a glass of cold Chardonnay and pulled up a chair to see what was what.

WEDNESDAY, JUNE 17, 2009 • 1:30 A.M.
PACIFIC DAYLIGHT TIME

7 Candle (Engaging with the Matrix)

Max and Pam were lost inside each other's bodies and souls, balanced on the edge of orgasm, on the crest of the opalescent Universe. Their bodies and minds were alight, dazzling, sizzling, and endlessly so—surrounded by vast pastel-colored waves, singing like the aurora borealis. They knew who they were with perfect clarity, and Pam saw clearly that the meeting of the straight and the curved was the basis of everything.

Pam knew pi.

7 Candle (Engaging with the Matrix)

Diana was still working her computer when she heard Michael come home. She had to smile at that because Greg checked out all along the line. His biggest sin was being barred from the MGM Mirage Group for counting cards, though this seemed to be more for winning too much than for any specific technique. He'd also been accused of leaving a Miss Amanda Louise Jericho at the altar of the Wee Kirk o' the Heather Wedding Chapel, but that had been quickly resolved in an amicable fashion.

So he was human, and he was real, and that was a good thing.

Day Three

. . . .

WEDNESDAY, JUNE 17, 2009 • 6:00 A.M.
MOUNTAIN STANDARD TIME

8 Earth (Connecting with Humanness)

When their wristwatch alarms went off, Aaron and Craig rolled out of the twin beds at their motel in Wikieup. They had showered the night before so they could simply slip on their clothes and go. By 6:15 they were having breakfast at Luchia's down the road. The lighting there was bright but their waitress was tired. She was probably working two jobs.

Aaron and Craig were working their job, and they were damn glad to have it. By 6:45 they were headed on down 93. It was going to be another hot one.

WEDNESDAY, JUNE 17, 2009 • 11:40 A.M.
CENTRAL DAYLIGHT TIME

8 Earth (Connecting with Humanness)

Rita Diamante entered the forest behind Tower's house the way she'd once entered crack dens, her H&K P2000 in her right hand, alert for anything. It was cool in there, and dark even in daylight, thick with old trees that didn't grow in South Florida. Jackson Tower told her on their flight to Suriname that he ran through the forest every night, but this was an investigation she had put off as long as she could. She went where the wizard went when the sun was high.

She followed an old path through the trees, listening for birdsong, looking for buildings, seeking out anything that would tell her anything useful. She didn't expect to see magick, but she hoped to see *something*. The path was not straight, but it would be easy to run along—flat, with wide curves. From time to time it crossed other paths, or maybe itself twisting back. Very quickly she realized that there was no birdsong, no sign of anything living besides the ancient trees, which sighed and shifted in the breeze. She didn't like it at all.

She was goddam ready to shoot something, anything to let loose a little of the tension she kept inside her as she, the patrona, acted the good peón. All she needed was one thing, one little thing, to let her and Pete get ahead.

But she found nothing.

WEDNESDAY, JUNE 17, 2009 • 1:07 P.M.
EASTERN DAYLIGHT TIME

8 Earth (Connecting with Humanness)

Breckenridge strode across the Manhattan Bridge on a very pleasant day. It was partly cloudy, in the high sixties, though cooler in the open air above the water. The twelve-foot steel-mesh wall to thwart suicides loomed ominously over him, with the eight-foot steel-mesh fence on the other side of the walkway humming with the passing trucks and cars. Only one bicyclist and two pedestrians shared the walkway, as far ahead as he could see, which was why this was one of his favorite walks.

The Plain Man   169

Another man in his position—if there were one, which there wasn't—would never venture out of doors without at least two bodyguards. But Breckenridge wasn't worried; he was carrying a simple, traditional, brown-leather attache case. He noted with interest that the briefcase seemed heavier today, the third day away from Aleksandra, and wondered if her absence was reducing the life-force she provided him, weakening him. But his stride was as springy as ever, his pleasure in the day undiminished. Perhaps it was not a lessening of life-force but a lessening of the narcotic effects of her presence. Going cold turkey had made him more aware of himself in all his aspects, physical as well as mental.

LoBianco's report had gone well last night. He had never supposed that the man would make him wait for it.

In the shadow of the massive bridge towers, he stopped and peered through the steel mesh at a passing barge below. He took out his cell phone—retrofitted by Hanrahan's people to the highest security, though outwardly unchanged—and called Carole van Dusen.

"Quick work on Ensign," she said.

"Yes, and I want to do it again."

"What's gotten into you, Lawrence?"

"Call your friend at *The Post*. This is going to be a week no one will ever—"

He was struck across the left shoulder, causing his phone to spin from his hand and clatter to the walkway. He lurched forward against the fence, but rebounded as the steel mesh sprang back into place, turning to face his assailant with agility belying his apparent age. The bicyclist was straddling his bike ten feet away, a lead pipe in his hand. There was no one else within a hundred yards upon the walkway. Vehicles were passing just two yards away, but their speed and the mesh fence may have blocked their view. Certainly none of them could stop and do anything.

"I want your wallet and your case," the cyclist said. He was a Latino teenager, high on something as he swung his leg over and let the bike clatter to the walkway. He stepped forward. "Now, *cabrón*!"

Breckenridge smiled. It was not a smile of nervousness, or calming influence. It was the teeth-baring smile of a predator. "This case?" he said softly, barely audible over the sound of traffic, and held the case out at shoulder height toward the boy, who was rolling too strong to notice the incongruities. Neither did he notice Breckenridge's brow tighten, or eyes squint, as the older man stared past the case at him.

The air around the case began to shimmer, like a mirage in the desert. Finally the attacker noticed. But the next moment, he dropped the pipe with a clang, to paw at his face. He was trying to rip the air apart, or something; in any event, he was having trouble breathing. His eyes bulged and his face turned red and he struggled for air, there high above the open water in the freshening wind. It was a struggle he lost. He dropped to his knees. He dropped to his face with the sound of his nose breaking. He lay still.

Breckenridge lowered the briefcase. It had not seemed heavy at all just then, even though it held a twenty-nine-pound *stone*.

WEDNESDAY, JUNE 17, 2009 • 10:15 A.M.
MOUNTAIN STANDARD TIME

8 Earth (Connecting with Humanness)

Aaron and Craig had covered the highway south of Wikieup that would have encompassed two hundred miles from Tucson, if the van had come this way. It was a completely different experience, driving that two-lane in the light, but a completely familiar result. Nothing. Since there was no sense going back into Phoenix, they turned west again on U.S. 60, toward the California border and Interstate 10.

8 Earth (Connecting with Humanness)

"What's today, Pam?"

"Connecting," she said, "with the Universal."

Sly, doing one-armed push-ups, spoke up. "What the hell does 'the Universal' mean?"

Max said, "I've actually started calling it 'Humanness' instead. I'm always trying to express the energy as precisely as possible, and 'Humanness' gets a little closer, I think."

"A man who makes his living with words," said Sly, shaking his head sadly. "I preferred the pioneers; they were strong but silent."

"Puritans, too," Pam said sweetly.

"Finding the right words is an art," Max said. "There are no two words that mean exactly the same, and the right words define the exact truth. That's the nature of all incantations. 'Humanness' defines the life we're all living here—the life we all take part in. You can also call it 'Nature.' It's everything that makes up the human experience on this planet."

"As opposed to the moon?" Sly asked.

"Nah, we've taken ourselves to the moon. What it's opposed to is the stuff we don't see, either because it's invisible or because we choose not to see."

"Like the Matrix?" Pam asked.

"The Matrix, yesterday, is the underpinning. The opposite to Humanness comes tomorrow. I used to call it 'The Unique'; now I just settle for 'Magick.' That's the stuff that isn't part of life as we know it. That's the stuff most people, even at Wickr, would deny even exists. That's where the Universe does what it does and only a master could attempt to say why, or join in. Humanness is hard-put to provide an explanation when magickal things happen, beyond calling them 'miracles.'

"But that's tomorrow. Today we're reaching out, wanting to connect with our natural urges, the stuff we all *do* understand. We're living our animal nature—our human nature."

"You're saying I couldn't get laid if it were a different day?" Sly asked, a little offended or pretending to be.

"Sure you could. Anybody could, and especially you, my friend," Max said. "But today it'll be real easy."

WEDNESDAY, JUNE 17, 2009 • 10:45 A.M.
PACIFIC DAYLIGHT TIME

8 Earth (Connecting with Humanness)

When he rolled out of bed, Michael felt great, but then he remembered that he'd promised Maya she could shower in his coach today. He looked around for whatever he could plausibly maintain was art and found nothing, so he took his dirty clothes and some heavier apparel and rolled them into balls, then stuck them in half-closed drawers to make it look like he'd put something away. He'd never specified what kind of art he was working on, so it would be some textile thing. For his brother-in-law, who was in the fashion business. That's why he'd had to be so secretive, and why he couldn't show her what he was doing even now. She might have a woman's or a hippie's curiosity and lack of respect for boundaries, so he'd have to keep an eye on her, but it should suffice. The shower and the bed were all she needed to see. This was doable.

The next step would be to check on Diana's schedule for the day. If he could at all convince her to go exploring before noon, it would be better. If he couldn't, well, he'd cross that bridge when he came to it. He had his political skills, and she loved to look at things; he could tell her about the nuns in the desert.

So he walked over to her coach to see what her plans might be, and met her coming out her door.

"Hey there," he said.

"Hey back," she said.

"Good time last night?"

"Pretty good. How about you?"

"Yeah, okay. You off somewhere?"

"Just gonna look around."

"Gonna be gone long?"

"Why?"

"No reason."

"Well, I don't know," she said. "I thought I might see what was on the other side of the city. What are you up to?"

"About the same. If you're going to be gone for a while, I can get some work done."

"Always trying to stay a step ahead."

"Three steps is my rule."

"Well, that'll be fine. I'll probably be gone a couple of hours."

"Okay. Our masters will appreciate it. You want some breakfast before you go?"

"Nah. I already ate." For some reason she seemed anxious to get moving, and all at once Michael's antennæ went up. *Could* she . . . ? he wondered.

Diana kissed him good-bye on the cheek, and left the camp at a leisurely pace. When she entered the street, however, she turned decisively to the left and started moving right along. Michael looked at his watch. Maya wouldn't be here for another hour.

WEDNESDAY, JUNE 17, 2009 • 11:01 A.M.
PACIFIC DAYLIGHT TIME

8 Earth (Connecting with Humanness)

Diana made her way purposefully along Saturn. She wasn't late but she was eager to see Greg again. She turned inward through the city, toward the Sun, and went down to Mars, enjoying the colors in the people she passed, some of whom she now recognized. She'd been here two days now and it was all becoming familiar. She was good with faces.

When she arrived at Mars, Greg was not yet there. She felt a pang of disappointment, but had to remember that Wickr didn't run on clock time. Events took place when they took place. If Greg stood her up, she'd hunt him down and have his balls, but she couldn't assume that yet. So she looked around and spotted a tent where the campers were giving out ink tattoos. She strolled over to it and looked through the samples while keeping one eye peeled for her new man. A medieval dragon caught her attention, and she called the "proprietor" over. He wiped her forearm with alcohol to clean the sweat and sunscreen, let it dry for thirty seconds, then inked and oh-so-carefully rolled the rubber stamp over the spot. He was just finishing when Diana saw Greg enter the intersection, so she thanked the proprietor with a blinding smile and went out to meet him. Greg was grinning that grin of his back at her as he took her in his arms and kissed her, while she held her inked arm to the side so he wouldn't smear it.

If Michael'd had a gun he might have shot him right then.

8 Earth (Connecting with Humanness)

Scorpio Rose arrived at the coaches to find Ron in a bleak and bitter mood. "I can't deal with *you* today," he snapped.

She showed surprise. "What do you mean—?"

"I'm here with someone. Or I *was*."

Now Rosa was tracking. She said soothingly, "She has found someone else?"

"Apparently."

"But so have you, Ron."

"It's not the same when she does it to me. And lies about it."

"Your pride is hurt. Of course. But we can soothe your hurt. And what better way of showing her that you do not care than by having your own affair?"

"That's the way she talks about it—'a Wickr affair.' I was good with it, till it became real."

"You are a loyal, passionate man."

"I am. People think—" He stopped himself. "I don't know why I'm talkin' to you. Just go."

Instead, she glided forward, using every trick she'd learned in four hundred years to make herself desirable. Her walk, her look, and the drabardi magick behind it, all were trained on Michael Salinan. She pulled the image of the «Lust» card from four hundred years of mental experience and mentally enveloped him in it. He was nowhere near the man to ignore her spell. She reached his side and tenderly laid her hand on his forearm. "I do not want to go, Ron. I came because I want to be with you."

He tossed his head like a nervy stallion, fighting his attraction. "And I want to be with you, Maya. But I'm not in the mood anymore."

She leaned against him, raising his arm until it rested between her breasts. Her nipples were hard; a simple trick. "You cannot control this other woman. You can only control yourself, and me. She will do what she will do—and so will we." She kissed his neck.

"Just go, goddammit!" He wrenched his arm free. "Sorry about the shower, now go the fuck away from me!"

Sadly, touchingly, she went. But he did not give in to it.

WEDNESDAY, JUNE 17, 2009 • 3:00 P.M.
EASTERN DAYLIGHT TIME

8 Earth (Connecting with Humanness)

Lawrence Breckenridge stood in the cupola of a narrow Brooklyn office building built in 1906. The airy dome was metal, greenish from years of weather, and here and there things had built nests, in the eaves and in the corners. His briefcase was to hand, just in case. But he was concentrating on the view through a high-powered sniper scope pointed toward an alley four blocks away. The cupola was situated so that his view was almost straight down that distant urban crevasse, and the time had been chosen to provide the most sunlight. Dick had set this up well.

A woman was waiting in that alley, hugging the shadow. She was a plain-looking woman, late thirties, who had dolled herself up for her meeting. It was not, Breckenridge knew, that she had romantic expectations of the messenger; it was that she had romantic expectations of life, so she made herself as attractive as she could as a general thing. Unfortunately for Breckenridge's tastes, she ruined her natural beauty with the makeup and the hair. He thought, without any irony, *Military wife*.

She was looking around, growing distrustful of the dark end of the alley. She checked her watch, and clearly said (visibly, not audibly), *Goddammit all to hell!* But then she heard something, probably footsteps, and moved farther into the dark.

A man came to the mouth of the alley. He took out some keys on a chain and swung them around, three times, clearly. Then he walked five feet into the alley, off the beaten path, and waited.

She came forth. Asked him a wary question. He nodded, and took off his backpack. He put it down, bent facing the mouth, looked around, gave it a minute. Then, assured no one was likely to witness it, he opened the pack and removed a package. He turned, handed it to the woman, turned back to keep watch. She, furtive, turned away before breaking open one corner of the package and checking the contents. The green contents. As she gazed astounded on all that money, the man silently sprayed her with an odorless mist.

Nicely done, Breckenridge thought. *But I was better.*

The woman said *Okay* and turned back to the messenger. He told her (not visibly—it was too hard to read it all—but Breckenridge knew the drill) that he would keep watch while she left, make sure no one would follow her. Then he did say, clearly, *Are we good?* She answered him: *We're good.* Breckenridge felt a surge of triumph.

She left, watched by the messenger, and the messenger's boss from the cupola four blocks away. The boss knew he could never get any closer, but he still felt the triumph of being there because he had been the messenger, more than once, in his time. Maybe, if Aleksandra stayed away for a while, Hanrahan could figure a way to make it so again.

WEDNESDAY, JUNE 17, 2009 • 12:20 P.M.
MOUNTAIN STANDARD TIME

8 Earth (Connecting with Humanness)

Aaron and Craig reconnected with I-10 just outside of Quartzsite. That was the extreme edge of the van's range if it had come this way, and there wasn't a whole lot on the 128 miles between Quartzsite and the Phoenix area on 10. If the van had come this way and had not bought gas before, they had to have bought it here.

The two men took the West Main exit and rolled into the Chevron. Craig got out, stretched, and went inside.

Within two minutes he was back, shaking his head.

They drove on to the Shell and Craig went inside. Within three minutes, he came back running. "Got 'im!" he snapped excitedly. "We got the son of a bitch!"

"When?" Aaron demanded.

"Sunday night."

"How does the day shift know?"

"The guy running the place has just one worker, and they each take twelve-hour shifts, twelve to twelve. He says it's the only way he can keep up with the rent. And the only way to make it bearable is to check out the girls coming through. He remembers the woman in the van, packed with camping gear. And because of that, he saw which way they went—up Ninety-five!"

"Thank you, Jesus!" Aaron said. "Go get us some gas station food and coffee, and we are out of here!"

8 Earth (Connecting with Humanness)

Hanrahan got the call he'd been expecting.

"My wife says it's all there," the man on the secure line said. "I still don't know why you paid her in cash. . . ."

Hanrahan read everything in that digression, but he said, evenly enough, "One reason is, she saw the money; it wasn't just some computer printout from an offshore account. The bills are large but she can cash them at our branch in Bismarck with no record whatsoever, and if somehow there's a problem, she can cash them anywhere with the paperwork on her aunt's death. We don't want you to worry."

"I'm not worried," the man said. "I'm good. Only . . ."

"Yeah?"

". . . talking with her . . ."

"Yeah?"

". . . look, you know I'm dying, that I want revenge. You know that's true. But I'm not dead yet, and, talking with Marianne . . ." He sighed. "Can we put this off for a while? Maybe a month? I'm not gonna get any better. I can't screw you. But what about another month? That's okay, isn't it?"

"Another reason we met your wife," Hanrahan responded, "was to spray her with a substance that bonds to the skin, that we can ignite electronically, which we will do if you don't carry on as planned. Don't call her, don't warn her, just do your job and the substance will wear off in about a week. Do you agree?"

"I . . . of course I do," the man protested. "I always agreed with the *idea*."

The surrender of others was an old and familiar routine to Hanrahan. There could be no glimmer of hope remaining. "You are a prominent figure on our satellites; we know where you are at all times. I'm watching you now . . ." he peered into the third monitor built into his desk, "between buildings AF-19 and -21." He saw the man glance up, his face only slightly pixelated at this magnification. "Hold tight for the next thirty-six hours, and this will all be a chapter in American history."

WEDNESDAY, JUNE 17, 2009 • 1:45 P.M.
PACIFIC DAYLIGHT TIME

8 Earth (Connecting with Humanness)

Diana got back to the coaches to find Michael in a very dark mood, and it didn't take long to figure out why.

"Have a nice time?" he asked sharply.

She knew immediately what he was talking about. "I did," she said simply. "You?"

"You didn't waste any time finding a lover."

"We talked about that, Mike."

"Yes, we talked about it. But my God! We've only been here two days, and you must have met the guy yesterday! While you and I have made love exactly *once!*"

"We can do it right now."

"Sure, because you're horny from him!"

"Well, what if I am? We talked about it."

" *'We talked about it.'* May I remind you that we are

sneaking around on some very powerful people so we can be here? We, us. I thought we were doing it to be together, Di."

"We are! We're together. And we'll be together after this week is up. But this is Wickr."

"Fuck Wickr!"

"I don't know what to tell you, Mike. I thought we were clear that this week was for experiencing *everything* we could. You for your job, me for mine—"

"So you're sleeping with another guy *for your job?*"

"No!" she said. "I'm sleeping with another guy for *me!* And I may sleep with a dozen more if I feel like it! And then, when we go back to the real world, I'll go back to sleeping with you exclusively, if you stop acting like a jerk. I've never cheated since we got together—and as you pointed out, getting together *is* dangerous. But I did it because I like being with you—"

"You *'like'* being with me."

"You think I should say *'love'*? We haven't been together *that* long."

"Nearly four years!"

"Yeah, and how many actual days has it been?" Di asked. "We've had to steal every moment; it probably adds up to a few months at best. And I don't know about you, Mike— maybe I *really* don't know about you—but *I* have had a lot on my plate when we're not together. I haven't sat around mooning."

"Nor have I!"

"Well then, what are you talking about? We like each other under tough circumstances. And I want that to continue. But we've got a chance for some un-tough circumstances, for you and me to be together, *and* for you and me to be free, and I'm not giving that up."

"You're a bitch. You know that?"

"Yes, I know it. And you're a bastard. That's why we do

what we do, and that's what I like about you, and that's what you like about me."

"I don't like this one bit, Di."

"Yeah," she said. "And just so you know, I may spend tonight right here with my new friend. So I really think you should go find one of your own, and listen to me when I tell you that I *want* us to be okay when this is over."

"I hear you. But I don't know if that's enough," he said.

"Well, it's all you get, Mike."

He couldn't look at her any more right now, so he spun on his heel and stalked away.

WEDNESDAY, JUNE 17, 2009 • 1:52 P.M.
PACIFIC DAYLIGHT TIME

8 Earth (Connecting with Humanness)

Scorpio Rose watched and listened from concealment across the road. Though she was within twenty feet of them, they did not see her.

WEDNESDAY, JUNE 17, 2009 • 2:02 P.M.
PACIFIC DAYLIGHT TIME

8 Earth (Connecting with Humanness)

When Rosa returned to her own camp, only Max was there, writing in his *Codex*. She moved directly toward him and took his hand, but spoke in measured tones.

"Michael has rejected me."

"What?" snapped Max, scrambling to his feet. "Why?"

"He saw Diana with Coyote, and he is a Taurus, so now he is balked and steaming. I tried everything I knew but he was unreceptive."

"So much for gypsy witchcraft," Max said.

"So much for Humanness."

"No, that's everything we humans do, including jealousy. I just didn't figure that jealousy was part of this equation. He had no interest in you at all?"

"None. He must truly care for her, to his manifest surprise."

"And you didn't get inside his coach."

"No."

"Try again this evening."

"I do not think so, Max. He has sent me away; returning would either make him suspicious or lower me in his estimation. Neither gets us forward." She shook her head, crimson hair catching the sun. "No. It is all on Coyote now. And he will have better fortune. He is a creature of fortune."

Max smiled tightly. "Is that an official drabardi prediction?"

"Yes."

"But he does tend to screw himself up from time to time, thinking it'll go his way no matter what—and now it has to."

"Well, what do *you* predict, with your Mayan time counts?"

"Listen, everything I know says this is a day for focusing on love. I mean *everything*; this is an *exceptionally* powerful and propitious day. You struck out but I have to believe Coyote will succeed—and let's not forget that in the simplest terms, Di wants him to."

" 'Everything' includes . . . ?"

"The Mayan time counts, the asteroid of the day, all the relevant planets, the Yijing, the Tarot . . ."

"*Only* those?"

"Not all of us can be drabardi. Some of us have to work it out on our own. And you use Tarot."

"Too true. But I see what I see by blending into the flow, and you see what you see by prizing out the truths of many systems . . ."

"Which I then blend into one flow."

"But not *my* flow. I work in a much older tradition of direct contact. I cannot feel human emotion but I can know the universe. While you feel only *after* you have used your mind. It may be better that way—you can explain your craft, to newcomers like Pamela. I can only say what I feel, with no explanations."

"And yet I'd hate to see which of us has the better track record."

"Then it will be interesting to compare, over the longer term."

Something in her tone made him study her face for a moment, but her face gave nothing away. Perhaps there was nothing to give. Still, he didn't forget it.

–o–

When I was thirteen, Russia suffered its great defeat in the Cuban missile crisis. It was then that the powers we were demonstrating at Academgorodok became the highest priority for the military.

Dr. Leonid Vasiliev, chairman of psychology at the University of Leningrad, took the day-to-day duties of Comrade Director, while Wolf was tasked with concentrating on the twelve most promising students. I, of course, was the most promising, and the following months with such personalized instruction, as outside the box as seemed right to us both, brought me forward even faster than before.

One day, I happened to overhear Wolf on the phone, talking with his masters in Moscow—though he wouldn't have labeled them as such. They were inviting him to a meet-

ing, but he, having grown ever more intoxicated with his absolute power in Academgorodok, told his caller rather brusquely that he would consult his calendar and get back to him. On hanging up, Wolf told Drysi, whom I knew to be his "official" mistress, to stonewall all calls from the ministry until the beginning of the following week, as he had his own pressing business to pursue.

I saw an opportunity to test myself.

Knowing the details of Wolf's illustrious career by heart after all that time, I remembered his incursion into Secret Police headquarters. I also knew that I was no longer satisfied with simply projecting my invisible essence to faraway places. So it was that the following day (allowing for time to have flown in an airplane), I hovered invisibly just outside KGB headquarters in Lubyanka Square. Then I concentrated as I had never concentrated before, hardening my thoughts to harden my essence. After nearly a quarter of an hour, I took visible form on that Moscow byway—the form of Wolf Messing.

At first I simply floated forward, but further concentration caused my—Wolf's—legs to move. I walked up and down the square, hoping against hope that Wolf's prestige would keep anyone of lesser rank from accosting him, and that the few men of equal or greater rank would be busy. Such was the case, and after another quarter hour, I felt ready to proceed.

I walked across Lubyanka Square to the ugly yellow building and announced my arrival, to see Director Semichastny. They were surprised to see me but no one questioned my legitimacy, and I once again appreciated the power Wolf wielded by the speed with which I was conducted to the director's office.

"Good of you to make the time to come," Semichastny told me by way of greeting. Not wishing to test my voice, I merely inclined my head, with all the disdain Wolf himself would muster. The director was evidently accustomed to this attitude, and accustomed to accepting it, which I duly noted.

"We have had a significant report on the activities of Cornelius Agrippa," my host told me, picking up a file from his desk. "He was seen in Detroit, Michigan, in the Negro quarter. His eternal quest for the 'new' took him to a company called 'Motown,' where he inquired about a singing group called the 'Supremes.' They are a failed act, having released eight records with no success. Agrippa, seeking to become their manager for whatever reason, suggested a song called . . ." he consulted the file, "'When the Lovelight Starts Shining Through His Eyes.' Unfortunately, we have no Negro agents in the American central states, and our man in Chicago was too visible as he tried to close contact with him. Agrippa left Detroit without acquiring the Supremes and is once more lost. But our man gathered a good deal of information about his current appearance and interests."

Semichastny pushed the file across the desk toward me, got up, and turned to stare out the window. "I must confess," he said, "an enemy who consorts with Negro musicians is not one I care to have, so I'm all too glad to leave him to you." For my part, I was reading through the file, turning the pages with my mind. I couldn't trust my "fingers" to do the job, and was taking advantage of my chance to work unobserved. But then I realized, this would not seem strange in Wolf himself, and so I took a chance by continuing to turn the pages mentally after Semichastny turned back around.

"Here," he said, picking up the file. "Take it with you." He handed it to me. I had no choice this time but to try to take it from him. It fell right through my "hand."

He gaped at me.

I vanished.

That night, Wolf came to my room in Academgorodok, but not for love. With both Drysi and Svetlana there to back him up, he beat me badly. I fought him, but the combined power of the three of them was too much.

"You're lucky I don't have you taken out and shot," he

hissed in my ear as I lay sprawled in my blood. "But I still believe that you can amount to something. That's the upside of your little stunt today. The downside is, I'm onto your tricks, and if you do anything that makes me look bad ever again, I will kill you without hesitation. I have worked hard for my position and I will not allow anyone to endanger it. Do you understand me?"

"I do," I moaned.

"Then be in class tomorrow at nine sharp," he said. "With no excuses for your poor body."

"Yes, sir. No excuses. It will never happen again."

All LIES.

WEDNESDAY, JUNE 17, 2009 • 10:04 P.M.
BRITISH SUMMER TIME

8 Earth (Connecting with Humanness)

As the day wore on, Eva Delia's body got stiffer and stiffer, while her mind grew more and more confused. Her little flat, which had seemed so cheerful, became a mausoleum of gloom, its ancient window crusted with the grime of the city and probably the fire that had killed Nurse Koomari. The light which came in, reflected from the old brick across the way, was gray and somehow twisted. The sounds from the street were increasingly serpentine. More than once it sounded like Lexi laughing out there. And sometimes it sounded like the blonde girl. Eva Delia knew she needed her meds but she couldn't get up off the floor in the corner and go outside. Where would she go? The clinic was in ruins. There was another but she didn't want to walk that far, didn't want to find a new doctor who would be nice to her and then die.

But as night began to fall over London, she began to get really hungry. She got unsteadily to her feet and went to the fridge. There was food inside but none of it looked appetizing. She could see the germs inside the food, fighting to get out like the fragments of her mind. The thing that appealed to her then was curry, nice Paki curry. There was a restaurant where she was always happy. She could go there if she didn't frighten the owners. But curry was easy. You said the words and they gave you food and you gave them money. She knew she mightn't do well with counting, but she could give them enough and then she could eat.

She put on her jacket and went down the stairs like water in a drain, flushing herself into the street. The lights were too yellow and the cars too blue, but just like last night, nobody objected to this treatment of her. She ambled along, sometimes stopping to be sure she remembered where she was going, and it was during one of those stops that she noticed she was outside Rusterman's, right where Lexi had hit her. She flinched, thought of turning back, thought of running on, thought of the book with the lines that made her feel better. Feeling better. That was what she wanted really, more even than food. Her stomach chose that moment to grumble but it was, as always, her mind that she focused on, and she went inside.

Through the first room, and the second room, and the third room, and the fourth room, and the fifth room, and the sixth room, and finally there she was somehow, in the seventh room. And there was the book. She couldn't hold herself back from it, driving toward it in a straight line, knocking books from the tables, knocking customers aside. They grumbled like her tummy but they did no more, and so she reached the book and opened it and looked on the lines of ancient type . . . and felt her mind grow more orderly.

The lines of the foreign language were like little caterpillars, with their soft undulations and endless marching. Eva

Delia could lose herself in there, and even though the voices in her head were almost as garbled as the words on the page, talking over each other unlike the words on the page, she could hold on to the orderly progression until it came to the bottom of the page, then she could turn the page and watch it go on and on. It was not a thick book but if she came to the end she could go back to the beginning or look at another book . . . until Rusterman's closed and they asked her to leave. The thought made her anxious and she bent closer to the pages, trying to drown herself in the lines.

"Eddy! Thank God I found you!"

Eva Delia jumped backward, as far as she could, slamming the small of her back into a table, rocking the stacks. She hardly felt the pain through her terror, and started staggering sideways down the aisle. But Lexi was in front of her, with her hands on Eva Delia's shoulders. "It's okay!" Lexi said, her face a mask of deep concern. "It's okay!"

Eva Delia screamed.

But just like last night, the other people paid no attention, and Lexi was talking rapidly, the words tumbling from her mouth. "I had to do it, Eddy! They were watching me. If they knew you were my friend you'd be in danger. I had to do it to save you!"

The words made no sense to Eva Delia in the state she was in, but the tone of them said she should make them make sense, and using her recent linearity of mind she laid them in a row and worked her way along. When she got to the end, she understood the words . . . but she didn't understand.

Lexi saw. "Eddy, I'm a secret agent. On Her Majesty's Secret Service. I found out something horrible about Corsican gangsters and they followed me to London. I thought I'd given them the slip but they saw us together on Monday so I had to pretend I hated you, or else they'd have killed us both on the spot." Lexi looked at her with the utmost concern, straining to see if she'd gotten through.

She had. Eva Delia could follow what she was saying. . . . "You don't hate me?"

"Oh God no! I never did! I had to lead them away from you."

"But won't they kill us now?"

"No," smiled Lexi triumphantly. "I caught them and turned them over to the police. I've been looking for you ever since. Look." She held out her hand, and there were Eva Delia's meds. "You lost these last night. I'm so sorry I took so long to find you."

The little bottle was like cake to a starving man. The desire for them crashed over Eva Delia like a golden wave, and she snatched them from Lexi's hand. She fumbled getting the top off, but she did it, and got her pills and popped them in her mouth and swallowed them, even though her throat was dry.

"Poor baby," said Lexi. "We need to stay together while they take effect. Have you eaten?"

"No," said Eva Delia. "But, I'll go alone."

"No, dear. You might do yourself a mischief. You need me." A thought seemed to strike her. "Or are you still afraid of me?"

"Yes," said Eva Delia, totally devoid of pretense. How long would it take for the meds to work?

"I understand," Lexi said, stepping back. "I'd be afraid of me, too. But I swear to you, the bad times are over. Let me go along with you, and I won't get too close. You can run away whenever you want, if you want. But in the meantime, I can be on hand if you need anything. And we can talk, even if we're not close. I just want you to trust me again, Eddy. I want us to be *such* great friends."

8 Earth (Connecting with Humanness)

Aaron and Craig arrived in Vegas, and took the 215 to 4615 West Sunset, where the Freeway and Arterial System of Transportation (FAST) was situated. It was also a center for the Highway Patrol, but that didn't bother two solid citizens like Aaron and Craig. They parked at the rear of the lot, facing away from the complex.

Craig consulted a map, and compared it to the locations of the cameras. He chose the spot where 95 left town—CCTV 38, Rainbow and Westcliff—as the best one to start with, and dialed up video from three o'clock Monday morning. Once it appeared, he ran it at double speed. By now he would spot their van at any speed. If CCTV 38 didn't work, he'd check the other cams, one by one—but Craig had a hunch about this.

Aaron's secure phone vibrated. The two men exchanged a look before Aaron answered.

"Hello, sir." Craig could hear Hanrahan's harsh tones from the earpiece. "Yes, sir," Aaron said. "But we're close now—very close. We've got video evidence of them being in Las Vegas." Craig gave his partner another look, of warning. But Aaron was committed. "One day, two tops. It's a big town, but—" More from Hanrahan. "Yes, sir. Friday by sundown. Yes, I understand."

He thumbed the End button, and looked around at Craig. "Two more days to find them, then our time's up."

8 Earth (Connecting with Humanness)

At the video feed's 09:47:17 mark, Craig spotted the van.

"Son of a bitch," he sighed happily. "I was going to quit if it got to ten. They must have stopped for a while on the way."

"But he went up Ninety-five," Aaron said. "I would've bet on the Extraterrestrial Highway, the guy being a Code Red and all."

"Nope. Ninety-five. In any event, he's out of Vegas."

"Fuck you, Hanrahan!" Aaron shouted. "We're taking this bastard *down!*"

They pulled out of the Highway Patrol's lot and drove away on Sunset.

8 Earth (Connecting with Humanness)

Peter Quince snapped, "What have you got for me, chica?"

Rita Diamante said, "I dunno, Pete. I need you to check it."

"Check what?"

"I went into the forest out back this morning. Tower told me he liked to run through it every night."

"The guy had a mechanical heart, and he didn't fuck. He needed to work off his excess energy somehow."

"You're probably right. I walked all through the place

and didn't see anything that would help us. But I'm not a wizard."

"So you want me to go outside?"

"If you can."

Quince hesitated, caught up in his own momentum. "I've got to get *into* my sanctum and get back to work, Rita." Then he shrugged. "That's all you've got?"

"Listen, Pete, the guy left hints of clues at best. There's no list of ways to get inside his head, let alone get inside the FRC. He wasn't from Duluth, either, so they probably made him live here just like you—but tonight, yeah, asking a wizard to check on a wizard is all I got. Maybe it's nothin', but you're the one to say."

"All right. All right." He felt around in a pocket of his robe and came up with several Provigils. "You want some?"

"Sure."

They both used his coffee to swallow them, then she led him out the back door, across the soft lawn, and into the trees.

"There's a path here," she said, and he could see the lighter color against the dark green of vegetation. "It runs into other paths farther in, a regular maze. But everything's more or less level, so I can see how a guy could run."

Quince was looking around the forest, his eyes bright. At first he seemed to be searching, but suddenly his head stopped. "There may be something . . . ," he said in a contemplative tone.

"What is it?" Rita asked with an edge. She was ready for anything sane, but there was always the *insane*. Like zombis . . .

"I don't know yet. The Oomph hasn't fully taken hold. But there is life in the forest."

"You mean, other than trees."

"And little baby fawns, yes. Higher life . . ." His scrunched face took on a hunter's gleam. "Why don't we run?" he asked, and started out immediately. Rita followed him, loping among the trees along the path. And she noticed, as the drugs began to work on her, that he was following the dim path perfectly. She noticed that the path had a rhythm she hadn't seen in the daylight . . . a musical rhythm. . . .

"You've never been out here before, have you?" she called.

"Never," he called back. "I never wanted to have anything to do with this place. The sanctum was my focal point, but I think I've missed something fantas—"

He stopped so suddenly that Rita almost ran into him, but her mind was as sharp as his and she caught herself in time, up on her toes with a sort of amazing grace. She looked toward where he was looking and saw a kind of golden haze between the trees. But Pete clearly saw something else.

He saw a flaming cabin with golden fire leaping into the overhanging trees but not consuming them. The front wall of the cabin teetered, then toppled, exploding a shower of sparks. Illuminating an Indian, wearing soft buckskin, also watching from among the trees.

"Pete—"

"Shh!"

The Indian heard them, and ducked into a defensive crouch. Quince thought of arrows flying from the darkness, unseen until they buried themselves in your chest. But no arrows flew, and the Indian stood up again.

"I am Yellow Beaver," he said, in a language other than English, but perfectly intelligible.

"I am Peter Quince," the wizard answered, and added, "I have replaced Jackson Tower."

"I have not seen you before," said Yellow Beaver. "*We* have not seen you." Now there were others beside him—an Anglo crone, an Anglo man in a threadbare suit, two more Indians in garments that were different from the speaker's. Quince knew at once that he had found what he'd been seeking all this time.

"I have been busy," he said. "There was much to do, replacing a man like Tower."

"Aye," said the crone acidly. "Such as bidding us welcome in your life."

"I didn't know," replied Quince. "Tower died unexpectedly. He left no mention of you."

"But what kind of shaman might you be," asked the oldest of the Indians, "not to know of your own accord?"

"A good question. A learning shaman, I suppose."

"Oooh, he has a silver tongue," cooed the crone.

"No," he said. "I do not excuse myself. I was told to live in Tower's house, and I found wonderful things there, but I should have lived in Tower's *world*." The spirits in the forest looked at each other. He followed up. "Are you the reason I cannot pursue my work?"

"Perhaps," simpered the crone. But Yellow Beaver believed in plain speaking. "Yes," he said. "No one can work his spells on this land without our approval."

"What must I do, then?"

The man in the old suit spoke for the first time. "You have done it. You have crawled out of your own skull to marvel at the wonders around you!"

"You have to know where you are," said the crone.

"Make us proud, Peter Quince," said the youngest Indian. And the phantom horde passed from his sight, along with the flaming cabin, leaving only silent woods.

Quince stood and let the spirit of the forest fill him, attuning himself to its ancient space and majesty. He had been unforgivably stupid, but now he knew why the Necklace wizard always lived in Duluth, Minnesota—why he would live here. Tonight he would soak up all he could of the magick in this land, and tomorrow he would charge his *stone*. It was all right there for him now.

While Rita had seen and heard nothing.

8 Earth (Connecting with Humanness)

Aaron and Craig pulled into Beatty, Nevada. With a population of just over one thousand, it was the largest town on the fringes of the Nellis Air Force testing site. That site was off-limits to ordinary mortals, but they weren't chasing one, and big-time military secrets sounded like something a Code Red would be into. The camping gear added to the idea that he and the girl were doing some infiltration.

The people of Beatty weren't the kind to spend all day in the casinos. They were desert people, and they traveled the legal roads fairly regularly. But no one had seen Max and Pam, and so the two hunters did not learn that they were finally within fifty miles of their quarry.

8 Earth (Connecting with Humanness)

Michael was a lover, but he was also a fighter. That was his problem. Others would have to deal with it—one other in particular.

Greg was strolling up Saturn, on his way to meet Stacy. Or rather, Coyote was going to screw Diana, in more ways than one. He was getting into that coach tonight.

Michael found a long stretch of shadow between the bright-lit areas. He had a wrench from his coach's toolbox. It felt long and heavy in his hand. It swung good. Michael's teeth showed in the shadow. It was just that primitive. You took my woman. I've got a weapon.

Greg walked into the shadow. Far ahead, in the light, some admirable women's bodies were lit in red and green. *Thank Great Spirit that I live in Vegas, too.* He could hardly hear himself think. *Really—I've got Crazytown and I've got desert, two sides of a very strange coin. I love 'em both, got to have both, but=MOVE!=*

Coyote threw himself hard to the left!

Michael's wrench broke the bastard's right arm!!!!

Coyote cried out in pain, a mournful sharp bark. He struck the ground with his left shoulder and rolled, cradling his broken arm. The pipe or whatever the fuck it was smacked his head and he went out like a light.

• • •

Michael stood in the dark and looked down on his enemy. The bastard was lucky to get off easy, but a full-scale murder would blow this whole place to pieces. People were moving his way so he faded back among the tents of the desert camp.

It was just that primitive.

WEDNESDAY, JUNE 17, 2009 • 9:49 P.M.
PACIFIC DAYLIGHT TIME

8 Earth (Connecting with Humanness)

Coyote half scampered and half staggered into camp, holding his arm, the vibration of movement rubbing his bones at the break. Coyote knew broken bones; he was a desert creature. He went straight to Max, as Pam and Rosa rose to their feet.

"Listen," Coyote said, straight to Max, "I'm out of it, so you have to be Greg, right now!"

"What happened?" Max asked.

"I'll tell you while you do your Alchemy. You've got to look like me and act like me, and I'm supposed to be there in ten minutes."

Max looked in his *friend*'s eyes, and saw that this was no trick.

He raised his right hand, palm toward his face, fingers open. A pale gold nimbus began to play around it, as if it were on fire, aflame. Just a small, compact flame, like a fiery glove. The bones of his hand showed through. He moved his fiery palm as if he were sculpting the face six inches away and his face rippled.

"Wait just a minute," said Pam in a deadly voice. She was standing right there. "Does this entail what I think it does?"

Coyote turned his head to look at her, and let her look deep into his eyes, too. He kind of enjoyed that, actually. But Rosa spoke first. "Let the men do their work, Pamela," she said. "This is no time to attach emotion to the plan."

"That's easy for you to say!" Pam snapped back heatedly. "But I don't have the same dynamic that you have with Sly. This is not what Max and I agreed on."

"Can you think of an alternative?"

Max's face now resembled Greg's, though he had more work to do. "There are no cut-and-dried answers in magick, Pam," he said with Max's words but something resembling Greg's voice. "We had an answer but it's gone, and nobody else can spring the trap now. You understand that, right?"

"Not really," she said, looking at the face she didn't know. "Not on a gut level." When he'd first shown her his ability to bend light and create a disguise, he'd made it possible for her to see the real him at the same time. Now, though, he was becoming nothing but Greg. She stared hard at that alien face, before flicking her hand, shooing away her annoyance.

"All right," she said. "All right, if there's no other way." She squared her shoulders and added, "Let me look at Sly's arm."

Coyote smiled at her. "Soon. Let me tell Max what he needs to know. Then I'm all yours, Doctor Pammy."

So, quickly and concisely but also entertainingly, he ran down the details of what he'd told Diana and what Diana had told him. Max took it all in and didn't miss a thing. But truth to tell, he saw even more problems—albeit different ones—than Pam did.

He was going to need every bit of his old deejay bullshit to pull this one off.

WEDNESDAY, JUNE 17, 2009 • 10:15 P.M.
PACIFIC DAYLIGHT TIME

8 Earth (Connecting with Humanness)

Michael lay back in his camp chair, beside his coach, and took a long swig of his forty-five-year-old Laphroaig Private Reserve. He had not known such a thing existed until Rita Diamante had extended her gratitude to the Necklace for taking her on, and shown why a Miami drug queenpin was a good friend to have. The single malt was so good that the first time he tried it he decided to save it only for very special occasions. And this was surely one.

Diana was perched on the steps of her coach, waiting for her boy toy, who would not be coming now. So to speak.

"Nice night, isn't it?" Michael drawled. His tone was carefully balanced: not quite knowing, but not quite innocent, either. She caught it.

"Don't you have something to do?"

"Not really. As you know . . ."

"Yeah, yeah, you don't screw around."

"Would you like to hash this out right now?"

"We already hashed it out. You didn't like the way—"

A third voice joined the conversation. "Hi there." It was Greg's voice, from Greg, striding toward Diana with real pleasure.

Michael's head popped forward in what was almost a classic double-take.

Diana stood up, a big smile on her face. "Hi yourself, Greg."

"Sorry I'm late, Stace," he replied. "But I stumbled onto a roller disco and got to watching. You wanna skate?"

"Yes, I do," she said. "Let's go." She ignored Michael, evidently preferring to avoid any further confrontation. But Greg waved at him, said, "Hi there."

"Hi," Michael said blankly. The guy was waving with the arm Michael would have sworn he broke. *Holy fucking Christ on a stick,* he thought bleakly. *I whacked the wrong guy!*

• • •

Greg and Stacy walked cheerfully into Saturn's swelling crowd as the night began to really roll.

"I didn't know you were a skater," she said. "I thought you were a desert guy."

"I live in Vegas, don't I? We've got ice rinks. We've got everything. Down in Phoenix there's even an NHL team, for the moment. The Coyotes. Big, ugly guys."

"What I meant was, I thought you'd prefer the desert tonight. After last night."

"And so I would. After roller disco," Greg said.

"But I like the desert."

"Well, I can't argue with that. But why repeat ourselves? Let's go back to your coach and inspect some clean sheets instead of snake holes."

"There were no snake holes. And we can't go to my coach."

"Why's that?"

"Oh, the guy you saw. We work together, and he had some ideas we'd sleep together on this junket."

"Sexist pig."

"Well, some of my best friends are sexist pigs."

"Legal secretary, right."

"But because I work with the guy, I can't afford to rub his nose in the situation."

"I'm a situation?"

"A good situation. But still—"

"Fine. But as you can tell, I haven't had a shower for a while now."

"That's all right. I like a man who smells like a man." They came to an intersection, and she took his hand, to turn their path outward toward the open space.

Ah, well, Max thought. *I hope you're back there, Rosa.*

WEDNESDAY, JUNE 17, 2009 • 10:33 P.M.
PACIFIC DAYLIGHT TIME

8 Earth (Connecting with Humanness)

Pam carefully finished wrapping tape around the splints she'd taken from her medical kit and placed along Sly's arm. "Does that hurt?"

"Believe me, I would let you know," he said. "If I bite you, ignore it."

"Bite me?"

"If you insist. But no, if a broken arm can feel good, that feels good."

"Good. One thing I've learned from being with Max," Pam said, "a doctor comes in handy sooner or later."

"Am I the first guy other than him you've patched up?"

"No. There were zombis, in Barbados and Suriname, and some lumberjacks in Brazil."

"Barbados, where we first met."

"Uh-huh."

"You were cute that night."

"Thanks."

"You're cute this night."

"You're in shock."

"Not at all. I mean, I am, but I've thought you were cute since Barbados."

"Where I was with Max and you were with Rosa."

"What's that got to do with your being cute?"

"Okay, I'm cute, but I'm not available."

"You're as available as you want to be. I know I am."

"What about Rosa?" Pam asked.

"What about Max?" Sly answered.

"Well, what about Max? You two are supposed to be friends."

"We are friends. But he's Max, and I'm . . ." He cocked his head, evidently deciding his next course of action. When she finished her splinting and sat back, he said, "You need to take your mind off things, Pammy. It's time I told you who I am."

As with Rosa, it caught her off guard, but this time she took it more in stride. Maybe she was still numb from this turn of events. "Okay," she said casually. "About time. I'm having a mojito. Maybe two. You want one?"

"I want three," he said. And so she went to Randy's camp and took the whole pitcher, before settling down in her camp chair.

"Well," he said, after savoring the cold concoction. "One time Great Spirit said there should be stars in the sky. He called his dog and gave him a bag full of stars, saying, 'Put these where I tell you.' "

"What's this got to do with you?" Pam asked.

"Shh," he said, and went on. "Dog said to Great Spirit, '*All* these stars? This bag weighs more than a buffalo, and smells worse.'

"Great Spirit said, 'The winds will clear your nose when you reach the sky. I have written the names of the animal people there. Imitate it.'

"'Why isn't my name first?' demanded Dog. But he was Dog so he did as he was told.

"At least, he started to, but after a time he said, 'They'd look prettier if I didn't have to run so far to see them.' So he threw the bag out ahead of himself and created the Milky Way. It was pretty.

"But Great Spirit was very angry. 'Now many of the animal people will not know who they are. But in tricking me, you tricked yourself, because you forgot to write your own name. You are no longer Dog. You are now Coyote.'

"Coyote said, 'I like it. It's sexier.' But really, as Dog he lived in the chief's tipi, and as Coyote he had to live down on the earth. Still, once Great Spirit had shifted his shape, he was a shape-shifter. So he—"

"Wait a minute," said Pam. "You're saying . . . that's you?"

"That's what I'm saying. I'm a shape-shifter because I'm a Totem."

"A totem? Like a pole?"

"No, not like a pole. Well, Diana would disagree. So would hundreds of others—"

"Got it."

"I'm a Totem-*spirit*. The poles are just pictures of us. Totems are the primal spirits of the land and the people— here because the land and the people are here. I'm part of the land, and the people of the land, and the sky over all."

"So you're actually a *spirit,* not a human?"

"I'm kinda both. Shamans say the coyote spirit is the same as the human spirit." He grinned. "Of course, they say that because they think I screw up every once in a while, and they *know* humans do. But even if I do screw up, I get out of it. Every tribe has a Trickster, and I'm it."

"But you're an *illusion?*"

"Hell no. I just don't have a fixed shape."

"So how come they can break your bones and whack your head?"

"My shapes are real."

"What's your *natural* shape then?"

"Anyone I want. I'm a Totem. So since you're wondering, this shape is as real as any other for me. You can touch it if you like. In fact, please do."

"But four legs and a tail is real, too?"

"You got something against a tail? My tail is beautiful. And four legs"—he lifted his bandaged forearm—"well, four legs allow you to lose one and still get around all right."

Pam took a long swig from her glass, sat back, and studied him. Rosa's story at least made sense, in human terms. His story . . .

"Max has told me Amerindian legends, when he was sketching some larger picture—Raven, Buffalo. The tales he told of Coyote were different."

"Well, he couldn't tell you my real story, now could he?"

No, she thought, *he couldn't. And I would never have thought this far outside the box on my own.* All of a sudden, she felt more like a wannabe than ever.

"I think I'll have three mojitos, too. But that does not mean we're gonna fool around."

"Have the three mojitos first, Pammy."

"Watch out or I'll pour them on your head."

8 Earth (Connecting with Humanness)

With Beatty a nonstarter, Aaron and Craig spent the night at the Ramada Tonopah Station, right where 95 meets 6.

8 Earth (Connecting with Humanness)

Scorpio Rose padded silently through the streets of Wickr. An attentive observer—could he observe her—would have noticed that no dust clouds rose with her footsteps, unlike everyone else's. But no one did observe her. She was drabardi, and that meant that even though she walked among many people, she did not register. There was something about her that negated the sense of her presence, that instinctive feeling we all have when someone is nearby. No one saw her pass.

Throughout, she remained some ten feet behind Max and Diana. Those two would slow and stop and she would slow and stop. At one point, Diana turned back to look at the city at night, and she did not see the quiet woman in the dark.

But Max did.

This impersonation wasn't hard in the broad strokes. Greg was just a gloss on Coyote's usual sly self, and Max could play that part. Max was very accustomed to playing parts. He looked like Greg, and would until the wave of energy he was drawing from moved on, in some six hours.

He sounded like Greg and he remembered everything Coyote had told him. But Coyote's mind wasn't a steel trap at any time, so at any time something could come up that Max had no answer for. That's why he needed Rosa.

"I still can't believe this is really going on," Stacy told Greg as she turned away from the city again, toward the waiting desert. She began to walk and he went with her.

"There's probably been festivals like this, somewhere in this desert, since the first people lived here. The ground is so flat when you look away from the mountain, and it leaves the sky so huge."

"You know what it needs, though. More clouds, for context. Like *Dexter* and *Burn Notice* and *CSI: Miami*."

"I can't stand *CSI: Miami*."

"I thought you said you didn't watch TV. Which I still find astounding."

Max felt Rosa move behind them, and said quickly, "I don't. But I lived in Miami once."

"What was that like?"

Good; he could steer her onto that. "I was big on jai alai—totally into it. You ever been to a match?"

"I have, actually. I went down for a legal convention and the guy I was with wanted to go."

"Smart guy."

"Not smart enough to be here."

"Did you invite him?"

"No, I haven't seen him in forever." She pointed toward the sky. "What do they call the North Star again?"

Max looked up, said nothing. Rosa's voice spoke quietly in the back of his mind: *Qui-am-i Wintook Poot-see.* She hadn't lived with Coyote all these years without learning his ways. "Qui-am-i Wintook Poot-see," he said.

Then he pointed toward the boulder blocking a chunk of the sky. "They call *that* our rock."

"Where," purred Diana, hugging his arm, "we *roll*."

8 Earth (Connecting with Humanness)

Coyote was sound asleep, snoring in his tent. Pam was pacing the camp area, unable to sit even for a moment. For all the amazement of Coyote's story, she'd returned to the main story soon enough.

Her boyfriend was sleeping with another woman.

Oh, it was all fun and games when other people were involved. Sly—Coyote—could sleep with Diana, just like Rosa could sleep with Michael. The good guys were making their own decisions, and they were operating on bad guys. But Max had been forced into this situation. (But he'd still made a decision.) *Goddammit!*

This was a war—alchemists with guns. Only this time they weren't using *guns*.

Okay, this was a war. All's fair in love . . . No, that's no good.

This was a war. If the bad guys continued unchecked, they would end up ruling the world. If Max had to sleep with a skank to stop that, it was a small price to pay. Only, who would do the paying? She and Max had been very happy to this point, with every day delivering some new delight for her, which delighted him. He wanted to be with her. After a year and a half, she knew that was true. (Even though he kept a place open for Val—the impossibly beautiful and talented and wonderful Val. But he thought Pam was beautiful and talented and wonderful, too. Hell! With *two* women, there was no way he would fall for a third, even if she weren't a total bitch—)

Pamela.

It was Rosa's voice—in Pam's thoughts. The witch was *calling* to her. And *calling* was Pam's primary magickal skill.

I hear you, Rosa, she answered.

Come to me.

What? Where are you? Pam asked.

In the night. Come to me in the night.

Pam understood her. Pam should travel down the same vibe as the *call*. Mama Locha had told her: *"Vodou uses the energy inside the body and sends it* ALONG *that energy to do its work, like a radio wave. Vodou* LIVES *in the Darkness."*

When you thought about it, there probably wasn't much difference between gypsy folk magick and slave folk magick.

Pam took hold of the *call* with familiar ease and did something completely unfamiliar.

WEDNESDAY, JUNE 17, 2009 • 11:40 P.M.
PACIFIC DAYLIGHT TIME

8 Earth (Connecting with Humanness)

The next thing she knew, she was standing on the desert plain beside Scorpio Rose. Twenty feet away, Max and Diana were lying beside a huge boulder. The two women were in shadow, but Pam stepped back instinctively.

"They cannot see us," said Scorpio Rose.

In truth, Pam could hardly see herself. She seemed to be, if not a ghost, then something made of fluid light, now visible, now not visible. And Rosa, though clearly more substantial, was just as hard for her to see.

"I am here physically," said the gypsy witch. "But Diana cannot pick me out. You are here only as a *shade*—an *as-*

tral, Max would say—and neither one of them can see you. Let me repeat: Max cannot see you."

"Where's my body?" Pam asked, surprisingly calmly. The unfamiliar still felt familiar.

"See for yourself," Rosa said. And Pam did. Without even turning her head, she looked back at the campsite, at least a mile away. She saw the site clearly, with her unmoving body sprawled in the dust.

"In the future, you will want to lie down before *flying,*" the witch said.

"Am I hurt, there?" Pam asked.

"A few bruises, no doubt."

"I didn't know I could do this," Pam said, staring at her ghostly hand.

"No, but I did," the witch said placidly. "Now look." She raised her own hand and pointed with a long, slender finger at Max and Diana. He was now on top, pounding between Diana's wide-spread legs.

Pam felt the blood rise in her face, even though her blood and her face were *astral.* "Why are you showing me this?" she demanded raggedly.

"Because you need to see it," answered Scorpio Rose. She was looking hard at Pam, but Pam was looking harder at her boyfriend. She could tell, because she knew him so intimately now, that Max was a little withdrawn over there. But only a little. He had to be into it, by the nature of the thing. More than Pam liked.

Connecting with Humanness. Living our animal nature, Pam thought. And then *Fuck Humanness!*

But she realized Rosa was still talking to her. "I know what Max tells you, because all masters tell their apprentices the same thing. He says to apply your logic to your experience, so as never to take anything on faith, no matter how famous the master may be who tells it to you. But that is not just advice for times when you are calmly meditating.

You need to apply logic even when your emotions are raging—especially then. Until you can do that, you can never be a master."

"*You* can say that!" Pam snapped, not even bothering to hide her displeasure. "But I'm not like you."

"Oh yes, Pamela—you are." Rosa fluttered a hand. "Despite my affliction, we are both women. All women know that there are two worlds, that of the God and that of the Goddess. All women are by nature magick, and can channel their magick more easily than can a man."

"All women are individuals. Especially that one over there." Diana was beginning to make little moans of rhythmic pleasure that really grated on Pam's ears.

"She channels it downward; thus, she is a threat to you. But some channel it upward, and among those are the ones you must truly fear, for Max's sake as well as your own."

"Like Aleksandra?" Pam asked.

"Like Aleksandra."

Pam stiffened, suddenly aware again that she was a disembodied spirit standing open to the universe. Watching her lover screw another woman. Just as he'd screwed Aleksandra twenty-nine years ago, when he was five years younger. Despite herself, Pam was beginning to see a larger dimension to her situation, like the vast, dimly lit darkness surrounding them, the two women who knew they were magick.

"I have met Aleksandra," said Scorpio Rose, quietly.

Pam was brought back to earth. "You have?"

"Yes. It was in the fall of 1963, when she was fourteen—as the nights were growing longer. . . ."

12 Dog (Fulfilling Embodiment)

Scorpio Rose had come a long way up the smuggling routes of Afghanistan, though no one had seen her come. These were not the Carpathians, but mountains were mountains, her earliest home, and she liked the mountains and the strange secretive people who lived there. She was satisfied to be standing quietly before a sharp-edged cavern at the bottom of a narrow gorge. The impossibly blue sky was high overhead but there was only gray and brown down here.

"Come out, demon!" she commanded the thing hunched in the cavern. Its eyes flashed but it didn't obey, so she called upon her drabardi power and propelled it into the crevasse. The creature, a young woman with floating hair and very long nails who fed upon fresh corpses, came surging out at her. Rosa calmly stepped back and vanished from its sight, though she'd moved just two feet. The creature, confused, tried to readjust in mid-leap, and was suddenly jerked backward by an orange cord around her neck as Rosa snapped her spine. The broken young woman went =pop= and dissipated in a foul-smelling fog, another mountain troll gone to its reward.

The Afghans didn't call it a troll, of course—to them it was an "alk"—but Rosa had been eradicating trolls since she was just a little girl, eight or nine. Magick was alive when Scorpio Rose was a girl, and for many years thereafter, but now it only survived in places where civilization had failed to find a foothold.

• • •

That night the tribesmen threw a celebratory feast for her, making her sit close to the fire while men with swords danced past and around. It reminded her strongly of the night she had danced for the stranger, and she dared hope that she might feel just for a transcendent moment what she'd felt then . . . but it didn't happen. It was just men moving in firelight—all the same to her.

Then she noticed, for the first time, a scrawny young girl sitting quietly next to the wood piled for the fire. She was perhaps fourteen, and definitely not an alk, but clearly of no importance to the men, who ignored her very existence. But the girl leaned ever so slightly toward Rosa, who nodded her onward. The girl got up and ran to sit in front of Rosa, her back to the fire, throwing her face and form into silhouette.

"They say you are the supreme drabardi," the girl said. "Will you tell my fortune?"

"What is your name, child?" Rosa responded.

"Aleksandra," the girl said.

Rosa opened the leather pouch on her belt to remove her deck, then handed it to the girl. "Shuffle until the cards feel right to you," she said.

Aleksandra took the cards and tried to shuffle, but she apparently suffered from some arthritic disease; her hands were stiff. She managed three shuffles, then laid the cards back on the dirt, defying Rosa to feel pity for her. Rosa could not feel pity; she calmly reached down with her left hand and began to turn the cards over. She put the top card on the ground and laid the next one across it, perpendicular. The next four cards went around that cross, and the next four made a separate line to the side. It was a layout as old as the cards themselves.

By now, reading Tarot began with the cards for Rosa, but involved everything around them, including the questioner. She slid into her familiar waking trance as she manipulated the symbols—the cards, the girl, the fire, the night—and shuffled them into place. When they formed a pattern she recognized, she spoke with quiet certainty.

"You will know great power, Aleksandra, but it will gain no acclaim from this world. The Americans say they are going to the moon. Perhaps the world of space will open within your lifetime, and you will find your destiny there."

The girl smiled.

"One man will know you, and you will know one man, and they are not the same. The man who will know you is the King of Coins. The man you will know is the Prince of Wands."

"This Prince," Aleksandra said. "This is not, simply, the space?" Rosa noted that her Afghan was less certain than her opening request for a reading, but attributed it to the girl's motor difficulties.

"No. It is a man. But the more I think on it, the more I think that space, or wherever you go when you are away from the world, will be your salvation. The limitations of the body will not trouble you forever. I give them thirty years at most, and probably less. You will live to see yourself . . ." But all at once, Scorpio Rose felt a new reality fall into place. Symbols which had refused to line up smoothly abruptly did so, forming a new pattern, darker and more disturbing. This girl—

—was gone.

Where Aleksandra had sat, there was open space, flooded in firelight.

"Who was that girl?" Rosa demanded of the man to her left.

"What girl?"

8 Earth (Connecting with Humanness)

"She fooled me," said Scorpio Rose. "She came as an *astral*—a much more accomplished *astral* than you, though she was half your age. It explains not only her vanishment but her difficulty handling the physical cards. But—she handled them well enough. She was not ready but she was well on her way."

"Why did she come to you?"

"I think she was testing her powers. I think she was testing mine as well, and I think, if I turned out to deserve my reputation, she wanted to hear her future."

"But you didn't know her nature from the start."

"She did not project all of herself; she hid the evil. I saw it soon, but not soon enough. After that night, I kept an eye out for her on my travels, but I never encountered her again. Max has told me what he knows of her subsequent life . . . how she transcended her physical body completely and became a diabola. . . ."

"Living in space," Pam said. "When I met her, she was a crimson star. But she took on human form, and there was nothing scrawny about it."

"Her idealized image of herself, I imagine."

"*Too* idealized. Too . . . porcelain."

"Yes."

The two women looked directly at each other for the very first time.

"She is the ultimate enemy in the war Max is waging, Pamela," Rosa said.

"That I know," Pam said, and couldn't resist looking back

at Max. Evidently, he and Diana were going for round two, but the sting had gone out of it, at least for now. She looked at Rosa again. "I'm trying to imagine projecting myself like that and having so much control."

"You will learn. She did."

"She started when she was six, Max says. I'm twenty-three years behind."

"If you achieve Timelessness, twenty-three years will be as nothing," Rosa said. "You are learning quickly, your *astral* strong and certain."

Pam looked down at her ephemeral form. From what she could see of it, it did look like her body. "This old thing?"

"You have an aptitude."

Pam stole another glance at Max and Diana as the two of them dissolved into gasps, and groans, and as sex sometimes does it now seemed comical. "Is this power *drabardi*, Rosa?"

"It is, but it is vodou as well, and witchcraft. Being a woman of magick is what you make of it." Scorpio Rose touched Pam's arm, and even though it was only *astral*, Pam felt it as clearly as she'd felt her blush. "There are great forces at work," the witch said. "There are great emotions in play. Do they conflict? Yes, they do. But you must decide if the emotions help or hurt you, and act accordingly."

"Will you read my fortune, Rosa? Tell me what you see in the cards?"

"Not tonight. When all of this is behind us."

Pam took a final look at the lovers, now lying spent. "Thank you," she said. "I could stand to know."

8 Earth (Connecting with Humanness)

When Max got back to his tent, Pam was sound asleep. He debated waking her . . . but not for long.

Somehow she'd picked up a bruise on her cheek.

Day Four

9 Flint Knife (Being Magick)

When their wristwatch alarms went off, Aaron and Craig rolled out of the twin beds at their motel in Tonopah. They had showered the night before so they could simply slip on their clothes and go. By 6:15 they were having breakfast at El Marques down the road. The lighting there was bright but their waitress was tired. She was probably working two jobs.

In the next booth, two women began talking about camping in the desert for Wickr—fifty thousand people where last week there was nobody, buncha pagans and hippies. The two men stood up, leaving their breakfast half eaten, Aaron tossing a twenty on the table as they all but ran to their car.

Aaron and Craig were working their job, and they were damn glad to have it. By 6:45 they were headed back down 95 to the Wickr turnoff. It was going to be another hot one, but it might be the last one.

9 Flint Knife (Being Magick)

Max awoke to find orange Gatorade and granola bars laid out for him. It was already eighty-five so he rolled out leisurely, brushed his teeth, got dressed—he wanted a sponge bath but that didn't fit today's agenda. Finally, he ate his breakfast, and only then did he venture outside.

Pam was sitting composedly in her camp chair. To his experienced eye, her spirit was elsewhere, in the *astral*. If so, she saw him from there, because she opened her eyes. "Good morning," she said, neither friendly or unfriendly.

"Morning, my love," he replied. "Listen, about last night—"

"Had to be done."

"Yeah, it did. But I never wanted to hurt you."

"I'm fine."

"Really?"

"Don't you want me to be fine?"

"Sure, if you really are."

"I really am," she said. And then added, somewhat obscurely, "Today is Being Magick, Max."

9 Flint Knife (Being Magick)

"Funny, huh?" said Coyote.

"Is it?" asked Scorpio Rose. They were strolling along one of the outer roads, letting the sights and sounds entertain them. A woman in an elaborate orange dress covered with dozens of tiny mirrors sashayed by, twinkling. A woman carrying two blue umbrellas and wearing nothing at all sauntered by. A trapeze artist swung back and forth at the top of a geodesic dome before somersaulting into a block of thick padding below.

"You and I were supposed to be the great seducers, and we came up empty." He raised his right hand palm up to symbolize emptiness, and winced at the torque on his broken bone.

"The work is being accomplished."

"Well, sure, because I set it up. Max just had to follow my lead. But poor Diana. She must have wondered why Greg lost his zip."

"Greg's 'zip' was fine. It greatly affected Pamela."

"Did it really? But you know what I mean. He harvested everything I gave considerable effort to sowing. I take full credit."

"You never give considerable effort to anything."

"Dammit, Red! What's the matter with you this morning? I'm the one with the broken arm."

She just looked at him, placidly.

9 Flint Knife (Being Magick)

> WASHINGTON—*The Washington Post* has terminated its relationship with liberal columnist/blogger Dan Froomkin.
>
> "I think that the future success of our business depends on journalists enthusiastically pursuing accountability and calling it like they see it. That's what I tried to do every day," said Froomkin. "Now I guess I'll have to try to do it someplace else."

Breckenridge was attending a reception at the White House when the news broke. His cell vibrated to alert him to a text, and once he read it, he allowed himself another shrimp puff.

The reception was to honor E. Emsley van Wilgen, the President of Suriname. Breckenridge quite enjoyed shaking the man's hand, since he'd almost had the man murdered by zombis just twenty months before. It meant far more to him than shaking Obama's.

"Thank you for all your hard work," the President of the United States said, and Breckenridge replied, "I *enjoy* my work, Mr. President."

9 Flint Knife (Being Magick)

Aaron and Craig pulled up to the entry portal at Wickr. Tickets on site were three hundred dollars each, to discourage "tourists," but the two men paid without a murmur. The lone greeter, so close to the end of the week, asked them to get out of their car and get a hug, but received flat stares in return. The greeter decided to hell with it, and waved them through. People who came this late never had the right spirit. Craig took off in a cloud of dust and the greeter chased after them, yelling that they had to slow down. They decided to comply.

So they drove the ring road at a miserly five mph to the first available parking spot, where they parked, got out, and locked the car. Then they began to jog the long dusty road ahead of them with the patient, ground-devouring pace they'd learned in Iraq. They still didn't know for sure that they would find their prey in here—but they had a job to do.

9 Flint Knife (Being Magick)

Diana showed up at Michael's door with hot muffins, cold jam, and bacon.

"Look, I don't want to fight," she offered. "We obviously came here with different ideas, but we're halfway through it, and when we come out the other side, I want to be with you. That said, you'd probably be happier if you went for a walk."

"You're a real sweet-talker," Mike said.

"I want what I want, and so do you. If you can't accept that in me, then say so. I've done enough trying to make up around here."

"I can accept it if I don't have my nose rubbed in it. My business deals in personal relationships; I take them seriously."

"But you know they're all bullshit!"

"Not all of them. And not this one with you. But we did have an agreement. I'll go."

"Haven't you met anyone here, Mike?" Di asked.

"I haven't been looking."

"You don't have to look! They're everywhere!"

"But you have to be looking, Diana. *I* stayed true."

THURSDAY, JUNE 18, 2009 • 12:15 P.M.
PACIFIC DAYLIGHT TIME

9 Flint Knife (Being Magick)

"We need some ice," Coyote told Pam. "Come on with me."

"Why?" she asked. "You only need one arm."

"I'm a desert dweller," he said. "I can't hold ice all the way back here."

"Well, all right." She got up. "But if this is just a diversion, I don't need it."

"Diversion from what?"

"You know what."

"Your boyfriend off making his big move on poor defenseless Diana?"

"Don't make me laugh."

"Just part of the plan, huh, Pammy?"

"Are you trying to undermine it?"

"Not me. I'm trying to undermine your resolve."

"My resolve not to sleep with you?"

"Yeah, I think that was it."

"Not gonna happen."

"He doesn't appreciate you, Pammy."

"He appreciates me fine. And you appreciate every woman you meet."

"Is that supposed to be a bad thing? I think women are great. They're cute and mysterious and make life worth living, for men and kids and the tribe as a whole."

"You got that right. But some men—like your friend Max—manage to keep it in their pants. Usually."

"Men are *supposed* to make love to women. That's what men are here for. That's what women are here for, too. So why be coy?"

"Right time, right place, right guy."

"Nuts. If it feels good, do it."

"I'll punch you in that arm and you can see how that feels. Then you really will need ice."

THURSDAY, JUNE 18, 2009 • 12:20 P.M.
PACIFIC DAYLIGHT TIME

9 Flint Knife (Being Magick)

Greg arrived at Stacy's coach fashionably late; having come this far, he didn't want to seem too eager. With his three coconspirators' avid coaching, he had made himself as attractive to women as possible, while smelling more than a little ripe.

"Ready to go?" he asked cheerfully, deliberately stand-ing upwind of her. She wrinkled her nose.

"You need a shower."

"True, but unless that thing has one . . ."

"It does."

"It does?"

"Hell yes it does. Get on up in here."

"I thought the guy next door would have a cat."

"Let him."

Greg shrugged and went up the steps, just as if he hadn't been scheming for this for days. Max had last been in a coach like this in 1999, and they hadn't changed much in ten years. The flat-screen TV was the most noticeable difference; otherwise, the over-lacquered dark wood and over-stuffed couches were more than familiar. The bathroom was in the back, and there he found a shower stall, a curved plastic cabinet set into a corner of the room. It had a wide shower-head, and the spray nozzle on a flexible tube that infiltrated showers in the 1990s. It was just large enough for two.

"Join me?" Greg asked Stacy.

"Love to," Stacy told Greg. "I'll soap you all over."

"We might break this wall."

"It's a rental. What do I care?"

He started taking off his clothes and she started taking off hers. When they were nude, he started up the water. She started running her hands along his hip and he held her back with his longer arms. She laughed, and he laughed, but he kept her at bay until the water was right. Then they both went inside and closed the curved door behind them. True to her word, she picked up the soap. He pulled her to him, pressed her against him with his right forearm, and kissed her hard.

He raised his left hand and made a half swipe through the air, alongside her face, quick, left-right-left. She had her eyes closed and didn't see, then suddenly went limp in his arm, a robot switched off. He used the closest wall to help balance her as he drew forth her essence.

A luminous nimbus, sapphire blue in color, blurred her features. The last time he'd seen this was with Nancy Reinking, the spy in Pam's CDC lab, but this glow was far more radiant. Max, his face just inches from hers, read it easily enough. This was a woman simultaneously farther up the power grid than Nancy, but no more magickal. Diana had had long exposure to the FRC's magickal *stones* but almost no natural aptitude or affinity for magick.

Max used his free hand to turn off the water, then he opened the door and carried Diana out, draped in his arms. He laid her head and shoulders on the fluffy rug, her legs on the bathroom tile, and took one of the ready gray towels to dry her thoroughly. He didn't want her catching cold in the air-conditioning. Then he dried himself before picking her up and carrying her to the bed.

He sat beside her, his naked hip against her naked breast, but he didn't notice. He placed his palm against her forehead, his fingers in her hair, and concentrated on the wall. A golden nimbus played around the hand. He was visualizing all the things that he and she would have done if only he'd really been there for that. Sweat popped out on his own previously cool forehead. And then, with a harsh grunt not unlike sexual climax, he rocketed the images into Diana's brain. She cried out exactly like her own climax, a series of climaxes, leaving her lying sprawled and spent and smiling.

Max stood up. He was trembling slightly. He'd felt it all, too, even if he'd only visualized it.

He turned to survey the interior of the coach. He raised his left hand, held it palm-outward near his right shoulder, then swept it from right to left. He looked through the area he'd "cleaned," then brought his hand back again. Each time he wiped between himself and the coach, he saw new levels of interest and usage from its occupant, Diana. On his third wipe, he spotted the nightstand and the storage cabinet.

The false floor of the cabinet was no surprise to anyone who'd learned the arts of safe-cracking. The safe itself was factory-installed, not a product of the FRC, so it had to have a key, and a quick search of Diana's purse turned that up. Inside the safe lay the laptop, and that, of course, was FRC-made, which meant he wouldn't touch it with a ten-foot pole, yet. Somehow, something in the nightstand would be needed for the next steps.

He stood up and backed halfway between the cabinet and the stand. He turned perpendicular to them and spread his legs slightly, centering himself. He raised his hands chest-high.

His body remained where it was but his consciousness began to expand, radiating outward from his brain like sunlight. Around himself, he mentally marked the letter "pi," with its one straight leg and one curved leg and a bar above connecting them. He stood in the middle of it, feeling the vast flow from one end of the Universe to the other, sweeping through the room from one leg to the other. The pi around him began to glow with golden light, Max began to glow with golden light; everything in the room was glowing as he stepped *through* the pi like a gate. . . .

Max saw the flashlight in the drawer, saw the flashlight at the cabinet, shining on the laptop. He could have stopped there, gone back to the physical world and taken the flash and used it, but instead, he took the light from the flash with his magick, and rubbed it over the surface of the computer with his magick. He took the *sense* of the configuration on the back of the flash and pressed it into the computer and the computer opened.

But the flow was not yet unimpeded. There was a last obstacle. He focused on the computer, saw Diana's left ring finger pressing the power button. Again, he never physically moved as his awareness spread even farther, enveloping Diana's body. But he only wanted her sense of that finger.

He let the sense flow across the room, come to rest against the button, press it in. The computer turned on.

It was good to be the Alchemist.

THURSDAY, JUNE 18, 2009 • 1:49 P.M.
PACIFIC DAYLIGHT TIME

9 Flint Knife (Being Magick)

But the Alchemist was no computer genius, so he wasn't going to cut any corners while hacking Diana's data. He returned to physical reality, pulled the device Dave had given him from his pocket, and plugged it in.

"There's an app for that," he intoned, sending the secrets of the Necklace into cyberspace.

THURSDAY, JUNE 18, 2009 • 1:49 P.M.
PACIFIC DAYLIGHT TIME

9 Flint Knife (Being Magick)

Dave yanked the headphones from his ears, alerted by the flashing light on his homemade modem. Information was arriving, and he knew exactly what it had to be. He padded quickly to his kitchen and fired up the electric coffeemaker while the transmission was written to his handmade version of a Cray XT5, then completely disconnected from the

Internet. He went to his bedroom and grabbed two hits of Provigil, not surprised to see his hands shaking, his fingers clumsy.

Here it was: the holy blood of the holy grail, at last! Now it was all on him.

THURSDAY, JUNE 18, 2009 • 4:49 P.M.
EASTERN DAYLIGHT TIME

9 Flint Knife (Being Magick)

The Necklace's IBM Roadrunner supercomputers under the hard earth of West Virginia detected the transmission and flagged it due to its unorthodox encryption. Immediately, the full thrust of their decryption algorithms went to work on it, and sent an automatic signal to Dick Hanrahan.

Hanrahan had a visceral reaction to encryption his people couldn't break: he did not like it *at all*. So he made certain his rooms were securely sealed, then ran as fast as he could to the subterranean shuttle connecting his mansion with a farm in Moundsville, fifteen miles away. That was where the supercomputers were already grinding away, and where he would be until they succeeded.

Then whoever used and whoever devised that encryption would disappear from the face of the earth. The Necklace would see to that.

9 Flint Knife (Being Magick)

Lawrence Breckenridge, more and more enjoying the simple freedom of walking the streets of Manhattan with nothing pulling him into another world, came upon a Tea Bagger rally. It made him laugh.

First, of course, the name. None of those geniuses know what it means.

And second—WE were the ones who destroyed their lives. We were going for our own enrichment and we went too far, so we had to be made whole, and that destroyed them. So naturally, they hate . . . the people we've always told them to hate.

They love living the fantasy of revolution, feeling what people felt in 1776. If only health care were the same as subjugation to an insane foreign despot—and so, of course, in their minds it is! "Give me liberty or give me death," actually fits perfectly. They love the storyline, and they NEED the storyline, because otherwise they'd have to face the truth that they're fighting the guys they hate instead of the guys who are continuing to screw them.

They don't hate guys that screw them because they want to be screwers, too. Like they'll ever get the chance. We've got their money and we're not giving it back.

Roll on, Tea Baggers! Roll on!

The Grimorium Gris, *earliest surviving book of magick,
was written by Maslama ibn Ahmad Al-Majriti in thirteenth-
century Spain. It was an open doorway to worlds beyond
this world, and lives beyond this life. There were said to be
but three copies of it, because the knowledge in that grimorium was far too powerful to be disseminated freely. Scorpio
Rose had taken one, and she protected it relentlessly. Those
who knew sought one of the other two, and I was one such,
determined to gain the power I'd need to destroy Wolf.*

*In October 1968, men took the first photographs of Earth
from space, and that moved an old woman in Haverhill, New
Hampshire, to evaluate her life. She had inherited a copy of
the* Gris *from her grandfather fifty years before, along with
dire warnings of its potency and potential for disaster. That
hadn't stopped her from trying to work with it, but she quickly
found she had neither the will nor the stomach, and so she
buried the book in an oilskin wrap behind her house and
prayed that it would be lost forever. But seeing the earth for
the first time as the small blue ball it is, she, in her old age,
began to worry that it WOULD be found by someone in the
future. She thought she should dig it up and burn it. In that
moment, the book, which had lain dormant for decades,
awoke to its danger, and I awoke to its power.*

*But mere moments later, I was summoned to Wolf's office,
along with the four other students still within his inner circle.*

*"I have work to do," he told us, "sensitive and important
work, and your minds create too many cross-currents. I am
sending you to a house we maintain in Balchik, Bulgaria, on
the Black Sea. It is a luxurious villa, usually reserved for far
more important people than you, but the timing was fortunate. You may treat it as a well-deserved vacation."*

The old bastard was going after it himself, and I was clois-

tered with the others, before being put on a plane to Krasnodar and riding to the north shore. What we found there was unimaginable for the other four—the warmth, the architecture, the open pool overlooking the sea—because they had never been to a place like that. I had been along this coast twice in the past five years, in my astral self.

The five of us settled in, and I pretended to enjoy it as much as they did, while chafing for a way to get some time alone to pursue my quest.

That evening, the others decided to go to the fishing village ten klicks up the coast, and I was able to plead a headache. I would lie in the hammock and sleep. They gave me good-natured abuse, especially Mika, a peasant girl, and Hamish, the Scottish renegade. But then they left, and I went to Haverhill. I would have to hurry, but I would be all right; I could sense the Wolf waiting for midnight. I could not afford to wait. I came to the spot and threw myself to the ground, clawing at the dirt.

• • •

I became aware that I was being observed—not in Haverhill, and not in Academgorodok, but in Balchik. I stayed where I was in New Hampshire, while I opened my eyes in Bulgaria. It was Mika. She had known I was up to something, and sneaked back to catch me; she was better than I thought she was. I stayed where I was in Haverhill and I thrust into her brain in Bulgaria, with no lack of power at either spot; I was far too old a hand. In her brain I was ASTRAL at first, but I could solidify so easily, and she, for all her arrogance and envy, had no answer for it. I ruptured her mind from the inside, crushing her gray matter against the interior of her skull, pressing her eyes from their sockets. She collapsed on the tile.

Simultaneously, I clawed my way down to the grimoire. I reached down and took it in my hand, and felt its acceptance, and its calculation. No doubt it felt the same from me. I also *felt someone coming very near—Agrippa, I later found; not yet the Wolf. I left America.*

Once more wholly in Bulgaria, I knew I had to disguise my murder, because I was the only logical suspect. I had mastered the ability to solidify my essence, but I'd never used another's physical body before, and that seemed like what I needed to do. I had the Grimorium Gris, so I flipped it open at random, to see what it would give me; and there was a spell of necromancy. Once more I felt the flow between the book and myself. So utilizing its gift to me, I sent most of my ASTRAL into the corpse and caused it to rise, so terribly awkwardly at first—then spent the next hours practicing, improving, and learning. I kept a small part of my ASTRAL for my practiced skills, like thought projection.

When I heard my fellow students returning, Mika dove into the pool. When they entered our area—all feeling the impact of the local wine, which didn't hurt—they saw Mika finishing a lap, then pulling herself out of the pool. "While you were getting drunk, I was making good use of the villa!" she seemed to call gaily.

"I thought you had a headache like poor Lexi," Rhymers called back.

"I just found you lot boring," she said.

"I'll show you boring!" he yelled, and started toward her.

Squealing, she bolted up the ladder. As she reached the top, her foot slipped, she lurched backward, and as they all stared in horror, she fell heavily to the tile, landing on her head with a loud crack.

They raced to her side, and even I sat up in the hammock. They found her with bulging eyes, dead. We all agreed: a terrible, terrible accident.

I, Aleksandra Korelatovna, had the ultimate book of POWER.

9 Flint Knife (Being Magick)

Eva Delia and Lexi were strolling along the South Bank, two figures among hundreds celebrating the pleasures of London summertime. A rasta rolled by on inline skates, a boom box balanced on his shoulder playing N-Dubz' "Strong Again," and gave Eva Delia a wide grin, which she returned. As the music faded down along the river, it seemed the perfect anthem to Eva Delia. *"I never-ever-ever thought that it would ever get better!"*

She was back on top of the world. For one thing, her meds had stabilized her. For another, Lexi had been *so* solicitous as to be almost embarrassing. And finally, even her dreams had found the blonde girl in a rage.

"Did you get enough to eat?" Lexi asked.

"I did. You're spoiling me."

"It's the least I can do, after what I did Tuesday night."

"Really, Lexi, I understand. I'm fine."

"I know you are. You're doing so well tonight. Top of the world!"

The people they passed looked at them and smiled. Eva Delia thought of two nights previous—and last night, though she wasn't sure of her memories from then—when the people had ignored her. It must have something to do with how well she was feeling. "You catch more flies with honey than with vinegar," or however that went. The nurses used to say things like that. When she was happy, people wanted to relate to her, and when she wasn't they didn't. That was simple enough. It was all on her.

The two girls passed the London Eye, huge and still after

closing hours. Ahead, the round light strung out along the Thames, past areas of people, lights, and sound, past areas of shadow and silence. The buildings across the Thames, the bridges, all of them were lighted, lines of color in the night, like some alien encampment in the desert.

Desert? Eva Delia thought. *It's a sodding river!* She laughed, a sound of pure delight.

But even before the laughter faded, the people around her stopped their smiling. It wasn't that they were scowling; simply that they were no longer interacting. They laughed or fought or kissed among themselves, but no one was looking at Lexi and Eva Delia. Eva Delia decided that she'd been reading too much into a random event, just the way her psychs had said, and she looked around them—

—and saw small creatures with fangs following them!

She stopped. She blinked. They were still there. And there were more of them, pouring forth from a small thick cloud hovering a few inches above the sidewalk. A cloud . . . with eyes.

"Eddy?" asked Lexi, solicitously. "What's wrong?"

"This isn't real," said Eva Delia, very firmly.

"What isn't?"

"Don't you see them?"

"See what?"

"Them!" She pointed right at the little monsters.

"Eddy, just relax."

"They're surrounding us, Lexi! They're closing in!"

"Don't make a scene. They'll come take you again."

"Them?"

"The nurses, the guards."

"But these things—*they're on my feet!*"

"I'll take you home, Eddy."

"They won't let us!" This she knew for a fact; the look in their eyes—the same eyes as in the cloud—was sly and ravenous. "They want to kill us!"

"Not *us*," said Lexi triumphantly, and the nearest monster struck. His claws punctured Eva Delia's calf and she shrieked and jumped back, yanking her leg free but leaving blood on the pavement behind. The others surged forward, a herd of murder. Eva Delia skipped backward. And even then, she was craning to look at Lexi. "What's happening?"

"You can't trust anyone, Eddy. You can't trust any*thing!*" shouted Lexi, erupting into triumphant laughter.

Eva Delia scrambled backward but the monsters followed her, their numbers thickening as more and more poured from the sighted cloud. The cloud itself began to crackle with lightning. And no one else on the street paid the slightest attention! "You said you weren't bad!" Eva Delia whimpered.

"There's no escape for you, Eddy!" Lexi shrieked, like a witch. "No escape with your *life!*"

Eva Delia looked at her desperately. The girl was holding a rope in her hand, a black rope that glinted in the streetlight as Lexi tossed one end over the nearest lamppost. That end was a noose. The monsters were clustered around Eva Delia's legs now, bumping her, raking her with their claws, but it was the sight of Lexi's noose that drove Eva Delia completely out of her mind.

THURSDAY, JUNE 18, 2009 • 4:58 P.M.
PACIFIC DAYLIGHT TIME

9 Flint Knife (Being Magick)

It had been a long, hot day. Aaron and Craig had jogged at least ten miles, around one long curving street, then back along the next one in, then back along the next one. They passed two large buses on Saturn and thousands of other vehicles, of all shapes and sizes, but the only one they wanted was a beige Volkswagen van, license plate ZAR9197. And now, just before five o'clock, with the sun's baking heat in no way lessened by a rising wind, along a street called Venus, they found it.

The two men knew for certain that their quarry didn't know them, so they slowed to a stroll along the dusty road, letting the bikers and strollers pass them by, and looked the area over as if seeking a lost friend. The other campers were few and far between, many taking siestas in preparation for the full night ahead, or simply dodging the sun. The men could make out several groups of people, drinking and talking under shade structures, but none of them looked like much opposition.

The campsite itself was occupied by two sleeping men, with no sign of the woman. Aaron and Craig did not recognize either of them, but they didn't expect to.

"You think one of them's Blackwell?" Craig asked casually, as they came to the bank of porta-potties at the intersection. "They do magickal disguise, right?"

"Maybe," Aaron answered, looking back. "But they've always been a man and a woman before, according to previous sightings. I think we should give it half an hour, see if the woman comes back."

"On the other hand, it's two on two right now, and August is the real prize."

"But we need both to complete the mission—and we *need* to complete the mission, Craig."

"Should we call Hanrahan?"

"And have him tell us to hang fire until he sends some woman to replace one of us?"

"Yeah, you're right. It'd be just like him."

"I'll go back to the car, drive it up close. You stick around. When I get back, if Blackwell hasn't shown, we'll go anyway."

"Our best bet is knives—quick and quiet. I wish we could wear the Kevlar."

"Why can't we?" Aaron demanded.

"Because everyone—oh yeah."

"Yeah. It's just another costume."

It was really beginning to sink in: all their work had finally paid off! Aaron set out toward their car at a dead run, helped along by the rising wind.

THURSDAY, JUNE 18, 2009 • 5:45 P.M.
PACIFIC DAYLIGHT TIME

9 Flint Knife (Being Magick)

Rosa and Pamela stopped before six pickup trucks welded into a hexagon and stood on end to loom against the stark blue sky—just one of the art pieces positioned on the plain. A hundred yards beyond lay the low orange-mesh fence marking the edge of Bureau of Land Management desert. In the far distance, a dust cloud was rising on the wind.

Pam thought she heard Rosa sigh.

"Did you just sigh?" she asked.

"I have memories, Pamela," the witch replied. "I have memories of my first eighteen years, and memories of how I felt then." She stopped. There was no one within forty yards of them. "I was meant to live in a forest, in the mountains—in a time when magick was alive. Every bridge had a troll, and every well had a kelpie. Trees had their ancient spirits, gathered in forest conclave. Magick was everywhere, and everyone knew it, not just the drabardi. It was a time when demons were easily summoned, and just as easily banished. A time when half the land was wild wood and the other half divided into innumerable duchies and baronies, each its own secret enclave, plotting against its neighbors, hiring magick if it could—a rich and fulfilling time to be born a Roma."

"The sixteen hundreds?" Pam said. "I could be wrong, but I think nowadays that's the tail end of the Dark Ages."

"Aye. The end of the world as magick."

"The world is still magick, Rosa."

"And how many know that now?"

"Point taken," Pam said.

The dust cloud was rising above the plain, turning the far horizon hazy.

"Are you unhappy with Coyote?" Pam asked.

"I am never unhappy."

"Whatever you call it."

"Why? Are you interested in him, Pamela?"

"No, of course not."

"Then are you *un*interested in Max?"

"Of course not." She was about to elaborate when she noticed the gypsy's eyes focus on four girls who were strolling some twenty yards away. Their low voices carried on the wind, though Pam could not hear precisely what they said. Rosa said, "Excuse me," and abruptly moved to intercept the girls, leaving Pam to follow along behind. "This is what I came for."

"Pardon me," Rosa said brightly, using a less-seductive version of the personality she had donned for Michael to address one of the girls, a short, rather pretty brunette. "Would you mind if I read your cards?"

"What?" The girl had been in deep conversation with her friends, and had not noticed Rosa's approach.

"I am a simple gypsy and feel that I could be of help to you."

"Nice costume," said one of the friends.

"Well . . . thanks . . ." the brunette began.

"Five minutes at most," Rosa said. "This is Wickr; you must try new things, no?"

The girls looked at each other. Then the brunette shrugged. "Sure, why not?"

"Awesome!" said one of the friends.

"Then gather 'round, my dears," Rosa said, gesturing to the girls and to Pam. "We will need a windbreak." The dust cloud was splitting the sky gray/blue, so the women formed a tight circle to windward; in their ears the wind was singing softly, brushing them with the finest of dust. It rustled everyone's clothing, but where the cards would lie on the ground the air was still.

Rosa handed her deck to the brunette and asked her to shuffle. "What is your name?" she asked her.

"Kitty," the girl said, shuffling.

"I am Rosa."

When Kitty felt the cards were right, she returned the pack to Rosa, who swiftly and decisively dealt the top cards into the familiar layout. Then she sat and stared in silence at them, so long that Kitty looked helplessly at her friends and at Pam, wondering—before Rosa spoke again.

"Your brother is trying to cheat you, Kitty."

The effect of her words was galvanizing. Kitty recoiled, and her friend gasped.

Kitty said, "How—?"

"He has transferred his money to a private account . . . in your hometown."

"But he said he was laid off!"

"I know," Rosa said, apparently with real empathy. "It is hard. But I see he has an obligation to a man from the south, and he would rather betray you than confront that man."

"Gambling?" asked Kitty, now bitterly. "Or drugs?"

"Neither," Rosa answered. "It is worse than that."

"Worse than—?"

"It is an obligation. Leave it at that."

"Oh my God! But if I don't give him the money—will he be hurt? Physically?"

"No. He has other means of repayment—means he would rather avoid, but are still available to him."

"But he—he's my brother. He loves me!" It was almost a question.

Rosa took her hand. "Of course he does. He is simply not thinking clearly under the stress. But you must send him on his way, to make him think, to make him grow up. He cannot hide from his problems forever; he must *solve* his problems. Promise me you will do this, Kitty."

"I—I'll think—"

"Screw that!" said her friend. "We all know she's telling the truth!"

"Elizabeth!"

"Well, she is!"

Rosa said, "Excuse me, gentle ladies," and swept her cards back together. She stood up, slipping the pack back into its belt-case, and began to walk away, into the wind. Pam, caught by surprise again, hurried to catch up again.

Rosa told her, "Kitty's brother is a blackguard of the first water. He is going to commit a murder and be killed in the act. But that I could not tell her."

"You were looking for her all along," said Pam, impressed. "I haven't seen this side of you before."

"When I am not working for Max, this is how I help others, but there has been little time for it here."

"Is that why you haven't read my cards?"

"Yes."

"But you have no empathy. Right? Your manner with her was an act."

"But it is effective, and must needs be if I am to turn away darkness wherever I can. That is my sworn oath."

Pam walked beside her in silence for a moment, think-

ing, and then cocked her head at her. "How far should anyone trust you, Rosa?"

"What do you mean, Pamela?"

"I mean, I know how far Max is ahead of me, and he's
just started being Timeless. I know how different a world
he sometimes has to live in. So then, I imagine how much
farther along, and how much more different, you must be."

Rosa bowed her head in assent.

Pam said, "You decided that I needed to see Max and
Diana, the way you decided that Kitty needed to see her
brother. You may well have been right. But it would never
have occurred to me to invite the guy's girlfriend out for that."

"Someone with humanity would not have done it?"

"People can do anything, but it wouldn't have occurred
to *me*."

"You'd have preferred ignorance?"

"Maybe I would have."

"No, you are not like Kitty, Pamela. I do not need to read
you to see that you are on a path which can only be trod in
Truth. And Truth, it is said, shall set you free."

Then the dust cloud finally swept over them.

THURSDAY, JUNE 18, 2009 • 6:01 P.M.
PACIFIC DAYLIGHT TIME

9 Flint Knife (Being Magick)

Max and Coyote were languidly sipping mojitos, eyeing the
dust cloud coming their way. "We're gonna get a blow,"
Max said. "You want to go inside the tent this time?"

"No, thanks," Coyote answered, sniffing the air.

"You're insane. I'm putting on goggles, and a scarf over
my mouth," Max said, and did exactly that. "You should

have been a soldier sometime. This could be another white-out."

"Prairie dog," Coyote jeered.

"Uh-uh. Point man. I don't want to be blind and choking."

Coyote stood up and stretched. "It's a beautiful day," he said, then coughed as a small cloud of dust hit him square in the face, and twitched as the cough jerked his arm. "Pfffth." He sat back down. "When will you hear from your computer *friend?*"

The dust cloud swept over them. Coyote, just three feet from Max, became a gray shape.

"Two more hours," Max said, his voice slightly muffled by the scarf.

"Then let's get to the important things. How was it with Diana?"

"None of your business."

"None of my business? It was *all* my business *before!*"

"*Was.*"

"No way! I told you all about her! Tell me what *you* thought."

"I don't kiss and tell."

"You tricked me!"

"We never agreed on it. You tricked yourself—"

A golden glow flooded Max as his mystic alarms went off.

Max and Coyote leapt to their feet, turning to face two vague shapes rushing them from out of the storm. The assailants were surprised that men apparently sound asleep could hear and react so quickly, but they'd learned all the tricks in Iraq. Craig thrust at Max and Max oléd, sucking his belly tight. It was a near thing, but in the next moment Craig was defenseless against Max's counterattack. Craig knew it and threw himself aside; Max's elbow just scraped his ribs. Craig went over in smooth roll and came up, spinning back. Max prepared himself for the worst form of combat known to man—a knife fight.

Max had learned the art of the knife fight from Ricky Sing, king of Asian street fighters. The secret was, simply, wanting to kill. Not that technique meant nothing, but the best technique in the world meant nothing if the fighter weren't completely committed to murder. Not triumph, not execution, but murder—the idea that *anything* was possible if it would bring the fighter out on top. UFC extreme.

As indistinct as his opponent might be, Max could see that Craig knew the secret. So did Max, but Craig had the knife. He dodged the next thrust, staying completely centered over his feet, and the knife slashed one of the tent's support ropes. The tent sagged, began to flap-flap-flap in the wind. *Thank God for my shield,* Max thought. His neighbors might be blinded simply by the dust, but they'd certainly *hear* this war if he hadn't closed it in.

Coyote was hampered by his broken arm (and the pain that rattled up it every time his body jolted). He could have shifted shape, but an animal with a broken leg was worse off than a man—and there was more sport in man-to-man. So he stayed a man with animal instincts and an animal's desire to rip out his opponent's throat as he grabbed his chair and slammed it into Aaron's knife hand, sending the blade flying. Aaron gave it up as a lost cause and dove for Coyote's legs. Coyote jumped away but Aaron caught an ankle and heaved, sending Coyote higher so he fell farther, out of control, landing hard on his back. The pain in his arm exploded.

So he was slow avoiding Aaron's boot, and took a shot to his hip as he rolled aside. His arm *really hurt,* like a rattler bite, but his speed was undiminished, so Aaron couldn't follow up before he got to his feet, his arm dangling. Aaron came in for close-order combat. He feinted at Coyote's broken arm and got the reaction he wanted as his other hand hit Coyote in the face, drawing blood. But strangely, Coyote chuckled.

Max was no killer by nature, not even now. He grabbed his chair and snapped it closed, creating a solid metallic shield to hold Craig at bay. Craig waited for an opening, shifting his blade in a tight figure eight up and down, back and forth. It allowed him to strike from a number of arm angles—but not, as Max knew, from all. When Craig's arm was nearly at the top of the eight, his ability to strike was drastically reduced, and Max took that point as the moment to thrust with his chair. The rubber-tipped legs caught Craig in the gut below his Kevlar; he staggered away to avoid being driven to the ground. But he recovered almost at once and recentered himself as Max came toward him with the chair out front. Craig stepped back then exploded forward, essentially throwing himself onto the chair, stabbing over it as his weight tore the chair from Max's hands. The thrust missed. Craig hit the dirt atop the chair and rolled to his right. Max, now the one off-balance, danced backward as Craig swiped the chair at his shins.

Craig was up in an instant, coming hard. Max slammed his right arm against Craig's outstretched arm, shoving it aside, while he slammed his left arm like a club against Craig's unprotected temple. The blow stunned Craig but he still dodged Max's try at grabbing his knife hand. He danced sideways, clearing his head, looking for an opening, finding it, thrusting at Max's unprotected throat. But that was what Max wanted. He jerked his head back while keeping his eyes locked on his opponent, the most difficult move in all knife-fighting. As Craig's knife foundered on empty air, stretching out Craig's arm, Max drove his fist into Craig's throat.

Craig gasped, choked—tried to catch a breath and found his windpipe crushed. He threw his knife away and tried to administer self-correction, punching himself in the throat from the side, trying to shove the pieces of his esophagus into a new configuration that would allow air through. It didn't work. Craig took his throat in his hands and tried to yank his airway open. But it was too late. His legs went wobbly. For some reason he thought of his nephew, Kevin, and he wanted to say something to Aaron. He fell to the dirt and spasmed for thirty seconds, trying to suck in just one more breath, before falling still.

Max looked to Coyote. He was bleeding profusely from several serious gashes, but the blood dribbling from his mouth was Aaron's. It was all black blood, colored by the dust. Aaron looked astonished as he came forward with his blade again. His arm had chunks taken out of it, but his opponent should have been worse off. This time he caught Coyote in the upper arm and ripped outward, theoretically rendering the arm useless. But theory didn't square with fact as Coyote used that arm to drive his fist into Aaron's face. Aaron turned just enough to avoid the worst of it, but it still snapped his head back, exposing his throat. Coyote sank his teeth and ripped. Blood exploded in an arterial arc and Aaron, like Craig, tried to control the damage. But like Craig, the damage was done. Blood poured from between his fingers and he went to his knees. *There's no pony in this shit,* he thought, watching his blood form a black pool on the plain, then diving face-first into it.

THURSDAY, JUNE 18, 2009 • 6:05 P.M.
PACIFIC DAYLIGHT TIME

9 Flint Knife (Being Magick)

Coyote straightened. His blood stopped flowing, shimmered, and vanished.

"Why can't you do that with the arm?" Max asked, catching his breath above Craig's body.

Coyote gave him a look. "Blood is blood, bones are bones," he said as if Max were an idiot. "Why don't *you* go invisible?"

"Stuff like that takes revving up. I can't do it on demand."

"So you end up a soldier whatever you do. That's what you like, pally."

"Not entirely." Max fell to his knees beside Craig, rested his hands and bowed his head, gathering his power at the center of his mind. Then he thrust his mind into the man.

Coyote saw a golden lion's head flash around Max's head, and kept his eyes fixed on Max with avid interest. Max was a creature of skills, many of which were strange even to a totem spirit. He was as curious as a child when Max did things like this.

Within a minute, Max visibly returned to himself, but immediately looked to Aaron, and left this world again.

Finally, he came back for good, stretching his legs out and leaning back on his hands. He looked up at Coyote, the strain evident in his face. "I got one story from my guy, checked it with the other, just before he faded completely. We got very lucky, my friend."

"How's that?"

"They came from the FRC but they didn't report that they'd found us. They wanted to stick as partners and the FRC wants male-female teams now. We're still okay."

"They don't know about Diana?"

"No."

"Well, ring-a-ding-ding. So what do you want to do with them now?"

"Make us all invisible, tote them out onto the plain and bury them. If we leave them here they'll start to stink real fast in this heat."

"Right, but we can't take them past the fence around the perimeter. There's ground-based radar out there, to keep people from sneaking in for free. Rosa and I had to be very precise when we did it."

"Okay. We'll find someplace far from the farthest art pieces, where people have no reason to go. You take yours and I'll take mine. Ready?"

THURSDAY, JUNE 18, 2009 • 8:55 P.M.
CENTRAL DAYLIGHT TIME

9 Flint Knife (Being Magick)

Peter Quince was ready. He'd run through the forest just as the sun was setting, seeking renewed blessing from the spirits there. Having gotten it, he returned to the house—his house, now—and ate a large cheeseburger with tomato, lettuce, and onion, to provide amino acids for his brain-work. He added three oomph pills for dessert, then made love to Rita.

"What will you do?" she asked as they lay in the afterglow.

"What we see around us is what we see—not what *is*. You witnessed that last night. The Universe is a vast *cosmos*—an interconnected *system*—and we are standing in one small part of it, looking outward. We see space, because we cannot see the true nature of space."

"What does that mean, Pete?"

"I don't know, chica," he answered wryly. "I just know it's true. But once I charge my new *stone* with my magick, my magick alone, I may be able to open doors that have heretofore been closed to me, and then I'll tell you the answer."

"I don't know if I want to hear it."

"That's just another example of the ordinary human mind being unable to cope with the truth behind the illusion.

That's not your fault; it's how we all evolved, so we didn't go mad. But we only use ten percent of our brains. The other ninety percent is there for a reason, and that reason is to drive us onward, outward, to encompass more and more of the cosmos until we know it all and become gods."

"Gods?" *Elegua, Oya, and Oshosi. Santería.*

"Gods. When we know all that god knows, there will be no difference."

"Can we really do that?" Rita asked. "I mean, if the whole thing's a system, it's bigger than we are. Maybe we're supposed to be human and gods are supposed to be gods and that's the end of it."

"If that were true, we would still be apes on the plains of Africa. No, chica, you and I may not make it, but that's where the human race is going. We are like children whose parents want nothing more than to watch us grow up." He stretched magnificently. "And I intend to become an adult tonight."

"If you do—if you do *understand*—can you make *me* understand?"

"Probably not. You'd have to devote yourself to it, the way I have."

"So you'll be a god and I'll be a dog?" she asked, not liking the picture.

"Only when we're doin' it doggy-style," he said, probably thinking he was funny. His mind was on what lay ahead of him, not on her now. "We're a team, Rita—taking it all the way to the top. I get power from the other world, you get it from this one. We'll need both."

Rita, despite herself, was touched. But she would never admit it, so she smiled cynically and said simply, "Sure." Then went back to her first question. "So what will you *do* tonight?"

"Well, here's a very bad analogy. We're all, you and me and everyone, *right now,* like a man looking through a hole in a wall. I can only see a fraction of what's on the other side. But if I could somehow extend my eye through the hole, then I could look in all directions."

"Including back at the wall, where you wouldn't be able to see yourself or the world you came from."

"I told you it's a bad analogy. But if you like, it allows for the other eye to still be available on the original side. Two eyes can see two sides. However you want to imagine it, I shall be in this world and the other at the same time, two worlds at once, and my mind will be making connections that are impossible in one world alone, and I will be channeling everything into my *stone,* so that when I come down, as I inevitably must, it will all still be there for me, any time I want it. And it will be mine alone, the clearest power known to me or any other man, unadulterated by any other mind. I'll have a weapon unlike any that's ever existed. Naturally, I won't tell the FRC that it's that good; just that it's linked to me."

"I like when you talk magick; you sound like a priest. Did any of the old magicians do the same thing with a *stone* we've already got?"

"If any did, there's no record of it."

"Maybe it destroyed them," Rita said.

"Look, will you admit that you don't know the first thing about it?" he asked with some asperity. "I do, and I'll take all the precautions." He leaned over and took her wrist to look at her watch. "Now I need my time alone, to prepare myself inwardly. You should go to a movie or something."

"There's nothin' I want to see."

"Go anyway," Quince said, rising to his feet. "The magick in this house tonight has to be mine alone."

Despite her resolve, Rita was getting real tired of taking orders.

9 Flint Knife (Being Magick)

At 8 P.M. exactly, Dave made his prearranged connection with Max.

"I'm sorry, dude," the jedi said. "I haven't got as much as I thought I would. I'm really sorry."

"What *have* you got, Dave?" Max asked, bracing himself.

"I've been grinding it all day, but there's only two names—van Dusen and Rupp. There's always numbers around van Dusen, so I'm guessing it's Carole van Dusen in Boston, the Queen of TARP, so I'm looking for Boston. And I've got something with a lot of N's in it, but it's not Cincinnati. I really thought I understood their code better, Max. I thought I'd be farther along."

"Are you fuckin' kiddin' me?" Max demanded. "That's five names altogether—three besides Diana's and the Maulin' Mikester's. If I can't parlay that into a win with her, I am in the wrong business!"

9 Flint Knife (Being Magick)

Quince entered his sanctum and locked the door. He was quivering with power and anticipation, almost audibly buzzing, fully prepared. The *stone* lay before him in the center of the circle, just where it had lain two nights before, but its presence felt different tonight, even from across the room. He could easily tell that the impediments to working with it were gone. It felt . . . *open.*

He stepped into the circle. It, too, felt different, and he stopped before proceeding to the center, to analyze that. If it was residual magick from Jackson Tower or his predecessors in the warp and woof of this old house, he would have to banish that. But if it were the magick of the spirits of the woods . . .

Yes, it *was* their magick. It was the power of this house and land, not of any particular wizard or shaman, and it was merely affirmative, encouraging. They were opening the space around his house to him, outward, like a flower. He had wasted so much time before finding them. In Wyoming, there were sacred places, but not that many, and it had simply never occurred to him to look for one in Minnesota. He had been so anxious to get *past* this house that . . . well, it didn't matter now. He had made the connection with this land. Now he would connect with the Universe.

He began by striding purposefully to the east, where he looked outside the circle, not at the walls but at the *outside,* beyond the walls, in his mind. He prayed to the old gods out there, the gods of the sunrise direction, carefully pronouncing the words perfected by the medieval magi for this. Then he moved to the south and offered his prayers to the noon gods, then on again to the west for sunset, and finally the north for the deep dead of night. At last he strode to the center of his magickal realm and stood over the waiting *stone.* He spoke his formulæ one last time, to himself, where the four roads met.

He could clearly feel the bubble around him now, a field that quivered and buzzed like him. No magick existed in this sanctified circle except the magick he controlled. He was the One.

He was the Magus.

He knelt before the *stone,* and placed his hands on it with his peculiar two-fingered touch. The chunk of Almahata Sitta before him, so unresponsive before, peeled open, petals of stone rolling outward, turning the impenetrable block into an opening through which a man might go. With full knowledge of his actions, and a final prayer to the gods around, Peter Quince went, headfirst.

The plain of four directions appeared before him—and he fell through it, shattering it.

Screams followed.

THURSDAY, JUNE 18, 2009 • 9:10 P.M.
PACIFIC DAYLIGHT TIME

9 Flint Knife (Being Magick)

Michael was lounging on his coach's couch, reading Politico on his laptop, finishing his third Scotch. *The Post* had fired Froomkin. Michael and Breckenridge had pushed that one for a long time, Breckenridge in the boardrooms and Michael in the halls. *One down, Krugman to go.*

And maybe he should be back in the thick of that, instead of cooling his heels at this goddamn hippie-fest, *not* getting laid. If he weren't going to shtup Diana, why should he stick around? He had escort services to turn to in Columbus. He should have been there for Froomkin—

The doorbell rang.

He sat and glared at the door. He could just ignore it. It was probably Diana and he wasn't ready to let that go just yet. Well . . . maybe he was. He yelled, "Just a minute," and quickly returned his laptop to the safe. Then he answered the door.

It was Maya.

"What's up?" he asked, neither friendly nor unfriendly. She didn't look half bad in the night.

"I came to see if you have finished being angry with me," she said in her delightful way.

"I wasn't angry with you, Maya," he said. "I was angry about something else, and just took it out on you." Maybe the hippie-fest could measure up to Columbus, at least for the night. He looked around the coach. So long as he didn't fall asleep and leave her to look around, it was doable. "Come on in."

"Thank you, Ron, but I am not some piece of meat."

"What? No. Of course not."

"I came to invite you to buy me a mocha coffee, and talk. Perhaps afterward we can return here. . . ."

"I have coffee in the kitchen. And some nice tunes."

"Please. We can go to Center-City, get some mochas, and listen to the performers. You were unkind to me the other day, and we must get to know each other again."

She was on the edge between her hurt feelings and desire, Michael thought. He recognized it in her because he knew it in himself. Other people denied themselves things, but he never did, so he was always in a position to supply the taboo the denier desired. And then the denier owed him.

He smiled, the smile of a man closing the deal. "Sure, Maya," he said. "Let's go." He turned back and locked the door; he still had to be careful. Then he went down the steps and took her hand, leading her into the night.

Her delightful laugh followed.

9 Flint Knife (Being Magick)

Diana was watching *CSI*. She loved Bill Petersen, but he'd wanted out, so she watched the reruns to watch him play his part in transitioning from "Gil and the Guys" to "The Guys." *The Guys,* she mused, *who should be led now by Marg, the number two to the number one who left. But in the credits, Marg stayed number two and they got a new number one. So once again the woman loses to the man, but this time it's the black man. What if we really are in a postracial America—meaning we've cooked up a new plotline, but with all the same players and all the same parts, and we've just rearranged the deck chairs. What if we did* The Cosby Show *with Mencia—no, wait,* The Cosby Show *with—*

The doorbell rang.

It must be Mike, she thought as she slid off the bed and muted the sound. *He'd better be in a good mood. I need it low-key now, after Greg.*

She opened the door. It was Greg.

"Hey," she said, thinking, *Oh, man, not tonight!*

"Hey," he said, grinning warmly as he came right up the steps, inside.

"Hey, listen," she said, stepping back between the seats to give him room, "I was just kickin' back. You were—jeez, *incredible* this afternoon. But you wore me out, big guy. I was just gonna watch TV and go to bed. Alone."

He closed the door behind him.

"Seriously," she said, standing her ground but fully aware of how far behind her her pistol lay if this took a wrong turn.

Instead, Greg perched on the passenger seat's armrest and said, "You're Diana Herring."

"Who?" Stacy asked, sincerely puzzled.

"Diana Herring. Stacy's not your name. And my name's not Greg." He raised his right hand. It was on fire, except his hand didn't burn. The bones showed through. "I'm Max August. You know who that is."

In one primal reaction, Diana spun to run for her gun or her *stone*—but found her way blocked by an invisible wall.

"I had you alone here for ninety minutes today, and we didn't have sex."

Images of him all over her, her all over him, the incredible high of it, her licking his thighs, him biting her breast. "The hell we didn't!" she snapped, spinning back to face him.

"Check your breast."

She stared at him, eyes wide and set, furious. Then she pulled her gown down to look.

There were no bite marks. *I felt the bite! I saw the blood!* No marks.

"I'm an alchemist, Diana. You call me a Code Red. I implanted it all in your brain, just as I implanted the desire to stay home tonight and the idea that you can't pass the sofas. Now, why don't we get comfortable while we talk about what I *did* do while I was here on my own?"

Oh, fuck! Her face at last showed her true dismay. But she sat down on the driver's side sofa. Max moved across from her, to the sofa on the passenger's side. He sat on the edge of its overstuffed leather, which creaked as he leaned forward. She leaned forward, too; it's the way everyone in show business sits. They were within four feet of each other.

"While I was on my own today, and you were dreaming sex dreams," Max said, mixing in bullshit as needed, "I opened first your safe, then your laptop, and I sent everything on your laptop to my people. Yeah, I can do that. The encryption was as good as the sex we didn't have, according to the first report, but my people are far more familiar with that encryption than I am with you, so even though it's continually improved, it wasn't that much different from what we've seen before, for years now. And we knew some key words we could identify as starting points. Words like 'Diana Herring' and 'Michael Salinan' and 'Porter Allenby' and the ever-popular 'FRC'—oh, yeah, and 'Necklace.'"

He could literally watch the blood drain from Diana's face and down her neck as the enormity of her situation sank in. She even swayed as her brain grew momentarily black. She was known from coast to coast for her mask, but here, at last, was the real Diana Herring. Facing mortality.

Absolute mortality.

The final nail, as he had felt it would be, was the word "Necklace." That meant more than it seemed. He leaned farther forward, closing the distance between them. "Yes, they'll kill you," he said quietly. "You exposed them to their worst nightmare."

Her jaw carried her chin up, and she looked him in the eyes. She was not going down without a fight. "What do you want?"

"I want a sleeper agent in the group. I want *you* to go about your life as a card-carrying member, doing your job just the way you should. You don't have to do a thing for me when you're with them—nothing at all out of the ordinary that someone might notice. You do everything you can to help them with their little schemes, including killing me— because you know as well as I do that any other way would one day arouse suspicion.

"But when you're safely away from the group, I want you to slip me info on those schemes. Now, we're both pros here, so you're thinking you can short me on the intel. But you're not my only source, and I can read the group's code, so shorting me would *definitely* raise suspicion in me, and then I would burn you. I don't think they'd forgive and forget, do you? So we come back to our starting point: I hold your life in my hand."

Diana abruptly sprang to her feet, lunging back into the coach, reaching for her nightstand. This time she made it. She grabbed the pistol, spun and fired in one motion, but it only clicked. She grabbed for the *stone* the Necklace had given her, a powerful weapon they said, but when she raised it to point it at Max she came to realize that the buzz felt different. She was not a wizard but she knew it was a fake. Max had planted it, and clearly it wasn't going to do what she wanted. She threw it at him but missed.

Max was still seated on the couch, calmly watching her, and waiting.

Diana said, "If you bring them down, I walk," she said.

He nodded easily. "If you play straight with me, you *do*."

"You can promise that?"

"Diana, I don't have any bosses. What I say goes."

She gnawed her lower lip. "Whatever I tell you about the Necklace *has* to look like it came from somewhere else."

"Of course."

"How will I get in touch with you? You're a phantom. It's death—"

Her secure phone rang.

She stood and stared at him.

"Answer it," he said. "You're on the clock now, so whoever it is, shine 'em on. I'll be interested to watch you work."

She glared at him, but the phone rang again. She moved her right hand aimlessly, indeterminate . . . then a visible change settled over her, from the thousands of times she had pumped herself up to go on the air. If nothing else, she was used to working live, without a net.

She answered her phone.

"Diana!" boomed a familiar voice. "This is Lawrence Breckenridge. How are you and Michael liking Wickr?"

FRIDAY, JUNE 19, 2009 • 12:36 A.M.
EASTERN DAYLIGHT TIME

9 Flint Knife (Being Magick)

Her breathing stopped—Breckenridge could hear the sudden silence clearly on the secure line.

"I'm calling to inform you," he continued urbanely, "that the Necklace will detonate the Yucca Mountain nuclear waste site tomorrow night. This 'accident' will take nuclear power off the table, leaving oil as the only acceptable power source, thereby enriching us greatly and scaring the crap out of the world."

Diana's brain was whirling, but she forced her breathing to grow steady again. She said clearly, "Why haven't I heard about this before now, Lawrence?"

"Because you and Michael fucked up!" Breckenridge said, a sudden whiplash. "You two are within the blast radius, Diana. In point of fact, it was your decision to go to Wickr that helped shape the plan in my mind. There are other places we could have struck, but Yucca Mountain serves the added purpose of obliterating you and Michael. We've known about you two since you began this charade at Christmas 2005. We have videos—many videos. We've known but we've waited to see what else you were besides horny. If I had not felt the need, based on your service thus far, to make this merely an object lesson, I would have left you to your fate. But you and Michael must understand that the Necklace knows *everything,* and I hold your fate in my hands at *all times.* I'll give him the same message, so you two will have time to avoid annihilation—but you can *never* fuck with me again. Do you understand that, Diana?"

"Yes, sir."

"Good-bye!"

9 Flint Knife (Being Magick)

Diana hung up, her brain whirling, hyperventilating. "That mother-fucking son of a bitch!" she shouted, loud in the enclosed coach. Face set in rigid lines, she stood drumming her fingers on her rigid thigh—looked unconsciously to the left—made other slight movements as she worked her way through it. She let it sink all the way in. "No!" she said explosively. *"No!"* It had been years since she'd been to this place and *she did not like it.*

She sat down on her couch and looked Max in the face. "Fuck him and his videos!" she hissed with venomous contempt. "And fuck you, too! *Here's your lead story, asshole!*"

Max prepared his mind to receive everything she said.

"Our group's the Necklace." Diana Herring, reporting the news. "The FRC is the outer ring and we're the inner one. There are nine of us, operating out of nine cities—Boston, Mass.—New York—Carlisle, PA—Wheeling, West Virginia—Columbus, Ohio—Fort Wayne, Indiana—Chicago—La Crosse, Wisconsin—Duluth, Minnesota. Draw them on a map and they form a choke-hold around the neck of the United States, as it was at the time of the Civil War." Her pointing finger sketched the half circle in the air. He wanted to ask what the Civil War had to do with it but kept his mouth shut.

"Besides me, the media link, there's Michael Salinan, politics, Columbus—Dick Hanrahan, intelligence, Wheeling—Carole van Dusen, finance, Boston—Ruth Glendenning, agents, Carlisle—Franny Rupp, ordinance, Fort Wayne—Porter Allenby, values, La Crosse—Peter Quince, wizardry, Duluth—and Lawrence Breckenridge, fuck-face, New York."

Suddenly her pointing fingers stabbed at Max's eyes. He knocked her hand aside, moving only his hand, and grabbed her wrist, pulled it down, forcing her to lean in toward him till their faces were just inches apart. "You were thinking clearly a second ago," he told her. "Get it back together, Di."

"I just gave you the crown jewels! What do you give me besides promises?"

"So you think if you killed me, you could still redeem yourself? But you can't kill me, Diana. Even with a *stone* twice the size of the one you have, you don't have the power or the skill. *Jackson Tower* didn't have the power or the skill. I'm the only one with that kind of power, and I've got you where it hurts." The many, many radio commercials he had delivered as a deejay made him a better salesman than she, a newswoman, could ever hope to be.

So she showed sudden, sincere interest. "We can work that out, too—"

"Don't even try," he said. "Just tell me the rest of it."

But she yanked her hand free and sat back on the sofa, looking mulish. "That ought to be enough."

"It isn't. I want it all."

She glared at him. "There's a nuclear bomb set for Yucca Mountain tomorrow night! I don't know any more than that." She stood up again, unable to keep still. "But you say you've got power, so go screw the Necklace or save Las Vegas or however you want it, and show me what you've got." A sudden thought hit her. "Are you doing this to Mike, too?"

"No. You're the one and only. Much safer that way."

"Absolutely." She hugged herself. "So—you've got me, and me only, and I walk if you win. But you still have to show me what you can do to that asshole Breckenridge before you get anything else."

He nodded, his smile showing teeth. "And maybe I'll die dealing with the bomb." He stood up as well. "But okay, I can live with that. We both need to know what the other can actually deliver." He took her shoulder, kissed her on the cheek. "This time tomorrow, you'll know that I *will* bring the Necklace down. But I intend for you and me both to enjoy long and prosperous lives thereafter."

Then he laid out for her his plan for keeping in touch. He was glad it was so simple, because he had a bomb to abort.

※ ※ ※ ※
....

Quince tumbled screaming through a realm of no fixed dimensions, where parallel lines crossed and holes opened to reveal even stranger holes beyond and behind. No matter how long and how far he fell, he never hit anything; he was tumbling through space like a lost astronaut. But he wasn't freezing. He was burning as if in hell.

From time to time he would slide along something he could only hear, changing his course. He should have been able to use that feeling, or at least that sound, to orient himself, get some sense of personal space, but he couldn't. He prayed over and over to the old gods of the directions and there were no directions there.

No directions. Even the best-prepared human mind cannot grasp an utter lack of orientation. Quince's mind went protectively blank in a very short time. He fought it with all his power, the massive power of a Magus, but Magi are human, and the human mind . . .

He tumbled in nothingness. As the asteroid Almahata Sitta had tumbled for four billion years.

And then, the song of the curvature grew louder, most beautiful, and it was enough for his mind to connect with, enough for him to say, "It comes from my left—so I have a left—I have an *I*," he told himself. "I am—"

Peter Quince.

Quince came to a halt, sitting on a well-padded throne, inside a chariot of fire. There was a second throne and it was inhabited by a dazzlingly handsome man, wearing the raiment of a mighty and powerful king. It was he who had spoken, with a sound Quince could feel in his bones.

Peter Quince. The king repeated, his voice collegial. **Are you comfortable?**

"Yes," Quince said. "I'm Peter Quince." Was he? "Who are you?"

Belia'al.

"The demon?!" Quince said, fear clutching his heart. He had read of Belia'al in the oldest grimoires—in the Dead Sea Scrolls.

People say that I'm a demon. People say a lot of things. But you have to admit, you cannot understand the world I live in.

"Get thee behind me . . ."

That's for Satan. Ha! That's for certain! Belia'al burst out laughing; it was a very pleasing sound. **I'm not Satan, or the Devil, or a demon, Peter Quince. I'm an angel.**

"A *fallen* angel!"

And why did I fall? Not through any fault of my own. I fell because my brother Lucifer fell. And why did Lucifer fall? He defied God. But why did Lucifer defy God?

My brother was the Light-Bringer, the *King* of all the Angels, and he'd sworn undying allegiance to God. But when God created man, when God created *you*, He commanded all of His angels to bow low before His creation. Lucifer, my brother, loved God too single-mindedly to bow to anything less. He was caught in an impossible situation. And so he defied God from complete devotion.

Now when an angel is cast from heaven, you know that it must enter Duality. Lucifer was banished to these outer realms, and I was created by necessity, so that now there is a Light-Bringer and a Night-Bringer. And I never defied God. I am fallen through no fault of my own! I have the power of Lucifer but not his curse. And I do not hate man like he does. I want to work with man—at least, those men powerful enough to make their way to me.

"Is that . . . what I did?" Quince knew he had to get it together, but this realm . . .

Yes, Peter Quince. You encountered pure power, unsullied power, an abyss. You soared through it and out the far side, into a world completely unlike your own. It is a test, and a severe one, but you have passed it. Now you may call upon my power as your own. We will be united from this night forth, I in my world and you in yours.

"And you get my soul?" Quince demanded. For all his faults, he was a brave man.

No, Peter Quince! I say again, I'm on your side. I am more than satisfied to simply participate in your triumphs over the Earth—of which there will now be many. Here, take my hand. . . .

Belia'al leaned from his throne, expectant. But Peter Quince had read the old grimoires. He remembered what they'd said about Belia'al. Charming, flattering—the Prince of Lies. Peter Quince was a brave man, and he knew he could never accept this bargain—knew his only escape route was death. He clutched his power inside himself and stopped his heart.

But too late.

No, Peter Quince!

His heart began to beat again . . . with a different rhythm.

THURSDAY, JUNE 18, 2009 • 10:19 p.m.
PACIFIC DAYLIGHT TIME

9 Flint Knife (Being Magick)

Max, Pam, Coyote, and Rosa rode out from their camp as fast as their bikes could carry them. The dust storm had passed, leaving the plain marked with drifts of soft sand that slowed them randomly, but they plowed on, straight out Noon toward the desert, and on out toward the perimeter and its low orange fence.

At several points they were reduced to walking their bikes through particularly soft stretches. The first time, Max took the opportunity to look back at the city. A cloud of dust in the far, far distance marked two buses making their way with all deliberate speed along the road to civilization. *Bye-bye, Di,* he thought. *It's been fun.*

Soon enough the foursome reached the fence, just ten feet from the graves of Craig and Aaron.

"Okay," Coyote said, "Rosa and I got in here because there are gaps in the radar coverage, but they're not big gaps. Sometimes they're not very big at all, so it's good we're all slim. I can lead us out of here, and Max can ride shotgun because he's learned what radar feels like on his own hook, but Rosa doesn't feel it and Pammy doesn't know it. So you pretty ladies stay between me and Max and pay close attention to everything we do or say."

"But first," Pam demanded of Max, "tell us everything Diana said!" He, however, shook his head.

"Wait till we're clear."

Coyote stepped over the knee-high fence into no-man's land. "Listen to the man," he said, "and watch me." He walked forward exactly four paces and stopped, waiting for the others to follow, grading their effort. Satisfied, he walked six steps at an angle to his first leg, and the foursome followed caterpillar-style.

Pam was bursting with curiosity, but she had to let it go for now if she was going to make this work.

Coyote came to a halt and turned sideways. Then he crab-walked for maybe twenty feet, up on his toes, his chest pulled in, making himself as thin as he could. When he finally stopped, he relaxed, letting his heels down and his breath out, and gestured for Rosa to follow him. With her dancer's grace, the gypsy was letter-perfect in her imitation of his passage. Pam strove to match her, but twelve feet along she stepped in soft sand and lost her balance. In an instant, Max had her arm, steadying her. She looked back. His face was unreadable in the night.

And then Coyote was moving again.

9 Flint Knife (Being Magick)

"All right," Coyote said. "We're out."

The foursome came to a grateful stop—then took a few more forward steps before relaxing, just to be sure. It had been nearly half an hour of concentrated effort and they were all surprised at the amount of relief stopping brought. The desert looked the same in front of them as behind them, save for the faint distant glow of Wickr in the sky back there. Ahead lay the empty plain, gray and grayer in the starlight, fading into distance and darkness.

"That was a lot of radar for a simple festival!" Pam said.

"Fifty thousand people is not a simple festival," Max told her. "It's a massive enterprise, and they're protecting their investment. If you want to go in, you pay."

"And I've seen much worse," Coyote added.

"Fine," Pam said. "But now that we're out, it's still a hundred miles to Yucca Mountain, at least."

"Got it covered," Coyote said, and Scorpio Rose placidly raised her hand to point to their left. She twisted her fingers and two Arctic Cat 4x4 ATVs appeared from nowhere. Each was big enough to carry a driver and a passenger behind; both had two helmets hanging from the handlebars.

"You didn't think we walked here, did you?" Coyote asked. "*I* could've; I could've *run*. But not Rosa. And those hundred miles ahead of us won't be as Crow flies; they'll be slow going, up, over, around, and through, for most of the day. It's not all plains like Wickr, and there's a mountain range. We need to get going."

"But first," Pam told Max, "I want to hear what Diana said."

"While we ride," he said.

"Oh no. You can't hear on those things. I don't care how far we have to go, I'm not moving till I get it all."

So he told them, as concisely as Diana had, of the nine people with nine centers in nine cities. "The important thing there," he said to Coyote and Rosa, "is if you come in contact with either the people or the places, let me know."

"Sure," Coyote agreed. "But none of those names means anything to me."

"Just file 'em away."

Pam said thoughtfully, "Carole van Dusen is a legend. The grande dame of finance. And Porter Allenby's got some humongous church there in Wisconsin." She clapped her hands with excitement. "I take back every bad thing I ever said about this plan, Max! That is, unless Diana changes her mind again and tries to kill you."

"She *will* change her mind," Max said. "She'll *want* to change her mind. But she's a survivor, and she'll come to see that she *can't go back*. She's as shallow a person on some levels as you'd ever want to meet—well, you know—but when it comes to determining her own self-interest, she's relentless. I watched her think it through after she got off the phone with the guy, weighing me against him, and she decided I offered more of an exit strategy than loyalty did."

"You may be giving her too much credit. She never struck me as a Mensa type."

"But she's one of the Nine in the Necklace," Max said. "She didn't get there by accident."

Rosa spoke for the first time. "What she lacks in raw intelligence she makes up in raw ambition."

"She thought through coming to Wickr," Pam said. "But she didn't know everything she needed to know to make the best decision. If she thinks she sees a way out with you . . ."

"Exactly. So I'll have to stay on top of her." He looked at Pam with an ironic grin. "So to speak."

Pam rolled her eyes and made her distinctive dismissive sound.

So Max turned to Coyote and Rosa. "This was worth everything we put into it, guys, and a whole lot more. We may have saved the world tonight."

"There's still the bomb in *my* world," Coyote answered meaningfully. "Which we won't abort if we don't get a move on."

"Absolutely," Max said. "You take the lead and I'll shield us from satellite view." He climbed onto the nearest ATV, with Pam taking the rear seat. Coyote and Rosa climbed onto the other, with Rosa in the front because Coyote's splinted arm couldn't stand the stress. Pam pressed herself against Max's back, her face in her helmet looking over his shoulder at the other couple, and thought how strange it was to see a gypsy witch on an ATV.

The two machines started up, and within thirty seconds, Pam knew this would be hard on her butt. But Max was enjoying everything about it. He was the man who put everything together, the grand alchemist, but that was because he *had* to put everything together; nobody else was going to do it for him. And what the grand alchemist really loved was being a point man.

They set off at a deliberate speed, so Rosa could get used to her ATV. Max drove his with ease, so Pam leaned closer and spoke in his ear.

"Why didn't you implant the sex in her mind, right from the start?" she demanded loudly over the engine noise. "If you could make her believe in a fantasy this morning, you could have made her believe it yesterday."

"No, I couldn't, for two reasons," he yelled back, keeping his face forward. "First, because she had to really feel the feelings before she could be made to believe in them so deeply. Hallucinations wouldn't have been enough to get us inside her door. Second, I just had to imprint her, not continue a conversation afterward. This morning's work was easier, made much easier by the fact that real sex had given her a lot of dreams like what she thought happened to her, so her visualization was vivid."

Pam, pressed against his back, yelled, "Nice work if you can get it." And then, "Coyote's a shape-shifter."

"Right," Max said.

"But not a shaman," she said. "Not an alchemist. Not someone who can implant visions in a woman's mind."

"Technically, shape-shifting involves visions—"

"Not like the ones you implanted, Max. It was always going to be you with her on the final day, wasn't it?"

Max shrugged under her arms. "Well, yeah. But it was always *not* to involve actual sex. We just had to change the middle part."

"So when were you going to tell me that part of the plan?"

"I figured I'd put it off, that's true. I wasn't actually sure if it was important in the overall scheme of things. And then when we changed the plan, it didn't seem necessary."

Pam said flatly, "You weren't actually sure if it was important."

"Pam—"

"Just drive, Max." And that was the last thing she said for the next three hours.

FRIDAY, JUNE 19, 2009 • 1:00 A.M.
PACIFIC DAYLIGHT TIME

9 Flint Knife (Being Magick)

The buses driven by Michael and Diana rumbled into USA Bus Charter off the Strip in Las Vegas. In many towns this would be well after hours, but that was not a problem here. Michael and Diana signed off on all the paperwork, and paid with Michael's untraceable credit card. That obviously wouldn't fool the Necklace, but there was no longer any reason to do that; it was the rest of humanity that should never know of their little excursion.

They took a cab to the airport, where they hired a private

jet to take them to Chicago at once. Waiting for the pilot to prep, they talked in low tones.

"We were fucking idiots!" said Michael. "We're lucky we're not dead."

"We are, though. Don't you see?" Diana asked.

"Are what? See what?"

"Lucky! We're *lucky,* because we learned our lesson and we're not dead. They want us, Mike. They need us. And we won't screw up again—not after this. We can walk the straight and narrow and it'll be like nothing happened."

"Straight and narrow meaning no more you and me?"

"I think you put a stop to that this morning."

"That was under extreme circumstances. I reserve the right to amend my remarks. . . ."

"*These* are extreme circumstances, don't you think? No, we're done. I'm going to be the fair-haired girl from now on."

"This just gets better and better," Michael said bitterly.

"Shit happens," she replied.

FRIDAY, JUNE 19, 2009 • 2:40 A.M.
PACIFIC DAYLIGHT TIME

9 Flint Knife (Being Magick)

The Taurus moon, a very thin gray crescent, rose to the left of the desert travelers, just north of east. It added no light to the dark gray land, but gave an exotic touch to the night. Also to their left was a sharply pointed mountain, and as the four-some's point of view changed with their approach to the peak, the moon seemed to hover on the mountain like a lover, or a vampire.

Rosa turned her ATV toward a canyon in the side of the mountain, and Max followed suit. They rumbled to within a quarter mile of it before Rosa drew to a halt. Both drivers shut off their motors, and all of the foursome slid gratefully off their seats, to stand and stretch in sudden and profound silence. It had been four nights since Max had met Dave south of Vegas in that silence. It hadn't changed, and it would never change.

Coyote whispered, "You three wait here."

Now, with the rims of both sides of the canyon in view, the composite shape of the mountain above them was much like the muzzle of a giant coyote. "Where are you going?" Max asked.

"Don't worry about it. We're copacetic—"

"'Copacetic'? When exactly did you get to Vegas, Sly?"

But for once, Coyote was not in a bantering mood. "Just stay here. I've got something to do." And he turned and loped toward the canyon.

"Show them, Coyote," Rosa said, perfectly placidly, perfectly audible in the silence of the night around them.

Coyote loped to a halt. He slumped, turned, looked back with a shrug. "You think?" He loped back to them. "Okay, fine. You three *stick together,* and *be quiet.* Rosa's in charge." He looked at her. "Yes?"

"Yes," Rosa said.

Coyote gave Max and Pam a sideways look. "Oh, what the hell. Whatcha see is whatcha get," he said, then he loped away into the desert, toward the cleft between the rims.

Rosa said, "This requires magick. We all have it." Her gaze moved from Max to Pam. "We are going to become invisible for the duration of this adventure, so we can spy. Then we will go forward together, I leading, Pamela behind me, and Max behind her."

Max looked at Pam. She deigned to notice him, and nodded. "Agreed," she said.

Max nodded back politely. He turned to Rosa and began. . . .

He put himself within the giant pi gate, felt the flow from right to left, stepped through it. He used the gravity there to bend the light around him, to flow past and leave him invisible.

Pam watched him vanish, then turned to Rosa herself. . . .

She loosed her mind from her body. She was her mind; her body was her body. She was not bound to the body and so she hovered forward, out of her body, invisible.

Rosa nodded to their empty spaces.

She slipped her thin fingers into the pouch on her hip and deftly pulled a card from the deck inside. She held it up, showed it to the invisibles. «The Moon». She pulled it back and pressed the card against her forehead. The card expanded to engulf her and became a gateway in the night, through which she stepped, invisible.

The three of them formed their line and began to trot after Coyote. He was just disappearing into the canyon. As they made their way across the plain, Rosa and Max had to work around cacti and rocks, but Pam floated smoothly through all that. From the canyon came a haunting howl, long and echoing. Rosa began to pick up the pace.

When they came to the mouth of the canyon, Rosa motioned Pam back to earth. The three of them would have to be side-by-side-by-side for what came next. She led them to the lip of the left side of the cleft, where they peered into the opening, and both Max and Pam saw that as notable. That was as far as the drabardi would let even invisible beings go. Then they understood why.

Inside the canyon, there was heaven.

It was the Paiute one, not any of the other ones, but it *was* heaven. The canyon before them glowed with a soft light of its own, a sphere of starlight on earth. In the center of the glow three figures were gathered. They seemed like the carvings on totem poles, simple, primal, pure, but they moved with the ease of living beings. They were translucent, marked with primal desert colors of tan, russet, and azure blue. One was an eagle. One was a rattlesnake. One was a Coyote, with a broken leg.

Max smiled, confirmed after years of speculation.

Pam recoiled, stunned. She could believe it, the idea of it, "Coyote/Totem-spirit"—but this was the *reality*. There were *three real Totem spirits* in conference, in the center of a world beyond this world—a world, she now saw, as primal as the Totems. The rocks were chunks, unweathered, and the green on the ground was ferns. All of it appeared as if in fairy light. Pam had never seen fairy light in her life, but if somebody were to ask her, this would be it.

"Eagle," said Scorpio Rose, "and Rattler. She hates 'Rattlesnake'; says it sounds too slow. This is a Council of Elders."

Coyote, standing on three legs, was making a point, and Rattler, from ground level, was not buying it. But Eagle, towering over them both, intervened. Rattler launched into some sort of recitation, probably of Coyote's many tricks. Coyote said what all three hidden onlookers read as "But this is real!" And—

TATZA MUHA

<hr />

"My friends and I need to reach Yucca Mountain with no delays."

"I have never heard of 'Yucca Mountain,'" said Rattler, darkly radiant.

Coyote said, "Out by Silver Wash."

The others looked at him blankly.

"By the purple arroyo."

"Oh," said Eagle, with ill-concealed disgust.

"We don't know your damned names," snapped Rattler.

"Well, you should," said Coyote. "They're the ones that are being used."

"Used by who?" snorted Eagle down his beak. "The newcomers?"

"They're in charge," said Coyote.

"For one hundred and fifty years," said Eagle.

"Besides which," said Rattler, "there *is* an actual purple arroyo there!"

Coyote shrugged. "Whatever. There's also a nuclear bomb, set to blow in less than a day, and getting lesser all the time."

"I don't believe it," said Rattler flatly.

"You heard me. So my tribe and I need to get there and stop it, and your tribes need to help us any way you can. No rattlers under rocks, warning of any approach. Let us concentrate on infiltrating a highly secure military base."

"This is a waste of everyone's time!" snapped Rattler.

"We can't afford to be wrong," Eagle told her, but he was clearly vexed. "Coyote never knows when to quit, but, we can give him a day."

"There's got to be a newcomer with him, maybe more than one. The desert is harsh, too. Rattlers *will* bite on sight."

"But not today," said Eagle.

"We need more Elders here," said Rattler.

"I'll take the blame for that," said Coyote. "This has to be quick, and nobody else was around. But we're doin' the right thing, aren't we, Eagle?"

"By a vote of two to one," said Eagle resignedly. "But Coyote, *why* won't you just be civilized?"

"I'm civilized."

"To the newcomers' civilization!"

"To the people who live on this land," Coyote responded. "I don't like how they got here any more than you do, but they're here."

"So you live like them, with them, instead of with us. And when you come to us, it's because you want something."

"It's my way, like yours is to be pompous. Not that I don't thank you for your vote."

"Is it your way to get your leg broken?" Eagle asked tartly.

"I gotta go."

He turned, a softly glowing russet and azure Totem carving, and padded lithely back toward the canyon mouth. As he came to heaven's edge, he rose on his back legs so he could wave good-bye with his unbroken foreleg, then returned to his three good legs. He passed onward through the edge of heaven, and as he did so he became an actual coyote, a small animal known from Panama all the way to Alaska, only to bark in pain as his broken leg re-formed without its splint. *"Ar-ar-ar-ar-arhh!!!"*

This animal did not glow, and the heaven behind it went away.

FRIDAY, JUNE 19, 2009 • 3:04 A.M.
PACIFIC DAYLIGHT TIME

9 Flint Knife (Being Magick)

As the coyote loped in the light of the actual moon, now hovering above the mountain like a moon should, he shifted himself back to Coyote, the man, only to cry out again. *"Yeeeeeeeee-oww!!!"* It was the cry of a man. A man Max, and especially Pam, now knew a whole lot better than before he went into that canyon.

She was just glad shape-shifting included clothes; he was wearing his leather pants. But she wished he'd hurry up getting out here; it hurt her to watch him jog with his arm wiggling.

He came through the cleft, looked to his left, saw nothing, looked to his right, saw them, and turned right to come straight to Pam.

"Little help," he said.

"Yeah, yeah," Pam responded. She was digging in her fanny pack, and came up with new splints and a bandage. "I don't have a zillion of these things," she told him, "so don't keep losing them." She took his arm and held the two parts stable, for perhaps a second longer than strictly necessary. He noticed, and their eyes met.

Day Five

10 Milky Way (Personifying Alchemy)

Peter Quince ran like a madman through the forest behind his house, stumbling but never stopping, as if the hounds of hell were on his trail. He collided glancingly with a willow tree and reeled drunkenly onward.

"Yellow Beaver!" he cried out, startling the birds fixated on the dawn and sending them into the deep leafy canopy. *"Yellow Beaver!"*

Quince was coming to a crossroads, and there in the intersection stood the shaman, in the gray between the trees, dead ahead. He was waiting impassively for Quince to reach him.

"Help me!" Quince yelled. *"Help me! You have to help!"*

"You are possessed," said Yellow Beaver.

"Help me!"

"I am sorry, Peter Quince. You have gone where none here has ever gone—or would go. This is beyond our powers."

"The witch! The man in black!"

"Beyond *all* our powers. We live on this land, drawing power from it. We have some power over things of the Earth, including demons of the Earth. But that which has taken you in is not of this Earth."

"No!"

"The only one with power over this thing is *you yourself. You* are the one man who knows it. *You* are the expert!"

"*No!*"

"*Yes!* You are the expert. You know the demon. Everything you need is within you. Use it!"

"That's all you've got, you fuck? That's *it?*"

"There is nothing else."

Quince stood in the crossroads and realized that everything he'd felt in these woods last night was gone. The spirit, the magick, it was all alien to him now.

"I can't do it!" he said, his eyes hollow, lips barely moving.

And then he said, **Too bad**.

FRIDAY, JUNE 19, 2009 • 7:18 A.M.
CENTRAL DAYLIGHT TIME

10 Milky Way (Personifying Alchemy)

Michael and Diana's private jet touched down in Chicago ten minutes early, rolling over the tarmac under a dawning sky. It was hot and humid as they disembarked in the private hangar they'd requested. Their pilot came down the steps a minute later.

"Will that be all, sir?" he asked Michael.

"I'm going on to Columbus," Michael said.

"Okay. I'll gas up. Give me fifteen minutes."

"No need," Michael said, and stabbed him through the heart.

The pilot yanked himself backward, off the blade, and tried to shout for help—but went down in a heap instead. His blood began to pool beneath him on the tarmac, which, Michael knew, could be easily cleaned. The man reached up at him and then fell back. "I'm going on a business special, commercial," he told Diana, ignoring the dying man at their feet. "We have to be ruthless in covering our tracks."

Diana gave him a hug. "And be seen to be, by our masters," she murmured into his neck. "I'm not happy about the way it went down, either, Mike. I was happy with you. But no more." She kissed his neck. "You know they see everything."

FRIDAY, JUNE 19, 2009 • 5:28 A.M.
PACIFIC DAYLIGHT TIME

10 Milky Way (Personifying Alchemy)

Dawn was creeping over the Paiute desert when the two ATVs stopped for breakfast beside a stand of cactus and willows. There was water there.

Coyote had Pam take the splints off again, then changed into his four-legged form. Still using only three of his legs, he put his belly low to the ground and began to slink perpendicular to the rising sun, disappearing among low cacti nearby. In a few minutes, there was a sudden rush of movement some fifty yards away, and shortly thereafter, he came back with a dead rabbit in his mouth.

Coyote had no deal with Rabbit.

Rosa prepared the meat for cooking while he went to get more. Pam, for her part, put Coyote's splints and bandage on the ground, and without looking up said, "What's today, Max?"

He looked at her for a long moment, not at all deterred by the fact that she still wasn't looking back, then said mildly, "Personifying Alchemy. Today we take everything we know and put it all together. We know the Human side, and we know the Magick, and we are masters of both together."

"They would have burned you once," said Scorpio Rose, her attention on the fire.

"That impulse has never died for some people," said Max. "Never will die. 'The haunting fear that someone, somewhere may be happy,' as H. L. Mencken said. It's as much a part of the human condition as anything else we do, and it has to be opposed at all times. You can't stop magick with anything, but you can stop magicians with fire, and then the time till we evolve will get longer. That, in a nutshell, is why Pam and I are taking down the Necklace."

Rosa nodded and tended her fire. So Max moved closer to Pam and said in a low voice, "Let's talk."

"I'm not actually sure it's important," she said.

"Come on, Pam. You know I love you."

"'Don't believe things because some master says so,'" she responded. "'Decide for yourself what's real.'"

She walked away.

10 Milky Way (Personifying Alchemy)

Rita Diamante was jolted from her breakfast of Honey Nut Cheerios by screaming—harsh, abrasive screaming. It sounded like the inside of her torture chamber in Miami. But that had been soundproofed; no one heard a thing from outside. And she had never heard anything like that in this house before.

She had her P2000 in her hand as she rose from the kitchen table. She went up the stairs at a dead run, stopping when her eyes reached the level of the second floor, and quickly sized up the hallway as deserted. So she ran the rest of the stairs and on to the sanctum sanctorum, arriving less than forty seconds after the first screams—which were ongoing from inside. She knocked hard.

"Pete! What's goin' on in there?"

There was sudden silence, and more silence. She began to eye the door with an idea of shooting it open. Then Quince's voice, strained but steady, responded: "It's okay, chica. I'm okay."

"Let me in!"

And he came back at her with savage fury. "Like hell! This is *my* space!"

She didn't like that change in him—but he was in charge. And still—"Pete! You're sure about this?"

"Go away!"

"And don't come back!"

That's how it sounded. The one voice, but somehow, not the same speaker. She gave up, and back down to breakfast. But she stayed acutely attuned to the room above her head throughout the morning.

FRIDAY, JUNE 19, 2009 • 6:00 A.M.
PACIFIC DAYLIGHT TIME

7 Candle (Engaging with the Matrix)

When their wristwatch alarms went off, Craig and Aaron did not get up, lying as they were beneath six feet of dirt.

10 Milky Way (Personifying Alchemy)

Lawrence Breckenridge rolled out of his bed in the Wheeling mansion with a song in his heart—much later than usual, but that was as he'd planned it. He was going to be up late tonight, monitoring the bomb blast and then the aftermath—the "fallout" in all senses. He didn't need more sleep when Aleksandra wasn't around; he just rearranged it.

With his feet on the floor, he could see out—well, it looked like the window, but it was actually a high-def screen showing the camera view of the estate from where his window would be. The Gemstone of the Necklace would not be sleeping in an insecure room. No matter; the view was spectacular, the ancient forest of witch hazels thick and lush at the border of the grounds. It was a far cry from the Nevada desert, and from Manhattan concrete, and Lawrence Breckenridge decided he liked the look of it.

10 Milky Way (Personifying Alchemy)

Rita Diamante had stuck around the house, in case Pete needed help after all—but after six hours of it, she wanted to get out. It was hot and it was rainy in beautiful Duluth fucking Minnesota, but she actually liked that; it was like

Miami. It was certainly better than sitting around inside. She pulled on a clear plastic rain slicker, still leaving little to the imagination, and drove down to the Duluth Hall of Records on First Street. The next step in her investigation of Jackson Tower was to check the history of the house the wizards had to live in.

In his sanctum, in his crystal, Peter Quince watched her go.

"That worked fast."

"Once you thought of it."

"*I've* been busy. Why didn't you?"

"Never mind. She's gone."

"Time to come out and play!"

FRIDAY, JUNE 19, 2009 • 3:00 P.M.
EASTERN DAYLIGHT TIME

10 Milky Way (Personifying Alchemy)

Lawrence Breckenridge stood beneath a huge witch hazel, sheltered from the sun. The old branches spread over his head and drooped so low around him that they formed a sort of tent—a tent that rippled softly in the West Virginia breeze. It smelled good, that witch hazel smell, warm and dry and summery. This little world was all his, just like the big one, but here he could almost expect to see rabbits in waistcoats or those elementals his wizards talked about. He had never seen any of that. There was Aleksandra and there was his *stone,* but otherwise he had no connection to the "other world" at all. He wished he did, he certainly wished he did, but he just wasn't built like that. And still, if he were ever to see something magickal, it would be in a green and private world like this. So he breathed in the wonderful air and gave himself five minutes of *waiting* to see if something would appear to him.

But it didn't. So then he used his secure phone to get back to his business of pleasure.

"You know who this is."

The trees rustled around him. He heard traffic behind the other voice of the line.

"Uh-huh. It has, hasn't it? But you'll like this," Breckenridge said. "Yeah. Well, here's a question: where's the governor?"—"You think? You might want to check that."—"No, he's not on the Appalachian Trail."

Now batting, the Governor of South Carolina.

10 Milky Way (Personifying Alchemy)

When Max, Pam, Coyote, and Rosa stopped for lunch, in the shade of a small group of trees flanking a barely extant brook, they were well across the expanse between Wickr and Yucca Mountain. The journey was proceeding pretty well, save for a certain lack of conversation. It was 115 degrees out there.

"Water," Coyote announced as he climbed off his ATV with stiff legs and a throbbing butt.

"You're sure this is safe to drink?" Pam asked, thinking of the breakfast water, too.

Coyote cocked his head at her. "Would I bring you here if it weren't?"

"I don't know *what* you'd do," Pam responded. "I know what *I'd* do, and that's boil any water—"

"—that animals may have pissed in?"

"Yes."

"I've been drinking this water for a very long time, Dr. Blackwell," he said with some dignity. "But I'm an animal. So let me assure you that both Rosa and Max have drunk it. It's . . . part of the land the way I am. It's as pure as I am." Coyote flipped a hand. "I'd be pretty stupid to poison you, Pammy."

"I wouldn't think you would, Totem Spirit. But—"

"—you don't trust my judgment."

"Would you let me finish my own damn sentences?"

Coyote grinned, shrugged, turned and went down on one arm and two knees to stick his face in the water and drink. Rosa did the same thing.

When Coyote raised his head, Pam asked, "Didn't you reveal the secrets of Eagle and Rattler to us, without their permission?"

"What do they care? They don't deal with people."

"I'm not sure that's the relevant point."

"That's exactly the point. They have no secrets. They're Eagle and Rattler all the time."

"Rattler won't be pissed?"

"Rattler's always pissed. It's her nature. And what are any of us but our nature? What are any of us but *nature?*"

Pam let it go—and Max took her arm. "Let's talk," he said, and this time led her away from the others, out into the sunlight, far out into the open. She went, but not unbendingly.

When they were out of even Coyote's earshot, Max stood by Pam and said, "I didn't mean that you weren't important. I meant important to the plan."

"Because I wasn't going to be in that room with Diana," she answered with asperity. "But I *was* part of the plan, or *thought* I was."

"Of course you are."

"You treat me like a second-class citizen, Max! Whether as your girlfriend or your disciple, I'm somehow not on your level. And I'm not talking about alchemical knowledge, I'm talking about human relationship—the prime concept, according to you!"

"It was *exactly* because of the human relationship that I didn't want to tell you I'd be naked with Diana at the end."

"Because you thought I couldn't handle it!"

"Well, you're *not* handling it."

"Oh, no! What I'm not handling is your thinking you needed to protect me—or protect yourself."

"Don't I?"

"You do not! If you had told me, I'd have said, 'Fine, good plan,' and that'd be the end of it. But you didn't see me as a partner. You're too used to being the point man, with no excess baggage."

"Pam—"

"I'm riding with Rosa."

–o–

I worked the Grimorium Gris *harder than I'd ever worked the drills at Academgorodok, and when I was twenty-three, I knew I had mastered it. I could see the other worlds and other lives awaiting me, though I knew there was still a path ahead. I was getting close, though, and the next step was obvious. I could not remain subservient to a flashy but ultimately limited old lecher. I spent night after night weighing every bit of magick I knew against his age, my skills, the watchfulness of Svetlana and Drysi, the forms bad luck could take. Nothing was a given. Wolf was approaching his seventy-third birthday and was still vigorous. Since the night he'd beaten me, I had been the most obedient of students, and lovers—even though my maturation had lessened his ardor for me. There were other, newer, younger girls for the banked embers of his quaint lusts.*

I chose the night of Midsummer, with the Sun at the peak of his power and the Earth at the peak of hers. But that year, 1972, Jupiter was opposite the Sun, which put the giant planet's power on the Earth's side. I chose the first moments after sunset, when the Sun was dying away. The sky was appropriately blood red in the window behind Wolf's old white head when I entered his office and closed the door behind me.

"What do you want?" he asked irritably, looking up from his neatly arranged papers.

"Have you ever read Lermontov's poem 'The Demon'?" I asked. "The great love between Tamara and her Demon?"

He looked at me as if I were insane. "I have had many other things to do in this country besides reading its literature."

So I quoted the demon's seduction of an innocent young girl:

> *Ah no! My lovely one, your morrow*
> *Is marked by different destiny,*
> *A different depth of ecstasy,*
> *A different scale of sorrow;*
> *Leave then your former thoughts, desires*
> *And leave the poor world to its fate.*
> *Then, in return, you may aspire*
> *To enter realms of knowledge true,*
> *And there I shall present to you*
> *The hosts of beings subordinate.*

"Go," Wolf snapped.

"It's very much like what you said to me," I told him.

"What is this now, Aleksandra? Schoolgirl regret? You entered your 'realms of knowledge true,' didn't you? This school has not failed you."

"And I have not failed the school. I'm a good student, master—a good girl. I learned my lessons, and I explored on

my own. But it is true that I learned the ultimate lesson here, from you. I learned how power is applied."

"Listen," he said, "go to the infirmary, get checked out. Go somewhere other than here."

"Exactly."

I raised my hands, formed a V, shook them sharply, just as if I were trying to flip water off them, and instead shot magick from them. A crackling spark snapped between my palms, and swelled into a tumescent cloud. Lighting flickered in it, and eyes . . .

The old bastard threw his power at me, but the Sun was gone.

Wolf Messing DIED.

FRIDAY, JUNE 19, 2009 • 9:25 P.M.
BRITISH SUMMER TIME

10 Milky Way (Personifying Alchemy)

The sun had risen over London at 3:42 A.M., and set at 8:21 P.M. In the eighteen and one half hours in between, Eva Delia sat hunched inside a walled-off construction site on St. Martin's Lane, diagonally across from *Calendar Girls* at the Noël Coward theater. Men were working all around her from seven in the morning to five in the afternoon, but she was in a small triangular room which had been closed off until all the electricity wiring was complete. They never saw her, and she kept very still. She was as far away from the world as she could be. She couldn't go back to her apartment because Lexi would find her there. The cloud and the monsters would find her there. The hanging rope would find her there. So she hunched in her little room, kept her hands near her neck to ward off the rope, and flinched at every noise on the street outside. She didn't grow hungry because she couldn't allow herself to venture out for food. In the same way, she didn't soil herself. She just sat, hunched.

But in that quasi-silence formed by occultation and lack of focus, with her mind a maelstrom, she had time to realize one thing. It was one thing out of millions, and it took most of the eighteen and one half hours, but as the light grew dim, she understood that the Voice was singing to her. And the Voice was not scared of the rope, or the cloud and monsters. Or Lexi.

It was singing something soaring, something with an uplift, like angels. It was holding to a beat. The words were unintelligible because Eva Delia could not comprehend English now. But what came to matter to her was the beat. It was steady, unscattered, like a heart when one's at rest, confident and unafraid. It was not buffeted by the world; it reveled in it. The Voice took most of eighteen and one half hours, but over time, Eva Delia found a single thread that ran through the labyrinth of her mind.

It only took twenty-nine minutes after that for her to realize a similarity between the thread and the lines in the book that always calmed her. And dimly, cautiously, like robins after a hawk has passed by, she was able to lean on the Voice and reach out. To understand that she was starving. To understand that she needed to pee. To understand that she needed that book to help herself.

To understand that she would go get it.

That book gave her peace. No matter how damaged she was, the Voice would not let her succumb. She could lose herself—her selves—but way down at the bottom, there was a self she could not lose. A self that was always there.

She went out of her cabin and went to where she could squat and empty her bladder. Had she been able to think clearly, she would have turned so her bum was downhill from her feet; as it was, she drenched her shoes. But as it was, she didn't much notice.

Once the sun set, she came out of her room and made her way out to the street. People looked at her—looked at her!—as she clambered into view. But she didn't much notice, and no one wanted to accost a girl who smelled like urine. She turned toward Rusterman's, her shoes squeaking.

When she entered the store, she felt a wave of peace, of sanctuary roll over her. When she entered the seventh room, she felt steadiness, and she became aware of her urine-smell, and aware of others' awareness, their moving away. But she felt steadiness, which only increased as she finally reached her book, surrounded by so many others. The book was even opened for her, lying on the table, showing her the lines. And looking at those lines, rolling so smoothly and inexorably across the page, she felt almost herself.

"You *are* a trooper, Eddy. I've got to give you that."

Lexi! Right on the other side of the table!

Eva Delia reacted without thinking as she flipped the table onto Lexi. The girl went down, buried under sliding books. But not Eva Delia's book. Eva Delia had that in her hand as she ran from the room.

Sixth room.

Fifth room.

Fourth room.

Third room.

Second room.

Main room.

Eva Delia ran toward the exit. But in her path was Lexi!

"Stop her! She's got a book under her jacket!" the girl cried out.

The clerk took interest, but didn't spring to action, giving Eva Delia time to get past him. Lexi was another matter, lunging at her, touching her, as Eva Delia ran out the door. Eva Delia's world immediately went psychotic, billowing with colors and sounds. She stumbled into the crowds as her world fell to pieces, ran into people, bounced off their verdant caws. She ran through Cecil Court, jacket bulging, buildings melting. All she wanted to do was get back to the construction site. But behind her a clerk was finally in pursuit, egged on by Lexi's shouts. His footfalls were black.

Eva Delia reached her goal and slid into concealment without hesitation. She skidded on the dirt but grabbed onto a stanchion with her free hand and cartwheeled around it, still almost smashing into her little cabin.

The clerk came to the construction site and stopped. He had no appetite for following a crazy woman into the dark. But Lexi was right there. "Get her. She can't go far!" Her tone touched his manhood; he went in.

Eva Delia was scrambling away between the four-by-twos, farther away than he'd have liked, but not so far away that he couldn't catch up. He thought of the work he was putting in for £16,000 a year, but he did his duty to his employer and ran after her (though not without deciding he'd get any damage to his clothes reimbursed).

When he caught up to her, she fought him, but not hard; she was weak and incoherent, using one hand to hold the book beneath her jacket. He got hold of the other hand, and twisted the wrist, not hard enough to break it, but hard enough to show her he might, if she kept this up. She tried to get free and couldn't. She burst into tears and collapsed in surrender, hardly aware of it, babbling uncontrollably. He retrieved the book from her coat. It appeared to be undamaged. Thank God for that.

"Good work."

To his surprise, Lexi was right beside him.

Eva Delia cried out one last time. "Evil! Evil!"

"What? Who's evil?" the clerk asked.

Lexi laughed attractively. "I think that's her name."

The clerk nodded.

Lexi leaned into her face. She smiled and said, "Good-bye, Eva Delia Kerr."

Her victim lost contact with reality forever.

10 Milky Way (Personifying Alchemy)

As Pam and Rosa rode across the desert, passing between two large, lumpy mountain ranges, one bright, one dark, the two women discussed Max August. They didn't have to yell over the engine noise; they could talk telepathically with now-practiced ease.

Max bases what he knows on two pillars, Rosa thought.

One is being a point man. . . . Pam returned.

And the other is sex magick, answered Rosa. *He began his journey to alchemy with sex magick. It was with his wife.*

Val.

There was no other.

Did you know her? Pam asked.

Yes. We three met in Egypt in 1981. Max and Valerie had been at the Great Pyramid . . . practicing sex magick.

Was she as wonderful as they say?

Who is 'they'?

Web sites. They love her, the way they love anyone great who died too young. And Max loves her, still. She really was great, as a singer and performer; I've watched her clips on YouTube. But what was she like in person, to you?

Just what you would expect, Pamela. She was a major goddess of rock and roll. Very beautiful. Very confident and strong-willed. And she and Max loved each other completely. There was nothing of 'show business' in their union;

their magick together was VERY *strong. I enjoyed her company quite a bit; Valerie was a good woman.*

Thanks, Rosa. You're always good for a laugh.

You need to know, Pamela.

I don't know what I need.

Pam sank her chin on Rosa's shoulder and let her gaze settle on the two men riding ahead of them.

FRIDAY, JUNE 19, 2009 • 2:07 P.M.
PACIFIC DAYLIGHT TIME

10 Milky Way (Personifying Alchemy)

Max drove the ATV with Coyote leaning back in his seat, his splinted arm resting in his lap.

You know you can't get in there, right? Coyote thought.

What do you mean? Max responded sharply. *Yucca Mountain?*

Yeah.

You've seen me in action. I'm looking forward to it.

But you can't get in there, Max. They've got ground-based radar, too.

And you're just telling me this now?

I thought you knew.

Nope. I didn't know a thing about it. Max took the next bump a little faster than usual. *But I can track in the way you did at Wickr, and confuse the radar with a little alchemy.*

Not even with a lot. Confusion would just draw them out to see what was up. All your masking tricks wouldn't get past what they have trained on the heart of their compound; there are no holes in their coverage. But when they see me on their screens, they'll only see a four-legged coyote. I pretty much always run my land like that these days.

Goddammit, Coyote!

It's copacetic, baby. Rosa and Pammy can't go, either; you guys get to party while I do the dirty work. But it ought to be me anyway. It's my desert.

And one way or another, it's also mine. Max thought furiously, running through his options. *All right. You go alone. But station the rest of us to the northeast of the base.*

Why? That's gonna mean a longer trip.

I'm going to give you some alchemical help.

I don't need any help.

Maybe not, but I need to give it.

FRIDAY, JUNE 19, 2009 • 5:18 P.M.
CENTRAL DAYLIGHT TIME

10 Milky Way (Personifying Alchemy)

Rita Diamante pulled into the driveway of her Duluth historical dwelling, and, for the first time, was struck by how nice it looked. It was most decidedly not her thing, this Midwestern, high-storied, wooden . . . thing. But it had its own style. It just took her a while to notice it. Kind of pretty, actually.

She went around back and found Pete lounging in the sun, as she'd hoped she would. He was out of his room, and he didn't look to be any the worse for wear.

"Hey, Pete," she said, feigning normalcy. "I tried another tack on Tower today, but struck out again. This house is in a sort of living trust for the family of a guy who died in 1904, only there's no record of anyone actually *in* that family. It's just one of those things where there's nobody to ever look into it. Taxes are paid on time. . . ."

"Hello, chica," he said with an insinuating drawl.

"Are you high?" she asked.

"Yeah. But it's a good high."

"Have you eaten?"

"Yeah. I have."

"So—how did it go with your *stone?*" Rita asked. "Did you get what you wanted?"

"Oh, yes."

"I gotta say, Pete, it didn't sound like fun."

"Fun comes in many forms, chica. It was like, how shall I put it?—it was like raping a virgin. There's no lubrication, no flexibility. There had to be *convincing.*" He laughed, delighted.

"But you did it," Rita said dubiously.

"Yeah. I did it. I'm very convincing."

"Well, I can be *your* virgin, papi."

"Exactly what I was thinking." His eyes lit up. "But if you're a virgin, I might need a knife to cut the clothes from your unwilling body."

Rita laughed low in her throat. "Bring it on, big boy! Let's see what you got!"

Quince laughed back at her, right into her eyes. "Yah!" he said. "*Let's see!*"

FRIDAY, JUNE 19, 2009 • 11:49 P.M.
BRITISH SUMMER TIME

10 Milky Way (Personifying Alchemy)

Eva Delia was booked into the Metropolitan Police station on Savile Row a bit before midnight. The charge was theft, and it was serious due to the high cost of the book she'd stolen. The copper who brought her in had a statement from the clerk, and Lexi had come along to tell them firsthand how the girl had scared everyone, how dangerous she was. The sergeant told Lexi he expected the girl would get treatment rather than prison, but she'd be institutionalized one way or another. It was too bad, really, the sergeant thought, looking over at his prisoner. Most of those he'd seen who'd gone into the system came out looking worse than when they'd started. Lexi took a deep breath, swelling her tee shirt, and said, "Thank you, sergeant." She bent to look directly into Eva Delia's eyes for the last time. "Poor girl," Lexi said, and made certain: *There's nothing there! NOTHING AT ALL! She's GONE!*

Eva Delia understood none of it. Her world was incessantly growing, erasing, filling, clattering, howling, *changing* moment by moment. There was no one thing she could base the world on, no one place she could stand and call her own. *She* was incessantly growing, erasing, filling, clattering, howling.

There was no *she*.

Her name was not Eva Delia or anything else. There was no *her*.

And in between she who was not her, in the collapsing spaces, there was howling, ecstatic laughter.

–0–

Aleksandra exploded back into SpaceTime, her laughter echoing through all dimensions. *VALERIE DRAKE IS FINALLY DEAD!*

I hung her by the neck. I plunged her soul into a newborn babe. She was schizophrenic and that should have been enough to at least neutralize her, but no! She continued to fight. A spirit like that—someday, she might have fought her way clear. She might have had that power. So she had to be COMPLETELY destroyed this time.

And she WAS!

Now you can have Eva Delia's body, Max! Don't mind the drool. And accept that your whole Timeless life is destined for eternal failure if you don't join with me!

The diabola laughed and laughed at the echoes sparking her angry red light, roiling back over her and taking her back down to flesh with almost sinful ease.

Now I CELEBRATE!

10 Milky Way (Personifying Alchemy)

Lexi reappeared in London, but not near Eva Delia this time. She was back on the South Bank, in the shadows of the Albert Embankment, where she had killed Valerie Drake through Eva Delia. It was just a few hundred meters to the north of a fine old London hostelry, the Regal on the River, and she walked south to book a room there. She was wearing a palace blue Carolina Herrera business suit with a stylish Nehemiah multi-stud belt. She ordered a magnum of champagne to be delivered to her room, which boasted a broad view of the Thames.

When the boy brought up her champagne, she tipped him twenty quid and gave him a dazzling smile. He thought for a second that she wanted him to join her, but she waved him out with cheerful finality.

She locked the door. She drank her bubbly. She stripped off all her clothes. She tied the stylish belt around her neck, with just enough slack to hang herself on the inside of her closet door.

Only one who could not die in flesh could truly savor autoerotic asphyxiation.

Now I CELEBRATE!

SATURDAY, JUNE 20, 2009 • 4:05 A.M.
BRITISH SUMMER TIME

10 Milky Way (Personifying Alchemy)

In between *she who was not her,* in the collapsing spaces, the howling, ecstatic laughter died gradually away.

It didn't mean anything to the chaos which was her mental world. That world kept right on growing, erasing, filling, clattering, howling, *changing,* right on and on and on, moment after moment, hour after hour, incessantly, endlessly, timelessly. She understood none of it.

But at one point she realized that in all of that chaos, there was no longer any laughter in between.

At one point, *she* realized it.

• • •

That was all. She was still completely mad, lost in a world of catastrophe. There was just this one infinitesimal dot that thought of itself, and that dot was in a universe, vast, endless, and strange, crashing and strangling.

Like the night she died.

She had a past. She had time.

And that dot began to send a message. It was just one word, one tiny little word out of all the words and all the chaos that was hers, over and over, again and again and again and again. A word that was silent, heard only inside the dot that was tossed on the storms of a mad universe.

The word of *she.*

At 4:05 in the morning, in her holding cell among other

denizens of London's mean streets, her *lips* began to form its sound. Silently at first, for minute after minute as the others laughed or looked away, but finally the word became barely audible. Again and again and again, droning on with no hope of stopping, no hope of anything. Just making the word.

"Koomari. Koomari . . ."

But *she* wasn't saying it.

She was *singing* it.

FRIDAY, JUNE 19, 2009 • 9:00 P.M.
PACIFIC DAYLIGHT TIME

10 Milky Way (Personifying Alchemy)

The sky above the desert to the west, where the sun had set half an hour before, was a deep, deep plum color. At ground level, below, there were three widely scattered lights—points in the Nellis Air Force Range, just ninety miles to the northwest of Las Vegas. In Nellis's heart was the Nevada Test Site for nuclear bomb experimentation. Yucca Mountain squatted like Jaba the Hutt on the southwest boundary of both the test site and range. Tunnels beneath the mountain held massive amounts of radioactive waste, from the tests and from industry—all of it supposedly safe, or at least necessary. Security was intense in all directions so no one way in was any better than any other. If it had been up to Coyote, they'd have come straight to it, but here they were well to the northeast, on the ridge above Area 51. It meant he'd have farther to go.

Area 51, aka Dreamland, was said to be closed now, a victim of exposure. The secret facility at Papoose Lake had drawn more and more people to the boundaries of the range, and more and more trying to slip past the boundaries, so it was decided in 1997 to let slip that the work done there had moved to the old Dugway Proving Grounds in Utah. There was still plenty of security around Dreamland, because that was a lie—but the number of intruders was way down, and they weren't usually alchemists, Totems, and witches. Security could be beaten.

Plus, as Coyote told them, "They can't get us *now*. I named this place back in the day—called it Pakonapanti."

"What's that mean?" Pam asked.

"I dunno," Coyote said. "It just sounds good. 'Pakonapanti.' 'Pack-on-a-panty.' I like it; don't you?"

"It's swell," said Max briefly, which made Pam smile in the dark. He lived to find the structure in things and Coyote's randomness drove him crazy. *Good,* she thought.

Coyote left the ATVs and led his party on foot up from Emigrant Valley, as the setting sun threw its long dark shadows below. Moving the way he moved was now second nature to them all, even Max, who had his own methods. Coyote would stride into the shadow of a rock, bob a little, feeling the way, and roll out again to the next hiding place almost as fast as if he were taking a straight line. His sense of the desert, and of electronic surveillance, was more than enough to get them through, and Max and Pam were adding their cloaking anyway.

However, none of them was *perfect*. All at once, an eagle's cry split the high desert air, and the intruders froze behind their boulders. Two jeeps, holding four men, came rumbling over the southern ridge, moving their way. What kind of surveillance had spotted them? Coyote looked around at the others, clearly indicating, *"They couldn't do this the last time I was here."*

The jeeps pulled to a halt not twenty yards away. Electronic screens in both vehicles lit the airmen sitting over them.

"Something twenty yards that way," one said, pointing toward the boulders. He slid sideways, stepped out of the jeep with his rifle at the ready—and fell back as if poleaxed.

"What the hell?" his driver snapped.

"Snake!" the man choked out. "Got me above the boot."

"Shit! There's arteries and things up there. Can you get back in?"

"Yeah," the man said. "Yeah." He crawled up into his seat, then grimaced as he pulled his wounded leg after him. The driver quickly tied a tourniquet below the knee; this was the third bite he'd dealt with since he got to Nellis so he was quick and efficient. Meanwhile, the occupants of the second jeep slid to their running board but not to the ground. Evidently, they'd all parked on a rattlesnake nest; a dozen serpents were slithering in all directions. With their helmet headlights sweeping the ground, the two men decided even the running board was too close and slipped quickly back into their seats.

"Shit, there's nothin' out here," the second driver called.

"I'm taking Urky to the infirmary," the first driver answered.

"Right with you," the second driver said, and both vehicles spun a sandy circle to drive away the way they'd come.

Coyote was grinning ear-to-ear, and threw his hands out. "Totems rule!" he proclaimed, and flashed a North Las Vegas gang sign. Then he started dancing in place. "All right. You guys wait here and play three-handed canasta. I'm outta here."

Now Rosa spoke. "Take Pamela with you."

Coyote made a gesture of dismissal. "Enough with your suggestions, witch. This is a one-man job."

Pam said, "Me—?"

Rosa said, "Pamela can *fly,* so she will not be seen by the radar. Her body will remain here in our care while her spirit walks invisibly and undetected beside you. I know, my Coyote, that you don't need anyone's help, but she can learn much by doing this—and I would not underestimate her skills or her courage."

"Well, thank you, Rosa," said Pam, blushing as usual, thankful as usual when it happened in the dark. Thankful she now spent a lot of time in the dark. "But I . . ."

"You can do it, Pamela."

"Oh, I believe you."

Max said, "You may have to keep it up for several hours, Pam."

"Yes, Max," Pam said sharply. "Don't *you* think I can do it?"

"No question about it. Go get 'em, cowgirl." He refused to be drawn into an argument. Instead, he gave her the intel he had. "You know the flow is Personifying Alchemy. Ride that hard: you can do what you want to do. The asteroid for that is Klytaemnestra. The Sun is conjunct Cyllarus, a CDO meaning 'pride in my work.' But the *Moon* is square to Neptune *and* Jupiter, because those two are conjunct, and all of that adds up to huge distractions. Moon square Neptune makes it easy to space out and let little details slip, without even thinking about it—but it's just as easy to stay *astral* if that's what you focus on. Moon square Jupiter makes it easy to go poking down side streets to see what's there, instead of focusing on the one goal. All squares show two distinct energies, both trying to enter the intersection at the same time. One will win and one will lose. Make sure you're the winner."

"Thanks. Appreciated," Pam said, now getting antsy. "But I'm not planning to forget a nuclear bomb."

Rosa slipped a card at random from her case. It was

«Princess of Cups». "All court cards are powerful," said the gypsy.

"And remember, I'll be out there with her," Coyote said.

"She'll be out there with *you,* pal," Max said. "But however you slice it, I'm glad we've all got *friends.*"

Rosa nodded slightly, as Coyote turned to Pam. "Lie down right here, Pammy," he said, pointing out a patch of earth devoid of vegetation between two small ridges. "The sand is soft, you'll be out of the wind, but completely open to the sky."

"Do you know every square inch of this desert?" Pam asked him.

"Duh," Coyote said. "It's mine."

So she lay down where he showed her, moving a little to get comfortable, and Coyote hunkered down beside her. There was the hint of a chuckle in his voice. "I'll see you out there because I can do that, and you'll see me because you're *astral.* But you'll get there about an hour before me, since I have to actually run, so scout the place completely while you're waiting. Just don't screw up."

"Jesus, you, too? Will you all just cut me a break?"

"Easy, Pammy, easy. People say I screw up all the time, but it's rarely true."

"I'll be fine," she said, adding defiantly, "and so will you."

"Okay then, I'm out of here," he said, standing up against the sky. "See you soon." He turned and loped beyond her field of vision, the right-hand ridge.

Pam lay and looked back up at the sky, which filled her vision. The stars of Boötes the Herdsman were directly above her. The invisible Haumea and Makemake were up there, and Saturn; she knew what they meant, at least in theory. But they didn't add anything to finding a bomb. So she went with what she knew.

She let the sky become, not a scenic backdrop, but an

environment, half of the globe around her, with width and depth. It was everything she could see, and all at once, with a simple mind-shift, she was not looking *up* at the stars, she was looking *out* at them, as if she were the figurehead on a boat. She wasn't lying flat on the Earth, she was pressed against the *front* of the entire planet as it flew forward through space. And then *she* was flying, soaring out ahead of the soaring Earth, out to where the stars fell into place *around* her, where she was one of them, a light in the dark like them.

Astral.

FRIDAY, JUNE 19, 2009 • 9:31 P.M.
PACIFIC DAYLIGHT TIME

10 Milky Way (Personifying Alchemy)

Pam looked down. She could clearly see her body far below, with Max and Rosa standing over it. And she could clearly see Nellis Air Force Base to the west, small clusters of reddish light on the vast black map of Nevada. She was at the peak of her arc, *flying* from the one place to the other, and it really didn't matter that her physical body wasn't making the same trip. *She* was making the trip. Pam Blackwell.

Twenty months ago, she had stumbled into the world that had magick in it and begun to study alchemy the way she'd studied tetrodotoxin. Now she could do *this*. The light around her was not fairy light, not the light of the Totem world; it was yellower, like starlight; and her *astral* body was the same.

She felt the wind as she flew, refreshing, not cold at all. Her *astral* body was a perfect body, unaffected by real world limitations unless she focused on them. Then she could interact with them. It was probably something like the way Aleksandra gave herself a form when she wanted, but Pam certainly couldn't do much more than touch things from the *astral*.

Below her, the Earth rose and expanded, the blotches on the black plain, shrubs and asphalt, coming closer. She was arriving at her destination already, arcing to a landing with steady precision and no shock whatsoever.

Her mind, her consciousness, was here, in the center of Nellis Air Force Base, five and a half feet above the ground, just as it would be in her physical flesh. She was standing, yes, standing, in the midst of a wide open area graded to perfect flatness, unblotched by any vegetation. The tarmac of the landing strip was to her right. To her left were three buildings, warehouses, low but long. Ahead was a complex, maybe twenty buildings, long and low ones closest, then higher, bulkier ones with smokestacks on top. The buildings were for the most part nondescript, functional, with large letters and numbers painted on the sides. Behind the ones that rose above the warehouses was the wall of the crater that had been dug to hide this very special base. At the base of Yucca Mountain.

Soldiers (airmen?) and civilians passed her by, talking among themselves the way coworkers do. Several men sat in mesh camp chairs, communing with the night. None of them saw her. They needed something solid for that.

She needed an atomic bomb.

She walked toward the nearest warehouse fronting the bigger buildings, until she remembered that she didn't have to walk. She could *fly*. She could sail along ten feet off the ground like a bird riding a thermal. She jumped up and she stayed up, able to go anywhere her mind could.

She *flew* right through the wall of the warehouse, through

the big numbers AF-27. Before her something like the Home Depot on HGH was revealed: long rows of crates, each nine feet square. Within each crate was an eight-foot cube of dark metal. They were all identical and there were a lot of them, and this was only one building. *But I don't dare* FLY *through those cubes,* she thought. *I forgot to find out if an* ASTRAL *is impervious to intense radiation.* It was a challenge, and she only had an hour before Coyote got here, so she got busy.

FRIDAY, JUNE 19, 2009 • 9:37 P.M.
PACIFIC DAYLIGHT TIME

10 Milky Way (Personifying Alchemy)

Coyote loped down the mountain. His desert had low, yellowish glows along the limbs of the cacti—the ancients' spirits, unmoving but living just the same. His desert had moonlight-gray glows around the rocks, earth magick—except when a rattler was coiled up underneath. Then the glow was crimson. Coyote and Rattler had hated each other from way back.

I know Great Spirit wrote his name in the bag of stars, so it's all part of a plan, but it's a plan I'm glad I don't have my name on. A jackrabbit broke into a scoot, off to his right. *Yeah, yeah, I kill, too. But I run 'em down. They see me coming, and sometimes I don't win. If I do win, it's over right there. I don't make 'em suffer for days.*

He saw a crimson rock. A low, red warning from the stone. Coyote leaned left and gave it a wide berth. He was mostly leaning left on this run, since his right foreleg was no good. There was a learning curve involved in running on three legs, but he had the hang of it now. It was just tiring for the one remaining foreleg. *Up* it came, down it came

and *up* it came, working with both of his two hind legs. . . .
I might be a little longer than an hour, he thought, brow
furrowed.

But he gave the ragged rhythm a pleasing chant.
Pamela, Pamela, Pamela, Pamela, Pamela.

FRIDAY, JUNE 19, 2009 • 9:37 P.M.
PACIFIC DAYLIGHT TIME

10 Milky Way (Personifying Alchemy)

Max stood watch over Pam's body for several minutes,
probing the cosmos for any signs of distress. It was point
man stuff again. Different darkness, same probing.

When he was satisfied she had passed beyond his ken in
safety, he turned away and made his way to the jumbled
boulders; there he leapt athletically onto the nearest one and
clambered up them to the highest spot he could find. Just this
small increase in height opened far more of the universe to
his view. The moon was still below the horizon, leaving the
sky pitch-black and highlighting every star. From long experience, he carried the general layout of the worlds in the sky
in his head, but he pulled out his iPhone and checked its current astronomical map against what he saw in the darkness.

Directly ahead of him, halfway above the horizon in the
southwest where Pam had gone, was the star Spica. High
above that, near the dome of the sky, was Arcturus. The
ancient Babylonians, the first to truly study the stars, called
Arcturus "the Lofty Patriarch" and Spica "the Virgin."
They saw a downward flow from Arcturus to Spica delivering the power of heaven. Knowledge of that particular flow
was one of Agrippa's secrets, imparted to his disciples,
which was why Max had pressed Coyote to bring them in to

the northeast of their goal. Anyone looking southwest, on this rock or beside Yucca Mountain, would see the same view, but from Max's point of view, those stars were above Yucca Mountain. An alchemist could use that.

In the flow between Spica and Arcturus tonight were the asteroids Irene and Flora, and the dwarf planet Haumea. Irene was "peace," Flora "body," and Haumea "hard truth." He read that as Pam enjoying her *astral* form, and maintaining it against all obstacles. For Coyote, the power of heaven would be an addition to his own power. For Pam, it could mean the difference between success and failure. Max held all those factors in his mind, merging them, melding them, to create a vision of what was possible—empowering that vision—and bringing it all down on Yucca Mountain like a hammer.

• • •

When he was spent, Max came back to himself, sitting on the rock—and found Rosa sitting quietly beside him. He nodded at her but said nothing, resting for a moment, letting the flow fill him up again, while desert wind fitfully riffled their hair. Finally, Max let out a deep breath and said, "This is killing me, Rosa."

"Not being there," answered Rosa softly.

"Exactly. I'm used to being the one who goes out there and wins or loses."

"You arranged for this. We would not be here without your generalship."

"Maybe."

"Certainly."

"Whatever. It still sucks just sitting here—no offense."

Rosa spoke with her usual placidity. "Max, you know I take no offense. I am interested in this astrology you use, with your handheld tablet. When I was a maiden, the planets stopped at Saturn—their power was more marked than it is now—and I have seen the addition of Uranus, of Neptune, and of Pluto. But you know so much more. What is this 'CDO' you spoke of?"

"It's actually pretty straightforward," he replied.

"Then I will certainly understand it."

He took another look at the sky. Everything there had drifted to the right, as the world revolved before the stars. "Well, as you say, for millennia there were seven factors in a chart—Sun and Moon, Mercury, Venus, Mars, Jupiter, and Saturn. With the Moon standing in for Earth, that was one Sun and six planets, and that's the way it always had been."

"Yes, Max. I know."

"Indulge me; I'm telling a story here," he said, warming to that familiar pleasure. "So after the entire history of the world to that point, in 1781 another planet appeared— Uranus. What everyone knew to be true—that Saturn patrolled the outer boundary of space—wasn't true anymore. Everyone had to recalibrate, expand, and work out a more accurate picture of the structure around them. Then just twenty years later, on the first night of 1801, Ceres appeared, followed by three other asteroids over the next six years. For thirty-eight years after that, things settled down again, but in 1845, a fifth asteroid appeared. In 1846, Neptune appeared, a whole new huge planet. In 1847, the sixth, seventh, and eighth asteroids were discovered, and there's been at least one and at most several thousand asteroids discovered every year ever since—so everyone stopped paying attention to them because it was too hard. Things solidified again till 1930; then Pluto appeared. It violated all the rules for planets, but once again everybody recalibrated, and by the time I was born, we had another stable system: nine planets. And some asteroids that didn't matter. Nine planets."

"Yes."

"And then, in 1992, something beyond Pluto appeared— and very soon thereafter, so did other things. From then to now, we've been finding even more things, a lot more things, some little and some pretty big. We got some context for Pluto and saw it was just one of those things, so now there are eight planets and a whole lot of other stuff.

"I've had the time and inclination to work on that stuff. What I tell you tonight is subject to change because we keep finding new things, but after seventeen years, here's what I see. The other stuff comes in five groups, with hundreds of members each.

"First come the CDOs—Central Disk Objects, with orbits between Jupiter and Neptune, in the outer reaches of the old solar system. They're all on the same plane, like the surface of a compact disc; thus the name. You know what a compact disc is, right?"

"Vaguely," Rosa said.

"Well, like a CD, they have an outer boundary; Central Disk Objects don't venture past the Plutinos. Astronomers call them 'Centaurs' but that's not their nature; they're normal members of society, not exceptional. Their element is Earth, and they speak to the common functions of common humans—the work we do on a daily basis. Cyllarus, the one I told Pam about, means 'pride in the work.'

"The Plutinos are a group of objects much like Pluto, which is now their leader instead of a planet. They orbit together like a larger asteroid belt, all at more or less the same distance—Pluto's distance—from the Sun. So they mark out the *edge* of what we were taught was the solar system, and the beginning of space *outside* the system—the place where things get weird. Their element is Water, and they speak to intense experiences—the *un*common experiences of common humans—the opposite of work. Simply put, Plutinos are all about our sex lives.

"Beyond the Plutinos, in an area where we didn't know anything existed, are the Cubewanos, in another, wider sort of 'asteroid' belt. The first one ever found was the first of these new 'things,' the one that began it all in 1992. It was given a provisional designation of 1992 QB_1 and somebody with a sense of humor named all the ones like it the 'Q-B-1-ohs.' The Cubewanos' element is Air, and they speak to the feeling that we're common humans out past our boundaries, so we need an all-powerful leader to take care of us. Cubewanos are tied up with religion, which we all feel—and no one can miss the rise of religion since 1992.

"However, out beyond the Cubewanos are the Scattered Disk Objects, or SDOs. They're like Central Disk Objects, staying on a plane, but they go out past the Plutinos, past the Cubewanos, and pretty much everything else—way out past, until each one is completely on his own. The farthest one we know about goes forty times farther than the Cubewanos, and there are bound to be a lot of SDOs we know nothing about because they're even farther away. Their element is Fire, and they speak to the idea that each and every one of us is a living spark of the Universe—that we're all part of the Universe—that we're all one. Thus, we can all learn to lead our own lives. This is where you and I live—the realm of Alchemy and drabardi. And because we can't count them, out beyond our most powerful instruments, there just might be an SDO for every man, woman, and child on earth."

"I doubt that," Rosa said.

"You and I will find out over time, I guess. And I look forward to it." He swept his hand across the sky. "So finally, in the midst of these four regions—the new solar system—the dwarf planets *are* their own leaders. Ceres, now the leader of the asteroids, is one, and Pluto, now leader of the Plutinos, is another. Makemake and Haumea orbit among the Cubewanos. Eris and Sedna and a new one that doesn't even have a name yet—2007 OR_{10}—orbit among the SDOs. Sedna, at the farthest reach of its orbit, is twenty-four times as far away as Pluto—not as far as an SDO can go, but Sedna is a planet, in a huge orbit around the Sun. So the new solar system is now twenty-four times as large as the one I was born with, and ninety-six times as large as yours.

"And last but not least, as we draw this little tour of the solar system to a close, we look inward again, to those scrubby asteroids people blew off a hundred and fifty years ago. There are hundreds of thousands of them now, and each one of them has a meaning, too. I'm pretty much alone in working all that territory, but once I learned those extra meanings, those nuances, I got an incredibly detailed picture to replace the one drawn from just seven factors. It's sort of high-def—if you know—"

"I know." Rosa sketched a slow series of concentric circles on his leg with her finger, apparently deep in thought. "What do the Plutinos tell you about Pamela, Max?"

He looked around, in the direction where Pam's body lay, but she was hidden by the dunes. "I don't need astrology to know Pam, Rosa."

"Coyote has made passes at her, and she is upset with you," said the witch.

"Coyote makes passes at every woman."

"And she is upset with you."

"Pam's a big girl. I hope it won't go anywhere, but it's up to her."

"And what would you feel if she did?"

"I would feel that she's a big girl."

"You are as detached as I am, Max."

"No. Not at all." His voice grew sharper. "And what's it to you?"

"Do not distress yourself, Max. I meant nothing."

"You'd probably convince me if I were still new at this, Rosa. But I know how you inhabit the word 'nothing' when you're *vanishing*. Everything about you conspires to make me believe 'nothing.' But I know your tricks."

"Well," she replied tranquily, "perhaps you do. We need not speak of it again."

"Actually, we do need to speak of it," Max said. "What's up with you?"

"Nothing."

"Wow," he said, "you *are* good." He put his hand on her arm. "Rosa, I do know you. You're putting the moves on me, in your own way. And now that I think of it, telling Pam to take control of openness . . ."

She smiled faintly, in no way coy. "It is obvious, is it not? I believe you should be with me."

"Instead of with Pam?"

"That would follow."

"Instead of you with Coyote?"

"That, too. Though Coyote would entertain the idea of a threesome."

"Good for him. I wouldn't."

"Then take me as I am, Max. You and I are the only ones who are Timeless. Coyote is primal; it is not the same thing. Time means nothing to him. And Pam, she's beautiful, yes, so bright and sunny. She is intelligent and she has real power, which you have developed as best you could, and which I have helped develop. But she is not Timeless."

"Yet."

"I have not read her, so I do not see her future, but the odds are against her."

"Because of your 'help'?" he asked, with an edge to his voice.

"Absolutely not. I would never seek to harm her," Rosa said. "But I would try to move her aside, if I read a response from you—and I do not believe you realize, or can realize yet, just how strong a bond our Timelessness is." He became more aware of her slim palm atop his thigh. "I cannot offer true passion, but I can offer knowledge and I can offer comprehension that Pamela cannot. You would like to be a simple point man, Max August, but you've become a general, leading a vast campaign. You cannot afford to think small. You need someone who sees the world unemotionally. I admit that I am not sunny, but I bring the moonlight of the Roma, and for all that, I remain a flesh-and-blood woman, appealing to look at, quite good at providing pleasure." She kissed him, and she *was* skilled. In the starlight on the sandstone above the sleeping desert, he went with it for a moment.

Then he spoke softly, his lips still close to hers. "I know what you're talking about, Rosa. I've had almost twenty-four years of it. Nothing to four hundred fifteen, but yes, I have a sense of you that no one else has. On that level, I do love you. But I love you as a great woman, a drabardi, and a *friend*, Rosa. On other levels, I love Pam. That's just the way it is."

He was not prepared for her reaction; she jerked away from him. Her face and her words were as placid as ever, but her voice had a timbre he had never heard before.

"I have only one thing to my name, Max—Time. I have nothing else. I need another who knows what my life is like." He started to speak but her hand quickly covered his mouth. "I love you," she said. "I only know love as a memory now, but I *know* it. If you were to love me I would learn its fullness again. I would feel what I would feel and know that *that* was love, for me. You must love me—it will save me from my void."

He took her hand away from his lips, gently but deliberately. "I'm sorry, Rosa. Love is not something I can do on demand."

"You love both Pamela and Valerie. You can love me."

"It doesn't work like that. You know it doesn't work like that."

She hung her head. "I *know*," she said. "All I do is *know*. That is my tragedy."

He tried to hug her again but she resisted. So they sat unspeaking as the wind blew past for what seemed like a very long time, but probably was no more than three minutes.

In the end, Rosa said, "What if Pamela cannot resist Coyote?"

Max said, "People have urges; sex is fun. But even if she did sleep with him, it wouldn't change how I feel about her, because I love who Pam is."

"Even if you don't have all of her?"

"That remains to be seen."

Rosa cocked her head at him. A look of interrogation came into her eyes. Then she slipped her slim hand into her card case and pulled a card at random. Even in the starlight, both could see it was the «Prince of Wands».

"You arranged this," she said slowly. "You arranged it *all*."

"I arranged the attack on the Necklace, and I needed cutouts," he said. "Beyond that—a night like this was bound to come sooner or later. Pam had to see someone like him—and I was bound to see you. Because for my part, I do understand what you and I share."

Rosa replaced her card in the deck. "You're as cold-blooded as I am, Max."

"No. That's what you don't understand, Rosa. It's not cold-blooded at all. It's burning me up inside." He brought his fist down on his thigh the way he'd brought down the hammer of stars. "But people like us have to lead our own lives."

10 Milky Way (Personifying Alchemy)

Peter Quince stood looking down at Rita Diamante's unmoving body—the end result of her encounter with the new Peter Quince. She was breathing, but otherwise, she was just a piece of meat. A piece of meat pulsing with energy, hot Latina energy, that was now his for the taking. They had put her into a deep trance, he and his master, so that he could feed on that energy. A few days earlier he would never have done this to her, but now, compassion was beneath him. He no longer cared about her as a sex partner, or a cat's-paw to investigate Jackson Tower. Just as he no longer hoped for dead Indians to save him. He had no need of being saved.

She will be a battery to draw upon, when you need even more power. You can never have too much power.

"If she ever finds out . . . She's as deadly as anyone I know."

She can't kill you now. Not with me beside you. So— would you like to explore the power she gives you?

"Very much, my lord!"

–o–

Aleksandra died seven times, each time more dazzling than the last. Her throat was marked and mottled, but when she'd had her fill, her flesh vanished and she returned to her red realm as the unsullied perfection she was.

I will always have a preference for inhabiting the female form. It is my natural state. But the night I killed Wolf Messing, I took his place.

In a city of telepaths, he had made certain to charm his chamber; no one knew what I'd done. I had only been in his room for ten minutes; the sky was still crimson in the west. So I rolled his corpulent form into the subconscious, ridding the room of it, then used the powers I'd mastered with the Gris to change my form. I became Wolf Messing—a man.

I went to my desk and sat down behind it, on my big butt. I pressed the first button on the intercom with my larger, thicker forefinger.

Svetlana entered. She looked tired, but ready to serve her master.

"Hello, Sveta," I said in a familiar voice, just the way I'd heard it all those years.

"Hello," she replied. There was nothing out of the ordinary here for her. So I got up from my chair, walked over to her, reveling in the floorboards creaking beneath my added weight. I took her by the shoulder, harshly, the way he did, and I kissed her hard. She kissed me back. Nothing out of the ordinary—for her.

For me, the first fruits of DOMINATION.

SATURDAY, JUNE 20, 2009 • 10:00 A.M.
MOSCOW SUMMER TIME

11 Lord (Owning All)

Lexi appeared in Moscow, in an alley just off Lubyanka Square. It was in the mid-fifties and raining, light the color of ashes, summer weather only a Russian could love.

Making certain she was alone and unobserved, she stood stock still for a moment, then sort of shrugged her shoulders, her flesh tingling, and let the movement ripple down her body. As it went, her body changed. When it finished, Lexi was gone, and there was Lex.

Lex swaggered into Nikol'skaya ulitsa, heading for a brothel he knew, and when he got there he ordered up twins.

FRIDAY, JUNE 19, 2009 • 10:39 P.M.
PACIFIC DAYLIGHT TIME

10 Milky Way (Personifying Alchemy)

Coyote loped into what he would always call Pakonapanti, and was no more disheartened than usual by what he saw. The Old World peoples looked at the New World and saw nothing. Only the New World peoples looked at the land and saw The World. Among the Old World peoples, the military was the worst, and among the military, the Air Force ruled. They didn't come here for the land at all, beyond their ability to flatten it; their eyes were fixed on the sky, like pompous Eagle.

Now where's Pammy?

In response, the lady herself came floating up through the roof of the fourth building on the right. *Hi, Coyote,* she *called. I felt you arrive.* He swung himself, a little gingerly, to the right, and scampered on over to where she was coming down to a landing.

As he reached her, he shape-shifted back to his human form, though remaining invisible to the rest of the world. His right arm was bent but he shook off Pam's instinctive attempt to check it. *It doesn't hurt; it's just a shape,* he lied. *Shape-shifting's much better than* ASTRAL.

Really? Could you have searched all these warehouses? Or even gotten into them?

You did that? What'd you find? he asked.

Nothing.

Oh.

Exactly. Either it's really well hidden or it's not here at all.

Phooey. Why would your Necklace tell Diana there was a bomb if there weren't one?

Just to freak her out. Which it did.

The guys trying to run the world have nothing better to do than play games? he demanded.

They were pissed at her. They wanted to teach—

He cut her off, throwing up his palms, wincing at the pain in his arm, but saying, *Stop, stop, stop. Alchemy makes you think too much. It's here, and if we can't find it, we'll get somebody to show it to us.*

If you think some trick—

I KNOW *some trick,* he said. *Come on.* He started jogging toward the nearest warehouse, and she followed along, gliding.

They went deep into the shadows beside the building. There, he shimmered and shifted into visibility, in the form of a full-dress three-star general.

Not four stars? Pam asked, inspecting the impeccable lines of his tailoring.

I'm not a show-off, Coyote answered. *No matter what everybody says.*

But as an officer, Pam said, pointing meaningfully at his right arm, *you'll have to salute everybody.*

Oh yeah, he said, and stood there for a moment with a scowl like a kid's. But then he brightened. He shimmered, and he became a pirate, the full Johnny Depp. His hair was long, dark, and curling, he had a pointed beard, and a bandolero rode diagonally over his ruffled shirt.

How do I look? he asked.

Like a refugee from Disneyland, Pam said.

Exactomundo, he said. *So here's the trick. I was gonna order inspections as the general, get things in an uproar, spook the people who know about the bomb—*

Why would any of them be here?

I *wouldn't be,* Coyote agreed.

No!

But there'll be some sort of defense. We just need to stir things up, get a reaction, and a swarthy brigand will do even better. That's where you come in, Miss Invisible. You watch for the weird stuff—any attention to anything that doesn't deserve it. He took her arm with his left hand, pulled her to him and kissed her. *For luck,* he said, as if it were the most innocent thing in the world.

Pam knew better. She said, *Well, good luck!*—Max's ritual before going into battle, Max and Pam's ritual now— and rose into the sky. This time, she realized the process looked a lot like Google Earth, but she could feel the night winds pass through her. And she could feel Coyote's kiss.

In about a minute, she reached a point where she could see the whole compound and still be as close to any action as possible. She favored the quadrant with the buildings, but kept alert for danger from the wide, graded plain. Coyote, just an ant now, was standing right where she'd left him. She waved. It didn't surprise her at all when the little ant waved back. He had Coyote eyes.

And now, he turned and raced, at a speed impressive even in miniature, to the front of the warehouse, skidding out into the streetlight illumination. Twenty feet away (one of Pam's finger-widths), two airmen, their uniforms clear, came to a confused halt on seeing him.

The pirate's head snapped back in a huge double-take. Then he turned and bolted back toward the shadows, at the speed of an agile man. As he vanished, the airmen raised the cry.

The pirate dropped it into some fifth gear, accelerating like a missile, swinging around the back of the warehouse and rocketing past the warehouse next door and the one after that. Mere moments after diving behind one warehouse he ran out from behind one sixty feet away. *"Arrr!"* he cried out in loud frustration.

Alerted, the two airmen swung around in time to see him run away, like an agile man, along the front of the buildings. The senior airman was on his com unit, shouting, "Intruders at Sector 44! At least two!"

The pirate's ears heard him clearly in the crisp desert air, so he swerved to disappear again, and once he did, he accelerated again, toward the big buildings, where the poohbahs slept.

Pam saw eight air police burst from the smallest building on her left. They ran in groups of two, fanning out into the compound. Their rifles caught random streetlight beams. Pam saw lights snap on in the biggest house and, oddly, in the third warehouse before her. She raised her hand, seeking Coyote's attention, even though she was about to *call* to him—

—when she saw one of the men in the lawn chairs jump up and kick his chair over in his haste. He began to run toward the second largest house, even though his right leg was stiff, causing him to hop. He hopped with a vengeance.

Pam dove toward him, soaring in an arc that brought her out just above and behind him. (Even though she knew he couldn't see her, she stayed in his blind spot.) *Coyote!* she *called.*

The pirate was about to try to break into the smallest of the big houses, noisily, when he heard her. He turned toward the front of the house and accelerated so quickly his feet went out from under him as he tried to make his turn, sending him skidding across the raked sand, ripping his pirate shirt—which he liked a lot. He scrambled back to his feet and ran like a rocket toward the *call*.

When he was halfway there, the hobbled airman and Pam burst into view ahead. In the instant, Coyote shimmered and went invisible. The airman snapped his head around but saw nothing and went on with his stiff-legged dash.

Coyote ran invisibly to intersect them, *calling, What?*

He took off without any contact. He's got to have a radio on him, and somebody contacted him when the air police were alerted.

Good work, Pammy.

Thank you, Coyote.

Be right back.

Coyote left her to run toward the warehouses fronting the big houses. His right arm was really beginning to feel all the wear and tear, but he ignored that to stop at the edge of the shadows. Two APs were visible, tense and visible, in the middle distance. He turned himself into the hobbled airman so he could jump out of the shadows, spot them, and jump back in. They started running toward him. Coyote ran toward the real hobbled airman.

He found him in the shadows beside the second largest house, checking a side door. Pam was nowhere in sight. The airman straightened up, his shoulders showing his relief at finding nothing amiss.

"Halt right there!" The APs had arrived.

The airman took advantage of the shadows and pulled his sidearm, fired and caught one AP in the chest, knocking him backward but not killing him, thanks to Kevlar. Still, the man was having trouble catching his breath and his partner was already firing back. The hobbled airman threw the side door open, fired again as he entered the house. The bullet snapped past the second AP's ear, punctuating his com report of "Man down!" and call for general assistance.

Coyote followed the airman inside, invisibly, and down a set of steps to a basement. The man ran to a cinderblock wall and reached as high as he could to push a certain block. It clicked and a section of the wall moved around, angling left, to reveal an opening eight feet by eight feet. Coyote saw Pam already looking out from inside, pointing at something in there. *This is it!* she *called* urgently.

The airman and Coyote both ran into the hidden room. There was a large crate, just the one, inside. The airman turned and pressed a more accessible button, causing the moving wall to return to its previous position. But before it could complete the maneuver, bullets from outside caught it low on the edge and it shuddered to a stop, still two feet from its goal. The airman took cover behind the bomb— what else would it be?—and started firing back. He emptied his magazine, then spun it out and snapped in another. But a shot from outside went into a wooden slat of the crate, ripping the wood and ricocheting off the metal underneath. A second tore a divot along the side of the man's head. Blood began spilling but the man grabbed the broken slat, yanking the splintered wood apart, opening the crate enough for him to yank more of the slat free, to reveal a small metal box on the side of the bomb. Shots from outside drove him to cover for a moment, but as soon as the shots stopped, he was back at it. He flipped open the box to reveal a panel of lights and buttons. He started punching numbers. Coyote said, "Hey!"

The man jumped a foot, jamming his shoulder into the broken wood, then yanking his arm as he spun/fell backward defensively. But there was nobody there. "Hey!" said Coyote again. Pam, silently watching, almost laughed at the airman's goggle-eyed amazement—which quickly hardened to defiance.

"Fuck you, then! This is for my wife!" the airman yelled

to the empty room. He turned back to the control panel and Coyote solidified to grab his arm. The man began whimpering in frustrated incomprehension, but it didn't affect his determination.

Pam threw herself outside through the partially open wall. What was taking the APs so long to get inside? Now there were three of them, the original and two new ones, conferring in low urgent tones. They didn't know there was a bomb in there; they thought they had their quarry boxed in, and it was simply a question of how best to get him out.

Pam came down next to them, got her phantom feet set, and *called* with all the magick she had in her, which was substantial due to the pace and adrenaline. *NUCLEAR BOMB!!!*

The AP farthest up the steps said, "There's something in there! He wouldn't choose to get in that box if there weren't something vital in there!"

His partner shouted, "Go! Go! Go!" and started forward, using the movable wall as cover, giving his two companions no choice but to slide into the movements they'd practiced so many times in simulation. The second air policeman dove past the opening to take up a position beside it, his back to the wall. Pam *flew* back inside to try her luck a second time, screaming at the hobbled man, *Stop! Stop! Stop!* He screamed to the universe, "I love you, Marianne!" The third AP got the ready sign from both of his compatriots and threw himself on his belly in the opening, firing to lay down cover. The other two came around their respective corners firing a spray of lead. In the first speedy second they each thought they saw two men inside, fighting, but there was only one when their bullets cut that man nearly in two.

Smoke filled the chamber as the APs at the door pivoted inside, probing for any other men in the corners, behind the crate. The man on his belly rolled back behind the open wall to regroup, then got to his feet and came in to join them. Pam was eyeballing her body, having seen the hail of bullets that went straight through it. "It still looks perfect to me," Coyote offered. The first AP in was eyeballing the panel behind the broken slats. "Holy Mother of God!" he shouted. "Bomb!" The third man felt a thrill run through him, not from the bomb but from somehow having known that. "Is it live?" he demanded.

"No," said the first man. "Launch sequence was never completed. But another twenty seconds—hold the phone!" He fired his assault rifle into the slats to either side of the broken ones, sending shards spinning. One caught the nearest AP in the cheek. The first man slung the rifle over his shoulder, grabbed the slats and yanked them outward, nails protesting, to give himself some extra room. Getting it, he thrust himself through the opening and began to type frantically on the panel.

"What?" asked the third man, but the second one hissed "Ssst!" with a sharp hand chop. Pam and Coyote both crowded forward to see, pressed tight together, craning.

The first man typed on, the *snik* of the keys a crescendo in the smoky silence.

And then his whole body relaxed.

"What?" asked the third man again, this time not to be denied.

"Our guy tried an immediate detonation, but it was already set to go off at 11:11. If I hadn't seen that we'd still have been history in . . . twelve minutes."

Pam was jumping up and down with excitement. *Max!* she *called. Max!*

I hear you, Pam!

The bomb's aborted! We're okay!

She broke the *call.* She'd done what she'd needed to. She realized she was right up against Coyote.

They came together like a wave and when they hit the

floor among the three APs the animal growls were coming from both of them. There was nothing physical to either one of them, but from their standpoint it was physical as all hell.

FRIDAY, JUNE 19, 2009 • 10:59 P.M.
PACIFIC DAYLIGHT TIME

10 Milky Way (Personifying Alchemy)

And then Pam thrust herself away, rolling to her side among the airmen who had no idea they were sharing the room with two *astrals. No,* she said, her voice muffled. *I won't!*

Pammy, Pammy, Pammy, Coyote crooned, reaching to pull her back. *You don't mean that.*

Yes, Coyote, she said. *I just don't want to go there. Don't hate me.*

But it was so GOOD . . .

She sighed. *I know. It was. It REALLY was. But I won't do it. SURE you will.*

No. I CAN'T do it to Max and me.

Max would understand. Sex is magick, magick's universal . . .

But the best magick is with him.

How do you know that? Try me and see.

No, Coyote. No. She sat up, becoming for the first time aware that the little cinderblock room was crawling with men and equipment now. It was pretty much standing room only; there were boots all through her. *Max might well understand, or claim to—the all-knowing alchemist. But he wouldn't like it. And tomorrow morning, I wouldn't like it, either.*

Pammy! he said. *I'm a GOD!*

And she was a woman, reaching back to touch his ephemeral hand. It felt warm and fuzzy, just like the real thing. Hers was warm, too. *You're sweet, at heart. And you're really, really hot. But I'm with Max.*

He's not THAT great.

Tell me again how you're his friend.

I AM his friend; that's why I can talk about him. He's just an alchemist; he's still figuring things out, and I already live here.

'Just an alchemist' is all I'LL ever be.

Pammy, you are SO much more . . .

As an alchemist or as a chick?

That stopped him. *Both?*

That's what I thought. Listen, Coyote, I am what I am. I WAS a young doctor. I LIKED my life, and I did GOOD, unraveling the mysteries of medicine, to help people. Then I met Max. He got me exploring, not inward like research, but outward like life. Now I can do MORE AND BETTER good, because of alchemy. I can do THIS, indicating her *astral* state, *because of alchemy.*

So you're sticking with him because he's your teacher, Coyote said.

Her gaze grew steely. *Listen, dipshit, I'm not a virgin, but neither am I a whore.*

He spread his hands, bobbed his head. *'Course not. I didn't mean—*

You talk about sex magick. I don't know how Totems see it, but it's two poles and the flow between. Well, it matters who the poles are. The flow between Max and me . . . it's . . .

Coyote screwed up his face, not saying what he was dying to say.

I know, she said, *he's got a wife out there somewhere. I know.*

I didn't say it.

We are headed toward the day that Valerie comes back. I know. And suddenly, her voice caught in her throat. *She— she'll never give up!—And she* SHOULDN'T! *Good for her!* Then came more tears. *And* HE *won't give up, either. And* HE *shouldn't! And so we're all just going there.*

Coyote put his one good arm around her, and she could tell that now it was only for comfort. She wanted comfort so she leaned against him.

You can't tell Max what I just said, she told him. *Promise me.*

What good's a promise from me worth? Coyote asked sourly.

Everything you feel like putting into it, she said simply.

All right, I promise. Max won't hear from me that he's a dick.

No! He couldn't leave her to die, and neither can I. It's just a terrible situation, but nobody's to blame—except Aleksandra.

A small robo-sensor used by bomb squads crawled through her ankle, and then through his. She asked, gently, *Isn't there a female Coyote Totem for you?*

No. I forgot to write my name in the stars, so Great Spirit made me, all by myself. I love to be reminded of it, by the way—particularly now—

I'm really sorry, Coyote. It would have been fun, but you're not my guy.

And thus, the moment passed.

Pam squared her shoulders. *Naturally, I promise I won't tell Max about any of this. I don't want to get you in trouble. Or me.*

Coyote's laugh was low in his throat; his spirits had already revived. *What happens somewhere near Vegas stays somewhere near Vegas? Don't worry, Pammy. It's all our little secret.*

What about Rosa? She can read me, and, I assume, you.

She doesn't care.

Really?

Really. It's all the same to her; she's funny that way. He shifted his broken arm, which lay between them. Pam looked down and yelped, *What the hell!?*

It's fine.

It's BROKEN OFF!

It's easier to move the rest of me without it. We're magick, Pammy—we're not physical!

I feel like I am. For God's sake let me fix that! I may not jump your bones but I like 'em to stay where they should be.

SATURDAY, JUNE 20, 2009 • 2:12 A.M.
EASTERN DAYLIGHT TIME

10 Milky Way (Personifying Alchemy)

Breckenridge and Hanrahan stood stunned in their command center.

"Nothing," Hanrahan said. "There was no blast."

"Malfunction?" demanded Breckenridge.

"No!"

"August?" Breckenridge said. "Probably, since you didn't see this coming. But where was our wizard?"

"To be fair, he wasn't told about the bomb," Hanrahan said.

"Finding August was part of his brief."

"This is a time for looking forward, not backward—isn't that what you always say, Renzo?"

"I say, this is what gets people *killed,* Dick. Get him on the line."

"Sure," Hanrahan said. He turned to the command module

and snapped one of eight red switches running down the right side of his table. Then he snapped the second and fourth in the row beside it; these were black. They were all circuit-breaker switches, heavy and hard to activate by hand; the old man thought buttons were just invitations to mistakes. When he contacted one or more of the others in the Nine, he wanted to know it.

Summoned at his end, Peter Quince walked into the high-def picture coming in on Channel Nine, the secure link just for Necklace members. He'd evidently been partying a little of a Friday night, being flushed, bright-eyed, and breathing heavily. But the rest of the Necklace knew they had to overlook the oddities of their wizards; wizards did that kind of thing. The test was whether they could function regardless. Quince looked at Hanrahan, with Breckenridge looming behind him, on the screen in his study and said, "Yes?" civilly enough. It was a start.

"Two minutes ago, we intended to set off a nuclear device at Yucca Mountain in Nevada," Hanrahan told him. "It did not explode. Find out why."

"Yes," Quince said again.

"Tell me what you're to do," Hanrahan demanded suspiciously.

Quince laughed, deep in his throat. "I'm to show you that I remember that you said to find out why your bomb didn't detonate, Mr. Hanrahan." He leaned forward, his face growing larger on the Wheeling screen. "This bomb was evidently one of those things you didn't tell me about. That might be my first answer."

Breckenridge himself leaned into the picture. "You might even be right, Quince, but I want better ones than that. Talk to me when you have them." He himself punched the button cutting the connection. Then he turned his back on the old man and began to think. *August. August with no Aleksandra to help out. This could be the most fun of all.*

Hanrahan, meantime, snapped two switches, and the third ones in the two rows. "Michael Salinan and Diana Herring!" he barked. "Bring them to Chicago!"

SATURDAY, JUNE 20, 2009 • 1:14 A.M.
CENTRAL DAYLIGHT TIME

10 Milky Way (Personifying Alchemy)

Well done.
"I couldn't have done it without you."
And the night is young.

SATURDAY, JUNE 20, 2009 • 3:17 A.M.
EASTERN DAYLIGHT TIME

10 Milky Way (Personifying Alchemy)

Michael Salinan opened his eyes. There was a gun in his face, the barrel so close as to be out of focus, and his start of surprise smacked his forehead against it.

"What the hell?!!" Michael shouted, only now thinking, *He could have shot me.* His head was back on his pillow and he kept it there.

"Take it easy, Mr. Salinan," came a voice from beyond the gun. The room was lit by the lights of Columbus. There was a woman beyond the man with the gun, in the shadows.

"You won't like how this turns out," Michael said. "I'm not the man you screw with."

"We know how it turns out. Now get up slow and put your clothes on."

"You have no idea—"

"Fourth Reich Commandos, Mr. Salinan. Fourth Reich Commandos."

Michael was stunned. Had he heard right? "FRC? But—"

"Don't play dumb. You've been a bad boy, and now you're going to tell Mr. Hanrahan all about it. Get up and get dressed, or we'll take you like you are. The jet's waiting and we're on the clock."

SATURDAY, JUNE 20, 2009 • 2:18 A.M.
CENTRAL DAYLIGHT TIME

10 Milky Way (Personifying Alchemy)

Diana Herring was walking Factoid, her little Cavalier King Charles Spaniel, along the lake. It was very late, but Chicago was hotter than Wickr at this hour, and humid—and she'd missed her dog and she needed someone, anyone, to be nice to her right now. She turned her problem over and over in her mind. There had been no report of a bomb blast. Either Max August had stopped a nuclear bomb on the fly, or there had never been a bomb in the first place. If Max August stopped the bomb, he had power nobody she knew could best. But what if there hadn't been any bomb? What if the whole thing was designed to see what would happen when Diana and Michael *thought* there was? Then they would be on very thin ice. Maybe it'd be better to tell Breckenridge she'd been approached and offer to be a triple-agent, leading August to a trap.

It was too consuming a topic. She paid no attention to the man and the woman strolling in her way until they were too close to her. Each of them took an arm and the man slapped a rag over her mouth. A van pulled to a stop beside them, the side door slid open—Diana was thinking she'd seen this scene a thousand times on TV as she drifted off to sleep. . . .

SATURDAY, JUNE 20, 2009 • 3:20 A.M.
EASTERN DAYLIGHT TIME

10 Milky Way (Personifying Alchemy)

In Wheeling, Hanrahan received the reports from Columbus and Chicago. He told Breckenridge, who said, "That's *one* thing that's gone right tonight." He brought his right fist down on the old man's console like a hammer. "Christ, Dick! Do I have to do everything myself?"

−o−

I ran Academgorodok for two years, and no one knew. They did think old Wolf had been working out, as his body grew stronger, healthier, but no, I just like a better body than the one he left me.

I ran the institute as he had run it, though with less rape. I didn't need to keep experiencing male sensations the way men do. What I did need was to refine my control over my illusion.

And when I no longer had to think about it, I began to create multiple illusions, where Wolf and Aleksandra would appear together, where Wolf and Aleksandra and his wife Nard and even others would appear together. I began to fill whole rooms with my power. I knew full well that Wolf was only a way station—that I was preparing myself for the day when I would come to this. As with Mika, I practiced and learned,

At the same time, I made full use of Wolf's networks, in the world of espionage and the world of show business, and found that my next enemy was Heinrich Cornelius Agrippa. He fought the Wolf, which meant he now fought me. The KGB was happy to keep track of him as best they could, but they did not challenge him. And neither did the Wolf.

But I would. I would track him and take the battle to him and destroy a true wizard. To become a diabola, I would have to DARE.

SATURDAY, JUNE 20, 2009 • 11:00 A.M.
EASTERN EUROPEAN SUMMER TIME

11 Sun (Owning All)

Lexi appeared in the Great Pyramid. This time she stayed a woman. In fact, she stayed six women. It was this posse that encountered Samantha Davies of Nelson, New Zealand. "Hey, we're going to slip down into the Queen's Chamber passage," one of her told the twenty-three-year-old, sandy-haired tourist. "Come with us!"

"I don't think that's legal," Sam said.

"C'mon, it'll be fun!" Lexi said.

"It's dark."

"What're you afraid of? There'll be seven of us. And look, Sarah has candles."

So Sam went with the group of girls, and when they were well and truly alone, Lexi killed her, then did things with the body that had been blasphemous when the pyramids were new.

10 Milky Way (Personifying Alchemy)

Pam fell silently back toward her body. It continued to lie quietly on the sands down there, eyes closed, calmly waiting.

She thought, *I'm not tied to Max. I could walk away if I had to. I'm not a whore.*

I stay because I want to—because life with Max means something. How much would it hurt us if I slept with Coyote? Max has risen above the average guy in a lot of ways.

But no. Before he was an Alchemist, he was a point man. And before that, he was a man.

No.

• • •

She settled into her body, and felt a sort of "click" as she locked there. She became aware of the soft sands underneath her arms and legs, the soft wind fluttering her hair, the hunger in her tummy.

She sat up, and looked down at herself.

She looked more real than her *astral* self, which was kind of a relief. It didn't seem like a good idea to spend too much time away from her flesh—look how well that worked out for Val. So she got to her feet, really enjoying the sensations of muscles moving, blood circulating, bones taking her weight. But the sensations of the *astral* were still echoing, and for one long minute she was able to stand in the night and savor everything at once.

Then she walked to where Max and Rosa were resting, side by side, on a rock. On seeing her, Max scrambled to his feet and came quickly down toward her. He took her in his arms as he asked her, "What took you so long, lady?" She liked it—his arms, his concern.

But then she lied, as she'd agreed.

"We had to make certain there was no backup plan to the backup plan," she said, her real voice in her real throat also making her happy. "We searched the base thoroughly. It's a big place."

"And you were too busy to *call*?" he asked, knowing he sounded like a mom.

"Well, I'm no expert in the *astral*. Maintaining myself there and *calling* here isn't so easy. Firing off one bulletin was all I could do."

"That's fine," he said. "I knew you'd do what you had to do. I was just getting a *little* uneasy, not hearing."

Scorpio Rose spoke in the night, from the heights. "How was Coyote, Pamela?"

"He was fine," Pam said.

"How's his arm?" Max asked.

"He was neglecting it. I stabilized it in the *astral* so he'd do better in whatever form he chose."

"You've come a long way this week, Pamela," said Scorpio Rose. "I applaud you."

Once again, Pam was grateful for the darkness, to hide the blush that would inevitably color her face.

But for the first time ever, it did not come.

10 Milky Way (Personifying Alchemy)

In the bunker, airmen and technicians were working fever-
ishly over the bomb, making certain it hadn't been damaged,
that it wasn't still a threat. Lights had been brought in to make
the bunker brighter than day. Members of the Security Forces
were pursuing Crime Scene Investigation. Guard dogs were
seeking any traces of those involved. Two different officers
were on secure lines, one to the Pentagon and the other to the
Atomic Energy Commission. The air police were directing
the guards at all the entrances to the air base. News vans were
just arriving from Vegas but they were being held at bay.

The bomb vanished.

10 Milky Way (Personifying Alchemy)

Quince staggered backward, almost blacking out, almost
putting a foot over the line which formed his sacred circle.
He stopped himself, and then smiling an unfocused smile
he *let* his foot cross the line, *let* himself stagger against the
wall and slide slowly to the floor, his feet sliding back into
the circle. He could feel its energy wall cutting through his
calves, but it was like a cat purring. He was like a cat purring. The Universe was . . .

Belia'al.

His secure phone rang. He focused; it was on the other side of the room. At least it wasn't the screen down in the study. He raised a hand and *pulled* it; it came flying to his palm.

"Quince," the wizard said. The world around him was just on the edge of his command. Just.

"Where'd you put it?" Hanrahan demanded.

The bomb. "Medicine Bow Mountains—" Quince slurred.

"What?"

"Medicine Bow Mountains. A meadow I know, high above Laramie. Safest place I know."

"I want precise directions. It belongs in the Fortress."

Shape up. "I can move it again."

"No. The location of the Fortress is still need to know."

He can't talk to you like that. "Excuse me if I'm wrong, Mr. Hanrahan, but I am one of the Nine, and keeping secrets from me does not work. Tell me what the other eight know and I'll be a full-fledged partner."

"All right, Quince, you *are* wrong. You're *not* a full-fledged partner. We know that, we make allowances. But you don't get to know everything until we reveal it. So never tell me to do anything. Just send me a topo of your bucolic picnic spot so my men can get out there by dawn."

Flatter. "I saved the bomb, Hanrahan!" **Flatter!** "I *don't* know half the rules, it seems, but I saved the fucking bomb! I deserve a little more than this constant hazing—" Quince seized up, a dark clutching hand on his heart—just on the edge. . . . He couldn't speak.

Hanrahan regarded him on the screen. Wizards were just weird. But he had done a lot in a little bit of time. "That's the way it is, Quince. This is the Necklace. You don't like it, leave."

The pressure inside Peter Quince eased up. But it was waiting, just beyond the border—waiting to hear what he'd say. So he said, "All right. I like it fine, Mr. Hanrahan. I like it enough to want to help it. But rules are rules. I get it."

"Do."

10 Milky Way (Personifying Alchemy)

Hanrahan clicked off the video bug in the wizard's supposed sanctum sanctorum with real respect for the man. He had done what needed doing, and done it without any hand-holding. He said as much to Renzo.

"That's what I picked him for. He's a butthead but he's quick on the uptake," Breckenridge answered, still fuming. "Now when will *you* have intel?"

"You've asked me that for sixty years—"

"Because I've never liked your answer."

"It comes when it comes, Renzo. Not a moment sooner, but not a moment later, either. Now, I've got to prepare for a session with our next newest members once they're brought in. I'm going to Chicago."

"Fine. Just get me some answers." Breckenridge had plenty of other things to do. He picked up the phone. By the time Hanrahan left with a nod, he was on his third call, lying with increasing attitude.

10 Milky Way (Personifying Alchemy)

Coyote jogged three-leggedly into camp. Only Max and Rosa were on hand to welcome him. Pam was sound asleep.

He was kinda bummed about Pam. But he'd get over it.

Day Six

11 Sun (Owning All)

Hanrahan arrived at Quince's house in Duluth just as the sun turned Lake Superior from black to gray. "Saturday," the old man thought. "Has that ever been a day off for me? Has there ever been *any* day off?"

He climbed out of his car and stretched his bones, hearing his shoulders crack, then walked purposefully to the middle of the front yard, took a handful of buckshot from his side pocket, and hurled it at the second-story window on the left side of the house. The buckshot clattered.

In a moment, Quince opened the window and leaned out. The old man had learned about a wizard's spells during his first four years in the Necklace; he could see the pale nimbus around Quince's body even if the sky was lightening. For his own part, he turned a flashlight on his face with one hand, and raised a finger of the other to his lips as a token of silence.

The two men regarded each other for a moment, in the freshness of gray dawn.

Then Quince turned from the window.

"Who is it, Pete?" Rita asked.

"Couldn't tell. I'll go see. You stay back."

Rita watched him go, and didn't really mind it. *Since he started playin' with that rock, he's changed. Not so much . . . "became" somebody else . . . as "added" somebody else.*

He was already full of himself, but now. Shit! And the sex?
Like a mechanical dynamo. I honestly can't tell if he likes
me at all when we're doin' it. It's like he's just watching.

She sat up, still tired from it, and leaned across to look in
the mirror over her dresser. She studied her face a lot, so
she knew she'd definitely lost a little weight—the face she
saw was tighter. And attractive in a sort of hectic way, like
Tyra Banks.

She thought about getting up and going downstairs. But
that might show too much equality to their visitor. And anyway, she was tired. *¡Mierda, would the gang laugh if they*
ever saw me get tired! She lay back and closed her eyes.

Downstairs, Quince opened the door for Hanrahan—
nodded and stepped back to offer entrance. The old man,
however, stayed where he was.

"I want a private talk," Hanrahan said, very softly.

"I gathered."

"Use your stuff and close Diamante out."

Quince inclined his head, his curiosity piqued. He looked
Hanrahan straight in the eye, then closed his own eyes and
touched between them with his third and fifth fingers. Hanrahan noted that it was an awkward gesture, one unlikely to
be formed by accident. Good spycraft.

Upstairs, Rita fell asleep.

Quince looked out the open door at Hanrahan, then nodded. Hanrahan came inside. Quince said, in a normal voice,
"We can talk anywhere now."

But Hanrahan shook his head and beckoned the wizard
to follow him. He led him through the dining room to the
kitchen. One wall of the kitchen was covered by three pantry
doors. The old man went straight to the left one and opened
it, to reveal a larder full of canned goods, many handmade.
Hanrahan reached to press a knot at the top of the doorjamb
and one by his right hip—good spycraft—and the larder slid
back into the wall, barely rumbling the cans and leaving a

space three feet wide, six feet deep. Quince went inside. Hanrahan was right behind him.

The pantry door closed. There were just the two of them in this coffin-shaped place, which, now that Hanrahan could take it in, was dingy with dusty cobwebs and a dead rat carcass.

"Mr. Hanrahan," Quince said, "you do not have to tell me anything. I understand. But I can still ask, how did you know this was here?"

"I put it here."

"That doesn't surprise me," said the wizard sourly.

"Would this?"

Hanrahan pushed his BlackBerry toward Quince's face and hit PLAY. On the small screen, Quince and Rita entered the sanctum through a door on the far side of the room; the camera recording it would be high on the inner wall, hidden in the landscape of the Great North Woods ringing dark Lac Seul. Quince closed the door, locked it, and made passes before it, saying in good-quality audio, even with the echoes of the wooden room, *"Jackson Tower kept this cupola as his sanctum sanctorum, completely insulated from electronic* and *from magickal surveillance. I've renewed and reinforced his spells because, despite my recommendation, chica, I don't plan to be monitored myself. And neither should you be, so I've made certain we won't be."* He turned. *"Moreover, Breckenridge and Hanrahan know far more than they were telling."*

"How could we have faith in them if that weren't true?" Rita asked.

"Exactly. They're our masters. So we have to learn their secrets in order to become masters ourselves."

Hanrahan clicked the playback off, almost casually, and looked into Quince's face. It was flushed with repressed emotion. Hanrahan had him.

"Quince, I knew about the sanctum in this house almost

before Stavros did, and he conceived it. *And* he *was* really good. But I made certain that my division had a legit operation that could only proceed if we had what I called 'spell-flatteners.' He made them for me, we used them on the operation, and then I had some of my people remake them. I don't have any wizards, but I have a few guys who know a few things. So I installed my mystic bugs throughout this house, except for this hidey hole. I'm the one man who can be sure that no one can see and hear us here. And I'm the one man who knows what Roland Stavros did in his sanctum when he thought no one was looking, what Jackson Tower did when he thought no one was looking, and what you do."

Quince's eyes flashed. "You bastard!" **Careful.** "You told me this was *my* house!" **Careful, I said! Do you want me to squeeze?**

"This is the wizard's house, Quince. He has to live here because of the power at the point of the lake, stored in the woods. He has to live here so I can watch over him. But wizards come and go. This is the Necklace."

Ask if he can see you after you've gone through your *stone*. "So now you kill me?" Quince said, and braced himself for an attack for disobedience within, and an attack for rebellion without. But neither came.

Instead, Hanrahan laughed—not a hearty laugh, but a laugh. "Believe me, Peter, if I killed everyone with a hidden agenda, I'd destroy not only the Necklace, I'd lay waste to the world. I just want you to know what I have on you."

"Why?"

"I want a secret alliance—just you and me."

Quince reacted as if someone had walked over his grave. *He doesn't know what happens beyond the* STONE. "A secret alliance?" he echoed, his pleasure evident. "You and me . . ."

"Yes. I had to wait to see if you measured up, and the events of this evening have shown me that you do."

"But if I say 'no,' *then* I die."

"This *is* a delicate negotiation." The old man was watching him narrowly, his free hand no longer free; it was holding a small device.

Quince ran his eyes up and down his visitor, calculating—much like Diana with Max the night before, if he'd only known it, and it would have been hard to say whether Diana's adrenaline had pumped harder. But like his fellow member of the Nine, Peter Quince understood self-preservation. "When you say 'secret,'" he said at last, "does that mean from Lawrence Breckenridge?"

"Especially him."

"He's your friend, isn't he?"

"Not relevant to this negotiation."

"But," said Quince, "even with your leverage, why would I want to cross the most powerful man in the world?" **Exactly**.

Hanrahan unbent, fractionally. "Because his power flows from mine. He knows what I tell him. And it obviously has to be *almost* everything. But I hold a little in reserve. You're not the only one who fears my files. But you're right; Renzo is *almost* unbelievably powerful. That's why it would take the two of us to get past him. He has gifts I don't, and you don't. He's a ruler." He smiled his evil smile. "But I run things."

"And you would give me access to your intel, in exchange for my wizardry and my extra set of eyes, in the face of Necklace vengeance?" Quince asked. "You think that's an equal trade?"

"Well, Renzo will kill us both if he finds out, and if he doesn't, we'll both rule the Necklace—but no, I don't think it's equal. I need you for one area where my intel's thin, and I offer you all the others. So you're gettin' the better of the deal. But the window on it's closing fast."

"And what's to keep me from killing you and freeing myself from your blackmail?"

"You can try. But my personal spell-flatteners, like Renzo's, are better than anything you've got."

That's what you think.

"And any idiot can see I'm worth far more to you alive," Hanrahan concluded.

"If I run to Breckenridge with this . . ."

"I'll know. You know I'll know. And then you'll be dead."

"So will you," Quince said, measuring it all out. "So why are you even asking? You've got that recording. You could make me do it."

"Like you said, I want your wizardry, and I know from my long years of experience that it works better when given freely."

"Long years, right. You won't live forever—not a threat, old man, just a fact. Why are you even bothering?"

"Because I joined the Necklace in 1953, and I recommended Renzo for the political link in '76—and when he became the Gemstone in '92, he ascended in his own mind and left me a rung below. Before I go, he's going to know a secret: he shouldn't have done that. I am not to be taken for granted." He waved a hand. "And once I go, *you* can have the Necklace with my blessing."

"If we survive," the wizard said.

"It's time for your answer, Quince."

Quince said frankly, "Well, I've been reading you this whole time, Hanrahan. It could be some elaborate loyalty test, but I don't think it is. I'll stake my life on that." He stuck out his hand. "I'm in."

We're in!

··

11 Sun (Owning All)

The other women in Eva Delia's cell were inured to the un-
pleasantries of life, but even they got sick of her incessant
singsong and complained to the warden. He didn't much
care at first, but the word "Koomari" reminded him of a recent case. He told his sergeant, who really wished he hadn't
added to his post–Friday night workload, but the sergeant
called the National Health an hour later, and the overnight
nurse who answered, a Jane Kimble, came to see the inmate as soon as she could, which was when her shift ended
at eight.

She recognized Eva Delia, who sat, completely unresponsive, save for, "Koomari. Koomari. Koomari. Koomari.
Koomari . . ." It had the slightest backbeat to it now.

Jane Kimble wondered if Eva Delia could have had
something to do with the clinic fire . . . and decided she
couldn't have. Eva Delia was harmless. And the more Jane
thought about it, the less she believed that Eva Delia had
meant to steal a book. She'd clearly just gone off her meds.
Jane told the police that Eva Delia was a familiar patient
who had never in the clinic's experience acted out before,
and asked that she be allowed to give her her meds. The
sergeant said he'd have to clear it, but Jane said it wasn't
right to keep Eva Delia in her present state, and he had a lot
of work to do, so he said go ahead. Jane dosed Eva Delia,
and after ten minutes, the inmate finally stopped her chant
and drifted off to a deep exhausted sleep.

The constable who'd arrested her, reached at home, told
the sergeant that she'd been cooperative, and Jane, fired with

the justness of her cause, took it upon herself to speak with the proprietor at Rusterman's when his store opened at nine thirty. He examined the stolen book carefully and had to admit that it had sustained no damage in the mêlée. By eleven A.M., everyone concerned felt that Eva Delia could be released if she would promise to take her meds religiously and stay in close touch with the clinic.

And so, as the bells of St. George's struck noon, Jane escorted a groggy and subdued Eva Delia into the gray rain of summer. They walked the flat, shining streets back to Eva Delia's flat on Greek Street where, standing in front of the spread-eagled sex doll in the shop called Shop, Jane bid Eva Delia good-bye, and good luck.

"Aren't you . . . coming up?" Eva Delia asked, still singsonging it.

"It's important that you do it," Jane said. "It's *your* flat, Eva Delia. It belongs to you. Just come see me tomorrow, all right?"

"Okay," Eva Delia said. "Okay, okay, okay." She gave way to her impulse and hugged Jane, who hugged her back. Then, with slow but rhythmic steps, Eva Delia went on inside.

When she got up to her single room, where her window looked out on the bricks of the building next door, she threw herself onto the bed and began to cry, great, wracking bursts of sorrow that went on and on. The other residents on Greek Street let her alone, even those who liked Eva Delia; they had their own problems.

Except this wasn't Eva Delia.

Eva Delia was gone, killed off by Lexi. What remained inside this body was the Voice and the Clown.

11 Sun (Owning All)

Max stood alone on the peak and watched the sun come up over the eastern plains. It was his favorite moment of the day, as he had aligned himself very early on with the golden energies of the Egyptian dawn-god Harmakhis, back in 1981. This particular day of the year was Midsummer, the day with the most sunlight. At the same time, it was the Mayan calendar's Owning All—taking charge of our true nature. There were good energies all around this day—as Max stood alone on the peak.

The growing sunlight on the horizon opened a day when the world would be very large. To Max, the world was large at all times, but today the energies added even to that. Great things would happen before the next dawn. His alchemist's heart sang with it.

But he didn't know where his love life stood, and that threw a cloud over everything.

11 Sun (Owning All)

Peter Quince ran through the forest behind his house, leaping and prancing in a victory lap, laughing maniacally. With his stocky build, he was not a natural runner, but he had to get out here and do what he could to shove it in those old spirits' faces. They'd had their chance but they'd refused to help him; they had to know what that had wrought.

"It was hard to sound rational with Hanrahan," Quince said to himself.

"But being too bent would have taxed the old man's faith in you," Quince said to himself.

"I didn't ask what you wanted."

"Initiative has its place, Peter Quince. You'll learn."

He looked ahead, to the crossroads. They were all up there, clustered together, waiting for him with disapproving scowls like maiden aunts. They were no longer immaterial to his eyes; they seemed full flesh-and-blood beings, because *his* power had been expanded. There was the Dakota shaman, small and dry like an old apple. There was a fat old witch, and a cadaverous man with slicked hair parted down the middle, accompanied by twin ectoplasmic clouds. There was a thing that was half man and half wolf, insane from the dichotomy. The forest was on fire.

They all disapproved of Quince now, and they feared him. As well they should. He laughed at them, a looping laugh for those old failures, and his laughter echoed through their forest. They were welcome to it; he didn't need it any longer.

He had Belia'al—or—he had Quince. It was all the same.

SATURDAY, JUNE 20, 2009 • 8:03 A.M.
CENTRAL DAYLIGHT TIME

11 Sun (Owning All)

When Hanrahan arrived at the interrogation center, Chicago was like a steambath. He stepped from his car into a light mist, even as bright morning sunlight blasted his eyes. But he never felt discomfort, at least not for very long. Weather was irrelevant and his plan was working. This would work, too.

He was in an older part of town, down by the docks. The weather sent waves crashing up against the rotting piers fronting a row of long-abandoned warehouses. The north and south ends of the area were cut by high mesh fences topped with razor wire, running across the asphalt from the warehouses to the lake. From time to time, some entrepreneur tried to buy the whole area with an eye toward gentrification, but the owner, a company in Delaware, always refused to sell. And so, the area sat unmolested, unconnected to the vibrant city around it, as it had since Hanrahan had bought it for the Necklace in late '54. It was one of his homes away from home. He might be based in Wheeling but an Intelligence man went anywhere and everywhere.

He loved the crunch of cracked asphalt, its tarred repairs already slightly gummy, and the scent of hot rain. This was the way it used to be, before he had to add wizardry to his worldview. This was *real*. He let himself into the third warehouse on the left, whose interior was as derelict as the exterior, but once he'd locked the outer door behind him, he opened a secure inner door and entered a modern, air-conditioned corridor. Two guards—the man and woman who had taken Salinan—were waiting for him.

"How are they doing, Barry?" Hanrahan asked the man. Barry shrugged.

"Neither one has more than a headache, sir, but they're no happier than you'd expect."

"They're about to forget happy altogether. Where's Salinan?"

Barry pointed down the hall. "Second room. Herring's in the third."

"Thank you, Barry. Thank you, Martina. Be ready if I need you."

Hanrahan walked down the hall, the sound of his foot-steps deadened by the plush carpet. What the hell was the point of that? He entered the indicated room—unadorned except for a metal table bolted to the floor against one wall, two metal chairs, also bolted, in the center of the room, and two metal U-bars in the floor. The chair that faced the door held Michael Salinan, both wrists cuffed to the U-bars.

"Hanrahan!" Michael shouted savagely, straining forward. "This is bullshit! Get me out of here *now!*"

Hanrahan went and sat in the other chair, the one that faced the prisoner. "Michael, you know you wouldn't be here if you weren't in serious trouble. Somebody sold us out on the Yucca Mountain project."

"I didn't even know about it!" Salinan shouted.

"Until you did. Then somebody—we think it was the Code Red, August—went down there and saved southern Nevada. Where you were. Don't shout at me."

"No no no," said Michael truculently, but lowering his tone, "I was back in Columbus long before the bomb was scheduled to go off; you could nuke the entire West Coast for all I care. But you're supposed to know everything, so *you know* there is no reason on God's green earth why I would betray the Necklace."

"Somehow, Michael, I suspect that you didn't take very kindly to learning we were onto you and Diana—that we could have blown you to pieces as easily as that." He snapped his fingers.

"I won't deny it," Michael said. "Of course I was pissed. But that's for us to work out among ourselves. We're the Nine. We're a team. I'm a team player. *You know that!*"

"Don't you preach a scorched earth policy when it comes to payback?"

"That's politics, goddammit! The Necklace is business!"

"So then what about the mysterious transmission yester-day afternoon?"

"I don't know what you're talking about."

"Michael, if you know so much about what I know, then you know that I'm going to know everything I want to know before we're done. I wouldn't care if you were the Gemstone himself; I am going to make you talk. Do it now and save yourself a lot of trouble. That's my advice as one of the Nine to another. Talk now."

"I am talking now, Dick. I am talking right now and I am telling you I don't know anything about a Yucca Mountain leak or a transmission. I do not. If you torture me, I may tell you I did to get you to stop, but I swear before God right now I did not betray us."

"I'm not going to torture you, Michael. Torture is unreliable, as you say. *You* will be blissed out of your skull. You will not only tell me everything, you will be begging to tell more. The problem is, these drugs have bad long-term effects."

"I don't know anything, I swear to God!"

"Then you're saying it was Diana."

"Diana wouldn't do it any more than I would. We're just a couple of people who wanted to party for a week. Everything in both our shops was set up and running smoothly. You've had no glitches, have you? We wanted to get laid. Who doesn't want to get laid? That's all we did."

The U-bars pivoted sideways, pulling the prisoner's wrists to the ground, and one-inch metal rods rose up from the openings the U-bars had been covering. The rods rose as high as the prisoner's forearms and stopped. Half-inch needles shot out from the top, like rattlesnake fangs, and drove into the prisoner's forearms. Salinan snarled.

"I'll be back," Hanrahan said.

11 Sun (Owning All)

Diana was frazzled by being left alone for so long, left to ponder her own situation and what Michael might be saying next door. She trusted him, he was hard as a nut, but there was no telling what Hanrahan was doing to him. She'd seen the video of waterboardings, and the unaired photos from Abu Ghraib. She didn't think she'd be able to withstand that for very long, so she had to put a stop to it. And meanwhile, her bladder was killing her.

Finally, finally, the old man opened her door.

"Dick," she said right out of the gate, "you and I have worked together on the journalism project for three years. You've seen me at my best and at my worst, but you've seen me. I'm not some data on a screen for you. You know me. And I swear to God that I have done nothing wrong."

Whereas Michael was used to lying to people's faces, Diana was used to lying to millions over the air. Hanrahan absolutely understood that she could fake sincerity with the best of them, but even so, he simply could not read her as well as he could Michael.

"Nothing?" he said sarcastically. "What about the transmission?"

"What transmission?"

He just looked at her, waiting.

"I don't know anything about any transmission that you'd be worried about!" she said. "I run a transmission empire, remember, but I haven't done anything to deserve this. Wait! Is this about the unauthorized access to the data bank? It had to be unauthorized because we didn't want you to know where we were, but you can see it was only to check on a guy. I am a girl. I was at a festival. That can't be worth this."

"I'm talking about the encrypted transmission Thursday afternoon."

"I don't know." She sounded baffled.

"And then there's tipping off Max August to the bomb."

"How the hell would I know Max August? And why would I tip anybody off? I like the Necklace; I'm not going to do anything to fuck it up. And you wouldn't be asking me if you had any information, or any feeling, that I would. So why are we even doing this?"

"Because it was either you or it was Michael, Diana. That's just a fact. And you both are extremely convincing, here at the start of your day. So I'll have to go to Plan B, which will hurt you for the rest of your life—and if you're truly innocent, that might be a long time, yet. So as your partner of the journalism project, and not as the man who will have to carry this out, I really think you're better off talking before I start."

"I—" the polished professional choked up; this sure looked like an honest moment, "I honestly don't know anything."

"Then you say it was Michael."

"No! That doesn't make any sense, either. It wasn't either one of us. You're looking in the wrong place."

The U-bars rolled over and the needles came up.

11 Sun (Owning All)

"Well, podner," drawled Coyote, as he and Rosa stood with Max and Pam beside their ATVs, outside the border of Area 51, "I guess it's time we were moseyin' on up the trail." The sun was still low in the morning sky and the day was just turning hot, but the vista around them was fanciful and it went on for miles. They'd all caught a few hours of sleep, eventually.

"Stick around," said Max; nothing in his face revealed his innermost thoughts. "Come back to Wickr. The big party is tonight; they burn the Sun."

"Nooo," said Coyote. "I think I've done all I can do here, at least on this go-round." His gaze swept over Pam and as soon as his left eye was invisible to Max, it shimmered and became a wink, then a wide-open happy eye, then the wink, then the happy eye. It was like a desert motel sign, big and brassy and flashing—and it was all in that one eye, just for her. His other eye, the one Max could see, registered an unchanging friendly regard the whole time.

"I apologize for not reading your cards as I promised, Pamela," said Scorpio Rose, "but I, too, have said all I have to say in this encounter." She was standing to Coyote's right, before Max, so she couldn't see Coyote's crazy eye, either.

"I was looking forward to it, Rosa," Pam said.

"It is best that I do not know you yet. I might have an unintended effect on your future. But we will meet again." Rosa's gaze moved placidly onto Max. "And you will be in my thoughts, Max, as our futures unfold." She took the image in her mind of «The Star», the naked maiden open to wisdom, and projected it from between her brows over the man before her. She had sworn not to magick Pamela, but hadn't said anything about Max.

He smiled back. "You're always in mine, Rosa." Was that smile a part of him or was that the spell? She couldn't tell—a true emotion or a false one, all the same to her. Her eternal problem.

"Well," Max said to his guests, "if you've had enough of us, I can't blame you. Which way are you headed? I'll set up a spell to keep you invisible the rest of the day."

Coyote said cheerfully, "So Rosa and I could, you know, in the middle of everything at high noon?"

"Be my guests," Max said. "Meanwhile, it's been a real pleasure, guys. Fun, and we definitely owe you one."

"I don't think that's true," Coyote said. "You gave us the bomb."

"Yeah, but I got the Necklace, and that's even bigger."

"Not if you're living in Las Vegas."

"That would seem to be true, but the good citizens of Vegas, and the bad ones, are being shaped by the Necklace every day. They just don't notice."

"Well, they would have noticed a bomb, that's for sure," Coyote said.

So Max gave Coyote a bro-hug, and Rosa a warm hug— and Pam gave Rosa a warm hug and got a long hug from Coyote. Then Coyote and Rosa climbed onto one of the ATVs, she still taking the driver's seat, and with Coyote's final jaunty wave of his unbroken arm, the oddest of odd couples rumbled away along the ridge into the desert vista.

"Fun folks, huh?" Max said to Pam, who was watching them go.

"Fun, yeah," she answered.

"And tonight we get our own fun, all by ourselves, just like the doctor ordered. It's the Sun Burn at Midsummer, for fifty thousand maniacs, including you and me."

She smiled. "I could use a party like that. I am more than ready to dance my ass off."

"There's an ass for that."

They were chuckling together as they took their seats on the remaining ATV, and with Pam nestling her head against his shoulder, they went their way. "What time's Midsummer?" Pam asked her wizard.

"Ten forty-six P.M."

"Lotsa time, then. We could even, you know, in the middle of everything at high noon," she murmured.

"Or at the first nice place we come to, away from here," he said, and gunned their ATV.

SATURDAY, JUNE 20, 2009 • 7:02 A.M.
PACIFIC DAYLIGHT TIME

11 Sun (Owning All)

Forty-five minutes later, Max and Pam were strolling naked in the hot morning sun, just because it felt good. They were five miles from the military, beside a trickling brook sliding over colored stones, and they were invisible. The battle was over with. So after they finished getting reacquainted, they donned nothing more than their boots and went for a walk to the top of a small ridge, savoring the crisp heat and cool breeze on bare flesh.

"Just so you know," Pam said, completely relaxed, "I did not sleep with Coyote."

He squeezed her hand. "I'm glad to hear it," he said, his tone reinforcing his words. "And just so *you* know, I didn't sleep with Rosa."

"Rosa?" Pam echoed.

"Yeah?"

"Why would you sleep with Rosa?"

"I didn't."

"Rosa has no sex appeal."

Max thought, *You don't know all her levels,* but said, "Right."

"But why would she think you would? I mean . . . *Rosa.*"

He spread his arms. "What woman wouldn't harbor hopes, once she beheld this body?"

Abruptly, she laughed.

"What?" he asked.

"I just thought—Coyote and Rosa—they can seduce anybody, you told me." She took his hand again. "But they couldn't seduce us. That's a hell of a testimonial to something, I'd say."

"We should have medals," he agreed. "But where would we pin them?"

–o–

In 1974, I had gotten everything I needed out of being Wolf Messing, so I had the old man "die." People certainly do try to live on after death, just like Val, so many in our shadow world did not believe he was truly gone, and I was free to bring him back afterward if I wanted. Agrippa thought Wolf was alive, right up until the end. But it left me free to take on other identities and live other lives, away from Academgorodok.

As I began to travel the world in the flesh, I could always FLY back to Moscow to read the KGB reports. I kept current with Agrippa's whereabouts over the years, and was often— but not always—able to comprehend what he was about. Early in 1976, he sought out an unknown young singer called Purina Dog Ciao. This was not unusual for him; he was addicted to popular culture to entertain his Timelessness. That summer, the singer, back to her birth name of Valerie Drake, had her first hit song. Over the next two years, Agrippa built her into a major act, culminating in a New Year's Eve 1978 appearance that was determined to be "legendary." The year of 1979 they were inseparable . . . until May, when he left her side for the first time in three years, to pursue what could only have been a wizard's quest.

There were no home computers as yet, so he went to NASA three times, and the KGB reported to Moscow that he'd shown an interest in a planetary alignment occurring on the final day of 1980, the following year.

It was four months before he finished his work and went back to the management of Val's career. Now I began to notice an emphasis on personal appearances by her at radio stations. Most of those transpired at stations owned by the Northcliff Corporation. So in November, I became Madeleine Riggs, businesswoman, and went to New York to assume my duties as president of an investment service, Atlantic Coast Counsel, which Wolf had run as a front since 1962. Through careful maneuvering, I put ACC into Northcliff's view, and in October of 1980, after more dithering than I'd have liked, they acquired us. I became corporate liaison to their holdings.

I intended to meet with "Mr. Cornelius" on Northcliff's behalf, but before I could, he made a sudden addition to Val's touring schedule. All this time, that fateful last day of 1980 had been open, but in mid-December, he booked her into San Francisco and arranged an interview with a disc jockey named Barnaby Wilde on KQBU. I took the next flight to Frisco and got to know that deejay—Max August. Soon enough I learned that Max had a lion talisman which both Agrippa and I had wanted for a long time—a talisman that could forestall, or insure, what we both now knew could transpire on New Year's Eve.

I thought Max was a pawn in Agrippa's game—that Agrippa was the only one who mattered. It was my first real mistake, and I PAID.

SATURDAY, JUNE 20, 2009 • 4:00 P.M.
SOUTH AFRICA SUMMER TIME

11 Sun (Owning All)

Lex appeared in Johannesburg. He walked across Nelson Mandela Square and on down Albertyn to Wierda Road, approaching an anonymous gray house standing by itself in the midst of a dense jacaranda grove. He rang the bell.

"I offer myself to Mistress Ginger," he said humbly when the bell was answered. "I've been a bad boy and I need to be punished."

"Come in, slave!" said the woman in black in the doorway. "On your hands and knees."

SATURDAY, JUNE 20, 2009 • 6:32 P.M.
BRITISH SUMMER TIME

11 Lord (Owning All)

Around dinner time, the Voice's stomach pulled her from her drug-dull thoughts. She got up, went to the kitchen, and made herself a large pot of tea, to go with a tin of Spaghetti Hoops. When everything was hot, she took her biggest knife from its drawer, and sat at her uneven table in her silent room with its view of nothing. She ate—and waited for Lexi to come.

With each forkful of pasta, she tried to see how long a line she could make with her thoughts, the way the books kept their thoughts in check. The meds were working against it, but still . . .

Eva Delia was gone. That left the Voice and the Clown, and the Voice was far stronger. The Voice had no interest in staggering and puking. The Voice was free to be herself for the first time in a long time. The Voice was free; the Voice was "Vee."

Vee ran this mind now. The Clown was there; Vee didn't have things all to herself. But Vee was the one who lived in the room, who picked up the knife and began to dance in front of her sightless window, weaving the blade in the air. It felt especially good to dance in the window. It meant something to Vee. Somewhere, sometime, she had known a man who danced in a window.

Lexi would be here soon. Unless she'd forgotten a night, this was a night of Good Lexi, so sorry for Bad Lexi. But it really didn't matter which night it was, because Vee had a knife.

"Come on, Lexi," Vee sang in a strengthening voice. "Come to *meeeeeeee*." She was new to this freedom; weakened, tentative, and still drugged. But there was nothing weak or tentative about Vee's vengeance.

SATURDAY, JUNE 20, 2009 • 11:22 A.M.
PACIFIC DAYLIGHT TIME

11 Sun (Owning All)

Max and Pam, dressed again, were making good time over the uneven desert plain when they spotted a dust cloud which swiftly grew closer and larger. The wind began to gust and they knew they were in for it, so they pulled to a stop in a low-lying wash and Max threw a gravity field over them for added protection.

"We'll be here for a while, looks like," Max said. "What have we got to eat?"

Pam checked her bag. "Granola bars and Gatorade."

"Yum."

They sat at the bottom of the wash and ate, watching the beige clouds of alkali dust scud across the gravity field above their heads. It was not too bad in the shade.

"If it was raining anywhere in the area," Pam said, "the bottom of a wash is the last place we'd want to be."

"I concur, Doctor," Max agreed. "But right now it's heaven."

"Heaven. Yeah." She watched the gravity field, held in place by simple alchemical skill. She was almost ready to do that.

"Granola bars and Gatorade . . . ," Max said slowly.

"Yeah?"

"Hang on a minute." He sat, his eyes looking far, far into the distance, his jaw clenching as his thoughts connected what he saw. He cocked his head just slightly, getting a better view of something. His lip curled.

Pam watched him with fascination and with love. This was the Max no one else knew—the young wizard, the man on the road to the heights Agrippa reached. He looked like an ordinary man (okay, maybe better-looking), but he did not live in the ordinary world. That world was just part of his Universe. And when his lip curled, she saw what he had learned in that world, before he became a wizard. She saw the hunter.

He turned to her. "Granola bars and Gatorade. Out here, they go together, but they wouldn't be your first thought at home. They only make sense in context." He pulled his iPhone and started running his fingers over it. "I was looking for clues in Dave's lists, and I saw that many girls' names are asteroid names. What I didn't see was two names together." He began to scan the list on screen. "Somewhere in the UK, there was an Eva Something. . . ." And then he had it.

"Eva Delia Kerr, born Thursday 31 October 1991, Cardiff, Wales."

Pam held her face together. "That's Val?" she asked, and not even Scorpio Rose could have shown less emotion.

"It could be. Asteroid 164-Eva. Asteroid 395-Delia. Oh *fuck!*"

"What?"

"It's an *anagram!*"

Eva Delia Kerr
Valerie Drake

They stared at each other as the dust scudded above. Max was the first to speak. "I am so stupid."

"Nonsense. It was a needle in a haystack, and you found it in a week. A very busy week," Pam said. "Just—do what you've got to do now, Max."

Instead, he leaned forward and kissed her, a long kiss, and not of good-bye. It was an affirmation.

Then he got up and went out through the gravity screen.

Pam told herself, *I wanted him to find her. I wanted him to find her.*

But not yet!

11 Sun (Owning All)

The northern tip of Scotland is two land masses which have come together. The seam between them is obvious, and nowhere more so than where it has become a very long and very straight lake—Loch Ness.

There is one inlet on this long, straight lake. Above the inlet lie the ruins of Castle Urquhart. It is said that when the castle yet stood, there was a secret passageway leading down to a pool which connected to the lake through an underground tunnel—and the monster lived in that pool.

But now the area's inhabitants clustered toward the village of Drumnadrochit, two miles inland. The older houses here were made of stone, proof against the winter's chill, cooling on the hottest summer days, and standing unchanged for centuries. In a glen a mile from the A831 stood a small stone home, exquisitely made, with ancient trees on all sides that looked like they'd been designed to frame the house, instead of the other way around.

Lying in a lawn chair beneath the largest tree, sipping iced coffee and watching the birds soar among the shafts of sunlight in the forest cathedral, was a woman. She was not at all a Scot, her skin darker than theirs, more like a Spaniard, with a mane of hair the color of espresso. A scar ran across her left eye. People called her Hoodoo.

All at once she forgot about the birds and sat up, thinking, *Max! What a nice surprise.*

As always, she was amused by his inability to project his body along with his mind, but his *call* was distinctive for all that. He said, *Hoodoo, I need you to find, and if need be protect, a young woman named Eva Delia Kerr. She's seventeen years old, last reported in a Cambridge halfway house called Yellow Gables, but that was a year and a half ago.*

(Max, standing in the desert dust storm, fingers to his temples as much to shield his eyes as anything, realized: Right when I met Pam!)

He went on. *She was a mental patient. She could be anywhere now—but if she's in the UK, you have to track her down.*

Hoodoo replied, *I'm in the north of Scotland, Max—a long and circuitous way from Cambridge.*

I know. But I searched for people I trust in the UK, and you're the only one there now.

Then I'll do it, of course. Just understand that it won't be easy. Besides the travel issues, we're completely past the Saturday workday, so NOTHING *is open. You should have asked me on a Tuesday.* Hoodoo paused. *And when you say "protect her"—you know my alchemy is limited.*

What I know is, you'll do all you can do, and you can do a hell of a lot.

Right, she responded. *Then I'll get started at once.*

Thanks, Hoodoo. The moment you get something concrete, I'll be on a plane. And I will owe you a major debt— anything you want that I can do.

Don't write checks your ass can't cash, Max.

Believe me, my ass will cash this one if you pull it off.

Don't you have a girlfriend now?

Yes, I do. So my actual ass, I cannot do, he said. *But I'll make it up to you.*

I'll get right on it. The case, not the ass.

Thank you, Hoodoo. Forget about my ass.

Never, Max.

....

11 Sun (Owning All)

Max came back inside the gravity field, dust spilling from him.

"Now we wait," he told Pam.

"Are you going to England?"

"If so, you'll go with me. But Hoodoo has to find her first."

"Who's Hoodoo?"

"A woman I met in Argentina, in 1996. She—" He stopped because Pam had raised her hand in a "stop" sign.

"You know what, Max? I don't really care," she said. "It is what it is. But I won't be going with you when you go."

"Sure you will."

"No. I've thought about this. You need to have total freedom when you find Val. You can't do it right if I'm there."

"You're presupposing my decision."

"No, just letting you make the right decision. I'm betting that's 'come back to me.' But if it isn't—dammit, I want you, Max! But she has first claim, and she deserves a fair shot. You deserve that with her. It has to be that way. But then I want you to decide for yourself that you love me more than her."

He came toward her and took her in his arms. She turned her head but he ducked his own so his lips still met hers. At first she was unresponsive, but then she couldn't hold out. This was their fate, and it had always been their fate. And with that thought in mind, she returned his kiss with all her being, and they stood there for a very long time.

Then Max took a step back, still holding her arms. He wanted to see her face.

"You and I are still going to Wickr for the party at the Burn," he said.

"And *we* are going to dance your ass off!" Pam responded.

Then he had to explain why he laughed.

SATURDAY, JUNE 20, 2009 • 8:11 P.M.
BRITISH SUMMER TIME

11 Sun (Owning All)

Near to Hoodoo's little stone house was the quarry from which the stones had come. It was a long, narrow defile, paralleling Loch Ness two miles to the east, with craggy walls reaching twenty feet high in some places. About a quarter of a mile into the cleft there was a section of the wall with strange grooves marked across its face, which were nearly worn away by centuries of Scottish weather. Sunset was still two hours away at this latitude, but the sinking sun's light caught the grooves and made strange markings. Hoodoo didn't speak the language but she knew they said "Heart of the World."

She had only been with Max for six months, back in '96, before deciding that she didn't want to follow his path. Timelessness was a wonderful thing, but something within her preferred to live the life she'd been given, as intensely as possible, and then go on to the next adventure. So she and Max had parted, on excellent terms, and while they were together he'd developed her innate talent for alchemical metals. Simply put, she could command the magick in the earth.

She had come to Loch Ness to live near this stone, so now she lay back against it, her hair spreading, her arms and legs wide, putting herself in sync with the energy it bore.

She felt her own magick extending into the rock, merging with the magick of the Earth . . . and then surging on through the rock, through the Earth, along subterranean strata in all directions. Blasting through the rift between north and south below Loch Ness was always a thrill, but she was seeking every major strata from Land's End to John o' Groats.

It would be foolish to take an airplane somewhere until she had more to go on, but if Eva Delia Kerr were anywhere on the British Isles, Hoodoo would find out.

SATURDAY, JUNE 20, 2009 • 2:21 P.M.
CENTRAL DAYLIGHT TIME

11 Sun (Owning All)

Hanrahan went back into Salinan's room, where the man himself was strapped to the metal table, shivering and shouting.

"Michael," Hanrahan said, "I'm going to find out about the transmission."

"I dunno, I dunno, I dunno!" Michael shouted, way out on some ledge. But was there still some note of defiance in his voice?

"Then tell me what you know about Diana."

Michael had steeled himself to keep silent, but in his current state he saw nothing wrong with talking about Diana. In fact, he wanted to talk about Diana, very soon. But he had to sell what he had to say, and that meant holding out, even if he didn't want to, just a little longer. . . .

11 Sun (Owning All)

Half an hour later, Michael couldn't stand any more. The bliss had become sickly, like his entire body wanted to vomit but could not. Spasm after spasm wracked him. He had to let it go—now, or never.

"Diana," he said. "There was an e-mail, just before we left for Wickr. It changed her."

Hanrahan promptly stood up and took a small box from his pocket. He removed a syringe and gave Michael a shot in the hip. It would ease things up a little—a reward. Then he contacted his people in the tunnels under West Virginia, pulling the most senior of them off the mysterious transmission and onto Diana Herring's e-mails.

11 Sun (Owning All)

Forty-five minutes later, Hanrahan got the report on Diana's e-mails. He read it once, then summoned the guard, and together they went into Diana's room.

She was fighting as hard as she could against the blissful nausea, and she did not like their demeanor. She was close to the end.

Hanrahan said, "On June 10, at 6:55 A.M., a single e-mail

was sent from one Gmail account to another, both of which were used just that one time. The message read, 'Apocalypse Now.' We were able to identify the sender as you, Diana."

She tried to sit up but the straps held her tight. "No!" she screamed.

Hanrahan continued, "At 7:14, a message from a new Gmail account was sent to another new account, both again used just that one time. It read, 'Gold Diggers of 1933.' The recipient, again, was you. At 7:16, one hundred thousand dollars was transferred to a numbered account in Guatemala. The Trust Agreement for the account lists a Guatemalan law firm as the account holder, but our man in the Finanzas Reguladas de Corporaciones was able to knock a few heads and trace the ultimate holder to you."

"No!" Diana yelled, more firmly. "Not true!" But her voice broke even on that.

"The information is solid," said Hanrahan flatly.

"Somebody—set me—"

"Who?"

"Enemies! Hundreds!"

"But who among them could burrow so deep into the electronic world that we wouldn't detect a fraud?"

"Don' know—"

"Because there is no such person."

Diana raised her head and then banged it down hard on the table. Tears spilled from her eyes but she said, lucidly enough, "You can't crack transmission! You'd tell me what it said!" She banged her head again in desperation. The window of lucidity was closing. "If you can crack this one, it's a setup!"

"This one was never supposed to be noticed. The encrypted transmission could not be missed."

"But, a hundred thousand! Chump change! I know exactly

what would happen to me if I sold us out! I would never do that, for anything, let alone a hundred grahhhh!"

Hanrahan did not answer. It was more of his mind games. Except—he was right up next to her, giving her a shot.

SATURDAY, JUNE 20, 2009 • 3:48 P.M.
CENTRAL DAYLIGHT TIME

11 Sun (Owning All)

Diana lay unmoving on the table for what must have been hours. She was sure the circulation had stopped in her backside; they would have to amputate. She felt better than she had for a while, except they'd have to amputate. If they didn't kill her.

The door opened. Hanrahan entered, followed by Martina, carrying lunch.

She set it on the floor, then went across and unstrapped Diana. She helped her sit up, and the full force of returning blood surged through Di's butt, tingling and burning. She was grateful to get all the way to her feet. The old man approached her with a bowl of cottage cheese and offered her some, while Martina held her upright.

"Last meal?" she muttered.

"No," said Hanrahan. "Michael confessed."

"What?!" Her eyes were huge.

"It *was* a setup, like you said."

"Michael?"

"Your point about the hundred grand was a good one. It *was* too cheap to buy you out. It was more like what someone would risk on an insurance policy, in case your week at Wickr ended badly. Or what a man used to buying politicians would think sufficient."

"But," Diana said, her head whirling, "he set me up, *before* we went away?" She shrugged off the guard's hands and stood erect on her own. This made no sense. "He doesn't have the skills to fake e-mails."

"But he knows people who do."

"But he was pissed when I met someone else at Wickr. He cared about me!"

"You met someone else?"

"Don't even start!" It was over! Over! The old Diana was already coming back to the fore. "I vetted that guy thoroughly, Dick, and it was just for the sex in the desert. He never came near my computer."

"I know how horny you are."

"I know you do. I hope you have graphs. But Michael loved me. He wouldn't set me up!"

"He loved what he could get out of the Necklace more. Going to Wickr was a dangerous move, even though you both thought you could pull it off. He covered his ass by setting you up. If everything had gone as planned, no one would ever have known. When it didn't, he held out as long as he could, to make it look real, and then he gave you up."

"But you believed him."

"I was willing to accept it at first, for all the reasons you just mentioned. But that hundred grand ate at me, too, so I went back to talk with him again. This time he broke for real."

"Is he dead?" Diana asked.

"Not yet."

"Can I kill him?"

11 Sun (Owning All)

Diana entered Michael's interrogation room, flanked by Hanrahan and the two guards. Martina was carrying a long leather whip, in a loose coil. Michael lay groaning on the floor, drawn into a fetal position.

Hanrahan went over and squatted down beside the captive. The old man's bones creaked, but he was able to do it easily enough. He held out his BlackBerry, putting it in front of Michael's face.

On the screen was Breckenridge's face. It showed an odd mix of satisfaction and disappointment. Breckenridge said, clearly enough for all to hear, "This is really a shame, Salinan. You were doing an excellent job. I had no complaints with the political link."

"You won't ever again!" Michael said with feeling. "This was just an insurance plan. It was never supposed to be activated."

"You betrayed the Necklace."

"I didn't!"

"What about Diana? She's one of us."

"I betrayed her but not you!"

"What about Wickr?"

"That's petty stuff! I was thinking the way a member of the Necklace should think! I was being devious." Michael tried to sit up but couldn't open himself. "Don't kill me."

"I'm not even there," Breckenridge said. "But you needn't worry; no one will kill you. We're transporting you to Bagram, in Afghanistan, to learn more about your ties to the Code Red."

"Not Bagram!" Michael blurted. "I don't deserve that!"

Breckenridge chuckled. "Guantánamo's closing, some-time, sort of."

"I don't have any ties to August!" Michael shouted. "The whole thing was a trick! I swear on everything I hold holy!"

"Diana has a going-away present for you," Breckenridge said. "She'd have liked it to be more." Hanrahan handed the BlackBerry to Barry, who pointed it at the scene so the Gemstone could continue to watch. Martina handed the whip to Diana.

"Oh God no," said Michael.

"You set me up," she said, moving toward him, uncoiling the leather. "Not when you were pissed at me, but before we even left for Wickr." She flipped the whip backward, with a sharp =crack!=

"I love you, Diana!" he shouted.

"Love *this!*" she shouted back, and drew deep blood.

SATURDAY, JUNE 20, 2009 • 5:15 P.M.
CENTRAL DAYLIGHT TIME

11 Sun (Owning All)

Rubber-legged with delayed reaction, Diana was escorted to the warehouse exit by Hanrahan, Barry, and Martina.

"These two will take you home," the old man told her. "They will stay and care for you if you want them to; other-wise, they'll leave you alone."

"Alone is exactly what I want to be," she said.

"Fine. But now you have a much more acute appreciation of what we know and what we can do. So I wouldn't expect you to ever find yourself in a position like this again."

"I didn't do anything—" she started, but he overrode her.

"You tried to put one over on us. It doesn't matter what that 'one' was. You did it, and you can be damn thankful that you didn't pay a steeper price. Most of the effects of those drugs can be remedied, but every time it rains you'll ache, for the rest of your life. So I wouldn't expect you to ever find yourself in a position like this again, Diana, and if you do, you won't walk away no matter how inadvertent your sins. Do we understand each other?"

No one but Diana knew what it took to look sincere in that moment, as she said, "We do."

"Good. I look forward to a long and fruitful relationship, as if nothing had ever happened. But I will always know that something did, and so will Mr. Breckenridge. Now go take a bath."

Diana started to say something else, but felt the last of her energy drain away in the aftermath of all that had happened. The old man was right; she had to watch her step every minute from now on, and probably for a long time. But at the same time, if she didn't give August something every now and again, that would kill her, too. As she walked slowly into the hot Chicago rain, she thought, *Jesus! What the FUCK am I going to do?*

–o–

Thinking Max was a pawn, I didn't kill him. I was too sure of myself, and he almost killed me on that New Year's Eve of 1980. It took reserves even I didn't know I had to survive, but finding those reserves actually made me stronger afterward.

On New Year's Eve 1985, I watched his mentor die from my psychic wounds, and I killed his wife. But Agrippa had taught Val everything he could as he approached his death, and she used her performer's strength of purpose to live on.

And I couldn't know that, because I had used the magick from
that double-death night to begin my transubstantiation.
*   Put another way, I went MAD.*

11 Sun (Owning All)

Lexi appeared atop Portillo, encased in air-tight latex and
aerodynamic helmet, at the very instant she went over the
edge to begin a savage descent of Juncalillo. The drop, the
sudden switch to dazzling wintertime, the crystalline snow
whipping past her face—it literally took her breath away.

She didn't have to breathe. She just needed to clear her
palate at seventy-five miles an hour, blow the stink of her
orgies clean away, before the grand finale. So many rôles
that humans can adopt, so many forms of flesh, and she was
mistress of them all—but here, inside the latex, she could
be her fleshless self.

11 Sun (Owning All)

When Max and Pam got back to the perimeter of Wickr,
they pulled their ATV into the exact same spot that Coyote
and Rosa had used, and Max used his own alchemy to turn
the machine invisible. "We can jog on in from here," he
said. "They'll see us on their radar, but anyone they send to

see us in person, won't." So they did, and were in fact past the orange perimeter fence and halfway farther on toward the city before the camp rangers arrived in a truck.

The city sat open in the desert air, but it was still appreciably warmer than the empty desert to those who had just spent two days out there. There were the fifty thousand bodies, the fire exhibits, and the general buzz coming from the anticipation of the burning of the Sun tonight. The change was remarkable in all aspects; this was the climax of the week, and everything was geared toward it.

Back at their camp site, Pam told Max in no uncertain terms that if she were going to appreciate the festivities tonight, she needed to take a nap now, and she went into their tent to do just that. Max stayed outside. He hadn't slept much but he was wired by the day's events, so he walked out to Saturn to see if he could learn anything from the spot where Diana and Michael had camped. It was, of course, just an empty space in the dust now. Except for the man and the woman with metal detectors, whom Max immediately pegged as a clean-up crew from the Necklace. He kept on walking, but as soon as he found an appropriate spot, he stepped out of sight, drew a pi around himself, stepped through its gate to become invisible, and walked back.

The two agents finished their electronic sweep, then each of them knelt where a coach had been. Each began to work his way forward, using a sharp metal rod to poke the dirt every six inches. When they both had worked the length of a coach, they turned and came back again, six inches to the right of their first paths, and when they got back to their starting lines, they turned and started forward again, six inches to the right. Had anything been buried there, they would have found it soon enough.

Max watched until they, and he, were certain that there wasn't anything. But Diana wasn't going to betray herself like that. She was one of the Nine; she knew how to play.

So the man/woman team walked away, as quickly as reasonable at Wickr, to the spot where they'd left their car, and left. Max watched until they disappeared.

Then he went down to Center-City and stood in line to order an iced chai. A brightly painted sprite nearby was handing out half-melted but half-not-melted ice cream. Max took a cup and surreptitiously made his *wipe* to be sure it was what it appeared to be; satisfied, he wolfed it down. It tasted unbelievably good.

Chai in hand, he sat on one of the scattered pillows at the exact center of the city and watched the scene around him. A damn good scat singer was up on the stage and he enjoyed her. The people around him were wearing grungy-looking gear now, saving the good stuff for tonight. "Ten forty-six," voices in the crowd said. "The Sun Burn." After a week of freedom and harmony, the fifty thousand were coming together for one event. Life in Wickr City was no longer strange to anyone. *We all live in Wickr now,* Max thought, and let the afternoon just flow by in the ephemeral city.

–0–

It took two years to adjust to pure Space. Two years of raving madness, until I became its master. And when I did, those two years became incomprehensible. Those two years did not exist—not for me. But in time and space, I awoke to my transubstantiation, on New Year's Day ANNO DOMINI 1988. I was reborn a DIABOLA.

And so in time I appeared to Tom Jeckyl. The Necklace had been in existence for two hundred and fifty years, and they'd always had wizards, but I offered Jeckyl something no Gemstone had ever had before—a PRIVATE arrangement with higher power. Unfortunately, as the months went by, I saw that he was not the man I needed. So on All Hallows'

Eve 1991, I tried recruiting Max. He would be something else. But Val's appearances had only strengthened his hatred of me. So I turned to the next man on my list, my
    RENZO!

SATURDAY, JUNE 20, 2009 • 8:00 P.M.
EASTERN DAYLIGHT TIME

11 Sun (Owning All)

"Diabola!"

All of his independence flew out the window the instant she appeared to him. He leapt up, sending his chair flying backward, and rushed around his desk to reach her. She reached out to run her hand along his side and all of his clothing disappeared. She was already nude for him. And for all of her debauchery today, all her other celebration, she liked this sex the best of all. Renzo had the one mind on the planet as twisted as hers, and Renzo couldn't live without her now.

They were made for each other.

SATURDAY, JUNE 20, 2009 • 8:00 P.M.
EASTERN DAYLIGHT TIME

11 Sun (Owning All)

Hanrahan heard that goddammed buzz begin to issue from his tap on Lawrence Breckenridge. What the *hell* did that guy do in there?

11 Sun (Owning All)

The sun was setting for the last time at this year's Wickr. The techno was louder, more insistent, and the things that lit up were all lit up—all the art cars, the neon-limned buildings, the people. Most of the camps were deserted or close to it as the people wandered their city at its apotheosis. A double-decker art car with a massive sound system trundled past playing "Poker Face" for its eighty partying pagans.

Max was standing beside his camp-stove in clean tee shirt and shorts, cooking good old pork and beans, working on his second mojito. He could feel its effect and gauge it; he knew he was within his limits but the buzz was good, too. He deserved a little buzz right now. The sun had gone behind the mountain at least an hour earlier, and finally the few clouds overhead were crimson going gray.

Saturn winked into view, the color of old gold, high in the southwest.

Max got up, feeling the first of the slightly cooler night breezes, and walked into the tent. Pam was sitting quietly in her own chair, the *Codex* open in her lap, but she'd been ruminating, her gaze far away.

"Want some dinner?" he asked.

"Okay," she said.

12 Nipple (Fulfilling Reality)

In one sense, Hoodoo had lain against the face of the rock called Heart of the Earth for nine unmoving hours. But in a truer sense, Hoodoo had expanded her consciousness into the land. Her reach had extended slowly but steadily southward, through the rocks underlying everything, striving toward Cambridge.

Once in the university town, beneath the halfway house Max had mentioned, she reached upward through the foundation, into the room which held Yellow Gables' computer server, into the server's metallic case, into the silicon and gallium of the chips inside, where the server's "mind" was at work.

She entered that mind, read Eva Delia's records, and left Cambridge for London.

In London she performed the same magick at the National Health, and found where they had put her. Number 7 Greek Street, Soho W1. She also read of the girl's brush with the law. Clearly things were happening.

Hoodoo pulled her mind back into her human body, all the way from London. After nine hours, she returned to herself and stepped away from the Heart of the World. This was a ridiculous time to charter an aircraft, but there was no commercial service at this time of night, and Max felt time was of the essence.

Money would sort it out, now that she'd found Eva Delia.

11 Sun (Owning All)

I have found him!

Quince was thrown sideways by the sudden weight within him, slamming his robed body against the wall, but he felt no pain. No! His demon master had done what he'd promised.

A fire festival called Wickr.

Quince knew what that was. He looked up at the wall, where the camera was hidden. "I've found August!" he shouted to Hanrahan, and began at once to expand into the higher realms. If the old man was going to watch and evaluate him, he would give him a show.

But not the real show.

11 Sun (Owning All)

Hanrahan was hunched over his table, chin in hand, trying to decipher that damnable noise from Renzo's room. It was pulsing now, like some honky-tonk siren, but he knew Renzo didn't have a babe in there, and Renzo himself couldn't go this long. It was still a mystery—

But Hanrahan had cut a deal with every wizard, and the first deal had been with Roland Stavros, the Great Wizard. That grand old man had provided Hanrahan with a charm to warn him if a certain level of mystical power was obtained, by anyone other than Stavros. Now it functioned, its power rolling over him like an orange wave.

The spymaster leaned to his right and pulled up an automatic video of the trigger point. It was Quince, doing some incredible spell, judging from his strain. Hanrahan switched off the sound on Renzo's tap, left Quince's on, and interlaced his fingers. He laid his chin on the interlace and settled in to watch.

SATURDAY, JUNE 20, 2009 • 11:17 P.M.
CENTRAL DAYLIGHT TIME

11 Sun (Owning All)

Quince slipped out of this world and into the other. It was now so easy.

SUNDAY, JUNE 21, 2009 • 12:17 A.M.
EASTERN DAYLIGHT TIME

11 Sun (Owning All)

Hanrahan saw him disappear. He set a watch on the feed, to alert him to the next movement in that now-barren room, then pulled a yogurt from his fridge and went back to pondering Renzo's tap.

11 Sun (Owning All)

Quince was floating above the plane, the perfectly flat endless plane, with the four directions crisply marked. But Quince began to *thicken,* and the plane began to turn to powder. . . .

11 Sun (Owning All)

On the plain of Wickr, in the farthest corner of the orange-fenced city, a dust devil began to rise. Dust storms never rose after dark here, lacking the daylight's heat, but this one did. It swirled and bobbed, not unlike a serpent. It rose from the ground, gathering size, until at last it rose up like a rattler, towering thirty feet above the desert, and seemed to leer at what it saw.

Its dust became gelatinous, but the dust of the plain didn't stick to it. It was an ectoplasmic tube, rippling, swirling, preening. And within the tube, from its blind, rounded top to its coiling tail, faces tumbled over each other. Hundreds of faces, thousands of faces, of those who had joined with Belia'al since the demon-king had first appeared to man. They were the faces of history, men and women with hair arranged in the styles of the twentieth century, the nineteenth, eighteenth, tenth, first, and beyond the zero line. Old Testament faces, side by jowl with flappers and nuns.

Among the masses was the face of Peter Quince, with wide, staring eyes and a slavering grin. But even Rita Diamante would not have found him in the tumult and shadow. He was just a detail in the massive thing that dominated the desert, gathering its strength.

For the next thirty-one minutes, that thing lay there and pulsed—and drew a crowd, Randy and Sara among them. This was the art project to end all art projects, and the Wickns were expecting great things from this night.

SATURDAY, JUNE 20, 2009 • 9:49 P.M.
PACIFIC DAYLIGHT TIME

11 Sun (Owning All)

From the eyes of each of the thousand faces, an ectoplasmic tube sprang, like hair, like legs. The smaller tubes quested blindly for the plain, and when they found it, they stabilized under it, slowly raising it, like legs. One of them moved, then another, but far back from the first one, in no pattern anyone could comprehend. Other rhythms began among the other legs, some moving forward but at different speeds, some moving backward with a sort of *hop,* so that in the end the thousands of legs were churning in some alien concord that somehow moved the whole thing forward, slowly at first and then with implacable momentum.

Anyone it touched in its path was instantly fried, so quickly his scream was lost before he ever uttered it.

Randy and Sara thought that was a hell of a show. Like some Cirque du Soleil on meth. They got back on their bikes like the others who weren't dead and rode off into the dark, unperturbed.

Belia'al's magick was strong tonight.

11 Sun (Owning All)

The demon came to Venus Street. Directly in front of it stood Max and Pam's camp—and Max and Pam, just leaving for the Sun. It was only when the demon crossed the road that Max felt it. Just before the demon engulfed them, Max thrust out his hands and barked one word—a trigger-word for a septet of spells that he called Agrippa's Seven. They had protected Agrippa for centuries, and they protected him and Pam now while he fought for time to build his own power.

Pam was gaping at the monstrosity around them, at the seeing faces behind its legs. But Max was beginning to glow softly gold, and told her calmingly, "This is a demon—Belia'al."

This is *the* demon, artist. I knew your master, and *his* unfortunate disciple.

"Agrippa?" Pam asked, and Max nodded shortly, his eyes never leaving the vast ectoplasmic horror. "Just remember the flow," he told her.

She did remember, and she still felt it. But the world around them started to disappear, the way it had when they fought Aleksandra.

He knew what she'd be thinking. "This is not Aleksandra," Max said. "It's gonna be weird. But it's still just power against power, and I bet on us."

A face at the end of a long viscous tube shot out of the blob—the face of a sobbing, terrorized witch, drenched with water from the drowning trials. It grew large but stopped before they could take it as a threat, the beaten midwife crying at Pam from twenty feet away:

I am Belia'al, Dr. Blackwell. You do not know me at all. My brother Lucifer was banished for loving God too much, and I was created through no fault of my own—much like yourself.

"Demons lie," Max said to Pam.

And alchemists think "Ride the flow!" But there's something to be said for not having to ride anything. There's something to be said for having all power in the first place!

"No, Belia'al—" Pam said, facing this.

You're going to stand beside him because that's what you want, Doctor. But you should know that I won't kill you the way I'll kill him. You will survive, so that one day you'll regret your choice and join me of your own free will.

"That will never—"

With its two thousand legs flailing in all directions, the demon attacked. Dazzling multicolored lasers exploded from tubes in random parts of its body, all swinging out of harmony yet right on time to focus on Max and Pam. But the Agrippa Seven, from the very first moment, had thickened gravity to a wafer-thin energy sphere surrounding them. The lasers ricocheted all over the night sky as the sphere began to flicker with the head of a golden lion.

"Well, good luck!" Max said.

"Well, good luck!" Pam responded.

Her power was a personal thing, not something she could imagine as separate from herself. She had strengthened the life-force within her, the power she learned to feel very quickly in South America. By the time they left last year, she could bundle that power in a ball, just like an old dress, and feel its magick zip back and forth between her palms. The ball was silver. She couldn't yet hurl it the way Max did—her *surges* of power were more URGES—but she could *give* it to him.

Max had two spots in the flow to work from, two fields of power, and what he made of that was more than the sum of its parts. He focused the currents of his alchemy into his own ball, at his own center, with their combined might. He loosed his own laser, not a thousand lights but one, the size of his sphere, a monumental blast. It exploded against the gelatinous blob and blew it nearly in two. As it was, the blob's left side was decimated, and it seemed unable to re-fill the space at once. But the plasm itself, though barbell-shaped, was still sentient, its seven hundred faces screaming curses at their attacker.

Max said, "It's hard for demons to hold their form on earth, but they can't operate without form here, and that's their weakness."

On the other hand, the plain around them was gone now, replaced by Belia'al's demonic geometry—lines that sagged through nothingness, meeting themselves in doorways that had no doors. Jagged stairways built upon themselves and went nowhere, sideways. There was no spot where line and curve met; there was no pi in Belia'al. Peter Quince, still hidden by thick legs, was fully aware that he was a mere speck in the malignancy, but he was part of his master and loving every second of it! Even the screaming all around him, in fury and in pain, was so *hot!* How could August defeat that rush?

Belia'al could not fill the hole but he sprouted tubes in his remaining flesh to once more reach one thousand. Max saw faces in the maelstrom torn apart, becoming two faces, each lost and mad, but filling the tubes. The damned tubes.

They erupted with a thousand green somethings. Max couldn't name them because they weren't flat or bent as they tumbled in havoc toward him and Pam. Max threw his hands wide and his golden sphere pulsed, as full of his ge-ometry as he could be. The pulse met the green things and lights exploded in all directions.

Under cover of the dazzle, the demon slipped through one of the mad doorways, its bulk gurgling in even as it gurgled out of a slot between tangles behind Max. For one long moment it was both before and behind him, and Max didn't know it. By the time he did, it was almost too late. Eighty-seven tentacles touched the gravity sphere and obliterated a chunk.

Max drove the demon back, and filled his own cavity. He was based in our reality; spheres could be re-formed at will. But the new shell was thinner there, thinner overall.

The lion's head around his sphere, his earliest magickal incarnation, snarled and snapped at the glob, ripping off another chunk of it. The chunk turned to acid in the lion's mouth, but the lion was *astral* so the acid just floated through its jaws and dissipated.

"How can he do this, master?" Quince shouted, and couldn't even hear himself. But the clutch on his heart showed Belia'al heard, and Belia'al was not happy.

Now the demon's weakness was even more apparent. It needed the thousand humans who were part of it now, but the thousand were not original. Over time some were lost, and had to be replaced by ripping others in half, at least until new humans could be enticed to join. But some of the humans were insane creations of the demon itself. They gave numbers and raw humanity, but they couldn't provide higher humanity, *Homo sapiens*. Those creations were just a mob.

And so Belia'al struck again with great power, but less accuracy. It was confused when it tried to operate on Venus Street, and growing more so. Max went after it, now fully committed to the form of Kalbu Rabu, the Great Lion, and Harmakhis of Egypt, Lion-Sphinx of the Dawning Day, and Max August, soldier. The jelly slithered back through the doorway, spilling into a new spot, and the lion surged to continue his attack. Belia'al regrouped, the din of its screaming madness growing more shrill, and exploded like a nova sun, its thousand filaments rocketing outward. Then the central form followed them as a second wave, filling the huge new space before collapsing around the lion head, engulfing it in slime, smothering it whole.

But what was this head but Max and Pam, themselves expanded? Pam felt weakness shoot through her as her power drained even faster. Max felt it too, on a much larger scale, but that power went to good use as it pressed back against the devouring slime, with the force of gravity behind it in a world where gravity was a force to be reckoned with. Belia'al knew he was losing. There had to be some recourse—

The bomb!

The demon vanished.

SUNDAY, JUNE 21, 2009 • 1:27 A.M.
EASTERN DAYLIGHT TIME

11 Sun (Owning All)

In Hanrahan's room in Wheeling, an automatic warning sounded. The old man spun around in a hurry—it was a Fortress alert. Someone had stolen—

SATURDAY, JUNE 20, 2009 • 10:27 P.M.
PACIFIC DAYLIGHT TIME

11 Sun (Owning All)

"The bomb, Max! I know its power! It's here!"

"Where?"

"Inside the wicker Sun!"

They spun toward the heart of the city, glowing in the

night two blocks away. They started to run, through people's camps, the most direct route, but then Pam yelled, "I'll meet you there!" and launched herself into the *astral*.

"Pam!" Max shouted, but she didn't listen.

Max ran after her, not like a coyote, but like a lion, with quick and agile strides, avoiding tent wires with a single bound and people with a slight touch—his gravity shield was on, so things moved out of his way. He hardly slowed as he went through the masses around the Sun. *I can't fly,* he thought. *But this'll do.* Arriving in the open circle beneath the hanging wicker sphere, he bent the light and became invisible, then slipped the tee shirt off his back and stuffed it down the back of his pants as he continued his run toward a tower and began to climb its two-hundred-foot height, commando-style, no single second wasted.

At the top, he crawled quickly out along the crane's arm to where the cable ran down to the sphere—a twenty-foot vertical sag in the lines. He held on with his right hand while his left hand reached back to grab his shirt and flip

The great wooden sphere was now hanging one hundred sixty feet above the plain. A ring of volunteer rangers kept the fifty thousand Wickns outside the fire ring below it. None of them knew that was now no modicum of safety. Pam, at *astral* speed, *flew* over them into the Sun. There was the bomb, hovering in the very center of the larger hollow sphere—and a stocky dark man half hidden beyond it.

Not the demon, thank God. It must be the wizard.

She reached back and drew upon the infinite power behind her, flowing through her, into the infinite future. Alchemist with a gun? She felt like an alchemist *in* a gun!

And she lost track of the *astral* and found herself bumping down the wooden staves. She instantly corrected that but lost her clarity in the larger flow.

The dark man bent and peered at her from under the bomb. "Pam!" he said. "Oh it over the cable. He grabbed the right side of it as he somersaulted forward, off the end of the crane arm, and let it take the friction as he slid. Just before hitting the Sun, he pulled down hard; the cloth burst into flame but it didn't matter; Max let go with his left hand to brace for impact against a wicker stave. He used his right hand to pull the burning cloth off the wire cable, arcing it around to have it slap his hip, and followed its flight with his right hand to crush the flames between hand and haunch. Then, rocking back and forth one hundred sixty feet in the air, he slipped into the sphere.

yes, I can see you in the *astral*." Energy crackled around his hands. It smelled like the demon. Even though it had taken the wizard's form, it was Belia'al.

Pam took all the power she could gather and hurled it at the man. It knocked him stumbling on the staves.

"She can't treat you like that!" the man said, to himself.

"She won't ever again!" the man answered.

Oh my God, thought Pam. If her best shot wasn't enough what else could she do?

Pam was about to *fly* into the man's head when Max's impact on the sphere sent it rocking back and forth. She refused to let it distract her, and threw herself through the *astral,* but Max saw what was happening and threw out a gravity shield to hold her back. "No!" he shouted, clambering quickly through the staves. "Belia'al's *inside him* now, Pam!"

"I know that, but there was nothing else I could do!"

"You wouldn't have survived it!"

"There was nothing else. It has to be done! There's no time!"

The dark man spoke. "She's right. The bomb is set. I wish I could wait for the solstice—bigger kill rate—but you forced my hand." He worked his way crab-wise down the wicker. "And why not show me your true face, Max August? I've seen Pam's."

"I'll pass," Max said. "But I know your face, Peter Quince."

That face darkened. "How?"

"I keep an eye on those who walk the higher paths."

"I've never been this close to your energy before. I'd know it."

"And what does that tell you?" Max asked him. "You didn't sense me because you weren't ready for this level, Pete."

"The hell I wasn't!"

"Well, you weren't ready for Belia'al!"

Peter Quince grinned, all teeth. **But I was ready for him,** he snapped, and vanished.

"Go!" Max shouted, throwing himself headlong toward the bottom of the sphere. Pam yelled, "There's only seconds!" as she *flew* alongside him. He landed on his hands and might have stuck the landing on the curved surface, but the Sun had increased its wobble when he pushed off and he had to roll instead, over the unyielding curves of the wood. He was going to have some bruises.

The bomb, on the other hand, floated steadily where the center of the sphere had been before the rocking. Its timer was at eye level as Max got his feet under him again. Pam arrived just as he stood up. The timer read **11.**

Max put his hands up, fingers widespread, palms cradling the circumference that would exist if the detonator had an invisible sphere around it, saying coolly, "Give me everything, Pam!"

10

Pam dropped into place behind him, put her hands on his shoulder blades, grabbing for all the flow she could—still *astral* but right there.

9

She focused her glow, out of her and into him. He felt it, an integral part of the vast flow, from the moment of the Big Bang when *everything* came flowing forward—

8

—to where he appeared and it was up to him what happened next. He was Harmakhis, Lord of the Dawn—and an alchemical master of gravity.

7

Feeling the strain, he forced his hands closer, closing the circumference around the timer. Nothing in the flow besides himself and Pam was providing the slightest help, but he focused on what he could control.

6

He pushed with the power of the Universe—tighter—

5

They pushed with the power.

4

Gravity crushed the timer.

• • •

There was no 3.

• • •

There was no 3, the countdown was over, the surge of adrenaline release—! They literally staggered on the rocking floor of the Sun.

But there was also a new certainty: they could *do* this. It wasn't a fluke or a one-off now: they could *do* this when they worked together. They had power together and they had fun together, and Pam was a real part of that.

There was no 3.

11 Sun (Owning All)

Quince spilled out in a heap on the floor of his sanctum. It was a wooden floor and it hurt when he hit it, but he made no sound externally. His inner voice was all.

We've won!

We've lost!

The bomb!

August blocked it.

Damn him! Find him again!

Modify your tone.

Find him, please, master.

I cannot.

Why not? You did before.

His master had a spell against me, which he is now speaking.

You're more powerful than he is!

Of course I am, but you are not—not yet. And you are part of me now. You are the weak link, Peter Quince.

So I'm expendable?

Oh no. We must build you up—give you power August can't ignore—that the Necklace can't ignore.

Then I am yours in all things!

11 Sun (Owning All)

Hanrahan saw Quince reappear in the room, sprawled heavily on the floor. Quince looked exultant to start with, but it soon became clear that the triumph he was expecting had not arrived. Hanrahan understood that he had failed.

But Quince, lying there on the floor, talking to thin air like all wizards, had proven himself, as far as the old man was concerned. He'd fought as hard as he could, *and* he'd stolen the Necklace's bomb. *I would have done that,* Hanrahan mused, *but not many others would have. He's resourceful, and he's got the balls of a burglar.*

Hanrahan smiled. It wasn't a nice smile. He'd picked the right horse.

11 Sun (Owning All)

The bomb appeared in the parking lot outside its Yucca Mountain home. Putting it inside would have crushed a dozen investigators—who instead remained alive to remember the strange things that happened in the days of Area 51, and how to just be glad when they were over.

11 Sun (Owning All)

In the sky, 93 million miles above Burma, the real Sun was as far north of the Earth's equator as it could get. In the northern hemisphere, Midsummer arrived.

In the sky two hundred feet above Wickr, the wooden Sun burst into flames.

11 Sun (Owning All)

The fire began at the bottom of the wicker sphere and licked its way gradually upward. The people who master-minded the city of Wickr had been at this for many years, and they'd found the right fire retardants to keep the sphere together until the fire got all the way to the top. Once the whole ball was ablaze, it would hang in midair for fifteen minutes before the lower staves began to drop away. For fifteen minutes, there was just the floating ball of flame high in the black desert sky, hovering like a UFO. Techno played from all sides and people cheered and got the party under way.

In the dark, Max and Pam were just two people among fifty thousand. Pam stood and watched the Sun burn, the flame-light limning her face and figure, while Max turned his back and encoded his first message to Diana in the ratings of WLS.

```
Peter Quince possessed. Evil. Guard yourself
at all times.
```

He hit Send. "Sorry," he said, slipping the phone back in his pocket. "I had to let her know."

"I know you did," Pam said. "You don't have to say 'sorry' to me, Max. I accept what we have to do. This is a war."

Max moved closer, took her face in his hands—the same hands that had crushed the bomb's steel timer. But he could not have been more gentle as he looked into her eyes. "Pam, I have to do a lot of things—and right now, I have to tell you that it's not fair, the way I've treated you."

"It's all right," she said, waving it off.

But he said, "No, the longer I live with you, the more I realize that I'm *happy now,* and I don't want to jeopardize that. Not in any way. I'm going to get Val back, and I hope you and I both can be her friend, but however that goes down, I'm with you, lady." He kissed her. "That's if you'll have me."

"Ha!" Pam said. "If you'll have *me.*"

"Why wouldn't I?"

"Because I'm not perfect. Not by a long shot."

"Neither am I."

"But you can't make that promise, Max," she said earnestly. "Getting your wife back and not falling in love again. If it's not the right decision, you may look at me and see someone who's not perfect."

"And then what?"

"And then you'll regret your promise."

"Not once I've made it," Max said. "And I just did."

"But I don't think you should. It's not fair to Val."

"I'm *not* walking away from you, Pam."

They hugged tightly. They were doing that a lot these days.

Then Max stepped back, reached out and took Pam's hand, started pulling her toward the nearest techno beat. "C'mon, my love," he said. "It's been a tough week but we got through it. Let's just go dance till dawn!"

"Impossible," she told him, laughing. "But essential."

Day Seven

. . . .

12 Nipple (Fulfilling Reality)

Vee waited all through the quiet night for Lexi to come, as she had come every night, but Lexi didn't come. It wasn't until dawn, at 3:43 A.M., that Vee began to entertain the idea that she'd been left alone—that maybe, just maybe, Lexi was finished with her. Or even that Lexi didn't know about Vee—that she thought Eva Delia was the sum of what she was. Wouldn't that be funny?

The meds had worn off with time and tea, leaving Vee to keep an eye on herself, continually checking to see if she were still in control. She was. The madness that was Eva Delia seemed to be completely gone, like a bad dream—the only kind of dream she remembered from Eva Delia's life.

But of course she didn't *know,* so she waited until she heard the city around her fully awaken. Then she carefully tucked the knife up into the sleeve of her jacket and went out onto Greek Street. Walking slowly and carefully along its long straight course, she saw neighbors she met on this Sunday morning as if for the first time. She saw *more* in them, human traits she had always missed before. She couldn't help herself and started to sing, but something with a tune everyone could appreciate—a pop tune. Cascada. It didn't matter what it was so long as she enjoyed it and no one thought her strange. She didn't want to be strange.

She crossed through Chinatown, leaving Soho, returning to the construction site where she'd been apprehended. She slipped inside and worked her way past the four-by-twos to the cabin she'd hid out in. Standing before it, she had a moment when she wondered if everything here had been the loonie's dream, that this was useless because she'd been useless, but she ruthlessly closed off that train of thought. She put her hand on the cabin door, pushed it open, and went inside. She went to her hidey hole, the loose boards at the back which opened into a space behind piled piping.

And there it was. She hadn't dreamed it. There was her book. Not the other book, the second book she'd snatched up with *her* book as she ran from the seventh room, thinking, with what must have been her last few moments as Eva Delia, how she could fool Lexi. She'd been struck by madness just a moment later, but she fought against it long enough to hide her book here so that when they caught her, as she knew they would, they would find *a* book but not *the* book.

She took her book out, careful not to scratch it. As Vee, she didn't remember why this book had held such a fascination for Eva Delia—but simply holding it meant something. Something just beyond her grasp.

Henry Cornelius Agrippa—His Fifth Book of Occult Philosophy

She opened the book and looked at the lines of the text again. She saw the great horizontal flow of words, as comforting as ever. But as she looked, she also saw, for the first time, the way some words flowed *down* the page. They made no sense as sentences, but they made sense to her with their shapes, their relationships. She began to sing those relationships.

She began to see an image, floating above the page—the

face of a man, maybe thirty-five years of age. He had a big nose and lank hair, under a little cap with a ribbon—from some time long ago. Certainly not now. The image stayed an image for just a moment longer and then became three-dimensional, the front of a face, like a mask, floating.

The face of the old-time man stared at the world ahead of him, somewhere near Vee's sternum, and spoke in clear if curious English:

Shouldst thou see and hear me, my friend, thou wert forsooth instructed at my table of art. Thus have I prepared this small treatise for thee. Any student may stray from the path, or be drawn from the path by divers wickedness, but any student of mine will come to this book in time, to speak this spell and know that I shall surely lead thee home. Sworn by Cornelius Agrippa on this 31st day of December, anno domini 1519.

She sat down on the cabin floor, abruptly, hard, legs simply giving way. She stared at the little face—the little image of a face, so cunning and so real—fading back to nothingness. And then she could feel the man taking the Clown with him, drawing that staggering puke out of her, leaving only Vee inside her brain. Her clear brain.

"My name's not Eva Dee!" she trilled, joy exploding throughout her being. "*I'm Vee, Vee,* VEEEEEEEEEE*!*"

It *was* her being, for the *first time in her life*. And she would never go back to what was!

12 Nipple (Fulfilling Reality)

Hoodoo's taxi from City Airport surged into Greek Street, the driver dodging the Sunday strollers—"half of them crazy people"—doing his damnedest to earn a fifty-pound tip. Hoodoo dropped two fifties on the driver's seat so that when the cab had only slowed for a stop, she was out the door. She hit the pavement in a jog and only accelerated as she ran into the building, up the stairs to Eva Delia's flat.

No one answered the door. Hoodoo gave it ten more seconds, then touched the knob. Her consciousness spread into it, so that she could then view the room inside from the point of view of the inside knob. It was truly empty, with no signs of a struggle.

Well then, I'll wait, thought Hoodoo.

It would be in vain.